SHIVERS VIII

SHIVERS VIII

Edited by
Richard Chizmar

Cemetery Dance Publications

Baltimore

❖ 2019 ❖

Shivers VIII
Copyright © 2019 by Cemetery Dance Publications.
All rights reserved.

Cemetery Dance Publications
132-B Industry Lane, Unit #7
Forest Hill, MD 21050
http://www.cemeterydance.com

First Printing

ISBN: 978-1-58767-662-8

Printed in the United States of America

Cover Artwork © 2019 by Desert Isle Design, LLC
Interior Design © 2019 by Desert Isle Design, LLC

TABLE OF CONTENTS

SQUAD D

by Stephen King

Billy Clewson died all at once, with nine of the ten other members of D Squad on April 8, 1974. It took his mother two years, but she got started right away on the afternoon the telegram announcing her son's death came, in fact. Dale Clewson simply sat on the bench in the front hall for five minutes, the sheet of yellow flimsy dangling from his fingers, not sure if he was going to faint or puke or scream or what. When he was able to get up, he went into the living room. He was in time to observe Andrea down the last swallow of the first drink and pour the post-Billy era's second drink. A good many more drinks followed—it was really amazing how many drinks that small and seemingly frail woman had been able to pack into a two-year period. The written cause—that which appeared on her death certificate—was liver dysfunction and renal failure. Both Dale and the family doctor knew that was formalistic icing on an extremely alcoholic cake—*baba au rum*, perhaps. But only Dale knew there was a third level. The Viet Cong had

9

killed their son in a place called Ky Doc, and Billy's death had killed his mother.

It was three years—three years almost to the day—after Billy's death on the bridge that Dale Clewson began to believe that he must be going mad.

Nine, he thought. *There were nine. There were always nine. Until now.*

Were there? his mind replied to itself. *Are you sure? Maybe you never really counted—the Lieutenant's letter said there were nine, and Bortman's letter said there were nine. So just how can you be so sure? Maybe you just assumed.*

But he hadn't just assumed, and he could be sure because he knew how many nine was, and there had been nine boys in the D Squad photograph which had come in the mail, along with Lieutenant Anderson's letter.

You could be wrong, his mind insisted with an assurance that was slightly hysterical. *You've been through a lot these last couple of years, what with losing first Billy and then Andrea. You could be wrong.*

It was really surprising, he thought, to what insane lengths the human mind would go to protect its own sanity.

He put his finger down on the new figure—a boy of Billy's age, but with blonde crew-cut hair, looking no more than sixteen, surely too young to be on the killing ground. He was sitting cross-legged in front of Gibson, who had, according to Billy's letters, played the guitar, and Kimberley, who told lots of dirty jokes. The boy with the blond hair was squinting slightly into the sun—so were several of the others, but *they* had always been there before. The new boy's fatigue shirt was open, his dog tags lying against his hairless chest.

Dale went into the kitchen, sorted through what he and Andrea had always called "the jumble drawers," and came up with an old, scratched magnifying glass. He took it and the picture over the living room window, tilted the picture so there was no glare, and held the glass over the new boy's dog tags. He couldn't read them. Thought, in fact, that the tags were both turned over and lying face down against the skin.

And yet, a suspicion had dawned in his mind—it ticked there like the clock on the mantel. He had been about to wind that clock when he had noticed the change in the picture. Now he put the picture back in its accustomed place, between a photograph of Andrea and Billy's graduation picture, found the key to the clock. And wound it.

Lieutenant Anderson's letter had been simple enough. Now Dale found it in his study desk and read it again. Typed lines on Army stationary. The prescribed follow-up to the telegram, Dale had supposed. First: Telegram. Second: Letter of Condolence from Lieutenant. Third: Coffin, One Boy Enclosed. He had noticed then and noticed again now that the typewriter Anderson used had a flying "o." Clewson kept coming out Clews^on.

Andrea had wanted to tear the letter up. Dale insisted that they keep it. Now he was glad.

Billy's squad and two others had been involved in a flank sweep of a jungle quadrant of which Ky Doc was the only village. Enemy contact had been anticipated, Anderson's letter said, but there hadn't been any. The Cong which had been reliably reported to be in the area had simply melted away into the jungle—it was a trick with which the American soldiers had become very familiar over the previous ten years or so.

Dale could imagine them heading back to their base at Homan, happy, relieved. Squads A and C had waded across the Ky River, which was almost dry. Squad D used the bridge. Halfway across, it blew up. Perhaps it had been detonated from downstream. More likely, someone—perhaps even Billy himself—had stepped on the wrong board. All nine of them had been killed. Not a single survivor.

God—if there really is such a being—is usually kinder than that, Dale thought. He put Lieutenant Anderson's letter back and took out Josh Bortman's letter. It had been written on blue-lined paper from what looked like a child's tablet. Bortman's handwriting was nearly illegible, the scrawl made worse by the writing implement—a soft-lead pencil. Obviously blunt to start with, it must have been no more than a nub by the time Bortman signed his name at the bottom. In several places Bortman had borne down hard enough with his instrument to tear the paper.

It had been Bortman, the tenth man, who sent Dale and Andrea the squad picture, already framed, the glass over the photo miraculously unbroken in its long trip from Homan to Saigon to San Francisco and finally to Binghamton, New York.

Bortman's letter was anguished. He called the other nine "the best friends I ever had in my life, I loved them all like they was my brothers."

Dale held the blue-lined paper in his hand and looked blankly through his study door and toward the sound of the ticking clock on the mantelpiece. When the letter came, in early May of 1974, he had been too full of his own anguish to really consider Bortman's. Now he supposed he could understand it...a little, anyway. Bortman had been feeling a deep and inarticulate guilt. Nine letters from his hospital bed on the Homan base, all in that pained scrawl, all probably written with that same soft-lead pencil. The expense of having nine enlargements of the Squad D photograph made, and framed, and mailed off. *Rites of atonement with a soft-lead pencil*, Dale thought, folding the letter again and putting it back in the drawer with Anderson's. *As if he had killed them by taking their picture. That's really what was between the lines, wasn't it? "Please don't hate me, Mr. Clewson, please don't think I killed your son and the others by—"*

In the other room the mantelpiece clock softly began to chime the hour of five.

—

Dale went back into the living room, and took the picture down again.

What you're talking about is madness.

Looked at the boy with the short blonde hair again.

I loved them all like they was my brothers.

Turned the picture over.

Please don't think I killed your son—all of your sons—by taking their picture. Please don't hate me because I was in the Homan base hospital with bleeding hemorrhoids instead of on the Ky Doc bridge with the best friends I ever had in my life. Please don't hate me, because I finally caught up, it took me ten years of trying, but I finally caught up.

Written on the back, in the same soft-lead pencil, was this notation:

Jack Bradley Omaha, Neb.

Billy Clewson Binghamton, NY

Rider Dotson Oneonta, NY

Charlie Gibson Payson, ND

Bobby Kale Henderson, IA

Jack Kimberley Truth or Consequences, NM

Andy Moulton Faraday, LA Staff Sgt.

Jimmy Oliphant Beson, Del.

Ashley St. Thomas Anderson, Ind.

*Josh Bortman Castle Rock, Me.

He had put his own last, Dale saw—he had seen all of this before, of course, and had noticed it...but had never really noticed it until now, perhaps. He had put his own name last, out of alphabetical order, and with an asterisk.

The asterisk means "still alive." The asterisk means "don't hate me."

Ah, but what you're thinking is madness, and you damned well know it.

Nevertheless, he went to the telephone, dialed 0, and ascertained that the area code for Maine was 207. He dialed Maine directory assistance, and ascertained that there was a single Bortman family in Castle Rock.

He thanked the operator, wrote the number down, and looked at the telephone.

You don't really intend to call those people, do you?

No answer—only the sound of the ticking clock. He had put the picture on the sofa and now he looked at it—looked first at his own son, his hair pulled back behind his head, a brave little moustache trying to grow on his upper lip, frozen forever at the age of twenty-one, and then at the new boy in that old picture, the boy with the short blonde hair, the boy whose dog tags were twisted so they lay face-down and unreadable against his chest. He thought of the way Josh Bortman had carefully segregated himself from the others, thought of the asterisk, and suddenly his eyes filled with warm tears.

I never hated you, son, he thought. *Nor did Andrea, for all her grief. Maybe I should have picked up a pen and dropped you a note saying so, but honest to Christ, the thought never crossed my mind.*

He picked up the phone now and dialed the Bortman number in Castle Rock, Maine.

Busy.

He hung up and sat for five minutes, looking out at the street where Billy had learned to ride first a trike, then a bike with training wheels, then a two-wheeler. At eighteen he had brought home the final improvement—a Yamaha 500. For just a moment he could see Billy with paralyzing clarity, as if he might walk through the door and sit down.

He dialed the Bortman number again. This time it rang. The voice on the other end managed to convey an unmistakable impression of wariness in just two syllables. "Hello?" At that same moment, Dale's eyes fell on the dial of his wristwatch and read the date—not for the first time that day, but it was the first time it really sunk in. It was April 9th. Billy and the others had died eleven years ago yesterday. They—

"Hello?" the voice repeated sharply. "Answer me, or I'm hanging up! Which one are you?"

Which one are you? He stood in the ticking living room, cold, listening to words croak out of his mouth.

"My name is Dale Clewson, Mr. Bortman. My son—"

"Clewson. Billy Clewson's father." Now the voice was flat, inflectionless.

"Yes, that's—

"So you say."

Dale could find no reply. For the first time in his life, he really was tongue-tied.

"And has your picture of Squad D changed, too?"

"Yes." It came out in a strangled little gasp.

Bortman's voice remained inflectionless, but it was nonetheless filled with savagery. "You listen to me, and tell the others. There's going to be tracer equipment on my phone by this afternoon. If it's some kind of joke, you fellows are going to be laughing all the way to jail, I can assure you."

"Mr. Bortman—"

"Shut up! First someone calling himself Peter Moulton calls, supposedly from Louisiana, and tells my wife that our boy has suddenly showed up in a picture Josh sent them of Squad D. She's still having hysterics over that when a woman purporting to be Bobby Kale's mother calls with the same insane story. Next, Oliphant! Five minutes ago, Rider Dotson's brother! *He* says. Now you."

"But Mr. Bortman—"

"My wife is upstairs sedated, and if all of this is a case of 'Have you got Prince Albert in a can,' I swear to God—"

"You know it isn't a joke," Dale whispered. His fingers felt cold and numb—ice cream fingers. He looked across the room at the photograph. At the blonde boy. Smiling, squinting into the camera.

Silence from the other end.

"You know it isn't a joke, so what happened?"

"My son killed himself yesterday evening," Bortman said evenly. "If you didn't know it."

"I didn't. I swear."

Bortman sighed. "And you really are calling from long distance, aren't you?"

"From Binghamton, New York."

"Yes. You can tell the difference—local from long distance, I mean. Long distance has a sound...a...a hum..." Dale realized, belatedly, that expression had finally crept into that voice. Bortman was crying.

"He was depressed off and on, ever since he got back from Nam, in late 1974," Bortman said. "It always got worse in the spring, it always peaked around the 8th of April when the other boys...and your son..."

"Yes," Dale said.

"This year, it just didn't...didn't peak."

There was a muffled honk—Bortman using his handkerchief.

"He hung himself in the garage, Mr. Clewson."

"Christ Jesus," Dale muttered. He shut his eyes very tightly, trying to ward off the image. He got one which was arguably even worse—that smiling face, the open fatigue shirt, the twisted dogtags. "I'm sorry."

"He didn't want people to know why he wasn't with the others that day, but of course the story got out." A long, meditative pause from Bortman's end. "Stories like that always do."

"Yes. I suppose they do."

"Joshua didn't have many friends when he was growing up, Mr. Clewson. I don't think he had any real friends until he got to Nam. He loved your son, and the others."

Now it's him, comforting me.

"I'm sorry for your loss," Dale said. "And sorry to have bothered you at a time like this. But you'll understand…I had to."

"Yes. Is he smiling, Mr. Clewson? The others…they said he was smiling."

Dale looked toward the picture beside the ticking clock. "He's smiling."

"Of course he is. Josh finally caught up with them."

Dale looked out the window toward the sidewalk where Billy had once ridden a bike with training wheels. He supposed he should say something, but he couldn't seem to think of a thing. His stomach hurt. His bones were cold.

"I ought to go, Mr. Clewson. In case my wife wakes up." He paused. "I think I'll take the phone off the hook."

"That might not be a bad idea."

"Goodbye, Mr. Clewson."

"Goodbye. Once again, my sympathies."

"And mine, too."

Click.

Dale crossed the room and picked up the photograph of Squad D. He looked at the smiling blonde boy, who was sitting cross-legged in front of Kimberley and Gibson, sitting casually and comfortably on the ground as if he had never had a hemorrhoid in his life, as if he had never stood atop a stepladder in a shadowy garage and slipped a noose around his neck.

Josh finally caught up with them.

He stood looking fixedly at the photograph for a long time before realizing that the depth of silence in the room had deepened. The clock had stopped.

SUMMER

By Tananarive Due

During the baby's naptime, a housefly buzzed past the new screen somehow and landed on Danielle's wrist while she was reading *Us Weekly* on the back porch. With the Okeepechee swamp so close, mosquitoes and flies take over Gracetown in summer.

"Well, I'll be damned," she said.

Most flies zipped off at the first movement. Not this one. The fly sat still when Danielle shook her wrist. Repulsion came over her as she noticed the fly's spindly legs and shiny coppery green helmet staring back at her, so she rolled up the magazine and gave it a swat. The fly never seemed to notice Angelina Jolie's face coming. Unusual for a fly, with all those eyes seeing in so many directions. But there it was, dead on the porch floorboards.

Anyone who says they wouldn't hurt a fly is lying, Danielle thought.

She didn't suspect the fly was a sign until a week later, when it happened again—this time she was in the bathroom clipping her toenails on top of the closed toilet seat, not in her bedroom, where she might disturb Lola during her nap. A fly landed on Danielle's big toe and stayed put.

Danielle conjured Grandmother's voice in her memory—as she often did when she noticed the quiet things Grandmother used to tell her about. Grandmother had passed three summers ago after a stroke in her garden, and now that she was gone, Danielle had a thousand and one questions for her. The lost questions hurt the most.

Anything can happen once, Grandmother used to say. When it happens twice—listen. The third time may be too late.

It was true about men, and Danielle suspected it was true about the flies, too.

Once the second fly was dead—again, almost as if it had made peace with leaving this world on the sole of her slipper— Danielle wondered what the flies meant. Was someone trying to send her a message? A warning? Whatever it was, she was sure it was something bad.

Being in the U.S. Army Reserves, her husband, Kyle, didn't like to look for omens. He only laughed when she talked about Grandmother's beliefs, not that Kyle was around in the summer to talk to about anything. His training was in summers so it wouldn't interfere with his job as county school bus supervisor. Last year, he'd been gone only a couple of weeks, but this time he was spending two long months at Fort Irwin in California. He was in training exercises, so the only way to reach him was in a real emergency, through the Red Cross. She hadn't spoken to him in three weeks.

Kyle had been in training so long, the war had almost come and gone. But he still might get deployed. He'd reminded her of

that right before he left, as if she'd made a promise she and Lola could do fine without him. What would she do if she became one of those Iraq wives? Life was hard enough in summer already, without death hanging over her head, too.

With Grandmother gone from this earth and Kyle in California, Danielle had never been so lonely. She felt loneliest in the bathroom.

Maybe the small space was too much like a prison cell. But she didn't fight the feeling. Her loneliness felt comfortable, familiar. She wouldn't have minded sitting with the sting awhile, feeling sorry for herself, staring at the dead fly on the black and white tile. Wondering what its message had been.

But there wasn't enough time for that. Lola was awake, already angry and howling.

Long before the bodies were found, Grandmother always said the Okeepechee swampland was touched by wrong. Old Man McCormack sold his family's land to developers last fall, and Caterpillar trucks were digging a man-made lake in the soggy ground when they uncovered the bones. And not just a few bones, either. The government people and researchers were still digging, but Danielle had heard there were three bodies, at last count. And not a quarter mile from her front door!

Grandmother had told her the swampland had secrets. Lately, Danielle tried to recall more clearly what Grandmother's other prophecies had been, but all she remembered was Grandmother's earthy laughter. Danielle barely had time to fix herself a bowl of cereal in the mornings, so she didn't have the luxury of

Grandmother's habits: mixing powders, lighting candles, and sitting still to wait. But Danielle believed in the swampland's secrets.

All her life, she'd known Gracetown was a hard place to live, and it was worse on the swamp side. Everyone knew that. People died of cancer and lovers drove each other to misery all over Gracetown, but the biggest tragedies were clustered on the swamp side—not downtown, and not in the development called The Farms where no one did any farming. When she was in elementary school, her classmate LaToya's father went crazy. He came home from work one day and shot up everyone in the house; first LaToya, then her little brothers (even the baby), and her mother. When they were all dead, he put the gun in his mouth and pulled the trigger—which Danielle wished he'd done at the start. That made the national news.

Sad stories had always watered Gracetown's backyard vegetable gardens. Danielle's parents used to tell her stories about how awful poverty was, back when sharecropping was the only job for those who weren't bound to be teachers, and most of their generation's tragedies had money at their core. That wasn't so true these days, no matter what her parents said. Even people on the swamp side of Gracetown had better jobs and bigger houses than they used to. They just didn't seem to build their lives any better.

Danielle had never expected to raise a baby in Gracetown, or to live in her late grandmother's house with an Atlanta-born husband who should know better. The thought of Atlanta only six hours north nearly drove her crazy some days. But Kyle Darren Richardson was practical enough for the both of them. Coolheaded. That was probably why the military liked him enough to invest so much training. *Do you know how much houses cost in Atlanta? We'll save for a few more years, and then we'll go. Once my training is done, we'll never be hurting for money, and we'll live on a base in Germany somewhere. Then you can kiss Gracetown good-bye.*

In summer, with Kyle gone, she was almost sure she was just another fool who never had the sense to get out of Gracetown. Ever since high school, she'd seen her classmates with babies slung to their hips, or married to the first boy who told them they were pretty, and she'd sworn, Not me. All of those old friends—each and every one—had their plans, too. Once upon a time.

Danielle wasn't sure if she was patient and wise, or if she was a tragedy unfolding slowly, one hot summer day at a time.

—

Lola cried harder when she saw her in the doorway. Lola's angry brown-red jowls were smudged with dried flour and old mucus. Sometimes Lola was not pretty at all.

Danielle leaned over the crib. "Go back to sleep, Lola. What's the matter now?"

As Danielle lifted Lola beneath her armpits, the baby grabbed big fistfuls of Danielle's cheeks and squeezed with all her might. Then Lola shrieked and dug in her nails. Hard. Her eyes screwed tight, her face burning with a mighty mission.

Danielle cried out, almost dropping all twenty pounds of Lola straight to the floor. Danielle wrapped her arm more tightly around Lola's waist while the baby writhed, just before Lola would have slipped. The baby's legs banged against the crib's railings, but Danielle knew her wailing was only for show. Lola was thirteen months old and a liar already.

"No." Danielle said, keeping silent the *you little shit bag.* "Very bad, Lola."

Lola shot out a pudgy hand, hoping for another chance at her mother's face, and Danielle bucked back, almost fast enough to make her miss. But Lola's finger caught the small hoop of the gold earring in Danielle's right earlobe and pulled, hard. The earring's catch held at first, and Danielle cried out as pain tore through. Danielle expected to see droplets of blood on the floor, but she only saw the flash of gold as the earring fell.

Lola's crying stopped short, replaced by laughter and a triumphant grin.

Anyone who says they wouldn't hurt a fly is lying.

If Lola were a grown person who had just done the same thing, Danielle would have knocked her through a window. Rubbing her ear, she understood the term seeing red, because her eyes flushed with crimson anger. Danielle almost didn't trust herself to lay a hand on the child in her current state, but if she didn't Lola's behavior would never improve. She grabbed Lola's fat arm firmly, the way her mother had said she should, and fixed her gaze.

"*No*," Danielle said. "Trying to hurt Mommy is *not* funny."

Lola laughed so hard, it brought tears to her eyes. Lola enjoyed hurting her. Not all the time, but sometimes. Danielle was sure of it.

Danielle's mother said she was welcome to bring Lola over for a few hours whenever she needed time to herself, but Mom's joints were so bad that she could hardly pull herself out of her chair. Mom had never been the same since she broke her hip. She couldn't keep up with Lola, the way the child darted and dashed everywhere, pulling over and knocking down everything her hands could reach. Besides, Danielle didn't like what she saw in her mother's eyes when she brought Lola over for more than a few minutes: Jesus, help, she can't even control her own child.

Danielle glanced at the Winnie the Pooh clock on the dresser. Only two o'clock. The whole day stretched to fill with just her and the baby. Danielle wanted to cry, too.

Kyle told her maybe she had postpartum depression like the celebrity women she read about. But her family had picked cotton and tobacco until two generations ago, and if they could tolerate that heat and work and deprivation without pills and therapy, Danielle doubted her constitution was as fragile as people who pretended to be someone else for a living.

Lola could be hateful, that was all. That was the truth nobody wanted to hear.

Danielle had tried to conceive for two years, and she would always love her daughter—but she didn't like Lola much in summer. Lola had always been a fussy baby, but she was worse when Kyle was gone. Kyle's baritone voice could snap Lola back to her sweeter nature. Nothing Danielle did could.

—

"She still a handful, huh, Danny?"

"That's one word."

Odetta Mayfield was the only cousin Danielle got along with. She was ten years older, so they hadn't started talking until Grandmother's funeral, and they'd become friends the past two years. The funeral had been a reunion, helping Danielle sew together pieces of her family. Odetta's husband had been in the Army during the first Iraq war and had come back with a girlfriend. They had divorced long ago and her son was a freshman at Florida State, so Odetta came by the house three or four times a week. Odetta had no one else to talk to, and neither did she. If not for her cousin and her mother, Danielle might be a hermit in summer.

Odetta bounced Lola on her knee while the baby drank placidly from a bottle filled with apple juice. Seeing them together in the white wicker rocker, their features so similar, Danielle wanted to beg her cousin to take the baby home with her. Just for a night or two.

"Did she leave a mark on my face?"

"Can't see nothing from here," Odetta said. But Danielle could feel two small welts rising alongside her right cheekbone. She dabbed her face with the damp kitchen towel beside the pitcher of sugar-free lemonade they had decided to try for a while. The drink tasted like chemicals.

"People talk about boys, but sometimes girls are just as bad, or worse," Odetta said. "We went through the same mess with Rashan. It passes."

Danielle only grunted. She didn't want to talk about Lola anymore. "Anything new from McCormack's place?" she asked, a sure way to change the subject. Odetta worked as a clerk at City Hall, so she had a reason to be in everybody's business.

"Girl, it's seven bodies. Seven."

Seven bodies left unaccounted for, rotting in swampland? The idea made Danielle's skin feel cold. Mass graves always reminded her of the Holocaust, a lesson that had shocked her in seventh grade. She'd never looked at the world the same way after that, just like when Grandmother first told her about slavery.

Danielle said, "My mother still talks about the civil rights days, the summer those college kids tried to register sharecroppers on McCormack's land. He set those dogs loose on them."

"Unnnnnhhhhh-hnnnnhhhhh..." Odetta said, drawing out the indictment. "Sure did. That's the first thing everybody thought. But the experts from Tallahassee say the bones are older than forty-odd years. More like a hundred."

"Even so, how are seven people gonna be buried out on that family's land? There weren't any Indians living there. Shoot, that land's been McCormack Farm since slavery. I bet those bones are from slave times and they just don't wanna say. Or something like Rosewood, with a bunch of folks killed and people kept it quiet."

"Unnnhhhh-hhnnnnnhhh," Odetta said. She had thought of that, too. "We may never know what happened to those people, but one thing we do know—keep off that land."

"That's what Grandmother said, from way back. When I was a kid."

"I know. Mama, too. Only a fool would buy one of those plots."

The McCormack Farm was less than a mile from Danielle's grandmother's house, along the unpaved red clay road the city called State Route 191, but which everyone else called Tobacco Road. Tobacco had been the McCormacks' business until the 1970s. Another curse to boot, Danielle thought. She drove past the McCormacks' faded wooden gate every time she went into town, and the gaudy billboard advertising LOTS FOR SALE— AS LOW AS $150,000. The mammoth, ramshackle tobacco barn stood beside the roadway for no other reason than to remind every-one of where the McCormack money had come from. Danielle's grandfather had sharecropped for the McCormacks, and family lore said her relatives had once been their slaves.

"How old's this baby?" Odetta said suddenly. "A year?"

"Thirteen months."

Lola had only been a month old last summer, when Kyle went off to training. But Danielle didn't want to talk about Lola now. She had enjoyed forgetting all about her.

"Your grandmama never told you nothing about summer and babies?"

Danielle stared at her cousin, whose eyes were slightly small for her face. "You lost me."

"Just be careful, is all. Especially in July. Summer solstice. Lola may seem strong to you, but you gotta pay special attention to any baby under two. It's always the young ones. And now that those bones have been unburied, you need to keep an eye out."

"What are you talking about, girl?"

"I'm surprised your grandmama would let you raise a baby in her house. When your mama was young, she moved in with her cousin Geraldine. She never told you that? Lived in their basement until your mama was two."

The story sounded vaguely familiar, but Grandmother had died soon after Danielle married Kyle, when Danielle had still been convinced she'd be moving to Atlanta within six months. She hadn't even been pregnant then. Not yet. She and Kyle hadn't planned on a baby until they had more money put together. If not for Lola, they might be living in Atlanta right now.

"What do you mean? Is the water bad?" Now Danielle felt alarmed.

Odetta shook her head. "Leeches."

Danielle remembered the flies. Now she could expect leeches, too? "You mean those nasty things people put on their skin to suck out poison?" A whole army of leeches could crawl under the back door, with that half-inch gap that always let the breezes through. "Those worms?"

"Not that kind," Odetta said. "Swamp leeches are different. It's just a name Mama used to call them by. You could call them lots of things. Mostly people call them demons, I guess."

Danielle would have thought she'd heard wrong, except that Odetta had a sense of humor. She had Danielle cracking up at Grandmother's funeral, of all places, when Odetta whispered to point out how everyone who gave remembrances called Grandmother by a different surname. Grandmother had been married four times. When I knew Mrs. Jenkins…When I knew Mrs. Roberts…And on down the line. Once Odetta pointed it out, Danielle had to pretend to be sobbing to stifle her giggles. That laughter was the only light that day.

"What did you put in that lemonade after I fixed it? I know you're not sitting there talkin' 'bout demons in the swamp like some old voodoo lady," Danielle said.

Odetta looked embarrassed, rubbing the back of her neck. "I don't know nothin' 'bout no voodoo, but just ask folks. Nobody has young children near the swamp in summer, or there's trouble to follow. Cece's baby got crib death. But usually it just lasts the summer. The babies change, but by fall they change back."

"Change into what?" Danielle said, still trying to decide if Odetta was playing.

Odetta shrugged. "I don't know. Something else. Somebody else. You watch this baby real close, hear? Anything happens, ask me to take her by Uncle June's. He's my granddaddy's brother, and he knows what to do. He says it's like those spirits flock to the swamp in summer, the way fish spawn. And they leech on to the young ones. That's why Mama calls them leeches."

Danielle almost asked about the flies she had seen, but she caught herself. What was she thinking about? Grandmother might have kept her candles lit, but this was plain crazy talk. The minute you start letting family close to you, turns out they're bent on recruiting you for the funny farm, too. No wonder Kyle was so happy living so far from Atlanta and his relatives. He might never want to go back home.

"Don't look at me like that," Odetta said, grunting. She handed Lola back, almost as if to punish her. Danielle watched the sweetness seep from Lola's face, replaced by the mocking glare she saved only for her mother. If Odetta hadn't been sitting here watching, Danielle would have glared right back.

"I got to get home and see my stories. Just remember what I said. Watch over this girl."

The swamp leeches can have her, Danielle thought. God as her witness, that was the exact thought in her mind.

—

Just to be on the safe side—and because she knew Grandmother would hound her in her dreams otherwise—Danielle brought Lola's crib into her bedroom so the baby wouldn't be alone at night. Danielle hadn't let the baby sleep in the master bedroom since she was four months old, and Lola never had liked the nursery. Now Lola fussed less at bedtime, and Danielle rediscovered how much she enjoyed the sound of another person breathing near her at night.

The strange thing didn't happen until nearly a week after Odetta's visit, when Danielle had all but forgotten the flies and Odetta's story about leeches. A loud noise overhead woke her one night. It sounded like a boot clomping on the rooftop.

Danielle opened her eyes, staring at the shadow of the telephone pole on her ceiling. Her bedroom always captured the light from the single streetlamp on this end of Tobacco Road. Sometimes her eyes played tricks on her and made her think she could see shadows moving. But shadows don't make noise, Danielle thought.

Kyle would have sprung from bed to get his rifle out of the closet. But Kyle wasn't here, and Danielle didn't know the first thing about the rifle, so she lay there and stared above her. That hadn't sounded like breathing wood or any of the old house's other aches and pains. Someone was on the roof. That was plain.

Not a rat. Not a raccoon. Not an owl. The only thing big enough to make that noise was a deer, and she'd stopped believing in creatures with hooves flying to the roof when she was eight. The clomping sound came again, and this time it was directly above her.

Danielle imagined she saw a large shadow on the ceiling above her, as if something was bleeding through. Imagined, because she couldn't be sure. But it seemed to be more than just the darkness. It was a long, large black space, perfectly still. Waiting. Danielle's heart galloped, and she couldn't quite catch her breath.

The thing on the rooftop made up its mind about what to do next. The shadow glided, and Danielle heard three purposeful strides on the rooftop above the mass. The sound was moving away from her bed—toward the baby's crib. The baby was still asleep, breathing in slow, heavy bursts. Danielle could hear Lola over the noise.

Too late, Danielle realized what she should have done: she should have jumped up, grabbed the baby, and run out of the room as fast as she could. It wouldn't have hurt to grab her Bible from inside her nightstand drawer while she was at it. But Danielle had done none of that, so she only lay there in helpless horror while a shadow-thing marched toward her baby girl.

As soon as the last clambering step sounded above—
CLOMP—the baby let out a loud gasp.

The rooftop went silent, and the baby's breathing was normal again. Well, almost. Lola's breathing was shallower than it
had been before, more hurried, but it was the steady breath of
sleep.

After listening in the dark for five more minutes, feeling
muscle cramps from lying so still beneath her blanket, Danielle
began to wonder if the horrific sound on the rooftop had been in
her imagination. After all, Lola woke up if she sneezed too close
to her door—so wouldn't the baby have heard that racket and
started wailing right away? Suddenly, it seemed all too plausible
that the sound had been from a raccoon or an owl. Just magnified
in the darkness, that was all. Served her right for letting family
too close to her. Just crazy talk and nightmares.

But although she didn't hear another peep from the rooftop—and Lola's breathing was as steady as clockwork running
only slightly fast—Danielle couldn't get back to sleep that night.
She lay awake, listening to her baby breathe.

—

The next thing Danielle knew, sunlight was bright in her
bedroom.

Lola woke up at six o'clock every morning no matter how late
she went to bed, so Danielle hadn't lingered in bed long enough
for the sun to get this bright all summer. Danielle looked at her
alarm clock: It was ten o'clock! Midmorning. All at once, Danielle
remembered the racket on the rooftop and her baby's little gasp.
She fully expected to find Lola dead.

But Lola was sitting up in a corner of the crib, legs folded under her cross-legged, patiently waiting. She wasn't whining, cooing, babbling, or whimpering. The baby was just staring and waiting for her to wake up.

Danielle felt a surge of warmth and relief, a calm feeling she wished she could have every morning. "Well, look at Mommy's big girl!" Danielle said, propping herself up on her elbows.

The baby sat straighter, and her mouth peeled back into a wide grin as she leaned forward, toward Danielle. Her eyes hung on Danielle, not missing a single movement or detail. She looked like a model baby on the diaper package, too good to be true.

And Danielle knew, just that fast. Something was wrong with the baby.

This isn't Lola, she thought. She would swear on her grave that she knew right away.

There were a hundred and one reasons. First, Lola started her days in a bad mood, crying until she got her baa-baa. The new sleeping arrangement hadn't changed that. And Lola never sat that way, cross-legged like a Girl Scout around a campfire. The pose didn't look right on her.

Danielle went through the usual motions—seeing if Lola's eyes would follow her index finger (they did, like a cat's), testing her appetite (Lola drank a full bottle and ate a banana), and checking Lola's temperature (exactly 98.6). Apparently, Lola was fine.

Danielle's heart slowed down from its gallop and she laughed at herself, laying Lola down flat on the wicker changing-table. The baby didn't fuss or wriggle, her eyes still following Danielle's every movement with a contented smile.

But when Danielle opened the flaps of the Pampers Cruisers and the soiled diaper fell away between Lola's chunky thighs, something dark and slick lay there in its folds. Danielle's first glance told her that Lola had gotten her bowel movement out of the way early—until the mess in her diaper shuddered.

It was five inches long, and thin, the color of the shadow that had been on her ceiling. The unnamable thing came toward Danielle, slumping over the diaper's elastic border to the table surface. Then, moving more quickly with its body hunched like a caterpillar, the thing flung itself to the floor. A swamp leech. A smell wafted up from its wake like soggy, rotting flesh.

For the next hour, while Lola lay in silence on the changing table, Danielle could hardly stop screaming, standing high on top of her bed.

—

Danielle didn't remember calling Odetta from the portable phone on her nightstand, but the phone was in her hand. The next thing she knew, Odetta was standing in her bedroom doorway, waving a bath towel like a matador, trying to coax her off the bed. Danielle tried to warn Odetta not to touch the baby, but Odetta didn't listen. Odetta finished changing Lola's diaper and took her out of the room. The next time Danielle saw Lola, she was dressed up in her purple overalls, sitting in the car seat like they were on their way to lunch at Cracker Barrel.

"We're going to Uncle June's," Odetta said, guiding Danielle into the car.

Danielle didn't remember the drive, except that she could feel Lola watching her in the rearview mirror the whole way. Danielle was sure she would faint if she tried to look back.

Uncle June lived at the corner of Live Oak and Glory Road, near the woods. He was waiting outside his front door with a mug, wearing his pajama pants and nothing else. A smallish, overfed white dog sat beside him. Odetta kept saying Uncle June could help her, he would know just what to do, but the man standing outside the house at the end of the block looked like Fred Sanford in his junkyard. His overgrown grass was covered with dead cars.

Odetta opened the car door, unbuckled Lola from her car seat, and hoisted the baby into her arms. As if it were an everyday thing. Then she opened Danielle's car door and took her hand, helping her remember how to come to her feet.

"Just like with Ruby's boy in ninety-seven," Odetta told Uncle June, slightly breathless.

Uncle June just waved them in, opening his door. The dog glared back at Lola, but turned around and trotted into the house, where it made itself scarce.

"Let's put her in the bathtub, in case another one comes out of her," Odetta said.

"Won't be, but do what you want." Uncle June sounded sleepy.

Lola sat placidly in the center of the bathtub while the warm water came up to her waist. Her legs were crossed the way they had been in her crib. Danielle couldn't stare at her too long before she was sure a madwoman's wail would begin sliding from her throat.

She looked away.

Danielle gasped when she saw a long blue bathrobe hanging on a hook on back of the bathroom door. It looked like a man floating behind her. And the mirror on the medicine cabinet was askew, swinging to and fro, making her reflection tremble the way her mind was trembling. Danielle wondered how she hadn't fainted already.

"I told you," Uncle June said, and Danielle realized some time must have gone by. Uncle June had been standing before, but now he was sitting on top of the closed toilet lid, reading a well-worn copy of The Man Who Said I Am. "Won't never be but one o' them things." When the water splashed in the tub, they all looked down at Lola.

Danielle didn't look away this time; she just felt her body coil, ready for whatever was next. Lola's face was moony, upturned toward Danielle with the same intense gaze she had followed her with all morning. But the water around her still looked clear. No more leeches. Lola had only changed position slightly, one of the rare times she had moved at all.

"That thing I saw…" Danielle whispered. Her fingers were shaking, but not as much as they had been up until then. "Was it a demon?"

Uncle June shook his head. "What you saw…the leech…that ain't it. Just a sign it's visiting. Evidence. They crawl for dark as fast as they can. Slide through cracks. No one's been able to find one, the way they scoot. Probably 'cause most folks head in the other direction."

"It's under my bed," Danielle said.

"Not anymore, it's not. It's halfway back to the swamp by now."

Danielle shivered for what seemed like a full minute. Her body was rejecting the memory of the thing she had found in her baby's diaper. She waited for her shivering to pass, until she realized it wouldn't pass any time soon. She would have to get used to it.

Lola, in the tub, wrapped her arms around herself with a studious expression as she stared up at Danielle. Lola was still smiling softly, as if she was going out of her way not to alarm her, but her creased eyebrows looked like a grown woman's. On any other day, Lola would be splashing water out of the tub, or else sliding against the slick porcelain with shrieks of glee. This creature with Lola's face might be a child, but it wasn't hers. Water wasn't novel anymore.

"If that isn't Lola…then where is she?" Danielle said, against the ball of mud in her throat.

"Lola's still in there, I expect," Uncle June said. "Dottie Stephens's baby was touched by it for a month…but come fall, it was like nothing happened. And Dottie's baby is a doctor now."

"Unnnnh-hnnnh…" Odetta said with an encouraging smile.

Danielle's heart cracked. A month!

"Course, you don't have to wait that long," Uncle June said. He stood up, lifted the toilet lid, and spat into the bowl. "I've got a remedy. They'll eat anything you put in front of them, so it won't be hard. Put about six drops on a peanut butter cracker, or whatever you have, but no more than six. Give it to her at midnight. That's when they come and go."

"And it won't hurt Lola?" Danielle said.

"Might give her the runs." Uncle June sat again.

"Lola's gonna be fine, Danny," Odetta said, squeezing her hand.

Kyle's nickname for her was Danny, too. She should call Kyle to tell him, she realized. But how could she explain this emergency to the Red Cross?

"What if…I don't give her the remedy? What would happen?" God only knew what was in that so-called remedy. What if she accidentally killed Lola trying to chase away the demon?

Uncle June shrugged. "Anybody's guess. It might stay in there a week. Maybe two. Maybe a month. But it'll be gone by the end of summer. I know that."

"Summer's the only time," Odetta said.

Danielle stared at Lola's face again. The baby's eyes danced with delight when Danielle looked at her, and the joy startled Danielle. The baby seemed like Lola again, except that she was looking at her with the love she saved for Kyle.

"So how many is it now, Odetta? At McCormack's place?" Uncle June said. He had moved on, making conversation. Unlike Danielle, he was not suffering the worst day of his life.

"Six. Turns out they'd counted one too many. Still…"

Uncle June sighed, grieved. He wiped his brow with a washcloth.

"That's a goddamn shame." The way he said it caught Danielle's ear, as if he'd lost a good friend a hundred years ago who had just been brought out to light.

"Nobody has to wait on C.S.I. experts to tell us it's black folks," Odetta said.

Uncle June nodded, sighing. "That whole family ought to be run out of town."

Six dead bodies on McCormack Farm. Six of Gracetown's secrets finally unburied.

The other one, in the bathtub, had just been born.

—

"Tel-e-vi-sion."

Lola repeated the word with perfect diction. "Tel-e-vision."

All morning, while Danielle had sat wrapped up in Uncle June's blue bathrobe on the sofa with a mug of peppermint tea she had yet to sip from, Odetta had passed the time by propping Lola up in a dining room chair and identifying items in the room.

Lola pointed at the bookcase, which Uncle June had crammed top to bottom.

"Bookcase," Odetta said.

"Bookcase," the Lola-thing said. She pointed up at the chandelier, which was only a skeleton, missing all of its bulbs. "Chan-de-lier," Odetta said.

"Chandelier."

Danielle shivered with each new word. Before today, Lola's few words were gummy and indistinct, never more than two syllables. But Lola was different now.

Odetta laughed, shaking her head. "You hear that, Danny? Ruby's baby did this, too. Like damn parrots. But they won't say anything unless you say it first."

The baby pointed at a maroon-colored book on the arm of Uncle June's couch.

"Ho-ly Bi-ble," Odetta said.

"Ho-ly Bi-ble."

At that, honest to God, Danielle almost laughed. Then she shrank further into a ball, trying to sink into the couch's worn fabric and make herself go away.

Lola gazed over at Danielle, the steady smile gone. The baby looked concerned. Mommy? That's what the baby's face seemed to say.

"Your mama's tired," Odetta said.

Tears sprang to the baby's eyes. Suddenly, Lola was a portrait of misery.

"Don't worry, she'll be all right after tomorrow," Odetta said.

All misery vanished. The baby smiled again, shining her big brown eyes on Danielle. Just like Odetta's joke on the day of Grandmother's funeral, that smile was Danielle's only light.

"Ain't that something else?" Odetta whispered. "Maybe this ain't Lola, but they seem to come here knowing they're supposed to love their mamas."

No, it sure isn't Lola, Danielle thought ruefully.

A deep voice behind Danielle startled her. "Gotta go to work," Uncle June said, and the door slammed shut behind him. Danielle had forgotten Uncle June was in the house.

"He never gave me the remedy," Danielle said, remembering.

"Later on, we'll carry Lola with us over to his gas station. It's just up the street. Besides, I'm hungry. Uncle June's got the best burgers under his warmer."

Some people could eat their way through any situation, Danielle thought.

After a time, Odetta turned on the television set, and the room became still. The only noise was from the guests on Oprah and a quick snarl from Uncle June's dog as he slunk past Lola's high chair. Lola didn't even notice the dog. Her eyes were still on Danielle, even when Danielle dozed for minutes at a time. Whenever Danielle woke up, Lola was still staring.

"What do they do?" Danielle asked finally. "Why are they here?"

"Damned if I know," Odetta said. "They don't do much of anything, except smile and try to learn things. Ruby said after she got over her fright, she was sorry to see it go."

"Then how do you know they're demons?"

"Demon ain't my word. I just call them leeches. What scares people is, they're unnatural. You don't ask 'em to come, and they take your babies away for a while. Now, it's true about that crib death, but Cece can't say for sure what caused it. Might've happened anyway." Odetta shrugged, her eyes still on the television screen. "They don't cry. They eat whatever you give 'em. And after that first nasty diaper, Uncle June says they hardly make any mess, maybe a trickle now and then. I bet there's some folks who see it as a blessing in disguise, even if they'd never say so. Lola, can you say blessing?"

"Bles-sing," Lola said, and grinned.

Danielle had never been more exhausted. "I need a nap," she said.

"Go on, girl. Lie down, and I'll get you a blanket. You could sleep all day if you want. This thing won't make no noise."

And it was true. Once their conversation stopped, the Lola-thing sat in the high chair looking just like Lola, except that she never once whined or cried, or even opened her mouth. She just gazed at Danielle as if she thought Danielle was the most magnificent creature on Earth. That smile from Lola was the last thing Danielle saw before she tumbled into sleep.

⟶

Uncle June had owned the Handi Gas at the corner of Live Oak and Highway 9 for at least twenty-five years, and it smelled like it hadn't had a good cleaning in that long, filled with the stink of old fruit and motor oil. But business was good. All the pumps outside were taken, and five or six customers were crammed inside, browsing for snacks or waiting in line for the register. The light was so dim Danielle could barely make out the shelves of products that took up a half dozen rows, hardly leaving room to walk.

Uncle June was busy, and he didn't acknowledge them when they walked in. Odetta went straight for the hamburgers wrapped in shiny foil inside the glass display case by the cash register.

"You want one, girl?" Odetta called.

Danielle shook her head. The thought of food made her feel sick. She had ended up with the stroller, even though Odetta had promised her she wouldn't have to get too close to Lola. But Danielle found she didn't mind too much. Being at Handi Mart with the truckers and locals buying their lunch and conducting their business almost made Danielle forget her situation. As she pushed the stroller aimlessly down aisle after aisle, hypnotized by the brightly colored labels, she kept expecting to feel Lola kicking her feet, squirming in the stroller or screaming at the top of her lungs. Her usual antics.

Instead, Lola sat primly with her hands folded in her lap, her head turning right and left as she took in everything around her. Odetta had spent the rest of the morning braiding Lola's hair, entwining the plaits with pretty lilac-colored bows alongside the well-oiled grooves of her brown scalp. Despite her best efforts, Danielle had never learned how to do much with Lola's hair. Mom hadn't known much about hair, either. This was the best Lola had looked in ages.

"I'll get to you in a minute," Uncle June called to Danielle as the stroller ambled past the register line. "I know what you're here for."

"Take your time," someone said, and she realized she had said it. Calm as could be.

Although Odetta was kin to Uncle June, she had to stand in line like any other customer. She'd helped herself to two burgers, a large bag of Doritos, and a Diet Coke from the fountain in back. It's no wonder she was still carrying her baby weight eighteen years later, Danielle thought. With nothing left to do, Danielle stood beside her cousin to wait.

"Well, ain't you cute as a button?" a white woman said ahead of them, gazing back at Lola in the stroller. The woman was wearing an ostrich feather hat and looked like she was dressed for church. Was it Sunday? Danielle couldn't remember.

"But-ton," Lola said, the first sound she'd made in two hours.

The woman smiled down at Lola. Danielle almost warned her not to get too close.

"Thank you," Danielle said. Lola didn't get many compliments, not with her behavior.

"How old is she?" the woman asked.

"Thirteen months," Danielle said, although it was a lie. As far as she knew, the thing in Lola's stroller was as old as the swamp itself.

"Lovely," the woman said. She turned away when Uncle June asked her pump number.

And Lola was lovely today, thanks to Odetta. There was no denying it. Maybe that was why Danielle could touch her stroller without feeling queasy, or getting goose bumps. The nasty thing that had crawled out of Lola's diaper that morning was beginning to seem like a bad dream.

"One minute," Uncle June said when it was their turn in line. He vanished through a swinging door to the back room. As the door swung to and fro, Danielle saw a mess of boxes in the dank space, and she caught a whiff of mildew and ammonia. Danielle felt her heart speed up. Her fingers tightened around the stroller handles.

"You sure you don't want your own burger? These are mine," Odetta said.

Danielle only shook her head. A fly landed on one of the ribbons on Lola's head.

Uncle June came back with a brown iodine bottle with a black dropper. He set the bottle on the counter next to Odetta's hamburgers. "Remedy's free. Odetta, you owe me five-fifty."

While Odetta rifled through her overstuffed pocketbook, Uncle June leaned over, folded his hands, and stared Danielle straight in the eye. His eyes looked slightly bloodshot, and she wondered if he had been drinking that morning.

"Remember what I said," Uncle June told her in a low voice, so the man in the Harley Davidson T-shirt behind them wouldn't hear. "Six drops. No more, no less. At midnight. Then you'll have your baby back."

Danielle nodded, clasping the bottle tightly in her hand. She had questions about what was in the remedy, or how he'd come to concoct it, but she couldn't make her mouth work. She couldn't even bring herself to thank him.

Another fly circled, landing on the counter, and Uncle June killed it with his red flyswatter without blinking. He wiped it off the counter with a grimy handkerchief, his eyes already looking beyond Danielle toward the next customer.

"Won't be long now, Danny," Odetta said.

Danielle nodded again.

Odetta opened the gas station's glass door for her, and Danielle followed with the stroller. She was looking forward to another nap. Hell, she might sleep all day today, while she had the chance. She hadn't had a good night's sleep since Kyle had been gone.

Danielle almost ran down an old white man in a rumpled black Sunday suit who was trying to come in as they walked out. "Sorry—" Danielle began, but she stopped when she saw his face.

Danielle and her neighbor had never exchanged a word in all these years, but there had been no escaping his face when he ran for Town Council in ninety-nine and plastered his campaign posters all over the supermarkets. He was Old Man McCormack, even though his face was so furrowed with lines that he looked like he could be his own father. He was also very small, walking with a stoop. The top of his head barely came up to Danielle's shoulder.

Odetta froze, staring at him with a stupefied expression, but McCormack didn't notice Odetta. His eyes were fixed on the stroller, down at the baby.

He smiled a mouthful of bright dentures at Lola.

"Just like a little angel," McCormack said. Some of his wrinkles smoothed over when he smiled, as if a great burden had been lifted from his face. He gently swatted away a fly that had been resting on the tip of Lola's nose. Danielle didn't know how long the fly had been there.

"Lit-tle an-gel," Lola said.

McCormack's smile faded as he raised his head to look at Danielle, as if he expected to find himself staring into a harsh light. His face became tight, like hardening concrete.

"Afternoon, ma'am," he said. His voice was rough, scraped from deep in his throat. And his eyes flitted away from hers in an instant, afraid to rest on hers too long.

But Danielle had glimpsed his runny eyes long enough to see what he was carrying. She could see it in his stooping shoulders, in his shuffling walk. She felt sorry for him.

"Afternoon, Mr. McCormack," she said.

He paused, as if he was shocked she had been so civil. His face seemed to melt.

"You and your pretty little girl have a good summer, hear?" he said with a grateful smile.

"Yessir, I think we will," Danielle said. "You have a good summer, too."

Despite the way Odetta gaped at her, Danielle wasn't in the mood to pass judgment today. Everyone had something hidden in their past, or in their hearts, they wouldn't want dug out. Maybe the McCormack family would have to answer to God for those bodies buried on their land, or maybe they wouldn't. Maybe Danielle would give Lola six drops of Uncle June's remedy at midnight tonight, or maybe she wouldn't.

She and this old man deserved a little peace, that was all.

Just for the summer.

Danielle rubbed the top of Lola's head, gently massaging her neatly braided scalp. Her tiny visitor in the stroller turned to grin up at her with shining, adoring eyes.

GAMMA

by Laird Barron

My dad shot a horse when I was a boy. The horse, a young sorrel mare named Gamma, slipped and fell while fording a creek way up in the Talkeetna Mountains. Dad had packed her saddle too heavily with supplies. I *knew* the load was too much when he was piling it on as if we were heading for fucking Mt. Denali, but I was a coward and didn't say anything, not a damned thing. Dad scared me. He had to cut the straps off with a Barlow knife as the mare thrashed in the frigid water and sprayed them in mud and twigs and piss.

Come on, girl, he'd muttered through his teeth as she fought. My god, she fought. *Come on, baby. You're okay, you're all right.* He danced at the end of the halter lead, a goddamned acrobat dodging those flying hooves. A bearded ballerina in a drover's hat and cowboy boots, shotgun slapping against his back as he leaped and capered. His antics were so hilarious that I laughed through the tears.

Gamma scrambled to her feet again, but after that she was never quite right, never quite the same, and as summer wore on toward autumn her health declined and she became sickly and weak. Her left eye went milky and her bones jutted. She stopped swishing the flies with her tail when they gathered in clusters upon her haunches. She stood in place for hours, muzzle in the mud.

One morning, Dad shrugged on his jacket and took down the big lever action rifle. He went into the barn and looped a rope around Gamma's neck and led her down the trail to a secluded spot and blew her brains out. I heard the shot, muffled through the log walls, from my bunk. He walked back into our homely cabin and put the carbine in its rack above the dining table. He sat without speaking at the table, waiting for his breakfast.

Mom poured him a cup of coffee and fried some of her world-famous pancakes. With blueberries she'd stashed in the root cellar. Fresh fruit was a cause for celebration at the ol' homestead, let me tell you. I recall being so grateful that I licked my plate clean. Like a dog.

—

If flatworm B eats flatworm A, flatworm B will inherit everything flatworm A ever knew. Even Snopes is on the fence when it comes to debunking this theory. But, look. When I speak of *when*, I mean now. There has always been and will only ever be the now. After the rats and the cockroaches succumb there's another order in the wings. Of course, eventually there won't be any carbon-based life on Terra, even the teeny fibroid shit that exists inside volcanic vents at the bottom of the sea.

Meanwhile. It's not just the flatworms, it's everything. Gimme a tomahawk, hell, a flat rock, and I'll show you.

—

About one hundred and eighty-thousand years ago a hominid slunk into a cave and murdered its brother with a spear of spruce wood, fire-hardened at the tip. The death scream echoed from the cave mouth and the birds in the trees began to chatter.

For reasons unknown, the murderer elected to remain in the darkness. Carrion eaters stayed away. *Everything* that walked or crawled stayed away. A vast and fecund mushroom bed existed within the depths, a portion extending unto the surface world in the manner of a gray tongue drooling from a slack jaw. In the hooting, glottal proto-language of the hominids, the cave was referred to as a cursed place. Eventually an earthquake happened and the mountainside closed in on itself.

Thank you, great worm that encircles all creation.

I eat pancakes, drive a Toyota, go hiking along nature trails. Camping at night in the wild, doing for pleasure what my ancestors did from necessity, I tell myself that stars are clouds of flaming gas, not the eyes of the old gods peeping through a black tapestry.

I tell myself a lot of shit.

—

I met Erin while attending college at the University of Washington. She worked part time at the Saturn Theater. Blonde, blue-eyed Norwegian honey with dazzling white teeth and a penchant for Catholic schoolgirl skirts. She smiled at me a couple of times as I shuffled past the ticket booth and eventually I worked up the nerve to ask her out. We fucked on the third date and the next morning went to breakfast at that little greasy spoon that used to be on the corner of 4th and Payne. Ruby's Grille and Disco. The disco bit was just pre-hipster humor.

We ordered blueberry pancakes with blueberry syrup, if I recall correctly. The café became a weekly hangout and after we got hitched and moved to Olympia, I still took Erin there every spring on the anniversary of our first date.

A couple of years ago I read in the paper that the frumpy, dumpy teen waitress who served us in the old days got murdered. An exchange student who came in for hash and coffee each and every goddamned morning developed an unrequited crush on her. The guy was a math whiz from Vietnam. His family pawned their souls to ship him Stateside for a shot at the major leagues. He tracked the waitress to her house and chloroformed her when she answered the door. Supposedly her choking to death was an accident. The guy decided not to face the music and snuffed himself in the back of the patrol car with a baggie of chemicals he'd stashed in his sock.

Ruby's went under with the recession, so I didn't have to make an excuse to Erin why we went elsewhere to celebrate our happy day.

Gamma died in a hollow. Scraggly spruce trees laced in black moss tangled together like teeth, marshy ground, stagnant water. A breeding pit for mosquitoes and gnats. Winter had come and gone. The birds and the flies and the worms had come and gone. All that remained of her were bones encrusted with verdigris mold sunk in the muck of a mushroom bed. Some of the mushrooms billowed as tall as my thigh.

Not sure what drew me there months after Dad killed her. I remember sitting in the shadows of the trees as summer sweltered the mountainside, and I remember the hum of a light aircraft traversing the eastern sky, and I remember thinking Gamma's skull was an abandoned palace of the ants, a museum of toadstools. I hadn't read any Baudelaire, but wow, fuck it would've resonated, would've blown apart my brain, just like Gamma.

What I couldn't grasp, or didn't want to, was that there were too many bones in that pile. The moss and the fungus obscured the mess, but down deep I knew the shape was wrong, knew I'd stumbled upon a dreadful secret, and I decided to play dumb.

The moss rippled and the ferns shushed with a passing breeze that warbled flute-like through Gamma's eye sockets while the gray and black and yellow-capped mushrooms dripped and oozed. The mushrooms whispered to me.

—

Fact or fiction: In 1951 the CIA secretly poisoned a village in France with a hallucinogenic fungus. The Company was interested in studying the effects of pharmacological mind control in the field. Some villagers died, others were sent to asylums due to lunacy. A royal fuster cluck, as my grandma would've said.

Fiction. The CIA had its hands full developing a small pox delivery mechanism at the time. Yes, mind control and pharmacology were the original hot topics down at R&D as the MKULTRA project testifies. Yes, there was a fungus involved, and yes, numerous villagers went berserk. However, it was simply a batch of bad bread that gummed the works. The baker's snot-nosed assistant fell asleep at the wheel, as it were. Blame him.

Not the CIA and certainly not H.P.'s bat-winged pals from icy Yuggoth. Pay no attention to rumors about them. No government has ever made contact with an alien species much less colluded with it regarding human experiments. It was the baker's apprentice in the mill with a sack of moldy flour.

Moving along, moving along.

—

For a while among certain fringe circles the Cordyceps discovery got scientists' hearts all fluttery. The zombie fungus, some called it. It hailed from before the days of the trilobite. Method of proliferation was to zap various insect species with spores, ants being the most infamous example until late in the 21st century when a rather horrible discovery was made at a monastery in northern Italy. Anyway, the lunatic fringe suggested doomsday might come in the form of a sporulating organism awakened from hibernation, or worse, adapted by one pharmaceutical company or another for military or private sector application.

The nutters were wrong about poor, innocent Cordyceps, but they had basically the right idea.

Lake Vostok was the epicenter of the latest and greatest extinction event to visit the planet. You know, the lake far beneath Antarctic ice sheets at the quaintly dubbed Pole of Cold where the Soviets built a station back when there were real live Soviets. Vostok Station. The Soviets stuck it out there and after they left, the Russians got ambitious and started digging, and digging. No money for bread, no money for car fuel, but plenty of rubles for military adventures and boondoggle science projects that included digging.

Into the ice.

That ice is thousands of years old near the surface and it just gets older until you reach bottom and there's a big, prehistoric lake teeming with…life. What kind of life? Oh, don't be coy, motherfucker. You know what kind.

The ha-ha part is, that "hypothetical" rogue star would've done the job down the road when it kicked loose that planet-killer asteroid and sent her tumbling our way. Every twenty-six million years. Look at the Yucatan, look at the *Grande Coupure.* Just look. Every twenty-six million years. Like a clock. Goodbye, lizards great and small, goodbye fish, goodbye you little troublemaking primates. Goodbye.

Except, it wasn't, isn't, goodbye this time around. It was, is, hello, baby. The living and the dead and those in between all merged. Separation no longer exists. Gives the old phrase "stuck on you" an entirely fresh definition. May as well resign myself to my new niche on the food chain. I got the feeling nothing is going to change until Nemesis swings by again.

—

Contrary to Mama's predictions, I didn't die in a hail of bullets.

My wife, I forget her name, slept with an English teacher at her school and decided he was an upgrade. She patted me on the hand and said, sayonara, sucker, or words to that effect. I left my happy suburban home and wandered the world for a while. It didn't cure my ills.

I read about this poor bastard over in Germany. He was so depressed he answered a personal from a psycho killer who was looking for a willing victim. The depressed guy went to the psycho's apartment and played the role of sacrificial lamb. A few glasses of burgundy laced with sedatives and depressed dude was unconscious. The psycho cut his guest's throat and cooked the muscle of his shoulder for supper. Yeah, there was some sick, insane shit for you. But, but…in the end, I sort of got where the depressed guy was coming from. The urge to self-annihilation occasionally overwhelms the best of us. Exhibit A: the atom bomb. Exhibit B: love.

Dad and Mom had moved on to greener pastures when I was still a teenager. Upon my return as a middle-aged wreck, I discovered our homestead in the mountains had fallen to ruin. Roof caved in, yard overgrown. Nobody went up there into our private valley. It surprised me how easy Gamma's death hollow was to find and how little it had changed relative to the obliteration of Dad's handiwork and the nearly erased trails that led there.

My god, my god, the bones, or *some* bones remained in a calcified pile, webbed in a strange skein of blue and yellow that clung to everything, dripped from the branches of the trees. Those mushrooms were bigger than ever-cyclopean giants the girth of my torso. They oozed dark sap. Thousands of insects and birds and squirrels were embedded in the webbing, the stalks of the towering fungi. Mummified, slightly shriveled.

The horror I felt was surpassed by a crushing sense of inevitability, of *rightness*. I hadn't come home with the conscious intent of suicide, so I hadn't brought a proper tool. No gun, no knife, no rope. When I tore a spruce branch from its trunk and rammed the jagged tip through my chest, I was very much taken by surprise. I collapsed into the bed of slime and muck, and waited for the agony to be replaced by the smooth, eggshell perfection of the void of death.

Laird Barron

The creeping appetite of that wilderness grave subsumed me over a span of decades. I remember every moment. Although, I am frequently confused. Instead of skewering myself with a homemade spear, I am staring down the barrel of my father's rifle and into his cold, dead eyes as he squeezes the trigger.

—

If visitors should arrive here from some distant constellation, they will find this a quiet, peaceful place. Nothing stirs except the water and the wind, the fronds and the blades and the stems of the plants and the fungi that cover everything from sea to scummy sea, from polar cap to polar cap. If the visitors are smart, and surely to travel so far from home they will be quite advanced, their equipment will safeguard them from spores and pollen and the crawling molds that have become ubiquitous. However, I doubt such visitors will ever become aware of me trapped in eternal amber, peeping at them from every keyhole, from every nightmare version of a sundew, a redcap, a pitcher plant. I doubt they will detect that the hiss of the grass, the drip-drop of sap, are the outward expressions of my cries of lament. They will gather their samples and mine their data, and leave, never guessing they've trod not a graveyard, but Sheol itself. I will watch them depart and I will not twitch no matter my anguish. I am in hell.

And by I, I mean we.

HOARDER

by Kealan Patrick Burke

Fifteen minutes till five and Art Miller's oversized metal suitcase weighed the same as it had when his day started. Even though he'd managed to sell three bottles of Mapleglow, the achievement had been undone by his disappointment in failing to sell the other seven. These were not good numbers, and that was before he even considered the four more boxes in the trunk of his company Lexus. Falkner, his biggest challenger for sales figures (though if he were truly honest with himself, Art knew that all but one of his fellow salesmen fit that bill these days) typically moved at least two boxes a day. But then, Falkner was also assigned the more lucrative neighborhoods where the residents didn't tend to be so tight or untrustworthy. How did they expect Art to move product when they kept giving him low-rent neighborhoods? The Catch-22 was crippling: Sell well and we'll give you more lucrative territories; sell poorly, you'll stay in the dead zone. But, of course, the theory was that a *truly* good salesman could move plenty of product anywhere, could sell ice to the Eskimos, or as Falkner nauseatingly put it: sell spectacles to the blind.

In the passenger seat of the Lexus, the neighborhood quiet around him but for the hollow resounding bark of some agitated dog, Art considered his options. The sun was like a baleful eye through his windshield and with a scowl he tugged down the visor. The smell of Mapleglow filled the vehicle, seemed to fill his pores, his lungs, and he wondered just how bad it would be if he woke up tomorrow and didn't have to smell it anymore, what it would be like to spend a day free of the need to hock crap cleaning products to people who didn't want them, to have just one goddamn day in which he didn't have to endure this demoralizing bullshit and nobody slammed a door in his face. It seemed like a dream (better than the one that greeted him every night in which he found himself trapped in a house that was all small rooms and locked doors), but unless they fired him, that's all it would ever be. He would never quit, was too old to find work elsewhere, so if they put him out to pasture, that would be that. He'd be screwed.

Slowly, he placed his hands on the steering wheel and closed his eyes. The collar of his shirt felt like a hose clamp that tightened with every shallow breath he took. Loosening his tie made little difference. Sweating, his heart like someone dutifully hitting a cold hammer against a hot pillow, he swallowed and opened his eyes. *Don't panic, old man. You've been doing this job for twenty-two years. And you used to be good. Surely that will count for something when all is said and done.* The obvious truth that it wouldn't cinched his collar tighter. Loyalty at the company was reserved for the young and the successful. Nobody there had even been present when Art had started there. Even the man who'd founded it was long in the grave, his name on the sign above the door the most respect likely to ever be shown to people from that bygone era.

Art tugged frantically at the door and all but fell out onto the cracked sidewalk. His lungs grabbed at the hot summer air and tugged the stink of garbage and fresh dog shit into his lungs. He retched, bent over with his hands on his knees, and begged calm back to his addled senses. It would be all right, he counseled. It had to be. If it wasn't and they canned him, well then maybe he'd find a more permanent way to end his despair. The appeal of that notion frightened him, and yet he didn't banish it. Terrifying to consider though it might be, it was also oddly soothing. In the end, it might quite possibly represent the only door yet open to him, a door which, sadly, nobody was likely to slam in his face.

"Are you all right?"

Art started, instantly regrouping, his salesman's face surfacing from behind his own, mouth split in a cheesy, well-practiced smile despite the beads of sweat speckled around it. Arms held tight to his body to keep the dark, damp half-moons beneath his armpits from being seen, he looked at the old woman standing behind the waist-high chain-link fence before him.

"Hello Ma'am," he said, and gave her a tip of his imaginary hat, an erstwhile cream fedora he missed every day. (Like so many other things, it had been lost to the wind.)

He watched her trepidation give way to a smile.

Someone else who remembers a better time, he thought.

"You look sick," she said. "Are you sure you're all right?"

He nodded. "I absolutely am, Ma'am, and I very much appreciate your concern. The heat just got to me for a second. I'm more of a spring and fall man, myself."

"Oh, me too. Would you care for a glass of lemonade?"

Art put a hand to his chest. "I'd hate to impose." Not only did it sound like Heaven, it was a way in, both to her heart and her home, and in his line of work both avenues of ingress were of equal importance. He quickly reached back inside the car and grabbed his case, then shut the door and turned back to face his prospective client.

She waved a hand at him and unlatched the gate. "Don't be silly." It made a tortured shriek he could feel in his fillings when she swung it wide to admit him. "Let's get you out of this terrible heat. It's even making me feel a little swimmy standing in it."

He nodded his gratitude, punctuating it with another tip of his invisible hat, and followed her lead up the path.

The house was a modest Cape Cod, not much different from those strung along the street on both sides of her, the biggest difference being that hers was badly in need of paint, the shutters around the window as cracked and gray as the woman to whom they belonged. The curtains inside were faded, or perhaps that was just the dirt on the glass, he wasn't sure. Some of the shingles had been blown loose from the roof, and parts of her red brick chimney were missing, making it look as if someone had tried to take a bite out of it. Her aerial was cocked at a jaunty angle and unlikely to stay tethered for long or receive anything other than further transmissions of rust. The yard was overgrown, the grass thick, tangled, and thriving, and at least two feet high.

Art repressed a smile. The condition of her house suggested she lived alone. If she claimed any friends, clearly they did not visit often, or care enough about the old woman to assist her in maintaining her home. Which made her vulnerable, open to suggestion, and more likely to be persuaded to try out the Miracle Cleaning Power of Mapleglow.

"Watch that step," she told him, pointing one bony finger down at the broken rectangle of concrete before him. "It's nearly got me more than once."

He hissed in sympathy and shook his head. "You should really have that seen to. I could call a repairman for you if you'd like."

She shrugged as she opened the door. "You're very kind, but that's not at all necessary. I'm used to it at this stage, and it'd kill me to spend any more money on this place than I already have with what few years I'm likely to have left."

"Oh now, don't talk like that," he said, sounding more and more like a character from a bad 1940s black and white movie the more he spoke. *Sayyy buddy, what's the big idea?* "You're in your prime, and if you're not, you could've fooled me."

"Oh, you charmer, you," she said with a chuckle, and shoved open the front door. It resisted at first, caught on something on the other side, and then gave way with a soft slithering sound like a wave of newspapers breaking on the floor.

"Do you need help?" he asked.

"No, no, it's clear now. Do come in," she instructed, and he joined her on the treacherously unstable stoop. She went inside, her floral dress as faded as the curtains, as faded as her skin. She was, to all intents and purposes, like a photograph that had been left too long in the sun. Her hair was a tangled cloud of silver and the only thing he could still see as she shuffled further into the gloom.

"Be careful you don't knock anything over," she told him. "Everything needs to be just so."

Embroiled in the rank odor of mildew, age, bodily wastes, and other things he could not immediately identify that breathed from the throat of the house to meet him, Art made no move to follow. He had been inside old people's homes many times before, of course he had—it was the desolate ground they had assigned them. The median age in this neighborhood and the next was 45-60. All that kept it from being a retirement community was the fragile illusion of free will and independence that came with owning individual homes. But few of them had reeked so badly. And none of them had been so calamitously unkempt.

At the far end of the hall, the old woman ducked her head and turned left into what he assumed was a doorway. He couldn't tell because the entryway was occluded from sight by the poor light and the two haphazardly stacked piles of broken chairs on either side of it. Gravity had pulled the uppermost chairs together so that the whole thing resembled a crude architrave. Closer to where he stood, and almost to his height, were four rough columns of old phonebooks, some of the more recent ones still wrapped in the plastic in which they'd been delivered. Beside them, numerous piles of magazines had been fused together by mold from a leak in the ceiling. Everywhere were swollen plastic grocery bags, all of them full, with what he didn't care to guess. They spotted the floor before him like fallen Chinese lanterns.

From the dark beyond the chairs, the old woman's voice crept out to meet him. "Are you there?"

Art cleared his throat. "Yes Ma'am. My lace was untied. Didn't want to tumble into your—" *Eiffel Tower of busted chairs,* he thought. "I didn't want to knock anything over."

"I appreciate that. Your lemonade's on the table."

He was gripped by apprehension at the thought of what else might be on the table, or on the floor around that table, or coating the inside of that lemonade glass. He had heard of hoarders before, had even half-watched an episode of a TV show about them once, but switched it off in horror after the cleanup crew removed dozens of dead cats from a weeping woman's fridge.

But, he reminded himself, as the old adage went: *a sale's a sale.*

Forced to breathe through his mouth, he steeled himself and carefully navigated his way to the tower of broken chairs.

⬤

If the hallway had been enough to stall him, the kitchen was almost enough to turn him to stone.

"There you go," the old woman told him, indicating with a gnarled hand the mercifully clean glass that sat in the only clear space atop the kitchen table. "My name is Gertrude, by the way."

"Art," he said when he finally remembered to speak, and it came out sounding like an awestruck description of what he found himself looking at, assuming Hell had an aesthetic.

"Sit, please, won't you?"

The idea held little appeal, though in truth he could have just dropped where he stood and he would have found himself propped up by any one of the myriad piles of garbage that filled the room. It was, he thought, as if a convoy of homeless people had infested the interior of the old woman's house, for it looked less like chaos and more like a series of crude dwellings with the kitchen table in the center of it all like some kind of communal gathering place, or a shrine. All that was missing from the picture were some burn barrels and a few hobos slinging cheap wine from paper bags. At worst, he had expected clutter, filth, but this...this was a level of fetidity almost too extreme to comprehend.

Her kitchen was a landfill, defined so clearly by the ordure that the table—the only ordinarily unburied thing in the room—looked out of place by comparison, a raft on a tide of detritus.

"Art, was it?" she asked him, and he nodded dumbly. "Won't you sit down? You're looking a mite more peaked than before."

Around him, the four walls were shielded from view by ramparts that reached to the ceiling. It was not immediately clear what might have been used to build them, so cloaked were they in shadow, dust and mold. Art could feel spores, whether real or imagined, tumbling down his dry throat and into his lungs, where he feared they might take root and grow, until he became just another ruined thing in this sepulcher of decay. As he took a step down into a two-foot high sea of discarded paper towels, newspaper, food wrappers, and Styrofoam containers, his throat clenched against the sudden urge to vomit, and he all but launched himself toward the table. Again he felt dizzy as his hand clamped down on the back of the nearest chair, which at the last almost threw him due to its unstable footing amid the same turbulent ocean of trash he had used it to escape.

"You are in a frightful state," the old woman said, and as he steadied the chair and all but fell into it, he tried to summon a smile to aim at her now incongruously ordinary face, but gave up. Instead he grabbed the glass, which at least was divinely cold, and brought the lemonade to his mouth, choosing to ignore the perils of whatever microbes and hostile organisms were likely to be swimming within. To his relief, it was cold and beautiful and sweet and perfect, and it instantly quenched the roiling acid in his throat. He closed his eyes for a moment to savor it, took another lengthy sip, and exhaled slowly.

"This is really very good, Gertrude," he said. "Thank you."

Kealan Patrick Burke

"Think nothing of it," she said, and wrestled a chair free from the claim of the garbage and joined him at the table.

Only then did he open his eyes. They made a bizarre tableau sitting amid the trash. Directly ahead, the window might once have looked out upon a thriving neighborhood. Now it looked out on nothing, the daylight fractured into blades by a tower of pots, pans, colanders, sieves, baking dishes, and other metallic objects he couldn't immediately identify, all of it glued together by layers of ancient grease and solidified leftovers. It was like some bizarre kind of modern art. He found it horribly difficult to stop looking at it.

"You have..." he started to say, but then paused to clear his throat of its obvious insincerity. "You have a very interesting home."

Between the window and the table where they sat were a series of small rabbit cages, all empty, all stuffed full of garbage. The tops of the cages were crowned by dozens of empty water bottles and soup cans.

"There's that charm again," she said, and lightly patted his elbow, which forced him to repress a flinch. "But I know my house is a mess."

Art raised his eyebrows. *A mess?* A mess would be one thing. This...this was Hiroshima.

"But at my age," Gertrude said, bringing up her hands to inspect them and to aid in illustrating her point, "it tends to get overwhelming."

Careful now, Art thought, taking another sip of the lemonade to clear his mouth of the taste of the air that seemed determined to invade him. "But isn't it dangerous?"

She nodded slowly, sadly. "Yes, of course it is, but you learn to live with it after a while. Learn the places you can go and the things you can do without threat to yourself. Not that I suspect it would be any great loss if I was to die in the morning. I'm afraid I've outlived anyone who might have mourned me."

Despite his discomfort and the miasma in which the conversation was unfolding, he felt a pang of sympathy for the old woman. He too could relate to that kind of loneliness, his wife having passed not four years previous. He had one son he spent many nights trying to convince himself he had done right by, that the boy's rebellion was at fault for their estrangement, but in his heart, he knew that wasn't true. He'd never admit to being a bad father; he just hadn't been a good enough one to keep his boy from becoming a stranger.

"Someone always misses us," he said, and patted the back of her hand. "Even if we don't know it. Someone always does."

In the shadows to his left, something shifted slightly. Boxes settling, he suspected, and oh how many of them there were. The small room felt suffocated by them, a room overstocked with waste in place of air and space and light. His skin crawled as if the dust had managed to infiltrate his pores and was even now burrowing deeper into him. Not for the first time he wondered if it was still worth trying to make a sale, if there was even a point anymore, now that he had been fully subjected to the degree of dilapidation in her inner sanctum. For all her awareness of the dirt, Art still assumed the old woman off-kilter, maybe even completely senile. How else could she live in such squalor and discuss it so matter-of-factly, as if she were merely acknowledging some dirty dishes in the sink?

"Oh, there will be someone," she told him, "at the end. It just won't be anyone I'll want thinking of me after the lights have gone out."

Kealan Patrick Burke

He had no more desire to probe any deeper into her life than he did into the layers of filth around them, so he withdrew his hand from hers and sat back in his chair. It was time, he decided, to make it or break it, and really, considering the unbelievable condition of her house, he knew there was less than nothing to lose.

"I could help you, you know," he said.

Something akin to a spark of hope flitted through her eyes, which in turn ignited his own. "You could? Really? How?"

He nodded and indicated the room around them, from the counter loaded three feet high with Tupperware, broken dishes, pots, glasses, soda bottles, cookie tins, mason jars, cat food bags and bowls (though he had yet to see any animals lurking within the madness), to the hidden window, and on to the far wall with its protective shield of sagging boxes. "I can get you a head start in cleaning it."

The light of hope diminished, replaced by a look of doubt. "You want to help me clean this? *This*?"

"Not exactly. For that I'm afraid you'd need more than just you and me. But to that end I do have a reputable company I can put you in touch with who would do a bang-up job in the space of a day. I've worked with them before. Used them on my own place from time to time, and they're the best. They'll take care of cleaning out the worst of the clutter."

"I see," she said, as if she didn't see at all.

Don't lose her, Art thought. "But after they've cleaned the place out, that's where I come in."

"And how's that?"

"With this little beauty," he said, and, employing a well-practiced one-handed open-retrieve-flourish technique, produced from his case an amber bottle of Mapleglow, which he set on the table between them as if he were an archeologist displaying his latest find to an acolyte. "Mapleglow Deep Cleaner. The premiere kitchen cleaner for over twenty years. Forget Lysol, forget Pine-Sol, my company has been producing the leading brand of kitchen cleaner since they came on the market." But when he looked at her face, he was not encouraged by what he saw. Her eyes had glazed over. If anything, the hospitality she had shown him thus far seemed to have been obliterated, replaced instead by an awareness of the kind of loathsome thing she had admitted into her house.

"If you'll permit me a brief demonstration—" He started to rise, but she put a firm hand on his wrist.

"Don't."

"I promise it won't take but a minute."

"Even if I could afford to buy what you're selling, Art, I wouldn't. As you can plainly see, I have no need for it, and Stephen wouldn't tolerate it."

Art sat back down. "And who is Stephen if I may ask? Your husband? Perhaps if I could have a w—"

Abruptly her face became openly hostile, her eyes shunning the light that already had to struggle to reach them. "You can't, and you wouldn't want to. He doesn't talk, not to you, and not to me. He merely whispers, and even then, I can't understand a single damn thing he's saying. He blames it on my ears when I know I hear just fine. He does it to torment me, as if his illness is my fault. And if you don't want to be the latest in a long line of unfortunates to find out just how ornery he can get, I suggest you leave now."

Art sat still, taken aback by her tone, confused by her words, but still reluctant to concede defeat now that he was already in full sales mode. He looked at the bottle, the amber liquid sloshing slightly due to the unevenness of the table on the carpet of trash. And then he looked at Gertrude.

We're not that different, are we? he thought. *We both live in filth. Yours surrounds you, mine is inside me, and neither one of us will ever be able to scrub ourselves clean because we've let the dirt get too bad. We've become it, and it's become us.*

It was time for the final play, the last-ditch effort, the Oscar-winner.

Without taking the bottle, the critical prop, from the table, he nodded and affected a look of apology. "You're right, Gertrude. I'm very sorry. I guess it's just an old habit of mine. Walking around out there from dawn to dusk schlepping products for someone else in shoes that long ago stopped being comfortable, and in this godforsaken heat…it just gets you down after a while." He let loose a sigh and watched the dust caught in a shard of window-light scatter before his face. "The truth is I'm not even sure I can do the job anymore. I'm not sure I'm any *good* at it anymore. I used to be the best, but you know how it is when you get on in years, everything changes, they bring in the younger guys and you find yourself waiting for the hammer to drop. So, really, I'm sorry." He slid his hand over hers again and was relieved when she didn't pull away. "I get desperate. I get ahead of myself and forget the world doesn't exist for me to sell it something, even though that's what the young ones tell me. I didn't mean to cause offense."

He was gratified to see her face soften, her eyes move to the bottle.

There you go…

Her eyes returned to him. "I didn't mean to snap at you."

"Oh, for Heaven's sake, I certainly asked for it by treating you like just another potential sale. You deserve more respect than that. Can we blame it on the heat and not bad manners, just this once? I'd never be able to live with myself if I thought I had offended or angered you in any way, Gertrude."

Her free hand found the back of his. And was that the hint of moisture in the corner of one eye? "Of course. Forgive me too, won't you? Stephen has been more cantankerous than usual lately. Perhaps it's been affecting my mood. It usually does."

"I'm very sorry to hear that. Marriage can be a trial at the best of times. Even good ones. I know that better than anyone, believe me. Does he work, your husband?" Which in Art-ese meant: *Does he have money he can spend on Mapleglow?*

"No," she said. "He used to, all the time. Worked in the city dump. But that was a long time ago. These days he does little other than lie around being of little use to anyone, which in truth is not much different than the way he used to be even when he could hold down a job. Sometimes I wonder what happened to him, why things ended up as they have. It makes me sad, makes me miss the way he was when we first met."

"Shame," Art said, with a cluck of his tongue. "I'd like to have met him."

The smile she gave him then was a very odd thing indeed. It was wistful, rueful, perhaps even bitter. "Oh no, I'm quite sure you wouldn't."

"And why, may I ask, is that?"

"You'd never understand. I've lived with him as he is now for twenty years and I still don't. What hope do *you* have?"

"As he is now?"

She frowned at him then as if he were the slowest person she'd ever found in her company. "Haven't you been listening?"

He released her hands and sat back. "I think so, yes, but it's entirely likely I missed something."

"Clearly you did. I don't keep this place like it is because I want to, or because I enjoy it. I don't thrive here, Art. How could I? This is Stephen's doing, all of it. Do you honestly think I just sat back and let it get this way? It disgusts me. But there was only so much I could do. Eventually, just like your job, it wore me down, and I guess without really realizing I was doing it, I gave up. I let him win. It was just easier that way."

"Win?" He took in the squalor once more, the clutter and filth robbing the very room of its definition. It seemed as if the terrible odor of waste was growing stronger by the second. "For God's sakes, what could he possibly have won?"

She sighed. "What he always won. His way. He got things the way he liked it. The way he needed it."

Outside a car drove by way too fast for a residential area and Gertrude scowled in the direction of its passing. "They'll kill some poor child one of these days. Then maybe they'll put up a sign."

Art sat forward again, steadied his chair and brought her attention back to him. "Why on earth would anyone need a place to be like this?"

"Again," she said, looking suddenly very old and tired. "You wouldn't understand, and I'm not sure I have the energy to help you. Even then, if I did, what would you do but try to go out into the world and tell everyone. Then they'd come and try to remove him and that would be that."

"That would be...what?"

Her watery eyes met his. "The end of *them*."

A cold trickle of unease began to winnow its way down between Art's shoulder blades, his mind already up and out of the chair and heading to his car should it abruptly become necessary to take his leave. And surely that moment was close. Already he couldn't imagine just how many showers it was going to take to rid himself of the awful crawling feeling of filth. "Gertrude. Are you saying he's violent?"

The old woman scoffed laughter, but it was completely devoid of humor. "What do predators do when other animals attack their nests, Art? They defend them at any cost. My husband simply does the same thing."

Out in the hall, more newspapers slid to the floor.

"Does he…has he ever hurt you?"

"No, not physically at least, though it's a miracle his incessant whispering hasn't driven me right out of my skull."

As if it had required him to be made properly aware of it, Art imagined in that moment that he did hear someone whispering, like the sound the pages of a book might make as the breeze browsed through them. It made him feel foolish when he realized it was nothing more than the a/c struggling to breathe cool air into the room. Still, his senses had become finely attuned, an unfortunate development in a place so full of unpleasant odors. But, he reasoned, better to be on than off, as that smarmy bastard Falkner liked to say.

"He would never hurt me," Gertrude continued, her voice more distant now. "He needs me. There are some things he can't do on his own."

From somewhere, in some other room, a door creaked slowly open. The a/c again, Art surmised, a verdict reinforced by the recurrence of that whispering sound. And if he thought maybe this time it did sound like words, it was nothing more than a side effect of the old woman's story.

"Like feed himself," Gertrude said, and looked at him with eyes so full of pain and regret it was almost debilitating. Before he knew what was happening—not that in a million years he would ever have imagined her capable of such a thing—she half-turned in her chair, twisted the cap off the Mapleglow bottle, and jerked the bottle toward him, dousing his eyes with the cleaning fluid. He screamed, blinded, the pain agonizing, and shoved himself away from the table. The chair toppled, tripping him up, and he went down on his back, hands raised before his eyes as the sea of garbage accepted him.

"Oh God, oh God, Gertrude...what are you doing? Why did...why?"

"I am sorry," Gertrude said. "You probably won't believe me. People seldom do, but this time I absolutely mean it. I am so, so, sorry. You seem like such a nice man."

He flailed, his hands lashing out to grab a hold of something, anything with which to extricate himself from the landfill, but despite the softness of those layers of old food boxes and burger wrappers and potato sacks, he felt as if something else had started to move beneath him, something less yielding to his weight, something bigger. Much bigger, as if someone had just dragged a knotted tree stump out from underneath him. He felt it tear against his back. And he was sinking, the layers separating, pulling him further down, further than should have been possible.

"Oh, Jesus..."

He felt hot breath on his cheek, breath like roadkill, powerful enough to compete with the lemon fresh taste and scent of the Mapleglow that was running down his throat.

"Stephen," the old woman said through her tears, "Please make it quick. This one was polite."

Something like wet ropes wrapped themselves around his chest and began to constrict his breathing, at the same time puncturing his skin with what felt like shards of glass. Pain blossomed seemingly everywhere as bones broke and organs ruptured, but when he opened his mouth to unleash a desperate plea for help, something filled it, something damp and stinking that pushed further into him until he began to choke. His tongue tasted sodden toilet paper.

At the last, he risked opening his eyes but the burning there fractured all that was left to be seen, rendering the already hideous, shapeless face with the rusted soda cap eyes all that much more terrible.

"This is my home," Stephen whispered into his ear.

And gave him the tour.

THE SHRIEKING WOMAN

by Bev Vincent

Burt isn't enthusiastic when Vicky asks if he'll drive her to upstate New York after she learns that the historical society will be holding its annual tour at the Willard Asylum for the Chronically Insane next Saturday. A few days later, though, he suddenly thinks it's the greatest idea in the world. She doesn't ask why he changed his mind. Her older brother can be obstinate and he might reconsider if she probes too much.

The trip from Pittsburgh takes six hours in Burt's old Mustang. They spend Friday night in a dive they can ill-afford, and arrive at the Grandview Building at nine a.m. for the tour, which lasts three hours and costs $10 each.

Conducted by local historians and former employees of the institution, the tour doesn't tell Vicky much she didn't already know. The most fascinating part is an exhibit of suitcases found in an attic after the asylum closed twenty years ago. She wonders if her great aunt's is among them. Identifying details were stripped away, so all that remains are the sad stories of anonymous people committed to this horrible place. Many were locked up for banal reasons: being the victim of abuse, displaying emotions publicly, being overtly sexual, excessive drinking. Some were committed simply because they couldn't speak English.

Several of the buildings were repurposed, but most are abandoned and in poor repair. A large, off-limits section of the campus was converted into a 90-day shock rehab clinic for drug addicted inmates from the nearby prison. Many of the places they're allowed into are dark and dismal. Hadley Hall is the exception, featuring a bowling alley, a movie theater, and a performance stage, but the morgue is dreadful. Vicky has a momentary flash of their great aunt on the post-mortem table being dissected before her remains are dumped in the nearby graveyard, the tour's final stop.

During its 120 years of operation, the asylum admitted over 50,000 patients. Nearly half died here, many of them buried in unmarked graves. The markers were removed to make the field easier to mow. Somewhere beneath this grassy field near Seneca Lake lie the remains of one of their relatives.

Until Vicky started going through the boxes she and Burt brought back from Cheshire, Ohio, after cleaning out Nana Wilkerson's house, she'd never heard of Great Aunt Nancy. According to documents and letters she found, her grandmother's sister suffered from depression and was a frequent inmate at various psychiatric hospitals. She died in Willard when she was 53. As Vicky learned subsequently, relatives of the deceased aren't entitled to information about former patients because of state mental health and national patient privacy laws, at least according to the form letter she received in response to her inquiry.

She and her brother have seen some inexplicable things in recent years that make her worry about her sanity. Given how flighty and unstable their mother was, and Burt's paranoia issues and affinity for conspiracy theories, Vicky wonders if there's a thread of madness running through the family. Her father's genes probably don't help—that's where Burt gets some of his wackier behavior. She hasn't had a long-term relationship yet—she's only nineteen, after all—but she doesn't want to turn out like her mother, running off to exotic-sounding places with strange men only to slink home weeks later, often after being bailed out of jail, until she ultimately went with the wrong man and ended up the victim of an as-yet-unsolved murder.

After the tour, Burt grabs Vicky's hand and leads her toward a fenced-in red brick building that looks like something out of a horror movie. Four columns support the rickety front porch. Vines cover walls, and many of the windows are shattered. The third-floor windows jut from the sloping roof, which is discolored from neglect. Sitting atop the building is a square cupola with two glaring windows from which Vicky imagines wives waiting for their loved ones to return from fishing expeditions on the lake.

"This is where we want to go," Burt says, tugging her toward the wire fence.

Vicky points at the sign posted out front: a red square with a diagonal slash.

Burt laughs. "I know how to get in. Follow me."

Against her better judgment, she does. Along the way, he explains. "After you mentioned Willard, I checked it out online. This used to be the main building. I found videos from urban explorers who've been all through it. They don't show how to get in, but they all started filming at the same place." He stops and examines the fence. "Look here." He indicates a spot where it has been cut, then pulls a few loops of curled metal free and peels it back like a door. "Come on. Before someone sees us."

She follows him through the hole in the fence and toward a set of angled cellar doors. Though on first glance they appear to be locked, they aren't. Burt reaches into his shoulder bag—the one she teased him for carrying—and brings out two powerful flashlights. He hands one to Vicky and then leads the way into a dank and smelly corridor that feels twenty degrees colder than it is outside.

The first thing they encounter is an abandoned gurney. A few yards later, they come across a wheelchair facing a graffiti-covered wall. When they round a corner, Burt accidentally kicks a pile of empty pill bottles that someone left strewn on the floor. Broken glass crunches under their feet like gravel.

On the ground floor, the cathedral windows admit plenty of light, but the place seems foreboding all the same. Photographs and paintings hang askew on the corridor walls. Many of the interior doors have been removed, revealing mostly empty rooms, although some contain random solitary objects. A toppled chair. A bedpan. An old Singer sewing machine. A stuffed animal. Then, surprisingly, at the end of a hallway they encounter one pristine room. No broken glass or peeling paint or graffiti.

In one wing on the second floor, the doorways are covered with streamers and other eerie remnants of festivities that probably took place long after the building closed. The fire hoses on the walls remind Vicky of the hotel in that movie about the guy who tried to kill his family with an ax. Ghosts had partied there, too.

They find a chemistry lab and, next door, the pharmacy, its floor littered with decades-old prescriptions and long out-of-date blister packs containing drugs like chlorpromazine and Zantac.

Bev Vincent

Vicky gets caught up looking through the patient names and doesn't notice Burt continue without her.

When she realizes she's alone, she dashes into the hallway, but there's no sign of him. She calls his name in as loud a whisper as she dares, but he doesn't answer. A lawnmower starts up nearby, drowning out any sounds he might make.

She dashes throughout the maze-like building. At the bottom of a rickety metal staircase, she steps into several inches of water, soaking her shoes and socks. She says a few bad words, then looks around in case someone heard her.

Since her feet are already wet, she decides to slog down the corridor to see if there are places people haven't explored recently because of the water. She ignores the part of her mind that tells her there might be *things* in the water, things like *rats* or *snakes*.

At an intersection, she turns right and is rewarded with a closed door. The knob turns, but she has to put her shoulder against it and heave before the door springs open, almost sending her tumbling to the floor. She shudders at the thought of her near miss.

The door swings shut behind her with a bang. The floor is raised, so there's only a thin layer of water beneath her feet. The room, like the others they explored, is filthy. She prays none of the dust she's inhaling is toxic. The paint on the walls and ceiling has peeled in huge, curled sheets, dangling like leaves on a mysteriously flattened tree. In the shadows cast by her flashlight, she is reminded of bats. Vicky shivers. She hates bats.

Her flashlight reveals filing cabinets lining the walls. Most of the drawers are open, with file folders bulging from within. Documents are scattered on the floor, soaked and ruined. There's almost no chance she'll find anything pertaining to her great aunt, but she isn't going to give up without trying. She picks an

X-ray up from the floor and shines her flashlight on it. Is the large cloudy shape on the patient's chest cancer or water damage? The patient's name, written in the corner, has faded.

Vicky tosses it aside and combs through the pages strewn atop the cabinets. Abstracted from their files and drawers, they're parts of a complex jigsaw puzzle with no picture to guide her. An expert with endless resources and time might be able to piece things together, but not her.

She looks for the drawer that covers Great Aunt Nancy's last name. Trapping the flashlight under her chin, she pulls the swollen files forward one at a time. A few seconds later, the light flares and goes out. "Shit!" she says. This could be bad. She'll never find her way out of this hell hole in the dark.

She holds her breath, suddenly aware of how quiet it is. The lawnmower is a buzzing insect a hundred miles away. She tries to picture her location relative to where they came in, but she's turned too many corners and descended too many staircases to be sure.

Something grazes the back of her neck. She swats at it, hoping her hand doesn't come into contact with a fat bug or a bat. Her heart races, her breath shallow. "Burt?" she says in a voice so feeble that he might not have heard her if he'd been in the room.

Someone screams. The sound is so loud it's like it's inside her head. At first, Vicky wonders if she's the one who yelled. She remembers the ghost the tour guide told them about, smirking as if it were a mandatory part of the script, told to sate her audience's craving for that sort of thing but not something she herself believed.

A moment later, the shriek is repeated. The deafening sound echoes in the small room. Vicky puts her hands over her ears. It's coming from everywhere and nowhere. Vibrations ripple through her body. It goes on and on, with pauses long enough for a person to fill her lungs. It's not the sound of someone afraid or in pain, she thinks. It's someone angry—no, mad, in every sense of the word—screaming out of frustration and fury.

What must it have been like for the people confined in this horrible place? Vicky read about the torture they were subjected to, as doctors attempted to cure their patients of their supposed afflictions. Shock therapy. Psychotropic drugs. Isolation. Vicky pities the screaming woman, as much as she's terrified by her.

She smacks the flashlight with her hand. Something shifts and suddenly there's light again, a golden beam that fills the blackness between her and the closed door two yards away. The light reveals a woman dressed in tattered rags. She has fiery red hair and her face is shriveled like one of those dried apple people Vicky has seen at craft fairs. Her eyes are wide, unblinking behind wire-framed glasses with shattered lenses. When the apparition opens her mouth to shriek again, Vicky sees that she has no teeth. That hideous noise fills the room again. Vicky almost drops the flashlight but regains her grip as she pushes past the woman…except, there's nothing for her to push against. Her outstretched hand meets empty space.

She lunges toward the door. A few stutter-steps and she's there, frantic to be anywhere but here. She doesn't dare look behind as she fumbles for the doorknob. Finds it. Twists.

It doesn't budge. She turns it in the opposite direction.

Still nothing.

The woman continues to wail behind her. The air in the room grows colder. Vicky turns. The woman is facing her, eyes still wide, face still contorted.

"What do you want?" Vicky yells, but she might as well be howling at the moon. She turns away, pounds on the door and jiggles the doorknob, determined not to reward the screaming woman with another glance.

She gropes in her pocket for her cell phone. Stupid, stupid, stupid, she chastises herself. It has a built-in flashlight, which she could have used a few minutes ago, but now she wants to use it to call Burt. She looks at the display. NO SIGNAL. Of course not, deep in the bowels of this ancient building surrounded by metal and pipes and who knows how many feet of earth? She stuffs it back in her pocket and pounds some more. The screaming makes her want to scream herself, so she does, calling Burt's name as she bruises her fists on the solid wood between her and freedom. Between her and sanity.

Finally, a light flickers under the door. She yells until her voice is hoarse, not caring if it's Burt or the police here to arrest them for trespassing, or breaking and entering, or whatever.

The knob turns within her hand. She steps back to make room for it to swing inward.

"Vicky?"

She's never been so happy to see her brother. She flings herself at him, hugging him hard enough to squeeze the air from his lungs.

"What happened?"

She has no words. She just wants to get out of here.

Before they go, though, she turns to take one last look at the room. It's empty. She plays her light around every corner. No medical records. No X-rays scattered on the damp floor.

And no screaming woman. The silence is almost deafening.

"Let's go," Vicky says in a raspy voice.

Burt leads the way as they splash through the ankle-deep water until they reach the stairs. They retrace their steps to the cellar doors, past the pill bottles, the wheelchair and the gurney. Burt glances around to make sure no one is watching before they emerge into the open.

Vicky fills her lungs with fresh air.

When they reach the car, she strips off her soggy shoes and socks. Burt does the same, driving barefoot. He starts telling her about all the cool things he discovered and, for once, Vicky is content to sit and listen as they embark on the long journey home.

When they roll past the former main building of the Willard Asylum, she looks up at the cupola windows, half expecting to see the redheaded woman staring forlornly down at her, but she sees nothing. She still hears the woman's lunatic cries, though. They reverberate in her mind, as constant as the sound of the tires against the road beneath them.

A God Unknown

By Tina Callaghan

"Every man for himself and God for us all." George Keane downed the last of his pint and stood up. Jim gave him a thump on the shoulder as a goodbye and George went out into a fresh night with the smell of autumn in it. There was a good sized moon up there, but it was covered by clouds. The fields were faintly visible.

Something in the shadows and half light made him long for the lost but he shook it off. It didn't do any good to think of what might have been. All he could do was work, as he always had done. He'd shed sweat and tears to make the land right. With no children to pass the place on to, he was doing it for those he followed, those who had suffered to put him where he was, and who gave him the two legs that he stood on. He was old now but he was still strong, stronger than most. He had kept his farm, when others had lost theirs. He would spill blood before he let anyone take it, his or theirs, it didn't matter.

He considered the jeep. He had drunk five pints. He felt straight and normal but if he got stopped on the way home, the breathalyser might tell a different story. He walked a few hundred yards down the road, climbed a ditch and set out across the fields. The moon was still hidden, but he knew his way across the country. He had hunted across it often enough. At the far side of the field, he climbed another ditch and stood at the top. The darkness was extra deep below him.

Hold on, girl, don't go without me. The mare's head disappeared as she looked down to gauge the gap. He had a bare second to get a good grip before the great grey head came up and with a grunt of effort, she launched herself into space. In the saddle, George was twenty feet above the bottom of the water filled ditch. Bella flew and George flew with her, head down, eyes closed against the whipping branches. The horse's front hooves gained the field but the hind ones had to scrabble against the sliding dirt. George threw himself forward over her neck to get the weight off her haunches. Somehow, with heart and luck, she managed to get back on solid ground. After a tiny pause, she heard the hounds begin to bay and she was off, a hunting machine, on to the next jump, the next dyke, all heart and muscle and fire and blood. He rode as hard as she did, no mercy, no hesitation, never giving up for anything or anyone.

Never give up, Georgie boy. After the unusually hot summer, he knew the ditch would be dry. He slid down and pulled himself up the other side, grabbing fistfuls of weeds. The rest of the way home was easier. When he climbed his own boundary ditch, he felt the pride of ownership wrap itself around him. He lay down in the grass and buried his face in it, inhaling the scent of the dirt. He had made once scrubby barren fields into meadows of rich grass, filled with fat glossy cattle.

He stood up, feeling his bones creak and his muscles pull. He had left a small light on in the kitchen and it called him home.

After a cut of his own homemade brown bread and a mug of tea, he fell into his narrow bed and slept.

He woke sharply in the night and lay listening. The noise came again, a distressed bellow. None of the cows was due to calve. It was hard to get up but it wasn't the first time he had risen in the night at the call of a distressed animal. He shoved his feet into boots and made his way down to the kitchen where he pulled a coat on over his pyjamas. In the yard, he stopped to listen. The cow bellowed again and this time he heard a low laugh. The cows were in the Long Meadow. His hand went out to grab the stick from its resting place in the corner of two walls and he set off at a run.

As he drew closer, following the rutted track, he heard more laughter and men's voices. He made out shapes between a flashing light. There were five of them, hunting and hitting the cows. They had one of them down and two of them were kicking her in her belly. Her hooves were lashing at them, but they were jumping clear. Five of them. There was a time that he could have taken down five good men on his own. Those days were gone, but a man had to step up all the same and with the darkness and surprise on his side, he might have a chance.

He took a moment to check their position, then he waded in. The first blow struck one across the temple and he fell with a short scream, dropping the torch as he hit the ground. George's eyes were more accustomed to the darkness than theirs and he had two more down before one of them caught him from behind, holding his arms back. He didn't release his grip on the stick, but he couldn't swing it. He brought his boot heel down hard on a shin bone, scraping down to the foot. The pressure on his arms relaxed and he tore free. He swung his fist and felt a cheekbone crack under his knuckles.

The last of them stood in front of him. George thought that as the last left standing, the man might give up, but instead he stood still, set solidly on wide spread feet. George thought he saw a gleam of teeth. Dawn, still a long way away, was nonetheless making the horizon brighter. He readied himself for an attack, but the other man just stood there. He waited until his companions struggled to their feet before turning away.

George followed them at a distance until they had cleared his land. His heart was thundering, his stomach on fire. If his hand had found the shotgun instead of the stick…He didn't go back to bed, but sat in the kitchen with mug after mug of tea until the daylight came. He did his work as normal, but his mind was on the night.

He watched the news that evening. It seemed worse than normal. Jim and the others had been going on about it in the pub. What the rest of the world did wasn't George's concern. Even so, the footage on the news showed gangs of people fighting in the streets. The reporter said that people were looting food, not televisions. George didn't hear anything after that. Instead, he went out in the twilight and twined barbed wire around the top bar of all the gates to the outside world. He put locks on the two main ones, but he knew it'd be a simple enough matter for someone to climb through the ditches.

Back in the kitchen, he buttered bread and put the kettle on to wait. He sat up all night, fully dressed, with the shotgun between his knees. No one came. He slept for three hours in the morning and then got on with his work. In the early evening, he walked to the pub to have a drink and collect the jeep.

The news was on in the snug. John pulled his pint without being asked and set it in front of him in silence.

Tina Callaghan

There were more scenes of trouble on the news and very little else. When it was over, John turned the TV off and men turned back to their drinks. After a few moments, someone spoke in a low tone and someone else answered. George drank his pint slowly. John went to pull him another but he shook his head. He wanted to be home. He drank the rest of his drink—the last for a long time, he reckoned.

As he stood up to go, Jim put his hand out to him. He took the offered hand, as hard and calloused from work as his own. A proper man, doing his work and having his pint without causing any trouble to anyone. He shook the hand. *Goodbye and good luck.*

He left the pub without looking back and drove the jeep home. With the last of the light, he drove the cattle to the paddocks nearest the house. He walked the boundaries and looked for signs of someone crossing. When he was satisfied, he went to the bull's field and drove him to the yard. The bull was the best he had ever had, and the most aggressive. He had tried to kill George several times over the last three years but his calves were so good that he was worth keeping.

George got him to the yard without too much trouble and left him there. He got over the rail into one of the open ended sheds and settled in, shotgun beside him. The bull trotted the yard and up the lane to the gate, snorting and claiming the new territory where he had never been allowed free roaming before. George heard him attacking the old jeep, just a shell now. After a long while, the bull came back to the yard and bellowed for the cows, getting as close as he could to the paddocks. A few answered him but by the time full dark came, they had settled down. George could hear the bull chewing on the bale he had rolled out. The peaceful sound made him start to drift off.

He woke to the sight of the almost full moon over the house. The bulk of the bull was in front of the shed gate. The animal's head was up and George could hear him breathing. They both heard a branch breaking and the bull was off. George stood on the gate and listened. He heard a yell followed by a higher pitched scream of pain. The bull bellowed and George heard more shouting and screaming. Then the bull made a terrible noise before falling silent. George climbed the gate and stood in his yard.

He heard them coming and raised the shotgun. He let them come around the corner before firing. Two of them fell, screaming. The others scattered for cover. George reloaded and waited in the shadow of the shed. He couldn't hear anything over the groans of one of the men on the ground. The other had fallen silent, unconscious or dead, George didn't care.

After some time had passed, he saw a slight shift in the shadows around the muck heap. They waited for a cloud to pass over the moon and then they ran for better cover. George fired again but missed this time. He reloaded and waited. The hair on the back of his neck was raised and he could feel the veins on his neck and arms carrying rage around his body.

They came for him in a group, roaring. He fired and one fell, but one of them grabbed the gun and pushed it towards the sky. He wouldn't let go but he couldn't use it. He struggled but two others wrenched the gun away from him. He fell backwards and wriggled under the bottom spar of the gate where there was a gap in the concrete. In the dark, he ran through the shed and out the other side and from there to the paddocks.

He got in among his stock and waited. He still had his knife. He would kill the intruders if he could and kill himself if he couldn't. He would rather die among his stock on his own land while it was still his.

The big moon showed him the group coming. There were more of them than he had thought at first, although a few looked injured, thanks to the bull, now presumably bleeding his last on the concrete of the yard.

"Come ahead your best, ye bastards. How do ye hold your blood? Because I don't hold mine so precious."

The quiet leader walked at their center, not putting himself forward. Clever and cowardly. The stock moved away from the strangers and George moved with them. They reached the corner of the field while the gang was still a distance away. George readied himself for fighting and for death.

He felt the rumble in his chest before he heard it. A deep rumble from somewhere beneath his feet. The cattle stirred around him, unsettled. George crouched down among the dangerous feet and put his hand on the ground. It was moving, full of long slow trembles as waves of vibration rolled from beneath his feet towards the intruders. He stood up and braced himself against the back of one of the cows.

The heavy ripples lifted him and set him back down. He had been on a boat just once in his life and it was like that. Rolling up and down on the back of waves. They came faster and faster until he was off the ground, gripping the backs of the cattle, which were milling together in terror, almost crushing him. They didn't run, but instead squeezed together in the corner of the field.

George heard the intruders begin to yell to each other. They started to run towards him. He heard a noise not unlike the rending scream the bull had made when they killed him. The men stopped and George saw something dark appear before them, some rising shadow. The cows drove themselves closer to the ditch, mounting each other in their effort to escape. A hard head struck George in the face and the pain of a broken nose shot through him, making his eyes tear up and his head swim. Still he clung on to any beast he could grab, trying to stay higher than their legs. His years of hunting came back to him and he swung his leg over the well fleshed back of one of his cows and clamped his knees to her sides.

From somewhere behind, he heard the rending noise again and the screams of the men, loud at first but then muffled and fading. After a long time, the cows began to settle. At last, one of them took a mouthful of grass and after that, they all began to graze and spread out. George, with blood crusting under his nose, slipped down to the ground and made his way towards the other side of the field. The moon was bright enough to show him his own shadow.

The ground was disturbed in a line across the field. A mound of muffin-soft dirt lay like a newly filled-in grave about an acre long. He poked it with his boot. Fresh earth too wide to step across. He took a long stride and planted his foot in the middle of the mound, pressing before he put his full weight on it. He leaned forward and brought his other foot up. Something hard gave under his boot, sinking further into the earth. He stepped aside, feeling himself sink a couple of inches. There, compressed under the mark of his sole, was a hand. He studied it for a long time and then stepped off the other side of the mound.

He went through the yard and found the bull. An axe had been buried in his neck, severing the artery. He was lying in a huge pool of blood, his great bulk hard to comprehend in death.

George went around to the side of the house with the view. The farm fell away from him in a shallow valley, rising to a distant hill. The moon showed him his stock moving peacefully about. It showed him the long thick line where the land had opened its throat and swallowed the intruders whole. It showed him that as he protected the land, it protected him. His sweat and tears and blood were mingled in its clay and the land was in his blood, his heart. He took a deep breath full of the scent of the night and the earth and the animals and went slowly off to bed.

Transfiguration

by Richard Christian Matheson

t is easy to become disoriented here. Snow is everywhere and the borders and corners of the world soften and disappear. Sometimes, when I dream, I watch myself drilling the thick, blue ice. I bore a large opening and stand over it, then slip through. I slide into the ancient sea beneath and, as currents gently sweep me away, my pained thoughts ease. I look up, through the ice, to see a place I never belonged, that never wanted me. Then, I close my eyes and fall asleep. I am finally home.

Angels come out at night, restless and far from heaven.

We like to move about when the sun dies and we can more easily pass for human. The night hides our secret and our tasks. It is not known where we dwell—whether in the air, the void or the planets, as some have noted, but whether by thrones or dominions, we were created to convey His will to men. We like cold places and are not subject to death, or any form of extinction, extradition or censure. As divine soldiers, we keep order in an impure, Godless world, and I do what I must to serve Him. No matter the cost.

I am seventy miles north of Fairbanks, where pavement dead-ends and the Alaskan Highway turns into the Dalton Highway; a hypnotic, gravel throat that stretches 414 miles across vast, plains of snow, all the way to Deadhorse, on the remote North Slope oil fields, at Prudhoe Bay. Bluish ice and dry snow surround the two-lane I'm on, as if infinite square miles of suffocated flesh and, at indefinable horizon, it collides with white-capped peaks that rise-up from the bleakness like paralyzed waves.

Dalton is the "haul road" for eighteen-wheelers like mine and when it isn't trying to kill you, the road takes you straight to where North America, for good or bad, finally runs out of land and surrenders to frigid sea. Along the way, I pass "Coldfoot" and "Beaver Slide" and, at mile 75, "Roller Coaster," where the icy, two-lane goes down steep, fast, then up steeper, making big rigs like mine slip and lose their grip. They'll tumble sideways, over and over, crushing the cab and driver, and when you come upon the mangle, it makes you sick. People should die for a better reason.

These plains are violent and primitive and it's a killing field when winter hits. I've seen bad ones at "Avalanche Alley," near mid-point; a man-eating gust flipped a married couple's rig and shoved them through the windshield, onto hard ice. Wolves finished them off. The weather's usually out to get you, so freezing to death is the easy way out. You can feel it. Arctic skies stare down at you, on the two-lane, where spruces huddle and the frozen Yukon River is still as sculptured glass. When I see it, I imagine fish posed, motionlessly, in the frozen river, like you see them sometimes in modern paintings. There is an incompleteness to this place that makes your mind fill things in. A gloom and need. But that isn't why I come.

To get to Deadhorse, I tank-up a grand of diesel, two big thermoses of black coffee and some candy bars. Sugar and caffeine wind me just right. I always have my notebook, too. I like to keep track. Dates; descriptions. My ride is a 13 speed, dual stack, diesel Kenworth. Whole shebang grosses out at 88,000 pounds fully packed. 475 horsepower, 18 aluminum wheels, tandem axles, Ultra-Shift, Air-Suspension. Sleeper, too. Only home I ever had and a hell of lot better than what I was born into. But even when a man dies inside, it's only the beginning. Hebrews 12:22-23 says that when we get to heaven we will be met by a myriad of angels, and spirits of righteous men will be made perfect. Myths of hopelessness are just that and do no one good.

My twin thirty-foot trailers get filled with groceries, medicine, cars; anything you can't get where it drops to fifty below. Deadhorse trucks-in everything life in a lifeless place needs, maybe some it doesn't. Truckers are a transfusion for the isolated workers of the Conoco Philips North Slope facility, every one of them trapped like cubes in an ice-tray. As for the road, the Dalton has strict rules:

1) ALWAYS DRIVE WITH HEADLIGHTS ON.

2) WATCH THE ROAD AHEAD AND BEHIND FOR PLUMES OF DUST OR SNOW SIGNALING ANOTHER VEHICLE.

3) BEFORE PASSING, MAKE SURE OPERATORS OF OTHER VEHICLES KNOW YOU'RE THERE.

4) DO NOT STOP ON THE ROAD. IF YOU CAN'T GET OFF THE ROAD, PULL FAR TO THE RIGHT AND ACTIVATE YOUR HAZARD LIGHTS.

5) RESPECT THE SPEED LIMIT. IF A RIG GOES TOO FAST, ITS WEIGHT WILL CREATE WAVES UNDER THE ICE THAT WILL MAKE THE ROAD BUCKLE AND COLLAPSE.

Now and then, overweight rigs, driving over the limit, drop through the cracking road where it thins and disappear like they were never there; I've seen huge carriers devoured by a big, jagged mouth in the road, the sloshing, polar sea beneath. Sometimes God needs a sacrifice. Sometimes the road is complicit. No life is sacrosanct.

Visibility is always an issue out here and when reflector posts vanish in white-outs, we chain our rigs together and ride it out, sitting in our cabs, listening to starved winds trying to get in. Snow can fill up the air intakes and choke you to death, so I keep my engine running even though the truck heater doesn't keep me warm. In bone-deep cold, blood slows and you can hear it throbbing in your ears like a dying heart.

Out here, no one knows you, no one cares, no one takes an interest. We come, we go. There's no cameras, no checkpoints. I could be anybody. Do anything. God's work requires the clandestine and though angels may have flesh which resembles polished metal or faces like lightning, I wander, free of such telling detail.

During the '74 oil crisis, the Dalton got carved in six months, borne of lies and avarice. It was clawed from denuded nowhere and runs alongside the massive veins of the 800 mile Trans-Alaska Pipeline that runs from Deadhorse to the port at Valdez. Long haulers do the four-hundred miles, but they all know it's a bad road, a bad bet. Some don't make it. The oil company doesn't care. There's always vultures. Ask me, people like that don't deserve to live. Add them to the fucking list.

Richard Christian Matheson

Driving the ice-road seems to go on forever; like being lost at sea. You can't get a cell phone to work past mile 28 but there's no one I want to talk to. People waste my time. Exploit my best intentions. I prefer being alone, in my rig, not having to talk or listen. I've heard it all. Lies disguised as prayers, lust masqueraded as faith. We live in dire times and I am sanctioned by our Father to do something about it. All things have been created by Him and for Him. And He is before all things, and in Him all things hold together. For He shall give His angels charge over earth.

Those who forget that cannot die enough times.

Going down a slope, my dual stacks belch scarves of exhaust and when weather's decent, I get lost in the locomotive hum of my tires on gravel. It puts me in a trance and lets me forget bad things; at least try. The worst nights, you come across accidents. Agonized faces, pinned under steel, begging for relief. Jackknifes, rear-enders, head-ons. I kneel and calm them as life seeps from their scared eyes.

Near the three-quarter mark, my rig strains through Atigun Pass, at 4,752 feet. Air gets thin and birds and animals don't come out much. The tundra is an un-crumpled sheet of white paper as I stare at my amber halogens, drink my fourth cup of black. Long-haul truckers are ants who never looked up, escorting cargo through frozen wasteland, and they don't realize that angels can take on the appearance of men when the occasion demands, and so they are imprisoned. It is said a book must be "an ax for the frozen sea within us," referring certainly to the Scriptures. Half frozen seas surround any life, threatening to wash people away. Life is a condemned promise and someone must pay.

They say drivers see things out here.

Apparitions or ghosts, or the lingering energy of those who have died, or whatever word you can live with. Once, on a brutal run, when I hadn't slept in almost forty hours, I saw my dead father standing, bloodied in the middle of the road, grinning in that hateful way he did the day he was taken from this world. But he was one of those people who never totally die because they leave a terrible dent inside you and your mind can't let go.

The aboriginal people up here say the dead seek salvation, but it is not because they are spirits that they might be angels; they become angels when they are chosen. And only the chosen are raised up. The rest burn; their debased souls punished, their flesh disemboweled.

Last month, snow flurries were hammering me from all directions, and I swore I saw my brother beside the road, in the white mayhem, screaming and running from something that terrified him, his long legs getting stuck in the deep drifts as he looked over at me with pleading eyes. He mouthed my name, though I couldn't hear it with my windows up. But the way he died all came back. Another day I'd like to forget. But those are the ones you can't.

Out here, wait long enough, everything comes back.

I've seen other people, too, in the hungry, falling snow, even though I know they're long gone. They stare at me, helplessly, as they dart in front of my headlights and the grille smashes their flesh and bones, and they're swept under the truck.

I know they were just mirages.

The Big Blank.

That's what long-haulers call it up here. It's when the outside world and your thoughts merge, a perilous weave that undermines sanity. Sometimes the soft powder takes on human shape. Milky silhouettes, without detail, that somehow want something. Fatigue breeds dark thoughts; every big-rigger and long-hauler knows it. The mind is a complicated thing and a childhood like mine is no help. Even angels suffer. God sees to that for his own reasons.

Things do bother me.

When I've been awake for too long, my mind loosens, and sometimes I imagine skidding off the road and dying in the crush of my overturning rig. I quietly bleed in the cold, and the snowy shapes circle me until I can't breathe. I fight them, but it is always too late. Angels can't die yet I imagine it.

A psychiatrist, at that place, once told me it was a projection. Like with movies. Light passes through the film and it gets bigger on the screen. I guess he was saying thought and faith have that kind of power. But he had no fucking idea who he was dealing with.

I reach the "Ice-Cut" grade, a steep climb with sheer drops on both sides, and grip the wheel tightly. When I'm going fast, my tires hiss on the frosted flatness, like a monster's sled, and the tire tracks disappear, as ice instantly re-seals. I rumble across the road, bite into a Butterfinger, watch the speedometer, and stay ahead of schedule so I can stop if I need to. Lick chocolate off my fingers and watch for approaching headlights, in my rear views and ahead. Scan for plumes of white, jutting and hovering over road-way, see none and finally know I'm alone.

I slowly pull over, in the solitude.

There is something sad out here. Sometimes I hear wolves, mourning in the desolation. If I'm very quiet and still, I can feel sleepless tides roaming under the ice. Mostly, I hear nothing until the winds anger, shoving my eighteen-wheeler like it's in their way. I glance at my watch and know I must move quickly. I pull on leather gloves, parka and goggles, leave the engine idling, get out.

The air freezes my face, as winds howl and tangle, and my amber halogens leave orange-peel streaks on falling flakes. Diesel ghosts from the chrome stacks as I lean down, unlock the storage space under my driver's door, and withdraw my rechargeable ice-fishing drill. I remove it from its case, quickly find a patch of thinner ice, beside my rig, trudge toward it. Fifteen miles behind me, headlights flare on a far rise; another rig will be here in ten minutes.

I re-check my watch, grip the drill with both gloved hands, press the five-foot long bit onto the frozen ground. The high torque and fast rotation allow me to work quickly, before the other rig shows. The bladed teeth bite into the hard ice and, as winds rake, I begin to drill: a fifteen-inch diameter. The grind of the motor makes my arms shake and curlicues of ice cover my waterproof boots. The whirling bit finally reaches the sea, five feet below, and I reverse the drill, pull it out, check the opening. Replace the drill in its case, toss it back in the storage compartment. Then, I grab the cinched canvas bag beside it.

I open it and begin to empty its contents into the hole.

I am at home out here. Angels have authority over the natural world, even when people don't realize their time has come. Hell is a self-inflicted state of mind and people get what they goddamned deserve, whether they like it or not.

As I work, I like it best when the snow falls audibly; a hushed downpour. Sometimes, what I drop in goes easily, sliding into the water beneath the ice road. Sometimes, I have to use a knife to cut it to size. Once the bag is empty, I fill the opening back up with snow, kicking it in, and pack it down with my heavy soles. It disappears fast, in the cascading white, as if miraculously healed, and I get back in my idling rig.

Richard Christian Matheson

I watch stars in overcast sky. Thank the Holy Father. In Genesis 18, Abraham welcomed angelic guests who appeared to be nothing more than common travelers. Truth disguises itself when necessary.

I flip on the overhead fog lights and they cast a sick glow as the other truck finally passes, with a high beam nod, and I lower my visor to block the glare. But I never look at myself in the hinge-down mirror. Prayer cannot repair flesh so ravaged. I have learned to accept shame and rage. There have always been sightings of angels who appear to be a man with unusual features. But I hate God for allowing this to fucking happen to me.

My tires leave grimy, waffle marks on the road and snow carpets the ground behind me as if I was never there. Snow is like time. It covers whatever it touches with a new layer of meaning that replaces the previous one, and the one before that. Out here, it paints over everything and this 414 mile, barren forever is a place of temporary fact; evidence erased.

Except for more headlights approaching from miles ahead, the Big Blank is shiny and black now, drawing me to Prudhoe Bay. I stare at my wide beams, the rushing dotted line. Longhaulers call it the Zipper and swear if you look at it too long, it gets inside you; does bad things. As I near Deadhorse, it's 3:36 a.m. and 17 degrees below. Tall sodium vapor lights spill on the road and there are no trees, only machines, mechanical shadows. There isn't even a church. It tells you everything. Where there is no God, impulse and pain rule. I have seen it.

Steam blasts from industrial structures and workers are up, walking around in parkas; shifts that come and go, twenty-four hours a day, an exhausted army of detached, clock-less zombies, deserted by friends and families who loathe them. Most are liars.

None can love. Thousands come and go, less than twenty-five live here. It is a soulless, transient dungeon and if they knew who I was, they would fall to their knees, ask for forgiveness.

Let them die for the sins they relish.

I drop my haul at the transportation yard, get paid, buy a hot meal at the diner, check into the Prudhoe Bay Hotel, a one-story outcropping that squats in this gulag.

The frozen Arctic, nearby, is mostly slush without visible tide and the local hardware store operates out of a thrashed double-wide. It's open 24/7, even during white-outs, and their policy is if they don't have it, you don't need it. I drop in to buy replacement gloves, hacksaw blades. Go back to my room.

Try to sleep.

Snow drifts are up to the windows, and I drink Scotch, watch septic swirls of smoke from the refineries. Listen to arguments, spilling from bars. Laughter and alcohol madness. The frantic despair of the voices, their pathetic, greedy noise. They are all damned. They will get sick and become empty and agony will ravage them.

Poison seeks itself.

From my window, I stare at the anemic expanse that leads back to Fairbanks. Measure the numbing monotony with blood-shot eyes. The undetected things beneath. Terrified expressions, twisted limbs, torn flesh. The couples and the ones who were alone. I imagine them all, under the vast ice, finally where they should be. Here, they will always look the same, forever preserved, unable to make bad decisions, demolish lives. I saved them. If they could, they would spiral-up from the countless openings I drilled, vaporous and sorrowful, wanting to be forgiven. But it's too late. Salvation is not given to the irredeemable.

Richard Christian Matheson

I can feel the Scotch and my skin hurts where scars seam my scathed features.

Sometimes when I dream, I watch myself drilling the thick, blue ice. I make a narrow opening and stand over it, step into it and slip through, sliding into the ancient sea beneath. As currents gently sweep me away, I finally relax. My bad thoughts and fears stop and I look up through the ice and see a world I never belonged in; that never wanted me.

People don't care.

They do what they want. They ruin their life. They ruin yours. They take and take. Smother everything good, give nothing back. Like my family did. It's the same everywhere I go. Every other truck route across this fucked-up country. I bring them here, where no one will find them. But none are missed. When I give them back to the sea, maybe there is some balance in a damaged, indifferent world.

I remember the one from last week. Refinery worker. Nervous. On his way to Deadhorse. Black oil under his fingernails, unslept eyes. We pulled out of Fairbanks as the weather got bad. The windshield iced-over and my rig's steel wipers ground at it. He glanced over at me, thanked me for the lift. I offered him coffee from my thermos and he said yes, in a polite voice. But I could tell he was a person who hurt others and derived pleasure when they begged. I could detect, in his casual conversation, that he cared only for himself and that anyone stupid enough to get close to him would suffer. As he sipped, he glanced at my pistol, mounted on my door bracket. Looked back at me. We hit a rut, duct tape rolled from under the seat, and the blizzard swallowed us whole.

That was that.

Just like the ones I met in San Diego. And down south. Back east. Tulsa. So many voices and faces. I get people talking, while we drink coffee, so I can write down the details later. Otherwise, I lose track. They're all narcissists. Bullies. All 361 of them talked about themselves, only a handful ever asked me a question about myself or faith or where their soul might be bound. Vain, worthless assholes.

The longest recorded night in Prudhoe was 54 days. The shortest was 26 minutes. No matter where you are, night falls when it is ready. Each must make peace with that in their own way. Heaven and Hell are not so different. Sometimes, in summer, when mosquitoes swarm, it gets warm here and the Aurora Borealis makes you swear you can see your life in its randomness. Time and places. Hurts. The faces of people who never cared. The strangers who did you wrong. The rape and torture.

The world is a diseased zoo.

As I listen to them, laughing like banshees on the icy street outside, I'm exhausted and sore. When generators die and lights go out and my room turns black, I stumble hard against the small dresser and hear its mirror fall and shatter. I always turn mirrors around in my motel rooms, even tape blankets over them, so I never have to see. But after a minute, the generator starts back up, the lights flicker and I glance down, without thinking, to avoid shards in my bare feet.

As the bulbs twitch, I see splinters of a terrible face I had forgotten. A scarred mosaic of every face in my family, the mouth an ugly slash like my father's, the eyes filled with sick contempt and futility like my mother's. The nose crammed and broad and common like my brother's. I stare at myself, reflected in vicious jigsaw fragments, and weep.

And though I fight its truth, I understand, at that instant, that I am guilty and damned. That I am not of Heaven but Earth. I take. Give nothing back. I am no better than anyone. Sadism and suffering is all I know; I was raised with it. I am one of them. My heart is an Inquisition, my thoughts are vile. God has abandoned me and I am forsaken.

I have been drinking sand.

When day breaks in Deadhorse, I am broken. Betrayed. I dress and shower and tell the front desk man I will pay for the mirror and he tells me it is seven years of bad luck. He smiles like a lizard and I want to put a bullet in his head. Outside, engines are freezing-up, plans changing. Workers need to get across the Big Blank, some with no means. I walk to the diner for coffee and a young woman with willing eyes asks me for a lift to Fairbanks. I refuse, tell her I'm not going all the way through. She doesn't know what I mean since the road ends where it ends and nowhere else.

Fuck her.

Fuck everyone.

God most of all. For his lies; for making me believe them.

I get in my rig and head toward Fairbanks, thinking about how the world is worthless and can never be saved. Like my family. Like me. The psychiatrist was right but I couldn't understand. He came to my ward and led me out into the garden and tried to help me. I thought he was evil, trying to cure an angel. I cut out his tongue with shears, got out of that place and moved on.

We all have regrets.

The falling snow starts to wall me in and I drive faster, ignoring the speed limit. I reach a stretch of the Dalton with thin ice and push the engine harder, speeding over the slick surface. My steering wheel shakes as the rig starts to create waves under the road that will make it buckle ahead, the undulations like a massive blanket, slowly shaken in wind.

As my tires wobble, I look over and see my brother, on hillocks of white, with the sawed neck I gave him; a gory joker's collar. Beside him is my murdering father and my sadistic mother. Both staring, unblinking, waiting for me because they know I am no better than they are and never will be; that I belong in the icy water, with them, for what I did.

I feel the sea shuddering, below the road, as the waves roll thicker and begin to break the ice, and the two-lane starts to crack under the weight of my rig. The road suddenly ruptures, like a pane of broken glass, and my engine is a roaring, wounded creature as a wide crack races toward me. Then, another. Then, more, wider and faster, the erupting waves tearing the road open.

I downshift, and my rig abruptly stops, hitching into the dark slush, tires spinning. My seat belt holds me tight against the sudden lurch, and my fog lights shine on the collapsing road, as it splits apart, currents churning beneath, leaking upward. The rig begins to make hideous, scraping noises and the huge front tires and grille nose into the shattered roadway, as the massive engine slowly dies and sea sloshes up to my doors, wanting me. I watch it without reaction and know I deserve this.

I slowly open my windows.

The freezing water gushes in, lapping at me, and I gasp at the aching cold, drinking in icy saltiness that fills me. I watch my belongings move, in slow motion, in the inundating cab, inked pages of my notebook running, details and names washed off the paper; my pious, repellant spree. The truck creaks and tilts, huge trailers wrenched and twisting, and I look up through windshield as we slowly descend into deep, green-black ocean.

TRANSFIGURATION
Richard Christian Matheson

My dreams were premonitions. But they were wrong.

As we drown, I begin to see murky images, drifting closer.

I can just make them out and am afraid, as they move toward me, with gunshot faces, slashed throats, many without legs or arms, mouths duct-taped. Pale crowds of them emerge through kelp, mutilations fresh, bloody clothes billowing. Wanting to hurt me, as I hurt them.

They tear at me and I look up to see a place I never belonged; that never wanted me.

The sea goes red and I am finally home.

THE BLUE CAT

by Keith Minnion

Miss Foyle was too old to drive, and she disliked taking the bus, but she tolerated it once a month to visit the Care and Share shop downtown to look for new Dresden porcelains to add to her collection. She had found her Woodsman and her Milkmaid there, both near pristine, and priced very reasonably. The volunteer behind the dinnerware, crockery and figurine counter clucked like a mother hen when she saw her. "Sorry, dear, no new Dresdens have come in."

"Just as well," Miss Foyle said. "I'm running out of mantle space anyway." They both shared a quiet smile.

Then Miss Foyle saw the cat.

It was a glass figurine, vaguely Deco, lacquered a pale powder blue everywhere except its face, chest, and paws, which were clear. Whiskers were hurried slashes of black enamel, and its eyes were awkward dabs of dark red. It sat on its haunches, front legs at full extension, tail curled around to cover one paw. Like a little

Egyptian god, Miss Foyle thought, instantly taken by the piece. She pointed to it. "Can I see that please?"

"The cat?" The volunteer's eyebrows rose slightly, but she took it down from the shelf and gave it to her. It was heavy solid glass through and through, with no chips or scratches. Miss Foyle turned it over to look for a mark or price sticker, but the bottom was blank. "How much is it?" she asked.

The volunteer made a face. "It just came in, estate sale, I think. Tillie does the pricing, but she's not due in today." She shrugged. "A dollar?"

Miss Foyle did not hesitate. "Deal," she said.

She didn't notice the tiny parallel cuts on her forefinger, or the accompanying small smear of blood, until she was home and the blue cat was in its place on the mantle. "That's odd," she said aloud, and put the finger in her mouth. "How did that happen?"

—

"Trouble!" Miss Foyle put her cat's dish down by his water bowl, then turned again to the hallway. "Trouble! Dinnertime!" Trouble never missed a meal, except when he was in the woods behind the house, hunting. She knew he was inside because she distinctly remembered letting him in before taking her afternoon nap.

Instead of the gentle tinkling of his collar bell, however, she heard another sound, equally gentle, but...different.

Tink! Ting!

Like one of her porcelains being lightly tapped by something hard and sharp.

Tink! Ting!

Was he up on the mantle again, living up to his name, traipsing through her porcelains? "Trouble!" Miss Foyle rushed down the hallway to the parlor, then exhaled in relief. The only cat on the mantle was the glass figurine she had purchased that morning. It looked across the room at her with its dark, ruby-red eyes. Then Miss Foyle saw Trouble. He was lying on the hearthstone, directly under the mantle.

"Trouble?"

The cat didn't stir. Miss Foyle went over to him, knelt, and stroked his fur. "Trouble?" Her hand came away wet. A warm, thick wetness. She saw fresh blood on her fingers, but it took a few seconds for that to register, then a few more for her to cry out and leap back, stumbling up against the settee.

Above her, the blue cat grinned.

Tink! Ting!

The first two days following Trouble's death Miss Foyle only entered the parlor to air it out, opening the front window in the morning, and closing it before going to bed. Today, standing in the hallway before the parlor door, the air in the room still smelled faintly...foul. Like dead things. Like death itself. Her neighbor was due soon for their weekly tea and game of Hearts. She should open the window again. She should—

The doorbell chimed. Miss Foyle turned, fingers to her lips, and saw a familiar shadow against the front door curtains. Goodness, she thought, was it that time already?

Mrs. Grimsby, her neighbor two doors down, bustled past Miss Foyle before she even had the door fully open. "I'm so sorry to hear the bad news, Anne! So very sorry you lost poor Trouble!" Mrs. Grimsby made a right turn into the parlor, went over to the settee, and sat down.

Miss Foyle hesitated at the doorway.

"Well what are you doing standing there!" Mrs. Grimsby opened the side table drawer and took out the deck of cards. "Is something wrong, dear?"

Miss Foyle gave her neighbor a pained expression. "No, nothing. You're right." She entered the parlor, carefully ignoring the mantle. Mrs. Grimsby put the card deck aside and patted the cushion beside her. "Come. Sit down for heaven's sake. We'll talk about it."

Miss Foyle took the seat offered, clutching her hands together on her lap. "I should make the tea," she fretted.

"Oh, forget the tea! We can have that any time." Mrs. Grimsby covered Miss Foyle's hands with one of her own, and squeezed briefly. Then she gave a brief gasp of quiet astonishment. "And who is this?"

A large cat, grey with white markings, had appeared in the parlor doorway.

"That's Max." Miss Foyle attempted a smile. "I just got him from the shelter this morning."

"Max!" Mrs. Grimsby bent and offered a hand. "Pleased to meet you!"

The cat stared at the hand, then her, briefly, then left the doorway, back the way he had come. Mrs. Grimsby chuckled. "Friendly little beast! I am glad you got another one, Anne. Back on the horse, as they say."

"I know, but..." Miss Foyle blinked away new tears. "Just look at me," she said, smiling helplessly.

Mrs. Grimsby pulled a handkerchief from her sleeve and offered it, but Miss Foyle shook her head, pulled her own from the sleeve of her housedress, and dabbed at her cheeks. "It's just..." she began, "...it all started..." She waved her handkerchief at the mantle without looking, "...that cat."

Mrs. Grimsby saw the blue cat for the first time. "Oh dear! Whatever possessed you to buy that?" She got up before Miss Foyle could stop her, went to the mantle, and took the glass figurine down. "Where on earth did you get this? At a carnival sideshow? It's positively hideous!"

"Be...be careful, Agnes!" Miss Foyle stammered. "You'll get cut!"

"Don't be silly. Cut from what, these little cracks?"

"Cracks?" That brought Miss Foyle up short. "What cracks?"

Mrs. Grimsby thrust the blue cat nearly under Miss Foyle's nose. "These, dear. At the base, and along the leg."

Miss Foyle saw a hairline pattern of cracks that she knew had not been present when she bought the figurine. They were new.

"Honestly, Anne!" Mrs. Grimsby returned the blue cat to its place on the mantle. She turned, dusting her hands ceremoniously. "What were you thinking?"

"Tink! Ting!"

Mrs. Grimsby paused. "What was that?" Then she looked down at her hand. "And why on earth am I bleeding?"

━━

The shelter smelled of pet urine and flea powder. Miss Foyle glimpsed row after row of cages in the ceramic-walled room behind the counter, all of them holding cats and kittens. "I'm sorry," the woman behind the counter said, closing her ledger with a loud thump. "No more cats for you I'm afraid."

Miss Foyle gripped her handbag tightly. "But...I only want one. Just one. My first cat passed away last week, you see."

The woman tapped the ledger cover with a stubby finger. "Our records show you adopted two cats since then, Miss Foyle."

"But I...I like cats," Miss Foyle said, pleading with her eyes. "And they like...company."

The woman frowned. "I'm sorry," she repeated, "but that's just too many. Too many in such a short time." She tapped on the ledger again. "People might ask why."

Miss Foyle brought her handbag up against her chest. "But—"

"I'm sorry," the woman said a final time, "but no. We have rules."

—

When Miss Foyle finished her weekly shopping, she saw a sign hung on the community board just inside the exit door, crudely drawn in crayon:

!!FREE KITTENS!!
10 MOTT STREET

Pushing her loaded two-wheeled cart slowly along the sidewalk, she detoured to pass Mott Street, and found another sign, very much like the first, taped to the picket fence of Number 10. As she pushed her cart up the walk a little girl with copper-red hair and lemon-colored overalls skipped across the front porch to meet her. Miss Foyle smiled at the child. "You have kittens, dear?"

The little girl nodded vigorously, pigtails flying. "Lots! Eight! Come see!" She led Miss Foyle onto the porch to a large open cardboard box. Inside, a fat grey tabby cat curled on a fuzzy towel, surrounded by her litter: three grey tabbies, one black with a white face, two mottled white and cream, another all black, and the last all grey. Most of them were asleep, but the black one and the grey one were wide-awake, tussling and pouncing.

"Mama says they're old enough now to give away," the little girl said, looking up at Miss Foyle. "Would you like one?"

Miss Foyle looked in the box again. The two kittens were rolling around like a furry grey and black ball. "Actually…would you mind if I took two?"

The grandmother clock in the downstairs hall struck five, its muted chimes filling the otherwise quiet house. Miss Foyle awoke from her nap to find both kittens—the grey and the black—asleep on her stomach. She deposited them very carefully on the coverlet beside her, then found her glasses, ran her fingers through her hair, and eased out of bed. She listened to the ticking of the clock downstairs, the quiet rush of a car going by in the street, and the far off muffled cries of children outside playing a street game. Olly-olly-oxen-free.

Then she heard it, and jerked her head toward the door. Dear God in heaven, she thought, so soon?

Miss Foyle went downstairs, and the kittens, half-awake, tumbling and stumbling, followed. She stopped at the parlor doorway. Across the room, sitting on the fireplace mantle with her Dresden porcelains, the blue cat stared back at her. She rubbed her forefinger against her thumb, feeling the tiny scars.

She heard the sound again: Tink! Ting! Glass gently touching glass.

Tink! Ting!

She brought her trembling fingers to her lips, looking at the blue cat, at its ruby-red, unblinking eyes, and at the space—at least an inch on either side—between it and the nearest porcelains on the mantle. Too soon, she thought, feeling tears begin to well, much too soon! She wiped at her eyes, and then looked down at the kittens, playing at her feet.

—

The next morning, she returned to Mott Street. The sign was still on the gate, and the big box was still on the porch. The little red-haired girl, however, was nowhere to be seen. Miss Foyle hesitated outside the gate, but then she saw a woman kneeling in a bed of tulips beside the house. She cleared her throat. "Excuse me?"

The woman looked up, wiped her forehead with a forearm, and got to her feet. She dropped her gardening gloves. "Can I help you?"

"I was looking for the little girl." Miss Foyle pointed to the sign. "The one giving away kittens. Your daughter?"

The woman nodded. "She's at play-camp." She dusted her knees, and approached the gate. "You interested in a kitten? We have a few left."

"Oh no, I'm sorry!" Miss Foyle fumbled in her coat pocket,

and brought out the grey kitten. "I took this one home yesterday...but I found I was allergic."

"Allergic?"

Miss Foyle could feel her cheeks burning. "Yes...to cats. I'm allergic to cats. I'm afraid I have to return her."

The woman reached over the gate, her expression neutral. "All right, hand her over." She took the kitten from Miss Foyle, and without another word went up on the porch and deposited it in the cardboard box.

"I'm so sorry," Miss Foyle said.

The woman turned and put her hands on her hips. "No problem. You're allergic. Have a nice day."

—

"Hello? Anybody home?"

Miss Foyle turned, creaking in her wicker chair.

Mrs. Grimsby peeked around the corner of the house. "There you are!" She picked her way along the overgrown path to the steps of Miss Foyle's back porch. "What on earth are you doing back here? It's a jungle!"

Their tea date. Miss Foyle glanced at her wristwatch with a sinking heart. It was past two! "Oh dear!" she exclaimed, "I'm so sorry!"

Mrs. Grimsby came up the steps. "It's just so buggy back here." She took out her handkerchief, dusted the seat of the chair beside Miss Foyle, and lowered herself into it. She reached across and fingered the sleeve of Miss Foyle's dress. "We look like twins today Anne. I always said you look your best in mauve."

Miss Foyle made to rise. "Shall I make us that tea?"

"No." Mrs. Grimsby patted Miss Foyle's knee. "Sit. Relax. You look tired, dear. You don't look well."

"It has been…a trying week," Miss Foyle admitted.

"You haven't been yourself since Trouble and Max ran away!" Mrs. Grimsby leaned toward her. "You haven't lost another cat, have you, dear?"

Miss Foyle's embarrassed silence was answer enough. Her neighbor looked out into the tall weeds of the back yard. "Cats are resilient. I'm sure they'll be fine." She patted Miss Foyle's knee again. "Still. Perhaps you should wait awhile before deciding about adopting another one, don't you think?"

Miss Foyle rose. "You are right about the bugs. Let's go inside and have that tea."

Mrs. Grimsby gave a sudden, nervous laugh. "Not in the parlor."

"Oh no," Miss Foyle said. "Never in the parlor."

———

The grandmother clock downstairs chimed five times, echoing through the little house.

Miss Foyle awoke from her nap but kept her eyes closed, pretending she was still asleep. If she opened her eyes, it would know; she was sure; it would just know. Outside, a little boy ran down the sidewalk, calling for a friend to come out to play. The faint drone of an airplane rose and fell in a slow, gentle arc. Downstairs, dust motes drifted through the afternoon sunlight of the parlor. On the fireplace mantle, she knew, the blue cat glared in ruby-red fury.

Tink! Ting!

Her hands, folded across her stomach, clenched white. She couldn't help it. Stop, she thought desperately, uselessly. Just…stop!

Tink! Ting!

She opened her eyes with a quiet sob, and sat up in her bed. Somehow, then, she gained the courage to stand. Somehow, she made her way into the upstairs hall, then down the stairs. Somehow—dear God! Dear God!—she entered the parlor, went around the settee, and approached the fireplace. Somehow, she raised a trembling hand toward the iron poker leaning by the ash shovel at the side of the hearth.

I will smash you! I will knock you to the hearthstone and break you into a thousand pieces! I will—

Miss Foyle cried out, jerking her hand back. Three of her fingers were cut and bleeding, each with four deep slices across the whorls of her fingertips. There was enough blood to run into her palm and drip in flat-sounding splats to the hearthstone at her feet.

"You are EVIL!" she screamed. "You are an EVIL THING!"

The figurine looked back at her with a sly grin.

Splat, another drop of blood fell. Splat.

"There aren't any more!" Miss Foyle sobbed, clutching at her hand, burying it in her chest. "I gave it back! You can't have it, you can't have any of them anymore, ever!" Her sobs ripped from her throat. "I'm done! I'm done feeding you!"

Tink! Ting!

She thrust her bloody hand forward once more, furious, beyond care, and again cried out at the new slashes of crystalline pain across her fingers. More blood, more droplets falling to the hearthstone. The eyes of the blue cat seemed to grow, to tilt, ever so slightly, laughing at her.

Tink! Ting!

Miss Foyle stood paralyzed, speechless, overcome with emotion and pain.

Tink! Ting!

She moaned.

Tink! Ting!

She swayed, but kept her balance. Why can't I run! Why can't I run away?

Tink! Ting!

Why can't I—

Tink! TING!

CRAACK!

Quite suddenly, the blue cat broke into several large pieces. They teetered on the mantle edge, then fell to the blood-splattered hearthstone below, shattering into a hundred, a thousand shards of glittering blue.

Miss Foyle, still rooted in place, stared open-mouthed. What did I do? How did I...? But she had done nothing, nothing at all. The cat, the insatiable, evil cat, had done it to itself. She moved, then, took a step back, then another, until she was out of the parlor. The remains of the blue cat lay scattered across the hearthstone like diamonds. No, like...like simple, harmless shards of cheap blue glass.

━━━

The grandmother clock chimed ten times; time for bed. Miss Foyle went down the hallway to the stairs, passing the open doorway to the parlor. She felt a small blush of pride when she did not automatically look into the room.

She went slowly, steadily, up the stairs.

Her bedroom door was solid oak, thick and sturdy, and she locked it from the inside out of habit. She was safe. She knew that. Finally, safe. She cradled her bandaged hand, warm under the covers. This would be the first night, she realized, the first night in weeks where she could sleep without fear, without dread. She smiled in the darkness. Tomorrow she would clean the mess in the parlor. Tomorrow...

At some point in the night she dreamed: of darkness, tiny pinpricks of pain, a heavy pressure on her chest, and the stench of something rotted and foul, pressed to her face. I am dreaming this, she told herself. I can dream away the weight, the pain, the smell; I can dream that I can breathe...

She woke up, tried to draw a breath, but the weight, the pinpricks, and the fetid smell were still there.

She opened her eyes.

To the ruby-red glare of the big blue cat sitting on her chest.

Gorilla In My Room

by Jack Ketchum

There's a gorilla in my room. Just because his favorite food is tender bamboo shoots and fruits and leaves that doesn't mean I can ignore him. His weight is five times mine. His elbow is the size of my thigh. His wrist the size of my neck. His eyes blink at me and I see light in them when he looks away.

How he got into my room I'm not exactly sure but I have a feeling he means to stay. He measures me as I measure him and I'm not insignificant to his world nor is he insignificant to mine or to my room though he grants me passage as I do him.

There's a gorilla in my room. We skirt one another for a while and then we settle in and stay.

I remember my first cat who was six weeks old and whose ear was thin as my fingernail and whose head I could have crushed in a single tight squeeze but who I embraced instead.

There's a gorilla in my room. I don't know how he got there. He's very big and I'm quite small.

When night falls I turn off the light.

—for Rita

The Chair

by Bentley Little

Somewhere along the way, Charlie had lost his interest in hunting. He didn't know when, didn't know how, didn't know why. All he knew was that killing animals no longer held the same appeal that it had when he was younger. He was still an avid hiker, however, and in many ways, had become a *better* hiker. Without the added weight of gun and ammo, without the responsibilities of stalking and tracking and endlessly waiting, he was free to explore, to delve far deeper into the woods than he ever had previously.

He also went out on his own now, which made for a much purer experience. Always before, he'd gone hunting with a group of friends, but the last time he'd gone with them, he'd felt restless in their company, and he could tell that they felt he was dead weight, dragging them down. So, these days he hiked and camped by himself, and not only did he go farther into the woods than he ever had before, but he encountered the wilderness in a much more authentic way. For he was not part of a group, lumbering around and bringing civilization with it. He was single, alone, and, like the other animals in the forest, he was an element of nature rather than an intrusion into it.

Not to get too Edward Abbey about the whole thing.

This time, he was on a five-day journey into the heart of the Kaibab. He had left the established trails back on the first day and since then had been blazing his own, encountering some truly spectacular scenery in the process. There'd been an ancient sinkhole, like a miniature canyon overgrown with vines and brush, housing a virtual fern forest at the bottom. There'd been a watering hole in a meadow where he'd seen a family of elk drinking peacefully. There'd been an unexpected ridge he'd discovered that overlooked endless acres of sycamore and oak stretching as far as the eye could see beneath a stratocumulus sky.

Since waking up this morning, however, he'd been hiking across flat land through thick forest with a canopy so dense that it seemed perpetually twilight. If he hadn't brought a compass along with him, he'd probably be lost, because it was impossible to tell by the sun in which direction he was going.

Ahead, the trees grew even closer together, so close that he would have to turn sideways in order to pass between them. It looked lighter, though, behind the trees, and while he could have changed directions and gone around, he was curious, and he took off his backpack, held it next to his side and slid between two oaks with intertwined branches.

He found himself in a small clearing, with no canopy of leaves above him, only open sky, which accounted for the brightness.

In the center of the clearing was a chair.

Charlie stood in place, frowning. There was no trail that led here, and he'd seen no sign of human habitation for well over a day.

Yet in this spot, as far from civilization as he'd ever been, someone had placed a high-backed wooden chair. It made no sense.

He looked around. The closely growing oaks encircled the clearing so precisely that they had to have been planted there. Many decades ago. And unless it had been lowered by helicopter, which made no sense whatsoever, the chair had been placed in this location at the same time, as it was far too wide to fit between the trees. Indeed, it did have an antique look, with a mission-style back and wide flat armrests. It was in perfect shape, though, its wood shiny and polished, not what one would expect for an object that had been exposed to the elements for any length of time.

He was starting to get an uneasy feeling about this. Who had brought it here and why? Moving forward to take a closer look, he stopped after only a few steps. He didn't *want* to see the chair up close, he realized.

He was afraid of it.

Charlie's heart started pounding. There was no logical reason for what he was feeling—the wood did not have demonic faces carved into it, there were no spikes on the seat—but something about the chair chilled him to the bone. It was not just the fact that it was in the wrong location, that furniture did not belong out here in the middle of nowhere. And it was not the bizarre contradiction that it remained in pristine condition despite its exposure to weather and bugs and animals and God knew what else. No, it was the chair itself that frightened him, something about the simple design of the utilitarian item that stopped him in his tracks, that made him back slowly away and exit the meadow the same way in which he'd come.

He hazarded a quick look behind him, saw, in the space between two trees, the flat seat of the chair and two straight legs, bathed in sunlight. Then he was hurrying through the darkness of the woods, running away.

It took him a full day to return to the wilderness trail he'd left when he set off into the forest on his own, and another eight hours or so to reach the trailhead and his Jeep. He walked nonstop, through the darkness, through the light, snacking and drinking water as he hiked, not sleeping, eyes constantly on the lookout for a sign of any other furniture.

Back home, back in the city, he tried to forget about what had happened in the woods. After all, Charlie told himself, it wasn't all that momentous. He'd seen a chair in a clearing. Big deal. But he couldn't stop thinking about it, and in his dreams, he came across the chair in numerous locations: on the sand of a beach, on the cliff of a mountain, in the yard of a house, in the center of a crowded restaurant. No one was ever sitting in it, and he wondered in his dreams if something would *happen* to a person who dared to sit on the chair.

He refused to tell any of his friends what he had found. They wouldn't understand. And how could he ever describe it? How could he make them realize the absolute *otherness* of this utterly ordinary object, the terrifying impossibility of its location, the horrible fear it engendered within him? Hell, if someone had tried to tell him something like that, he'd think the guy was a lunatic. And he'd laugh his ass off.

The dreams continued.

A week later, Charlie was in Home Depot, buying a new sprinkler head to replace one he'd accidentally damaged while mowing the lawn. He was about to walk over to the checkout stand when something caused him to glance toward the lumber aisles. On the endcap, facing him, was a deep stack of upright six foot two-by-twos. They were long and thin and looked to him as though they were meant to be made into...

Chair legs.

He suddenly knew what he had to do. Returning to the front entrance of the store, Charlie grabbed a cart and pushed it over to the lumber area, where he took three two-by-twos from the endcap, then picked out several flatter, wider pieces of walnut that could be cut to size for a chair's seat and back. He was not a woodworker, but he was handy, and he had no doubt that he would be able to make a chair. It might take a couple of tries, might involve a little trial and error, but he was sure he'd be able to pull it off.

He bought the wood, took it home and got to work.

The remainder of the weekend was taken up with efforts to build a chair, and though the phone rang several times both days, he ignored it and did not answer. His initial attempts were laughable, but he knew what he had to do—the perfect template was seared into his mind—and after several more trips to Home Depot, he had assembled a reasonable rough draft of what he wanted. For the rest of the week, he spent every spare hour, before work and after work, crafting the object of his obsession, fine-tuning joints and junctures, sanding, sanding, sanding, varnishing. Finally, mid-Sunday morning, after staying up all night, he was done.

Finished, he admired the product of his labor, walking around the chair, touching the arms, patting the backrest.

But what to do with it?

On an impulse, he closed the garage door, took off his clothes and sat down on the wooden seat. It felt smooth and cold against his buttocks, and the tactile sensation of it, the feel of wood against skin, gave him an instant erection. He stood slowly, still aroused, and walked around the chair, wondering what it would look like with a naked woman sitting on it. He imagined Myra from work, Judy from across the street, the blonde checkout girl at Safeway, two of his ex-girlfriends. He could put clamps on the armrests, he thought, shackles on the legs.

No.

As tempting as that might be, it would ruin the aesthetics of the piece. If a woman *wanted* to sit in the chair, that was one thing. But to force her to sit in it, to add chains and handcuffs? Well, that would be wrong.

His erection was fading. All this thought about making alterations to the chair had sapped his libido, and he realized that if the object remained here at his house it would probably not preserve the pristine perfection it now possessed. Even if he did refrain from reworking it, the chair would probably end up with boxes or books piled on top of its seat, like everything else in his house.

Maybe he should take it into the woods somewhere and leave it. Wasn't that what had been done with the original? The idea appealed to him. He could carry it into a forest, leave it there—

The sound of the doorbell caused him to jump.

Acutely conscious of the fact that he was naked, Charlie quickly pulled on his pants and underwear, slipping into his shirt but leaving off his shoes as he hurried out of the garage, into the kitchen and over to the front door. His friend Will was standing on the porch. "Hey," Will greeted him.

Charlie nodded. "Hey."

"Haven't seen you around, buddy. Where you been?"

"Busy," Charlie mumbled.

"Well, I'm headed out to Pineview. Last time I talked to you, you said you wanted to go with me and pick up some flagstone from that quarry if I was ever out that way again."

He was caught off guard and couldn't immediately think of a reason to beg off. Truth be told, he kind of *wanted* to go. Not because he needed the flagstone, though he did, but because he'd been spending a lot of time alone lately, and it would be good to see people again, hang out with his friends. His life since the hiking trip had become far too claustrophobic, and he thought that maybe if he got out a bit more, socialized a little, he might be able to get back on track, stop obsessing about the chair.

The chair.

Part of him wanted to show Will his handiwork, wanted to get an outside opinion, see if another person would have the same reaction to it he had. But another part, a stronger part, wanted to keep it all a secret, and he said, "You brought your truck, right? I'll meet you out there. Just let me grab some gloves and a chisel." He closed the door on Will so his friend wouldn't be tempted to follow him into the garage, then put on his socks and shoes, and came out with the work gloves and chisel a moment later.

Will had discovered an abandoned quarry just this side of Pineview, or, rather, had been *told* of the quarry, and he'd gone there and brought back enough flagstone to make a winding path through his wife's flower garden. Charlie had been thinking of building a backyard patio, and he thought that he could use flat rock and mortar instead of constructing a wood base. That project had sort of fallen by the wayside, but maybe now was the time to resurrect it. He wouldn't be able to haul enough flagstone for the entire patio in one trip, but he could get a decent start.

Charlie hopped into the pickup's cab, where Will already had the engine running. "Let's go."

Pineview was over an hour away, so they had plenty of time to talk. Will pressed him on where he'd been and what he'd been doing, but Charlie gave vague answers about being busy and having a lot on his plate, and the subject went away. Their conversation was easy, though, and moved on to other things, and he was glad that he'd come. It felt relaxing to be away from the house, out of his own head, and he was feeling pretty good as they turned right on the dirt road that led to the quarry.

A mile or two in, Will pulled to a stop in front of a dilapidated wooden house, a shack that abutted the road. "We have to stop," he whispered. "Pay respects. The old buzzard who lives here controls access to the quarry. We don't get in without his say so."

Charlie's good mood faded away.

On the porch of the hillbilly's shack was a chair.

The chair.

Holding his breath, Charlie got out of the pickup and walked slowly toward the porch.

"Ho there!" Will called.

An old man came out, stooped and grizzled, smoking a pipe, like some cinematic hillbilly straight out of central casting. "Yeah?"

"We wanted to go over to the quarry, take out some stone," Will said. "That alright?"

The old man nodded. "Yeah."

Charlie had glanced at the man when he'd come onto the porch but since then had not been able to take his eyes off the chair.

"I gotta take a whizz," Will said.

"Bushes over there." The old man nodded.

Will headed off in the direction of the nod, leaving the two of them alone.

"Where did you get that chair?" Charlie asked, trying to keep his voice casual.

"Made it." The old man stared at him, and as their eyes locked, each of them *knew*.

"Where did you see it?" Charlie asked quietly.

The man wouldn't answer, just turned away and walked back into the house. Charlie waited, thinking maybe he'd gone in to get something and would come back out, but the old guy did not return, and when Will emerged from the bushes and said, "Ready to roll?" Charlie followed him out to the truck.

It rattled him more than he would have expected, the fact that someone else had seen the chair—*somewhere*—and had also made a copy, and though Charlie was able to work with Will at the quarry for the next two hours, breaking up chunks of flagstone and loading them in the truck, he could not stop thinking about the chair. It seemed such a waste for it to be sitting on the porch of that hillbilly's shack. It seemed…

Wrong.

Yes. The chair deserved better. It was much too important to be left in such a location, though why it was important and what location would be better he could not say.

What of his own chair? What was he to do with it? His initial impulse had been to take it into the forest and leave it in the same secluded clearing where he'd seen the original. The chair had meaning, a purpose, and he knew that purpose was something greater than sitting hidden in his garage.

Would he even be able to find that spot in the forest again? He didn't know, but he doubted it. There'd been no trail to the clearing, and while he'd maintained a semi-steady direction on his hike in, there'd been quite a few zigs and zags, and in woods that thick he could pass within twenty feet of the spot and not know it.

Did he even *want* to find the spot again? That was a more difficult question. Part of him did, and part of him didn't. He hadn't forgotten how frightened he was of the chair, how its unnaturalness had kept him from even getting close to it. But he had often thought since about returning and sitting in it, and now that he had built a chair himself, he might feel more comfortable being around it, seeing it.

Touching it.

By the time Will dropped him off at home and the two of them unloaded Charlie's share of the flagstone, it was getting on to evening and the sun was setting. Will suggested they grab a burger, but Charlie begged off, saying he was tired, he'd been up all night and needed to catch up on his sleep before going to work tomorrow morning.

"Partying hard, huh?" His friend grinned.

Charlie thought of the chair sitting in the garage. "Yeah."

As soon as Will left, he locked the front door, closed the drapes and went into the garage, turning on the light. The chair sat shiny and new against the faded old junk that had been stored in here, the sawdust and castoff cuts of wood that had led to its creation littered about the concrete floor. It stood alone, simple yet flawless, and beholding its perfection, Charlie began to weep. He dropped to his knees in front of it, laid his head upon its seat and allowed the wood to absorb his tears.

When at last he stood up again, it was morning. The light of dawn shone in a single line through a space on the right side of the garage door. He checked his watch. Six thirty-five. He had spent the entire night kneeling on the floor of the garage, sleeping with his head resting on the seat of the chair.

Strangely enough, he felt refreshed. His neck was not stiff, his back did not hurt, and there was none of the muscle fatigue that usually followed a night spent sleeping somewhere other than his bed.

Charlie stared at the chair, wondering what to do with it. The chair he had found in the forest belonged there, and the one on the hillbilly's porch belonged...somewhere other than where it was. But what about this one? He was its creator—but not really. He was the *channel* through which it had been created.

He recalled the dreams he'd had and decided that *this* chair belonged on the beach. He didn't know why, but just looking at it, he knew that the chair should be sitting on sand, near an ocean, not in a forest, not in his garage.

He thought for a moment, then went into the house and called his work, leaving a message on the answering machine telling them that he was sick and would not be in today.

Then he got ready.

He drove for three days straight, making for the Atlantic, sleeping only once, when he stopped for coffee at a McDonald's and briefly dozed off in the plastic booth as he waited for the coffee to cool off. All the time, the chair sat in the back of his Jeep, untethered, untouched, unmoving.

When he reached the end of the continent, a beach in Virginia, Charlie parked the Jeep in a public parking lot, then picked up the chair and walked down to the shore. It was early morning, so there was no one else on the sand, but it was obvious from the walkways and the lifeguard towers that this was a popular stretch of coast. He needed someplace less used, more remote, and, still carrying the chair, he started making his way up the shoreline.

He walked for nearly an hour before he found a small section of sand between jetting rocks, beneath a steep bluff, far from both public beaches and waterfront homes. It was difficult to haul the chair over the rocks without scratching the wood, but he managed to do so and placed the chair in the center of the sand. Looking at it, he knew that it was right, and he was filled with a strange sensation, an unfamiliar emotion that had no name but that made him feel as though his purpose had been fulfilled, as though he could die right now and he would have accomplished everything in life that he was meant to accomplish.

As though he could kill himself and it would be...good.

Charlie moved back, moved away, climbed up the rocks and looked down at the chair on the sand. For a brief second, he wondered if he should have placed it farther from the water. Would it be encroached upon at high tide, washed away by the waves?

No.

If he knew nothing else, he knew that *that*, at least, would never happen. As long as it was here, the chair would remain untouched by the elements, in perfect shape. Forever.

He climbed down the other side of the rocks and walked back down the shore the way he had come.

Wondering who would eventually find the chair.

And when.

And what would happen when they did.

EYES LIKE POISONED WELLS

by Ian Rogers

The house said divorce work.

Actually, the first thing it said was money. It was a mansion in Forest Hill, one of the city's wealthiest neighbourhoods. Driving in I saw plenty of hills, but not so much forest. Toronto's rich and elite had ploughed most of it under so they could build their estates. A few trees remained, like ornamental reminders of greener, bygone days. To me they looked like trophies, the landscaping equivalent of animal heads mounted on the wall of someone's den.

Most of the places were vast estates with terraced lawns and sculpted gardens. I saw porte-cochères and private tennis courts, and even one with a three-hole golf course out back, the fairways as smooth and green as the surface of a pool table.

The Corwyn residence was modest by Forest Hill standards: a medium-sized Tudor sitting cosily on a lushly wooded lot that almost made you forget you were in the city.

I parked in the semicircular drive and sat for a moment staring at the house. When rich people enlisted the services of a private detective, it was usually because a marriage was in trouble. Rich people married for love, like everyone else, but when they divorced it was almost always about money. When adultery was involved, or suspected, a private detective was the belle of the ball. He's the cheater's worst enemy and the cheatee's best friend.

Divorce work makes up the majority of a PI's workload, but I tried to avoid it as much as possible. I thought of it like a trip to the dentist: an unpleasant, sometimes painful experience that fortunately only happened once or twice a year. Being so picky about my cases had its downside. I couldn't afford to eat in nice restaurants or buy suits better than off-the-rack, but I felt it was an acceptable trade-off.

Unfortunately, the time had come to get my hands dirty again. My coffers were low and I had rent to pay. And alimony. And an assistant. The money for the alimony and the assistant went to the same person, my ex-wife Sandra. We were still friends, and she needed the job, but it was a weird situation that probably went some way toward explaining why I hated divorce work.

I got out of the car and walked up the steps to the front door. Rich people don't call. They summon. I was hoping the rich person who lived here would tell me his marriage was just fine, thank you very much, but could I help him find his lost puppy.

I rang the bell and stood admiring the door. It was a massive piece of oak reinforced with iron braces. The sort of door that should lower down on chains like a drawbridge.

I was about to ring the bell again when the door was opened by a tall, attractive Filipino woman in a gray house dress. She smiled warmly and gestured for me to enter. I started to tell her who I was, but she was already walking away.

EYES LIKE POISONED WELLS

Ian Rogers

I stepped inside and looked around. I was in one of those cavernous foyers that make me want to yell out loud to see if there's an echo. I managed to restrain myself.

The Filipino woman was walking briskly down a hallway as big as a subway tunnel. I was moving to follow her when I noticed someone standing on the curved stairway. At first glance I thought she was a statue: her skin was white as marble and she was standing perfectly still. One of her hands was resting on the wrought-iron railing, the other held a glass of red wine. She was one of the most beautiful women I had ever seen outside of a movie or a magazine. A natural beauty—no make-up, no flare, no lifts or tucks that denoted plastic surgery. She had long honey-blonde hair, prominent cheekbones, and lush lips the same colour as the wine in her glass. Her eyes were a mesmerizing silvery-blue that seemed to change to violet as I stared into them. She wore a powder-blue gown with a slit up one side that revealed a heartbreaking glimpse of creamy thigh.

I said hello. At least I think I did. It was possible I only stood there drooling. Either way, the woman said nothing in response. She didn't smile or sniff in disapproval. She didn't even move. I waited a moment, then continued down the hall, feeling the woman's eyes tracking me the whole way.

The Filipino woman led me around a corner to another tall oak door. She knocked, pushed it open, then swept her hand in a graceful manner, still smiling. I nodded my thanks and stepped inside.

I was in a study with floor-to-ceiling bookshelves and a massive Scandinavian rug covering most of the floor. Two red leather wing chairs were positioned at angles in front of a black marble fireplace; a red leather couch was parked in front of the room's only window; and a red leather chaise lounge stood in the corner next to a floor lamp.

The only piece of furniture that wasn't red leather was the huge maple desk in the centre of the room. A man in a burgundy smoking jacket stood behind it. He was bent over slightly at the waist with his head down and his hands planted on the blotter. He looked like a man weighed down by heavy decisions. Like whether he should spend the winter in Aspen or Athens.

I cleared my throat and he looked up.

My first thought was that Michael Corwyn looked familiar. He was tall and tanned, his blond hair swept back from the type of brow that would have been called "noble" in a trashy romance novel. He had a broad nose, thin lips, and a blunt chin with a dimple in it that probably drove the ladies wild. I probably saw his picture on the society page of the newspaper.

"Mr. Renn?"

"None other," I said. "And call me Felix."

"Thank you for coming so promptly." Corwyn came around the desk with his hand extended. "And on such short notice."

Up close, Corwyn was still a handsome man, but I could tell he didn't come by his good looks naturally. His face had the chiseled look that came from the scalpel rather than good genes, his hair smelled faintly of its last dye job, and his tan was a little too perfect to come from anything other than a salon. He was a man in his fifties trying, by hook or by crook (and all the tools in his plastic surgeon's arsenal), to look like he was still in his forties.

"I had a cancellation," I said, shaking his hand. "Dentist appointment."

"Dentist, ooh." Corwyn made a face. "I hate going. Childhood fear, I guess."

"I think most people feel that way."

"Yes."

An awkward silence descended. Corwyn glanced down at his brown leather slippers. I stuck my hands in my pockets and refrained from whistling.

"I guess you're wondering why I asked you here," Corwyn said.

"It crossed my mind."

He gestured to the wing chairs and we went over and sat down. There was no fire in the fireplace. It was October and still warm enough to go without.

Corwyn took his time getting comfortable. He crossed one leg over the other, smoothed a crease in his pants, then folded his hands and propped them on his knee. Eventually he said, "My wife is very upset..."

Here it comes, I thought.

"Something was stolen from us, and I want you to get it back."

I perked up a bit. "Stolen?"

"Yes," Corwyn said. "From right here in the house. From this very room, in fact."

"Was it a book?"

A smile flickered across Corwyn's face, there and gone. "No, it wasn't a book. It was..." His voice trailed off. "I'm sorry, I forgot to offer you a drink. Would you like something? Coffee? Tea? Or maybe something stronger?" The grin reappeared, a quick flash of perfectly capped teeth, then disappeared again.

"Coffee would be great."

Corwyn picked up a silver bell on the table next to him and gave it a brisk shake. The ringing sound was very loud in the cavernous room. The Filipino woman appeared in the doorway, her smile permanently etched on her face.

"Two coffees, Mia." He held up two fingers just in case she didn't know how many that was.

She nodded and left the room.

"Mia is the keeper of the house," Corwyn said. "I prefer that to 'housekeeper.' It sounds less subservient. She works for us, takes care of our home, but she's not a servant. I don't make her wear a uniform."

But she comes when you ring a bell, I thought but didn't say.

"That's part of the reason I didn't notify the police about the theft. I prefer to have someone working for me in this matter. Someone who doesn't wear a uniform. That might sound strange to you, but that's how I feel. Uniforms bother me. They're too impersonal. Like masks. I think one gets better results by hiring individuals. Professionals. Not products out of a box. Uniforms are neat and orderly. I prefer a little chaos. Does that make sense?"

"Not really," I said honestly. "But it doesn't really matter. I can still find what's been stolen from you."

"Can you?" Corwyn sounded genuinely interested.

"Yes."

"You sound so sure."

"It's what I do."

"Yes." Corwyn ran his finger along the curved edge of the silver bell. "There are other reasons why I don't want the police involved." He grinned again, this one slow and sly. "Certain details about the item's history that I don't want divulged."

"Was it already stolen?"

Corwyn tilted his head to the side, considering the question. "Stolen is the wrong word."

"Is semantics a better word?" I asked.

Corwyn nodded. "Touché."

Ian Rogers

Mia came in carrying a silver tray with two cups of coffee, a creamer, a sugar bowl, and two spoons. She placed the tray on a low table between us, smiling all the while, then turned and left the room.

I put cream and sugar in my coffee. Corwyn took his black. We sat for a moment sipping our hot coffees in front of the cold fireplace. Then Corwyn said: "My wife has money. I have some, too, but there's a difference between rich and wealth."

"I'll have to take your word on that."

"My wife is wealthy," Corwyn continued, "while I am merely rich. Despite that, she doesn't care as much about money as she does certain heirlooms that have been passed down through her family for generations. These items have sentimental value, but the piece that was stolen is, quite literally, priceless."

"What is it?"

"A sword. A very old sword." Corwyn put down his cup and tented his fingers under his chin. "Do you know anything about medieval weaponry?"

"I've seen *Braveheart.*"

Corwyn nodded. "The Scots. They knew a thing or two about swords. But this one..." He shook his head. "You've never seen anything like it."

"How old is it?"

"It's practically primitive," Corwyn scoffed. "Made long before the craft of sword-making was even in its infancy."

"Do you think the person who stole it knew it was valuable?"

"That's the strange part. The sword itself isn't much to look at. It bears none of the grace or beauty of, say, a katana or a cutlass. It's an ugly weapon, to be perfectly frank. A thief wouldn't know it was valuable simply by its appearance."

"I guess looks really aren't everything," I said.

"Indeed."

"So, what makes this particular sword so special?"

Corwyn shifted in his seat. "Well, for one, the blade is made of stone rather than steel. Obsidian, or something like it. The experts I've shown it to don't really know *what* it's made of. Which I suppose isn't all that surprising, considering where it came from."

I shook my head, confused. "Where it came from…"

"The sword is from the Black Lands, Mr. Renn."

I didn't say anything for a long moment. The room was utterly silent. I stared at Corwyn, but his expression didn't tell me anything. Finally, I cleared my throat and said: "I don't suppose the PIA is aware that you have this…artifact in your possession."

Corwyn gave me the same slow, sly grin. "I'm aware of the laws pertaining to cross-dimensional imports. I'm also aware that the sword has been in my wife's family since before those laws were enacted. Which is beside the point anyway since the sword is no longer in our possession." He spread his hands. "And therein lies the problem."

"You're sure it's from the Black Lands?"

"Very sure. And so was the thief, apparently. There are a number of items in this house that could be sold for a great deal of money, but he—or she—took the one piece that was worth the most."

"I didn't know there was anything in the Black Lands that could make such a weapon."

"Apparently so." Corwyn's tone was dismissive, as if the subject didn't interest him. "It's crude, to be sure, but it clearly demonstrates a tool-making ability. The ones who made the sword were much more advanced than werewolves or vampires."

Ian Rogers

"The sword was kept in this room?"

Corwyn turned in his seat and pointed across the room. "Right over there."

Hanging on the far wall, between two of the floor-to-ceiling bookshelves, was a long, slender glass case with a pair of support hooks at the top, where the hilt of the sword would have hung.

"Was there a security system?" I asked. "A pressure alarm or anything?"

Corwyn shrugged. "I never thought I'd need one. The house itself is secure, and no one knows about the sword except me, Deirdre, her family, and the house staff."

"And the experts," I said, taking a sip of my coffee.

"Excuse me?"

"You said you had experts look at the sword."

"Yes," Corwyn said, without elaborating.

"Deirdre is your wife?"

"Yes."

"Your house staff has access to this room?"

"It's not locked, if that's what you mean, but Mia is the only one who'd have reason to be in here."

"She knows about the sword?"

"Of course, it was hanging right there on the wall."

"I mean, did she know it was from the Black Lands?"

Corwyn thought about it. "I don't think so," he said. "I don't see how she could."

"Maybe she overheard you talking to someone about it," I said. Then added, a little pointedly: "Maybe one of these experts."

Corwyn shook his head vehemently. "Absolutely not."

A thought tugged at my mind, and for the second time since we met, I was struck by the notion that I knew Corwyn from somewhere. It was a vague feeling, like a light turning on for a split second in a darkened room. I caught a glimpse of something, then the darkness came flooding back in again.

I pulled myself from this reverie and asked: "How did you come to acquire the sword?"

Corwyn pinched his wedding ring between his thumb and forefinger and turned it back and forth. "That has no relevance to the current situation." His voice was cool and firm. "And as I already mentioned, the sword belongs to my wife. Everything does."

"Everything?"

"The house, the cars, the money. She owns it all. The kit *and* the caboodle." He stopped turning his ring and dropped his hands in his lap. "I *was* rich but I'm not anymore. I suppose I should tell you that up front. You'll probably find out eventually, if you're as good as they say."

"They?"

"I was married before," Corwyn said. "My ex-wife cleaned me out in the divorce. I suppose I asked for it. I was having an affair and she caught me. She had a bigger and badder lawyer than I did. Oh well." He shrugged his shoulders like it was no big deal. "I had nothing when I met Deirdre. Nothing but my looks and a whole lot of anger." He looked away, as if staring into the past. "Nothing to give her but my heart. Which, consequently, was the only thing my ex-wife didn't take."

"I'm not sure why you're telling me this," I said.

"Because I'm the most likely suspect."

"Did you steal the sword?"

"No." Corwyn suddenly looked very nervous, although I didn't think it was because he was lying. His face had paled considerably and a nerve twitched in his cheek. He looked afraid. "If I did, Deirdre and her family would have taken me apart with their bare hands. They're a close-knit family, and not very forgiving."

"Do you think any of them might have stolen it?"

Corwyn gave me a look. "Why would they? It's been in their family for years. They gain nothing by stealing it."

I slugged back the rest of my coffee and put the cup on the tray. "I'll need to speak to your housekeeper."

"Keeper of the house," Corwyn corrected me.

"Right. I'll also need to talk to the rest of your staff."

Corwyn rose from his chair and came around to stand behind it. "I don't suppose it really matters," he said in a casual voice. "Deirdre said I was making too much of this."

"I thought the sword belonged to her family."

"Oh, I don't mean that," Corwyn said dismissively. "I mean *this*." He spread his arms wide.

"I don't understand."

"You weren't meant to, Mr. *Renn*." He put a strange emphasis on my name that I didn't particularly care for.

"This was all set-dressing. I suppose Deirdre was right. I do tend to take things too far. But sometimes that's the only way to take them. Sometimes you have to take things right to the very end."

I didn't know what Corwyn was talking about. I was about to ask him if he had put something in his coffee when I experienced a sudden wave of nausea. It came on so unexpectedly that it left me momentarily speechless. I lowered my hand to my stomach, and it was trembling—my hand, not my stomach. My stomach was churning like an overloaded washing machine. My feet started to tingle, and my shoes felt too tight. I looked down at them and they seemed an incredibly long distance away. I leaned over, trying to get a closer look, and my head felt it was going to topple off my neck. I pulled my head back, too fast, and the world shifted.

I was wrong. Corwyn hadn't put something in his coffee. He'd put something in mine.

"It's funny in a way." His voice seemed to come from the far end of a tunnel.

I turned my head and saw him standing over me, his grey eyes drilling into me.

"You'd think a private investigator would have a keener sense of perception. An eye for details. I guess it shows just how pathetic you truly are. You didn't recognize me at all, did you? Not my name or my face."

I gripped the arms of the chair and leaned forward, trying to peer into his face, but all of his features were blurring. Everything in the room was blurring, blending, separating, then reforming into vague, indistinct shapes before blurring and blending and separating again. It was like being inside a lava lamp.

I tried to focus on Corwyn, but he drifted up and away from me. I didn't realize it was because my chair was tipping forward until I made hard, painful contact with the floor.

I lay there motionless while the world continued to pull itself apart and meld back together around me. A wave of darkness suddenly splashed across my eyes like spilled ink. The only light that remained was a fuzzy moonface hanging above me. At first I thought it was Corwyn, but as I continued to stare and squint with the last of my fading vision, I realized it was his wife.

There was something wrong with her eyes. The hollows were too dark. The violet light I'd seen in them earlier twinkled like noxious water at the bottom of a deep pit. The light seemed to beckon to me. As I reached out for it, the world tilted and I felt myself falling into those dark hollows, those eyes like poisoned wells. A single thought trailed after me.

I really hate divorce work.

—

Consciousness returned like a corpse floating to the surface of a lake. I was the corpse. At least I felt like one. Then I realized that pain like this only affects the living. Which meant I was still alive. Hurray.

I opened my eyes to blackness. I blinked a few times, trying to get my vision back, but I still couldn't see anything. Then I realized it was okay, because it was night. I was lying on my back, staring up at the sky. I could see stars, but no moon. No moonface, either. I was alone, somewhere outside, and in a great deal of pain. My head throbbed from whatever Corwyn had put in my coffee, and my shoulder ached from where it had slammed into the floor.

My tongue felt thick and furry in my mouth. Like I'd been making out with a shag carpet. One that hadn't been cleaned in a long time.

Looking around, I saw I was in a clearing surrounded by trees. I couldn't hear anything except the low soughing of the wind and distant chirping of crickets.

I tried to get up and found that I couldn't. My hands and feet were bound together with thick bands of electrical tape.

I pawed around awkwardly for my gun, then remembered I left it back at the office. Divorce work didn't usually entail gunplay. But then this didn't turn out to be divorce work. It was a theft. And now it looked like it wasn't a theft, either. Unless I was the thing being stolen.

I'd walked into a trap, that much was clear. The question was why.

Working in the private-eye racket, one acquired a certain number of enemies. It was inevitable. The problem was trying to figure out who I might have pissed off enough that they would drug me and leave me tied up in the middle of the woods. Off the top of my head, I couldn't tell you if the list of possible suspects was long or short. The fact that there was a list at all might have suggested I was better off pursuing another field of interest. Dog grooming, for instance.

Corwyn had a grudge against me, but why? I didn't know him. Or did I? That niggling feeling rose again at the back of my mind, like an itch that I couldn't quite reach.

In terms of things I *could* reach, I had to wonder why Corwyn hadn't bothered to bind my hands behind my back. As it was, there was nothing stopping me from bending down and removing the tape from around my ankles. I was leaning forward to do so when a voice said, "Uh-uh, don't touch."

Michael Corwyn stepped out of the trees with his wife on his arm. Deirdre looked radiant in her powder-blue gown—and I wasn't just being colourful. Her gown really did seem to give off a cool luminescence, like it was lit up from inside somehow.

As they approached, Corwyn raised the arm his wife wasn't holding, and I saw the gun in his hand. "I'm glad to see you're finally awake," he said. "We must be quick. Time is of the essence."

"What's the matter?" I asked. "You got another kidnapping booked for later?"

Corwyn grinned at me without replying.

"I'm gonna take a wild guess and say there is no missing sword."

He didn't say anything to that either.

Ian Rogers

I held up my bound hands. "My keen powers of detection tell me you're pissed off about something. Care to tell me about it?"

"Snoops," Corwyn said.

"What?"

"Snoops," Corwyn repeated. "Isn't that what they call private detectives?"

"I suppose. Among other things."

"I like snoop," Corwyn said. "I think it fits you perfectly. It defines what you are, what you do. You insert yourself into a person's life—their *private* life—and you snoop. You spy. You look for things that are none of your concern, much less your business, and when you're done you run back to whoever hired you and you tell them all about it. You're nothing but a snoop and a snitch. And you do it all for money!" he added, as if this was the greatest insult of all. Coming from him it seemed rather funny.

"I have to take money." I lowered my hands out of sight between my legs and started flexing my wrists in small, furtive motions to loosen the tape. "I can't pay my bills with handshakes and thank-yous."

"You really don't remember me," Corwyn said.

"Refresh my memory. It doesn't work so good when I've been drugged."

"Please, Mr. Renn. You didn't know who I was even before you passed out."

That was true, and while I wished I could have said it was all coming back to me now, the truth was that I was still drawing a blank. But I didn't want Corwyn to know that. So, I scrunched my eyes shut and pretended to search my fuzzy, aching brain. I would have put a finger thoughtfully to my lips, but I was trying to keep Corwyn's attention away from my hands.

After a long moment, I cracked one eye open and said: "Are you an unsatisfied customer?"

"Try looking at things from the other side of the table," Corwyn said. He tilted his head to the side. "Or the other side of the lens."

Suddenly it came to me. It wasn't the face or the name, but that word, "lens," working like a post-hypnotic command that unleashed a flood of memories.

I'd been trying to connect Corwyn's name to one of my clients, to no avail. That was because he wasn't a client. He had been married to one.

Mary Stoddard. She had kept her maiden name, she told me, because she saw no reason to give it up simply because she had decided to share her life with a man. She had come to see me five or six years ago. She thought her husband might be having an affair. *An affair*, she'd said with a contemptuous snort. *That makes it sound almost dignified. Much better than saying my husband is fucking some little slut who's young enough to be his daughter.* After I discovered her suspicions were true, Mary Stoddard had given me a smile, one that managed to look both sad and satisfied at the same time, and said, *See? It was a good thing I kept my name.*

The man she had been married to—the man I had never met and had only seen once at three hundred yards through a telephoto lens—was Michael Corwyn.

"You remember," Corwyn said, nodding. "I can see it in your eyes." He looked at his wife. "You can see everything in a person's eyes, if you know what to look for."

"Is that what this is about?" I said. "You're pissed off because I caught you screwing around on your wife?"

Ian Rogers

Corwyn glared at me. "You interfered in my business. You took pictures of me and that whore and showed them to my wife. She didn't even give me a chance to explain. She just kicked me out of the house. *Our* house. Then she and her Jewboy lawyer raked me over the coals. Took me for everything I had."

I almost said *Not my problem*, then stopped myself. It was my problem, now. Instead I said, "You seem to be doing all right for yourself now."

"I paid for it," Corwyn said. There was a slight tremor in his voice. "I'm still paying. Every day."

"Alimony's a bitch," I agreed. "I can relate."

"Money?" Corwyn sneered. "This isn't about money. You ruined my life, you snooping piece of shit!" The gun trembled in his hand, his finger jittered against the trigger.

"I didn't do anything to you," I said, coolly and calmly. "Your wife already suspected you were having an affair. All I did was confirm it for her. You made your bed, Corwyn, and you screwed another woman in it. That was your choice."

I knew I might have been signing my own death warrant, but I didn't care. I wasn't going to lie there and apologize for doing my job. Other people had put me in the same position—usually without a gun pointed at my head, granted—and I hadn't backed down from them. I wasn't about to start now.

"Yes," Corwyn said. "I got caught and I paid the price. That's life, right?" His grip tightened on the gun. "Now the situation is reversed. I caught you and it's your turn to pay."

"How about you let me go and we call it even?"

Corwyn tapped his chin with the barrel of the gun. "I gave serious thought to just leaving you here to die from exposure. But then I thought, where's the fun in that? I want to be able to *see* you die."

"Exposure? It's October."

"I was thinking of a different kind of exposure."

Corwyn turned and smiled at his wife, but she wasn't looking at him. She was looking at me. She hadn't stopped looking at me since she'd stepped out of the woods on her husband's arm. She hadn't spoken a single word. It was a little unnerving.

"The house in Forest Hill," Corwyn said. "That's my home. This"—he gestured all around him with the gun—"this is Deirdre's."

"What the hell are you talking about?" I said, glancing at the dark trees that hemmed the clearing. "Where are we?"

"I'm disappointed," Corwyn said. He didn't look disappointed; in fact, he looked happier than a pig in shit. "I understood you were familiar with this place. I heard you'd been to the Black Lands before."

All the warmth suddenly left my body. It was like someone had doused me in ice water. In a small voice I didn't recognize as my own, I said, "You brought me to the Black Lands? Are you insane?"

"You made my life a living nightmare," Corwyn said. "It seems only fair to take you to the place where nightmares come from."

I looked at the trees again, but I was seeing them differently now. I was waiting for one of them to start moving. "You might as well shoot me," I told him. "Then shoot yourself. It would be quicker."

"I'm not in any danger." Corwyn slipped his free hand around his wife's waist. "Like I said, this is Deirdre's old stomping grounds. Although I'm not sure if she did any actual stomping." He turned to her, grinning. "Did you, my sweet?"

Deirdre finally showed some expression. She grinned. It was a small grin, just a slight upturning at the corners of her mouth, but it lit up her whole face.

Ian Rogers

"It's time," Corwyn said. He withdrew his arm from around his wife's waist and took a smooth, almost deferential step away from her.

At first, I didn't know what was happening. This whole time my attention had been focused on Corwyn. I hadn't considered his wife to be anything more than eye candy, a rich man's affectation. Now it seemed she had a role in this as well. Possibly even the lead role.

As she started to raise her hand, I knew I was right. Corwyn was going to pass her the gun, and she would take it and shoot me.

Only that didn't happen.

Instead, Deirdre's hand went up to one of the spaghetti straps of her gown and slipped it off her shoulder. She did the same to the other one and the gown fell to the ground in a hush of silk. As she stepped out of it, I saw that it wasn't the gown that had seemed to glow but Deirdre herself. Her skin, so pale it was almost blue, was possessed of a deep, inner light, as if a low electric charge was running through her body, just below the surface.

Any arousal I might have felt staring at a beautiful naked woman was immediately dashed by a pair of unsettling details— or rather, a lack of them. Her breasts, small and round and without the slightest hint of sag, didn't have nipples. And, as my eyes trailed downward, I saw she didn't have any genitalia, either. Deirdre Corwyn was as smooth and featureless as a Barbie doll.

"She's special," Corwyn said, by way of explanation. "We make quite the couple. But Deirdre has some appetites that I can't sate."

"I think they make a pill for that now."

Corwyn frowned. "I should have taped your mouth shut. But I want to hear you scream. You can start now if you like. No one will hear you out here." He took something from his pocket and tossed it on the ground in front of me. It was a small folding knife. I stared at it without picking it up.

"Deirdre prefers her meat free range," Corwyn explained.

I leaned forward and picked up the knife with my bound hands. I flicked it open and cut through the tape on my ankles, then turned the knife around and, moving slowly and carefully, did the same for the tape around my wrists.

Corwyn stood by and watched. When I was done, I started to pocket the knife, and he waved the gun at me. "Leave it."

I stabbed the knife into the ground and looked at him expectantly. *What now?*

When Corwyn didn't say anything, I panned my gaze over to Deirdre, who was staring at me with considerably more interest than before. It was not the kind of attention I preferred to receive from a beautiful woman. More like the kind a spider gives an insect unfortunate enough to wander into its web.

I knew better than to attempt to stand up right away. I scooted backward away from the couple while I rubbed the feeling back into my legs.

"Feel free to run," Corwyn said. "She loves that."

I barely heard his words. My focus was locked entirely on his wife.

The light that Deirdre had been giving off was now dimming. At first, I thought it was because I was moving away from her, but when I finally stopped and stood up on my trembling legs, I saw this was not the case. Her pale skin was darkening, as if an enormous shadow was falling over her.

As I watched, Deirdre suddenly bent over violently at the waist, like someone who'd been hit with an invisible gut punch.

Eyes Like Poisoned Wells
Ian Rogers

She heaved like something was stuck in her throat. Corwyn did nothing to help her. In fact, he took another step away from her.

I looked at her, then at the woods that surrounded me. I had to make a decision, and fast.

I ran straight at Deirdre.

It took all of my resolve because I was afraid of her. She was turning into something. Her skin wasn't just darkening, it was tightening, moulding to her frame and bringing out the lines and curves of her skeleton in a way that wasn't healthy even for a supermodel.

But I had no choice. If the trees around me were blackwoods, they'd tear me apart in seconds. My only chance was to attack Deirdre while she was in mid-transformation.

The only thing that told me this wasn't a completely stupid move was the slack-jawed expression I saw on Corwyn's face. He wasn't expecting this; it wasn't part of the plan.

Then I collided with Deirdre, hard enough to send us both to the ground. I clamped my arms around her waist before she could roll away, hoping Corwyn wouldn't try to shoot me for fear of hitting his wife. I was assuming that he actually cared about her. I was also assuming that I could keep her restrained long enough to use her as leverage in my escape. I was assuming a lot.

I needn't have worried. Deirdre didn't want to get away from me. The dark withered sticks that had become her arms snapped around me with the force of a bear trap. The bones in my shoulders creaked in agony. She heaved again, right into my face, and I nearly vomited from the thick, rotten-meat smell that issued out of her throat.

Turning my head from that awful stench, I saw Corwyn moving frantically around us, trying to draw a bead on me.

Even with my face averted, Deirdre continued to change. I couldn't see it, but I could feel it. You've heard the expression *his skin crawled*? That's what it felt like—except it wasn't my skin that was crawling. It was hers. And it was doing more than crawl. It was shifting, sliding, stretching like something inside wanted out, and wanted out bad. Her bones poked into me all over, making meaty cracking sounds as they bent into new positions.

I felt something tickling my ear, and forced myself to turn back to face her.

A pair of long, thin stalks had sprouted out of Deirdre's eyes. They bobbed in the air like antennae—which, I realized, was exactly what they were.

There was another cracking sound, this one louder and more drawn out, and Deirdre's skull split open, right down the middle of her face. Her skin peeled away like ancient parchment. Her flesh fell off in desiccated hunks and her hair blew away like dandelion fluff.

Within the shattered bowl of her skull, where her brain should have been, an inhuman face peered out at me. I stared at the thing eye to eye—my two to its eight—and felt a piece of my sanity crumble away.

I was familiar with some of the creatures from the Black Lands—I even had close encounters with a few—but this thing before me was nothing I'd ever seen or heard of before.

It looked like some sort of giant insect. Deirdre's slinky feminine body had been replaced by an exoskeleton of gleaming black chitin. The remains of her gown hung in tatters from a number of barbed appendages that had sprouted from her body—two of them the arms which continued to hold me in a viselike grip. A pair of serrated mandibles on either side of her head snapped rapaciously only inches away from my face.

Eyes Like Poisoned Wells

Ian Rogers

I struggled to break free from the creature's powerful embrace, but its arms, or appendages, or whatever you wanted to call them, were as strong as metal rebars. I tried twisting to the side and felt something dig into my back. I thought it was one of the creature's barbs, but when I craned my head around I saw Corwyn's knife sticking out of the ground.

I managed to squirm one of my hands around so I could reach the knife and pulled it out of the ground. I heard Corwyn say "Hey!" but I ignored him, turned the knife around in my hand, and plunged the blade into Deirdre's side.

She let out a sound that wasn't quite a scream—more like a high-pitched alarm. The sound a smoke detector would make if it could feel pain.

Her arms snapped open and suddenly I was free. My immediate reaction was to push myself away from her, but I knew the moment I did that, Corwyn would start pumping bullets into me.

Instead, I wrapped my arms back around the Deirdre-thing and pulled us both to our feet. It wasn't easy. She was heavier in her new form, and her limbs were flailing madly. One of her barbs opened a gash across the inside of my arm, while another knocked me a good blow upside my head, but I didn't let go of her.

Corwyn tried to step in close with his gun, but I swung Deirdre around and put her between us.

Then I played my gambit and pushed her at him. I didn't know what would happen, but at the very least I thought it would give me a chance to run. Run where? I didn't know. I'd had my chance before and I didn't take it. I was in the Black Lands; there was nowhere *to* run.

The Deirdre-thing slammed into Corwyn. She either latched onto him or one of her barbs got stuck on his clothing. I don't know which, but when Corwyn recoiled with a strangled cry, he pulled his wife right along with him. His legs became entangled with hers (Deirdre had a lot of legs in her present form), and they both fell to the ground.

I hadn't expected Deirdre to attack Corwyn—and clearly he hadn't expected it, either. She might not have been aware of what she was doing, or maybe she simply couldn't help herself. Some of the creatures in the Black Lands are intelligent, while others operate solely on animal instinct.

As do some humans.

The gunshot startled me, both in its intensity and its unexpectedness. The Deirdre-thing gave another of those smoke-alarm shrieks and her limbs moved even more rapidly than before. Corwyn began to scream—the high, piercing cries of someone who has found himself stuck in a piece of industrial machinery. There was another gunshot and the Deirdre-thing was propelled backward. She/It landed in a heap, her limbs no longer flailing, barely even moving. With a final spasmodic motion, it threw something onto the grass, then was still.

I stood motionless for a moment, breathing in the night air that stank now of cordite and a rotten pulpy smell that was the creature's blood.

Corwyn tried to push himself up, then flopped back to the ground. Something was wrong with his hand, but I couldn't tell what it was at first. Then I got it. He was no longer in possession of his gun. It took me another second to realize he wasn't in possession of his hand, either. Then I realized what the Deirdre-thing had tossed to the ground.

I went over to Corwyn. His wife had done a real number on him. His chest was a bloody ruin. I couldn't tell his shirt from his skin—they'd both been torn to ribbons. His throat had also been ripped open, and blood poured out in a steady stream.

Corwyn told me his first wife had taken him for everything he had. But that wasn't true. She'd left him with his life. It was his second wife who had taken that.

"She loved me…" he said in a thick, gurgling voice. "But she…"

He died before he could finish that thought.

I looked from Corwyn to his wife. He was right. They made quite the couple.

My eyes were drawn to something above the tree line. One of the stars was moving across the night sky. Moving and blinking.

It was a plane.

That meant I wasn't in the Black Lands. Corwyn had lied. Somehow, I wasn't surprised. He wanted to scare me, I guess. Make me feel like I had no chance of escape. I was probably somewhere on his estate.

I started toward the trees but my eyes remained fixed on the plane, pacing slowly across the night sky.

I was still in the city. I was still alive.

And I still hated divorce work.

ABOVE THE BURIED CITY

by Daniel Braum

I'm disappointed at how peaceful Gonzalez looks just lying there, eyes closed, his coffee skin tinged yellow in the morgue's fluorescent lights. I took some small comfort in the fact that he'd spend the rest of his days rotting behind bars, with nothing else to do but think about what he did to Naomi. But from the almost serene expression it doesn't look like he has it too bad now.

Warden Jeffries slams the clipboard with Gonzalez's death certificate and medical records onto the metal counter. "One day healthy as an ox, and the next, poof, he just drops dead, just like that."

"Yeah, I don't like it," I say.

He flicks his lighter, again and again. The constant sparking without a flame makes me nervous.

"Hell, it's way too late to be here. You should be home with that pretty little wife of yours."

"Girlfriend," I say.

Flick-flick-flick. The harsh fluorescent light finds its way into the deep lines in his face.

"Just sorry you had to come," he says.

"Only doing my job, Marty."

He's one of the few that knows a good DA is more than just a lawyer; he knows that I was there every step of the way. For the investigation. Meeting the family. Not just for the pretty stuff, like half the suits in our office who view the job as only a stepping-stone. So yeah, late or not, I'm here.

"Gonzalez's attorney and her freaky-hoodoo-mama sidekick are outside, waiting for the body," he says.

"She's a real piece of work."

She came to the trial. Every day. Wearing the same set of clothes. A stranger from another world. Her Mayan face, with its sloping nose, and deep-set brown eyes remained emotionless as I recounted Naomi Westin's last moments. Gonzalez wept like a girl.

Jeffries flick-flicks the lighter. "Your call."

"They couldn't have had all the paperwork just waiting and ready to go. It's like they expected it."

"Certainly are in a hurry."

"So, hold him," I say. "Can you do that for me, Marty? Ten million law-abiding citizens of the Tri-State-Area want us to err on the side of caution."

And Naomi deserved it. Close as we had to a royal princess, she was the shining spirit of New York. Of my New York. Despite the upper crust and their restaurants full of wealth, celebrity, and privilege, *my* New York is still the greatest city of the world, full of people with good old-fashioned virtue, like Naomi was.

She shunned the vapid socialite scene for charity affairs, and her politics classes at NYU; only appearing in public to aid her pet causes mostly having to do with combating Central American poverty and aiding New York's immigrant underclass. Still, her make up free, scar-lipped face was all over the magazine covers and Page Six. A photograph of us from one Thanksgiving, serving turkey dinners at the shelter downtown, hangs on my office wall. In the picture her smile looks the same as it did in school, when we were both wide-eyed rebels with a cause. I remember the feeling of my arm around her, our smiles beaming as the picture was snapped, and my chest feels full of rocks. Gonzalez took her from us. So, he belonged in prison. Dead was second best.

Jeffries abruptly stops his lighter flicking. "Good fucking god," he says.

Gonzalez is sitting up on the gurney, coughing. He throws the white sheet off his lower half then stops because he's coughing so hard. Jeffries radios for back up. And I'm frozen; staring right into Gonzalez's open eyes thinking this can't be happening, the rocks in my chest tumbling over and over.

Gonzalez looks confused, then disappointment dawns on him. Something akin to the forlorn expression of a suspect waking up in a holding cell I've seen countless times before. He looks past me to the double metal doors. On the other side is a long hallway, then the waiting room where his attorney and freaky groupie are, and then the parking lot and freedom beyond. I think he's gonna go for it and I'm gonna have to tackle him.

Two corrections officers burst into the room. They slam Gonzalez back down onto the gurney and tie the restraints. I'm suddenly aware I'm breathing heavy. Sweating as if it was I who restrained him.

"Naomi," Gonzalez cries, as they bump through the swinging doors and wheel him away.

A sweet smell rises above the disinfectant reek. The familiar mix of vanilla beans and flowers that Naomi wore. Whether it came from an expensive bottle or drugstore shampoo I never knew, it was just her. From the corner of my eye I think I see a woman standing there next to the examining table, and I turn, but nothing's there. A trick of the light on the stainless steel. I'm so tired I'm getting loopy. But if I hadn't been here, who knows what Jeffries might have done. It could have been a disaster.

Jeffries finally lights his cigarette, takes a noisy drag, and exhales. "Now I've really seen it all," he says.

—

I expect to find Marissa winding down from her gallery shift on the couch with a coffee, but all the lights except for her changing room are out.

Outside our windows the city lights blur into the skyline. Each light a life, overlapping, impossible to tell where one begins and another ends.

My phone rings. It's Abrams. I'd been wondering if he'd call tonight or take me into his office tomorrow. Dean and Gweneth Westin are hosting an event tomorrow, he tells me, and with what happened with Gonzalez, it's essential that I be there.

"I'd rather not go," I say.

I can't face Naomi's parents and there's no good way to tell him.

Marissa flits in from her changing room, a slender shape in the dark apartment. She's mastered the art of discerning when I'm on for work. She fills a watering can in the sink, apparently paying me no mind, but I know she's listening. Suddenly at 11pm, our neglected plants need watering.

"I'm sure someone else would be honored to come," I say. "Jan Manetti has been working hard on the Astor Place cases."

But Abrams wants me. The Westins want me.

Marissa stands on the table to reach the cyclamen dangling in front of the living room windows. The outline of her long blond hair glows faintly with city light. An edge of purple lace slides above her low riders as she extends to pour the water.

"Alright, tomorrow at seven, it is," I say, giving in to Abrams, then hang up.

"These need repotting," Marissa says.

"Going out?" I ask.

She is. Third time this week. And I'm too spent to get into what's at the heart of it. But she'll be back for the Westin's party. People from *her* New York, the New York she wants for us, will be there and she won't miss the opportunity.

A minute later she's out the door and I'm alone with the plants. I can almost feel their thirsty roots absorbing the water as I give in to exhaustion and let myself drift. In the blur of pink and white lights I see the shape of the silver mask that's been sitting in our evidence room since the trial. Naomi's face is beneath it. Her mouth moving. I can't hear the words as I fade.

—

The skyscrapers framing the Great Lawn fill the view from Dean and Gweneth Westin's floor-to-ceiling windows; a modern backdrop juxtaposed against their collection of Aztec masks and Mayan stelae. Jade statuettes and stone carvings are displayed on simple white pedestals throughout the penthouse. I can't wait for the fad to pass.

Marissa is chatting up Juan Farber, managing partner of Rivera, Larca, Weintrob and Associates. Her high-necked, black dress comes just below her knees and nicely hugs her curves. She stands straight, the stem of her glass balanced between her slender forefinger and thumb. I picture her holding one of her paintbrushes with the same grace and effortlessly manipulating her chopsticks on our first date. At Nobu. I'd made the reservations weeks in advance for Naomi and me, but she told me we would never be more than dear, dear friends.

I don't look away in time and Marissa calls me over.

"Richard, you remember Juan Farber, from the golf outing," she says.

He knows me from the trial. They all do.

"A pleasure, Richard," he says. "Even after you put the bastard away the motions never end. Is every judge in this town mad or what?"

I smile politely and when I don't speak, he does.

"She's quite the woman," he says, tipping his martini toward Marissa. "Suze is thrilled with the paintings you chose for our new extension."

"And we'd all love to see you at the gallery again soon," Marissa says.

"The way Suze spends I'll have to reel in a few more clients before doing that. Gimme a couple of days."

I force a laugh to match theirs. When Marissa laughs she is again the magical girl I met at "W" bar commiserating Naomi's rejection. The girl who had half my clothes off on the cab ride to my apartment. The girl from Nebraska who worked her way through F.I.T. tending bar. The woman who wants a life and all the world with me.

"How you two make it on Richard's government salary is beyond me."

Juan won't say any more. Not here. Not in front of Abrams.

Abrams is across the room with Dean Westin and a bunch of his Wall Street chaps in a huddle of cigar smoke, caviar, and laughter. I excuse myself and join them claiming "duty calls."

Marissa frowns. I'll hear about it tonight.

Dean's vodka-reddened face becomes serious as I join their circle. But after a second, the visage of the broken father passes and he claps me on the back.

"Cigar, Richie?" he asks.

I'm about to say no when Abrams' phone rings. He turns and steps back a pace to answer it.

"Yes. I understand. Right away," he says. His party face goes blank and he is once again my boss, the District Attorney of New York.

He folds his phone and finishes his Martini in one obscene swig.

"Mercurio Gonzalez flat lined, *again*," he says.

Gonzalez's attorney is in the waiting area holding paperwork up to the one-way window while arguing with the two corrections officers barring the door. She's just a dime-a-dozen suit from Legal Aid. It's the woman behind her who concerns me. Rosita Velez. The one Jeffries calls freaky-hoodoo-mama. File says she's Gonzalez's next of kin. Forty-five. Born in British Honduras. Belizean papers now. Declared address is a Yucatan resort village on the Mayan Riviera. Her long dark hair frames a face like one of the Westin's stelae come alive.

"Do something. Don't let this happen," I say to Jeffries.

He unzips the body bag. I'm not sure if to show me or to convince himself.

Gonzalez had been the cagiest cat burglar in department history. A string of thefts, all of Central-American artifacts like the Westins' collection, had perplexed us for years. Until Naomi Westin picked the wrong night to bring her weekend Romeo to the family's Greenwich Village brownstone. Gonzalez stumbled upon them necking amidst Daddy's priceless collections and pulled a gun, so the police report goes. And Romeo picked the wrong night to play hero. The gun went off in a struggle and that's where Naomi's story ended. They never found Romeo. I played it over hundreds of times in my mind. I figured him as one of the sons of the elite with a daddy who didn't want to get involved. Probably whisked him away to Europe faster than you can say big fat Police Benevolent Association donation.

Gonzalez, the cops said, was found weeping at her side. And the freak had placed one of the artifacts, a silver skull mask, on her face. I would have liked to have spoken to that Romeo. Just for that final look into Naomi's private world. With Gonzalez behind bars, the thefts stopped. But no amount of wishing brings Naomi back. Leaving through the morgue doors is not how this is going to end for him. Not with the stunt from the other day. No way.

"He's dead. For sure this time," Jeffries says.

I pull off the white sheet. Angry red lines of the autopsy incision divide his chest into a "Y."

"Come on, Marty. Do anything. I don't care. Lose the body. Burn him."

"Nothing I can do, Richard," he says.

"I'm telling you something's wrong."

He tries to put his arm around me. I push it off.

"I know this is the pits," he says. "But everything's in order."

The guards open the door and step aside.

My phone buzzes. It's a text from Marissa.

"Going to Montauk. Staying with friends. Not sure when I'll be back."

And just like that, Gonzalez is wheeled out the prison door.

—

Marissa being gone doesn't translate into big change, not with my hours at the office and her at the gallery nights and weekends. But she hates Montauk. Means she's staying with her sister and is thinking of leaving me, for real. I know I should call, that it's time we hashed it out. Worked it out, one way or another. But I don't.

I'm ready to leave for the office when the precinct calls on my cell. The Robinson-Dutt Gallery, in Soho, reported a break-in and theft, sometime in the early morning. The only object missing is a jade-lapis mask. Mayan. I go straight there.

Two police officers are pacing the top floor gallery, looking for prints and evidence among a few dozen pedestals displaying figurines and pottery. The room is as minimal and boring as the Westins'.

A man with salt and pepper hair, in a black shirt and dapper black suit, stands at the front texting on his cell, his silver thumb rings clicking on his phone.

"You look familiar," he says. "This doesn't have to do with-"

"No. Just asking a few questions."

He goes back to his phone.

"Such as, where does this stuff come from."

"Mexico's Yucatan Peninsula. Some Guatemala and Belize," he answers, full of attitude.

"I meant from whom."

"Why?"

His why implies "am I in trouble?" I know their sources are shady; the whole damn industry is questionable. But today I don't care. I know Gonzalez is responsible and I want him.

"Just trying to get an idea why only that one item was taken," I reply.

"Easiest answer is because it's the real deal."

"And the rest?"

"Honest answer?"

"Please."

"Maybe, probably, real. Depends on who's buying. Come look at this."

He leads me to a hardwood pedestal displaying an oversized coffee table book.

"The lore is fascinating. Full of lost civilizations and human sacrifice" he says while flipping through the large, glossy pages. He's talking like I'm a customer now. Good.

"The Mayans believed the cenotes, these deep natural wells next to their pyramids, were portals to other worlds and that they were sending their sacrifices through them. They suited them up with masks like this one."

He stops at a page with a stylized image of a shirtless Mayan priest pushing a sacrifice off a pyramid top. A silver mask is over the victim's forehead and nose giving his face the visage of a skull; a raw red hole is where his heart should be.

"Thing is, most of what we know comes from the art, like this, which is a restoration from a stela from Chi-Chen-Itza.

The practice went on for centuries but very few skeletons were found. That's why artifacts, like our stolen mask, are so rare, and valuable."

"So where are all the skeletons?"

"The cenotes, although all dried up now, were too deep for anyone in antiquity to retrieve them. So, it's a big mystery. Plays nicely with the lost Mayan civilization mystique."

"What do you think?"

"That it's a great story that sells a lot of pieces. Question for you. Do I get the form for the insurance claim from you guys or somewhere else?"

—

Back in the office there's a message waiting from Coop, my contact at Homeland Security.

"Shitty day," I tell him when I get him on the phone. "This better be good."

"You're not going to believe this," he says. "Go to your computer."

I open Coop's e-mail and an image of Gonzalez passing through airport security comes up on my screen, clear as day.

"This is great. Where are they holding him?"

"They're not."

I slam my fist on the desk and push all the files off.

"I had you flag his passport for a reason!"

"Easy. Easy. Shit like this happens all the time. I mean not like this. Records came up as deceased but he clearly wasn't."

"Don't tell me to take it easy. He's dead for fuck's sake. I saw him."

"Guy looked fine to me."

"He's a convicted felon. He belongs in jail not on the afternoon plane to Cancun."

Coop's silent. If he tells me the guy already paid his time or it's all in my imagination I'm going to kill him.

"I'll notify the field office in Mexico City," he says after a few seconds. "Uh, so, how's everything else. Marissa?"

"Everything's fine, Coop," I say, fighting to maintain calm. "I'm hanging up now."

I look at the photo of Naomi and me, then I ring Marissa. She doesn't answer.

—

One of Marissa's bras and a workout tee hang from the weight bench in our second bedroom. An empty canvas on her easel next to my desk is plastered full of invitations to gallery openings. I try her again and when she doesn't answer I read the trial transcripts again and dig through my old files but it's useless. I go online. At first just looking at maps and searching Mayan mythology but then I book a flight to Mexico.

Sometime in the night I hear the door slam and erratic foot clomps across the living room. I open my eyes to see Marissa standing in the bedroom doorway. She's holding the flight confirmation from my printer, alcohol emanating from her pores.

"You're not going to Mexico without me."

"Sorry, work." I say.

"He's fucking dead, Richie. And yeah, you were the one who put him away. But you can't spend your life as Abrams' dog."

Her fingers nervously grasp each other and I want to still them in mine.

Daniel Braum

"At least talk to Juan, please. For me," she says.

"I will," I say, sitting up in bed.

She didn't expect that. And neither did I.

"Really?" she asks.

"Really."

"Don't fuck with me just to shut me up, Richie."

"I said I will and I will. *After* I capture Gonzalez."

She thinks about this in silence for a moment, a sour look on her face. Then she walks over and sits on my lap. I can feel her heart beating, hear the shallow breaths in sync with the rise and fall of her chest. It's been so long since we were this close. I really smell the alcohol in her sweat now, along with a mix of cigarette smoke and her best perfume. Her seduction perfume, not intended for me. She runs her fingers along the back of my head and presses me to her and I don't care.

Marissa is asleep, naked among the tangle of sheets. Unable to sleep I crawl out of bed. I go to the closet and take out the locked metal case with my pistol in it. Abrams had us get certified and wasted a few Saturday afternoons at the shooting range before he lost interest. My paperwork is in order but I can't take it with me to Mexico. I put the case back, gently cover Marissa, and wait for morning.

I'm in the morgue watching them wheel Gonzalez away. This time I turn and the woman standing there does not disappear. Naomi.

Wearing the silver skull face mask. The world blurs and we're standing somewhere high. A sprawl of Mayan buildings beneath us. A giant green snake with white feathered wings flies overhead. Its spiral coils disappear behind a bright painted pyramid.

"No. Just go. Stop," she says. Her lips below the mask, tortured.

I wake up in the cramped plane seat with her words echoing in my head. Marissa is next to me flipping through my printouts and the photo of Gonzalez.

"You don't really believe it was him?" she asks.

"I know what I saw."

"You saw him dead. *And* this is a photo of a guy that looks like him."

"The burglaries started again."

"You're going to find him in his grave and we're going to spend the rest of the week on the beach."

"And then we'll have nothing else to do but drink margaritas and go sightseeing."

"And para-sailing. Don't forget shopping."

"They don't take credit cards in Mexico."

She smacks me playfully.

When we step off the plane the humid air hits like a puff of dragon's breath. Noisy birds chase lizards across the runway; lush tropical greens grow right to its edges.

The terminal walkway is adorned with stylized posters of idyllic beaches, romanticized bullfighters, and Mayan priests high atop pyramids.

An hour later we check into a fancy spa on the Mayan Riviera that Marissa selected. It is one in a row of hotels and shops on a steep cliff overlooking the long white beach and the turquoise sea. Remnants of Mayan ruins litter the grounds; gray iguanas of all sizes sun themselves on the ancient stones. The wall outside our room is covered in lush blood-violet bougainvillea and bright red hibiscus the same shade as Marissa's sundress.

A fist-sized humming bird whirs past with a click-click-click. The bright emerald greens of its feathers and ruby red throat catch the sun as it flits from bloom to bloom. For some reason I find this poignant and I feel an epiphany struggling to surface into thought, something about Marissa and me, but instead the image of the "Y" cut in Gonzalez's chest fills my mind.

A breeze laced with clean sea air and pleasant soap meets us as we open the door. I drag our bags into the bedroom. A gecko on the wall lazily eyes me.

"It's wonderful," Marissa says from the bathroom.

I hear the rustle of her shedding her clothes. She runs the shower.

The spacious sun-lit bathroom is covered in sand-beige tile, a few turquoise and whites thrown in here and there. Marissa's shape is softened by the frosted glass and running water.

"Join me," she says.

The past day with her has been wonderful. But I fear it is only a temporary shift brought on by telling her I'll to talk to Farber. It's easy to see how a carefree life like this, or even just a job that I leave at the office, could be so, so nice. But I don't want to feed her empty promises.

"Maybe later," I say. "No time to waste."

I feel the disappointment in her silence. I stand listening to the water run, the steaming glass obscuring her. Every inch of me wants to throw open the door and press her against the shower wall. But I walk away, stopping just a second for one last look before I go.

By the second afternoon I've questioned a host of locals, tourists, and the one policeman I found in the area, with no sign of Gonzalez. I'm ready to widen the net so I hire a cab to the little tourist trap towns at the edge of the jungle.

The first one is a just row of flimsy constructed shacks, open on one side facing the dirt road. They all sell the same things, Guatemalan crafts, Mexican blankets, and souvenir trinkets, the most common being little soapstone pyramids and replica masks. A few sun-burned tourists browse and haggle with disinterest as they wait for their tour bus.

At the jungle's edge, a dozen yards back behind the stalls, are rag-tag shelters. The real town. A teenage girl weaving bracelets looks up at me suspiciously as I walk over and start looking around.

"Do you know Senorita Velez?" I ask.

"No ingles," she says, and glances at one shack apart from the rest before looking down and avoiding my eyes.

The shack is the last of the row, offset from the rest by a garden of herbs and plants ringed by conch shells and stone. Looking at it that feeling of rocks in my chest returns.

As I approach I hear scuffling and moving around inside so I run over and open the flimsy door. The window is open and the table full of jars and herbs beneath it is in disarray.

I dash outside and around the shack. Someone is ahead, running through the jungle. I follow, swatting branches and vines as I run. Birds chatter angrily. Something the size of a cat darts across my path and disappears into the brush.

I emerge into a clearing in front of a huge mound covered in earth and trees, an unexcavated pyramid. Stone bricks protrude at the base, tree roots clutching them in place. Halfway up is a man. Long black hair, like Gonzalez. I scramble to catch up with

Daniel Braum

him, grasping onto saplings for footing. He circles around out of my view. I follow his trail of broken trees and crumbling earth to the far side of the mound where it stops for no apparent reason, like he jumped or just flew away. The cenote below holds only stagnant water teeming with insects, its surface undisturbed. For a half hour I circle the pyramid, peering up trees, and kicking rocks; checking for signs of a hideaway but find none.

He has to be here. But he's gone.

I buy a green coconut from one of the stalls and the lady chops off the top with a machete and puts a straw in it for me. I take out the picture of Gonzalez to try a little old-fashioned canvassing.

As I go from stall to stall a young boy follows me swiping a stick in the air like a sword. I'm met with a litany of nos.

"How about you?" I ask the boy in frustration.

He smiles and slashes the stick-sword.

"That's the boss. He's a great warrior. He told me someday a great army will come to take back Texas and California!"

"You saw him? Where?"

The boy's mother scrambles from her coconut stall.

"It's ok, tell me," I say to the boy.

The woman pulls the boy away by the ear.

"I'm sorry. I did not see anything, mister," he says.

"But I did," someone says from the stall across from us.

A Mexican teenager in cut-off jeans and a weathered black T-shirt with big red Rolling Stones lips leans against a pile of bright Mexican blankets. In his Nike sneakers and sleek black sunglasses, he looks as much a tourist as I do.

"Got any Marlboro reds?" he asks.

"Sorry," I say.

"I'm dying for a 'boro red. Come on."

"Don't smoke." I show him Gonzalez's picture. "But I might, if you've seen this guy."

"Is it worth a case of reds to you?"

"You're full of shit," I say, and turn to walk away.

"I can take you to his grave," he whispers.

That gets my attention. The women in the stalls glance at him with disapproving eyes.

"Walk with me," he says.

Everything else has turned up dry so I follow. He leads me five minutes into the jungle to a tiny clearing. A few dozen rectangles of earth framed with conch shells and whitewashed stones form three uneven rows in the moist rich brown earth. The dates on the wooden crosses show most of them died much too young. An old shovel, some two by fours, and beer cans litter the far corner.

The boy points to the freshest patch of earth. It has no cross.

"There's a body there," he says. "But it's not him."

"And how do you know?"

"How do you think?"

"You dug it up? Now why would you do that?"

"Ask my grandfather. I'd rather be in Mexico City but I'm back in this shithole till school starts again. And when I'm home, I work. He'll tell you himself, he's going to want to meet you with you asking all these questions."

"And your grandfather is?"

"I'd lose the attitude, mister. With all the questions you're asking he's someone you want to meet. His bar is the Serpent's

Daniel Braum

Nest. Best one we have around here. Plays dominos most nights around eight. And don't ask me why, 'cause I couldn't tell you."

I don't trust the kid. It's the boredom and arrogance in his eyes.

"You want a case of reds? Then let's start digging."

"Shit, not again."

"I'll tell your grandfather you're a good kid."

"Whatever, just don't tell him about the cigarettes."

—

The staff at my hotel said the Serpent's Nest is the place all the locals go but from first glance at the place I know they've lied. Marissa's happy to be here. The roof is thatched and cleverly designed walls slide open to the night. The dance floor sports expensive video screens and the bar looks ready for hordes of spring breakers.

"Come on, let's go burn off dinner," she says.

I pick at the last of the dirt under my nails. I wonder who that poor soul we dug up is. Gonzalez is out there, somewhere. I hope this old man helps me find him.

"I have to take care of something," I say.

"Then I'm starting without you."

The kid's grandfather is sitting at the bar across the dance floor playing dominos with the bartender. He's wearing a long sleeve linen shirt and god-awful plaid dress pants, despite the heat. The two goons flanking him are doing a better job than the bartender at masking their boredom.

"Your grandson sent me," I say, and the two men look at me like I'm nuts.

But the old man takes my hand, eagerly. "Oh, yes. I'm Don Luis."

Beneath his sleeve are green and blue blurs, tattoos so faded I can't tell what they once were. They're an odd backdrop for the smiley yellow character of his cheap Pokémon wristwatch.

"Makes my granddaughter laugh," he says.

"I'm sure your grandson's a bit too old to be impressed."

"Aye, my grandson. Every time he comes home from school, I know him less. I should be thankful he comes home at all."

One of the thugs nods with fake empathy.

I reach for the picture of Gonzalez. "Have you seen this-"

Don Luis stops me, then laughs and knocks on the bar top.

"Esteban. Miguel. We will be in my office."

I stand and look for Marissa. She's engrossed in the music and has attracted a circle of young men. The pang of jealousy is unexpected.

"She's safe," he says. "They know you are with me. They all do."

I follow him through a door behind the bar. As we walk the thumping bass of the dancehall reggae is enveloped by night sounds.

"Best not to talk in front of the men," he says. "They're superstitious fools."

The hulking shape of the buried pyramid looms over the trees. I picture it as part of the skyline of some lost city.

He takes me to the clearing where Gonzalez disappeared. He lets me take it in for a second.

"Treasures. Treasures. Beneath us, everywhere," he says. "One artifact can keep a family going for months. A much better alternative than working in the resorts."

"An honest day's work for an honest day's pay," I say.

"It's pitiful. One step up from servitude."

He produces a tiny figurine from his pocket.

Daniel Braum

"The people who made this are dead. They have no use for it. If they could know the world of good they were doing, do you think they'd object?"

"Do you?"

"I send things North. It's my business. It pays for the bar. Sends my grandkids to real schools in Mexico City. Our mutual <u>friend</u>, Senor Gonzalez, well, he's in the business of bringing them back. Bad for business. Having him locked in your jail was a blessing."

"This is where I chased him and he disappeared. You have people. We can stake out every giant mound of dirt from here to Belize."

"They say these are places where the dead cross between worlds. And I've told you my men are superstitious fools."

"But not you?"

"I know he's clever and he's hiding somewhere I can't find him. You're a clever man, shall we hunt together?"

He reaches into the crook of a tree overhanging the cenote and pulls out something wrapped in paper. He hands it to me. It's something solid.

"My grandson says you know where Velez lives. We've been watching but she's a crafty *bruja*. Gonzalez escapes every time. He will return, there, soon, a couple of days at most. The police will not question you if you leave right away."

"I'm not going to shoot anyone."

"Take it anyway."

"I didn't come here to shoot him."

"Then take him away then, back to your jails, if you can."

"I just came here for justice. The man's a criminal."

"Si. Si. You're the long arm of the law. I get it. Do what you have to do, Sheriff, just don't give my grandson any cigarettes."

I take out my roll of bills. "I owe him-"

"Keep it. Go to your girl. Dance with her. Enjoy the time you have. He'll be back."

In the morning there is a covered bowl of fresh fruit waiting outside our door. We take it to the beach. Marissa sketches me eating. She fills pages of her pad with the long line of the coast.

We pass the days in the sun. In the shade of the pool bar. I try not to think of the gun all wrapped in paper in the hotel drawer.

The afternoon of the third day Abrams calls. Marissa listens as I check the message.

"Gonna call him back?"

"No. Not now."

It is so hot we take dinner back from the restaurant and eat it on our balcony. After, she runs the shower and turns out the lights. We spend the rest of the night in the comfort of the quiet, dark room.

Toucans chatter outside our window. Marissa straddles me, my hand in the concave hollow of her lower back, her fingers spread across my shoulders. Beyond the noisy birds is the powerful lull of the breaking waves.

I become aware someone is in the corner. Naomi, the death's head mask above her razor thin white scar; her lips forming silent words.

"What is it?" Marissa says.

Daniel Braum

"Nothing."

Gonzalez has returned. I can't hear but I know it is what Naomi is saying.

The sun comes up filling the room with light. Marissa goes back to sleep. The bed is a twist of limbs and sheets, the clean smell of sweat, the smell of us not yet washed away by the morning air.

A hummingbird flits among the hibiscus. And in this still moment my mind is quiet. I see the bird loves every flower. Fully and completely. Drinking it dry before moving to the next. It has to to keep aloft. I wonder why haven't I moved on from the office? Why Marissa and I aren't married? And it dawns on me. Just like that. We have these beautiful moments. Always have. But they are moments. Islands in time, like chains of flowers. I know I will end up like Jeffries, a lifetime public servant, with her always second. And it's just not fair.

I take the gun out of its paper wrapping and leave, careful not to wake her.

—

The buried pyramid looms above the trees, a silent sentinel, guarding the closed stalls.

The row of shacks is alive with morning bustle as I walk to Velez's and stop at her open door. She is grinding herbs and seeds. A big fruit bat hangs upside down in the corner. Masks, knives, statuettes and pottery are crowded among her table packed full of jarred herbs. These are not the trinkets of the village outside, these are real. Gonzalez's illicit fruits. A treasure trove of evidence.

"What a fool you are for coming," she says, without looking up, as if she was expecting me.

The bat opens its eyes and licks its brownish-red fur. Then it opens and re-folds its fleshy wings.

"I know you've been talking with Don Luis. Why would you listen to such a thief?"

"I'm not here to judge anyone," I say.

"Then I hope that you will not. Mercurio has paid his debts. Two life sentences."

"I'm just going to bring him back. The rest isn't up to me."

She looks at a stone knife on the table.

I take the gun out of my pocket.

"Now look at you," she says.

With her disdain, I feel far, far away from New York, from the sterile halls of the airport, from the plush soft edges of the hotel room and Marissa's embrace. I could leave now. Take as much as I could with me to the authorities.

"Where is he?"

The bat tilts its head inquisitively.

"Such a fool," she says. "Even now you have no idea what they have done for you."

"You're under arrest," I say. A fear reflex. The words are feeble. The reek of herbs and humidity swallows them.

"And you think you are right, but you're just another outlaw."

I try to picture myself talking with Farber or running away with Marissa. But I can't. I can't summon the feeling of Naomi's arm around me. The gun feels heavy in my hand. I flip the safety off with a click.

"Don't hurt her," says a voice from outside.

My eyes are drawn to his white un-buttoned shirt, first, the "Y" scars on his chest, angry and inflamed. Everywhere else his olive skin looks sun-touched. But something's wrong, like that healthy glow is just a mask, a disguise that's fading. I wished the gun made me feel stronger. If I shot, I'm not sure what it would even do.

"You're alive?" is all I can think to say.

"No." Gonzalez says.

"Then what the hell is going on?!" I yell.

He traces the line of the Y from his shoulder and stops at his heart. "It does not beat. It stopped that night."

"Let's just make this easy, okay?"

"I loved her. I want you to know that now."

"You fucking killed her!"

"It was an accident," he yells. "You don't know. How could you? There was no one else that night but me. No break in. No missing boyfriend."

I keep the gun trained on him but he doesn't care and puts the items from the table in a bag as he's talking.

"Naomi wanted me to stop all this. And we argued. Someone called the police. Her parents, I think. They never approved. The rest is as you know."

"And you said nothing? All this time."

"Who would believe me? Not you. But ask her. She says you can see her. She's trying to tell you to just go. So please, go."

"And let you go free?"

"No, for you to go and live your life and stop holding on to her. It's not too late. The future is bright for you. This body doesn't have much longer. And after today, you'll never see me again."

He stuffs the last of the artifacts into the bag.

"I'm bringing you back."

"These don't belong in New York. Or as chits for criminals. I'm taking them where they belong."

"The cenote?"

He doesn't answer.

"Show me."

"I can not."

Something hits the side of my face and I realize I've forgotten about Velez.

Gonzalez bolts out the door and into the jungle. The bat drops from its perch and flaps out the window. I grapple with Velez and push her off me. She stumbles into the table, jars and bottles crashing around her.

I run after Gonzalez cursing his head start.

The jungle seems alive with obstacles, mounds of rubble and half excavated buildings. But I know where he is going.

When I reach the pyramid, he is already at the top and is throwing artifacts into the cenote. I raise the gun and take aim.

"Just go," he calls. "I forgive you."

I squeeze the trigger. Not sure if I meant to the first time, but with the second and third bang the sting of his words disappears. He shudders, stumbles left, then right and drops the bag. I take aim again but just watch as he closes his eyes and jumps. There is no splash.

I climb as fast as I can. But he is not in the cenote. I kick at the artifacts that have fallen from his bag. A stone knife. A bowl. A statute of a serpent. I pick up the serpent and throw it. The stagnant water swallows it with a deep glug.

This is not how its ends. I know Marissa and the hotel are waiting for me. Farber and New York are waiting for me. But I won't be a stranger in a world built atop my city.

I drop the gun and take the knife in both hands.

"I'm sorry, Marissa," I whisper.

ABOVE THE BURIED CITY

Daniel Braum

She'll wonder. She'll hurt. And I wish that the gates of glowing, glittering New York will open up and receive her because there's nothing left of our dream but a spent flower.

I hold the knife high, plunge it into my chest, and jump.

OPEN WOUND

by Darren Speegle

It was like any other frosty night, in any other city, smoke and mist turning the alley into a dream of destitution. Metal drums smoldered with broken chairs, sticks out of the park, a mouse carcass the fellow with the patch sleeves had found on St-Germain. The air smelled like piss, wine, guilt, obscured memories, rotting upholstery. It mattered not that the surrounding city was considered one of the most beautiful in the world, that within easy walking distance of this wretched cul-de-sac, the banks of the Seine sparkled with life, the Eiffel Tower rose like Babel towards the heavens. If anything separated this place in time from any other, it was the fact that two of the men present, one of whom had only thumbed in a little while ago, recognized each other from a former existence.

The recently arrived was named Thornton. The other answered to Harris. Two men of clearly American origin converging at a pocket of indigence in Paris. Thornton did not know where he remembered this Harris from, nor did the name ring a bell, but he could see in the man's eyes that the man remembered him all too well. Even now, through a billow of smoke rising from wet fuel, the other peered at him, invoking a definite negative feeling.

Through his wanderings, Thornton had come to regard himself as a bad customer. Expressions, tones, gestures, the occasional aimed word, other things he didn't want to remember had convinced him of such. He knew much of it had to do with the scar that lashed at the left side of his face, ruining his eye, pulsing with emotion. But it went considerably deeper than that. People had died at his hands. He knew this with the same sense he had for faces. The experiences behind the tenuous associations and moments of recognition wouldn't be revisited. He had shut down somewhere along the way. He had become like many of those with whom he shared beans and whiskey and ragged blankets. Sometimes he wondered if maybe he was dead, but then the scar would become inflamed and he would know his delusion.

Maybe Harris had the answers. Never mind that he championed the burning of rodent carcasses to "keep the city safe from bubonic plague," an English phrase he appeared to have taught the others. There was reason in those dark eyes. Thornton had caught a glimpse of it when their gazes first met over introductions performed by Josette, the cart lady. Harris did his reasoning behind a wildly profuse, wiry gray beard, making it less obvious, but he definitely weighed things in his mind. Maybe Harris had all the answers.

Thornton patted Josette on a knobby varicose-veined ankle and rose to try his luck. Harris showed blatant signs of recognizing his intentions, stiffening where he stood over the drum, eyes darting spasmodically through the smoke. As Thornton unpocketed his hands to put them over the heat, the other looked as if he might bolt.

"I only want to know how we know each other," Thornton said.

Harris trembled as he stared at the scar. "God…I'm so sorry, man. So goddamn sorry."

"Sorry?"

"For introducing you to them. If I'd known…" He was clearly distraught, his face wracked with emotion. Thornton was compelled to ease him.

"Calm down, friend. It can't be that bad." He paused, watching the dismay break across the other's features.

"You don't remember, do you?" Harris said. "You really don't remember."

"I'm afraid I don't. I don't know much about my past except that there was a lot of pain and a lot of pleasure. Extremes. That's what sticks with me."

"Oh God, Thorn," the bearded face said hopelessly.

Thorn. That struck. Thorn. Laughter. Naked flesh.

"Did you give me that nickname?"

"Not me, man. The squadron. Oh God, please don't be here talking to me. When I spoke to you while you were in the hospital, when you told me wrongs had been righted, penance had been paid, your voice chilled me. I hoped I'd never have to hear it again."

Harris had begun to shake. In an apparent attempt to reclaim possession of himself, he grasped the rim of the drum, cried out as it burned his bare hands. Looking down at his palms, then back up at Thornton's ruined features, he suddenly thrust his hands into the drum and brought up a pile of burning fuel.

"Don't you see?!" he screamed. "Michael told me it was going to happen. Your kids, your wife, all of it. Oh *God*!" As the last word came out of his mouth, he plunged his face into the contents of his hands.

Thornton backed away, step by strangely familiar step, shaking his head back and forth. No. Not this again. Didn't the last face that recognized him do harm to itself? Didn't she in fact destroy herself, stabbing glass shards into her eyes…? Where? Who? What was he, that he did such things to people?

The agonized sounds like an open wound behind him, he ran down the alley, out into the scant traffic of a lamp-lit street, hands waving meaninglessly. He was a moth, and it was cold, and he was dead, haunting the city. Where now? What to now?

A cab driver mistook his flailing as a signal and pulled up, rolling down the window. Thornton got in because he needed to be out of here, somewhere else, and no cab driver had ever caused him trouble that he could recall.

This one would test tradition. With no hesitation, and even less delicateness, the whiskered, vaguely Eastern face asked him how he had come by the scar.

"I don't know," Thornton said in English.

The cabbie shifted from the local tongue to his fare's. "You don't know how you came by a scar that runs across half your face?"

"Leave it alone," said Thornton, rubbing the frosted window with his sleeve so that he could look out into the night. "I'm the one who has to live with it."

He wondered where the footnote had come from. He could endure the scar; the reactions were what tore him down.

"Take me to the suburbs," he said.

"The suburbs? Where?"

"Out of the city." Where they couldn't know him, where he couldn't hurt anyone.

"You're going to have to be more specific, mister."

Thornton rubbed his eyes wearily. "Okay, where's the most well-to-do area?"

"This is Paris. There are many."

"A newer, more Americanized neighborhood," he found himself saying. "Take me there."

"You planning on panhandling? Prowling? They won't put up with that."

"Go."

"Let me see some money."

Thornton pulled out his wallet. "Here," he said, holding up a bill. "Happy?"

"Most."

"Go then."

"Whatever you say." He turned at the next light.

Thornton lay back his head and closed his eyes. *Thorn.*

—

When Ethan Thornton's secretary buzzed near day's end to let him know a Monsieur Duval was here to see him, a thousand emotions swept over him, not least shock. For a moment he found himself unable to breathe, a slave to his reaction, panicked. His voice, as he managed to summon the words, sounded in his ears like falling. "Send him in" was an invitation to the devil.

He rose, bracing himself against his desk as the door opened. The onslaught of memory impressions turned his knuckles white, his face to liver. All the power he might once have drawn from standing silhouetted in his office's nearly wall-to-wall window overlooking the heart of Paris now failed him utterly. When Michael was present, Michael was supreme, and that was that.

"Hello, Thorn."

"Michael," he acknowledged, nodding vaguely towards one of the leather chairs.

"May I close the door?"

God no.

"Yes."

As Michael sank into the chair, comfortable in his open, tailored-to-breathe jacket, Thornton imagined one or both of them crashing through the sixth-floor window.

"Why are you here, Michael?"

"To express my belated condolences for the loss of your children."

Despite himself, tears surfaced. "What do you know about it? I mean…" It required almost more restraint than he could muster to ask the question in an even tone. "Did you have something to do with what happened to my children?" He could not utter the word.

Michael's polish dimmed. "Why would you even suggest such a thing?"

Thornton stared at him for several seconds, then let his body, as if it was an extra thing, fall into the chair behind the desk. "Murder," he said.

"Pardon?"

"Nancy uses the word like a weapon while I can hardly even say it. Why I would suggest such a thing is simple, Michael. Fifteen years ago, when you and Marie showed up at the airport to bid me fuckoff, you told me if I came back again, it was to stay. The cult, you said, would not be my mistress."

"I highly doubt, Thorn, that I used the word *cult* to describe the Lovers of the Flesh."

"Whatever the case, you did use the word *mistress*. You were not pleased three years ago when I showed up for a weekend then left again."

Michael leaned forward, eyes starkly blue as they gathered in Ethan Thornton and his demons. "And for this, we had something to do with your children?"

"Did you?" The tears spilled freely now.

"As I said to you at the end of that weekend, Thorn, when the topic arose and you warned me about contacting your wife—"

"'I don't think we'll bother with that,' you said. 'Her betrayer will be sleeping in the same bed with her.'"

"I'm sorry, Thorn. Myself, Marie, all of us. Goodbye."

Through a mist, Thornton watched the door close behind him.

Ten minutes later he informed his secretary he was going home for the day.

He wasn't due to pick up his wife for a few hours yet, so he just drove around town, admiring the elegant ladies peeping from under the yellow and red awnings of bakeries and sidewalk cafés; the streetlamps coming to life as the short January day died a resplendent death; an African artist on the corner packing away his wire figures, planes and sailing ships reminding men like Thornton of their days in the service.

A horn sounded, but he didn't realize it was directed at him until his rear bumper was given a nudge by the nose of the car behind. He waved through the mirror, deliberately using up another precious second of the man's time before moving off. Once upon a time he'd wondered how he was going to make it in this traffic-wracked nightmare of a city. Funny how loud a salary could speak: even over the horn blasts and metallic crunches of a Paris traffic circle.

How foolish he'd been to come back to France. A stronger man might have been able to deal with it. A stronger man might have been able to conduct his affairs without any regard for the fact that a thousand kilometers to the south lay the Mediterranean coast. He might have been able to attend a business conference in Monte Carlo without succumbing to the temptation of slipping over to Nice to see if the gang was still around. Then again, a stronger man likely wouldn't have gotten involved with those people in the first place. How hard would it have been to tell Sergeant Harrison, who offered to introduce him to the Lovers of the Flesh, that his flesh had quite enough love and he didn't need to involve himself with sex cults to get his thrills?

Hard. For a kid in his twenties in an exotic land, hard indeed. And once he had tasted the fruit...

What began in Rota, Spain, his duty station at the time, culminated on the French Riviera in the most amazing weekend of indulgence he had ever spent. It was easy later to label the thing and laugh at its immature thrills, but at the time it had meant very much to him. So much that he had struggled over whether to re-up or move to the South of France, where they promised to welcome him with open arms. Indeed, had he not been sent TDY immediately following the weekend in Nice, and then, on the tails of that three-month assignment, back to the States for the remainder of his commitment, he wasn't sure what would have happened. As it was, they had met him at the airport with warnings about treating the cult as his mistress.

Little had he known then that he would return someday. When the Riviera conference came into the picture twelve years later, he convinced himself that Monte Carlo's decadences would be of an entirely different sort than Nice's; that they would be responsibly indulged in, with no threat to the family life he had made for himself. He would kiss his beloved Nancy seven times between home and the airport, enslaving himself to her flesh, as the Lovers put it.

He hadn't kissed her a total of seven times during all of the past year. Not since it happened.

When he turned onto the street, he wondered how she would be tonight. For that matter, how would he? The man's grotesque face always hovered there between them. Particularly here in this place, where it had last been seen. He parked and waited, looked at his watch, which didn't say anything. As she did every night, Nancy was out there searching the grounds of the private school Brent and Janie had attended, searching for that face. Ethan lay his head back on the rest, making no effort to stop the memories. It was he who had actually seen the face the first time.

They had been returning from a Wednesday evening activity at church. The man had been standing on the opposite side of the street, partially lost in shadow as he watched their family of four tumble out of the wagon. Ethan had naturally assumed he was visiting the neighbors across the street, had stepped out for a smoke. When they'd gone inside, he had asked his wife what she made of the stranger. "Who?" she'd said. And when they looked out the window, he was gone. Ethan had experienced an irrational disquiet, even a sense of dread, which he had kept to himself. He'd checked on the kids three times before finally joining Nancy in bed.

The next time the man appeared, it was Ethan's wife who saw him. She had called Ethan at work. "There was this man on the sidewalk, an ugly, scary-looking man. Then he was there at the school when I dropped the kids off. I know he was the same man because he was disfigured…"

The newer Americanized suburb was over the rainbow. Fountains introduced subdivisions, dogs on leashes trotted from potty tricks behind trim hedges. Not a few malicious glances, distorted in the dark, came from their owners walking them. Yes, Thornton thought, I can't hurt anyone here.

"You're going to have to come up with a spot, man. Even a cab can't just cruise indefinitely."

A guard shack stood ahead to the right, marking the way into a club of some sort. Opposite it, a street connected to the one they were on. "Okay, turn here," Thornton said. "Thornflower Avenue. Has a ring to it, doesn't it?"

"Whatever you say, man."

They drove a few blocks, noises from the cabbie indicating he was growing less pleased by the second. Finally, Thornton said, "All right, here will do." He handed up the bill. "Keep the change. What the hell do I need with money anyway?"

The cabbie kissed it, as if it hadn't just come off the grimy hands of a tramp, and bid his passenger goodbye. When Thornton had shut the door, the cabbie turned the taxi around. Before he could get away Thornton waved him to a stop.

"Yeah...hold up a minute, will you? Maybe I'll just soak it in."

The driver scowled loudly, but Thornton ignored it. Cold wrapped around him as he stood on the sidewalk smoking a cigarette, looking around at luxury and status, enjoying being the anonym. He didn't know why he had asked the cabbie to wait, wasn't sure what he feared exactly. One thing he was not afraid of was their calling the police; he couldn't hurt the police either.

A car rolled by, the face in its passenger window expanding as it passed. It turned into the next drive, opposite side of the street. She stepped out hurriedly, pointing at Thornton. A street lamp revealed her expression.

"It's him. It's *him*! He was the man I saw outside the school. *Why*? you twisted fuck! You monster! They were our children! Just little goddamn children!!"

Thornton stood there and remembered the voices of little goddamn children, bickering and singing and filling the world with life and frustration and meaning. Meanwhile the woman came, doubtless inspired—like all the rest—by the scar he wore.

"Why are you here? You want my husband and me, *too*? Here, take me then, you monster!" She ripped at her blouse, her neck, her face, her hair, as she came.

Thornton opened the cab door to the alarmed look of the driver.

"She has me confused with someone else," he said, slamming the door behind. "*Go*."

"No."

She landed on the hood, banging and cursing.

"Go!" Thornton shouted. He shoved the only thing he had, a tramp's weapon, at the driver. It was a penknife, and not even open.

"I'm pathetic. Can I be what she's talking about?" he croaked, working the little blade from its cradle. He jabbed the rusty sliver of metal at the cabbie's neck, misjudging the distance and actually puncturing the skin, inciting a yowl from the man.

"Just go!" Thornton screamed, the woman now having found her way to his door.

The cab lurched forward, tossing the crazed woman aside. Thornton turned to watch her run back towards her car, flailing her arms at the man who had been driving. As the cab sped around a bend in Thornflower, the man and woman were getting back in the sedan. Jesus, they were going to give chase.

The cabbie seemed to think speed would separate the front from the back seat, getting him away from the vagabond lunatic with the penknife and suburban enemies. The car pursuing was almost secondary until it raced up beside the cab, its far superior engine humming along without a gasp, giving over entirely to the woman who screamed maniacally from the passenger window.

"What the fuck! What the fuck have you gotten me into?" shouted the cab driver as the woman's face seemed about to devour them.

Her hand reached across space towards the cab's rear window, the features behind it distorted into an even more horrible mask by the breath-soaked glass separating Thornton and her. He smeared away at the condensation, needing to see that face, needing to understand why his world was what it was. When this feeble attempt at bringing it all into focus didn't work for him, he rolled down the window against the night and its terrors, meaning to bridge gulfs, to know her while he ran like a mouse from his unforgivable sins.

The driver of the cab had had altogether enough. He slammed on the brakes. The impact came hurtling back at them like the aftershock of a detonated A-bomb, withering misconceptions away on its journey to oblivion. The guard gazebo, uniform inside, shattered in a violent song of wood and brick and glass as the sedan barreled through, and the world, as the suburb knew it, came to a hissing state of static.

Thornton climbed out of the window of the overturned cab. Flames leapt around him, blood from the cab driver filled the street. Ahead, the tantrum of metal and rubble choked the entrance to the club. The guard shack had disintegrated. The car was the most recognizable part of the wreckage, and scarcely that. Thornton made his lumbering way there.

By some miracle she lived. She rose from the tangle and lived right before his eyes. "Babe," she said to him. "Baby…"

He didn't know what to say back so he just stood there.

"But…baby…" She looked behind her now as she spoke. Something caught her attention. With a murmuring glance back at Thornton, she proceeded into the wreck. "Baby," he heard again. "*Baby*!"

She threw herself on something, a heap, crying out in her anguish. Baby baby baby.

Jerking around, she had shards of glass, debris from the guard shack, in her hand. "This is what you wanted, you monster! To have us all. Well, here I fucking am!" Stabbing with the shards, stabbing out her eyes, yelling and dying and giving her own wreckage to the end.

Thornton loomed over the scene. Everyone was dead now. The only one fit for an open casket was the woman's husband, and even he was badly marked, the tear opening the side of his face.

As Thornton bent down to touch him, the man's good eye came open. "Where's my family?" he whispered.

SPICE

by David Gerrold

Alternating between gray and night, the world turns. I drive through desolation. What's left of the highway points toward a broken horizon. A hasty sign warns that the bridge ahead is out, take the detour.

The narrow road winds off to the right, then climbs up a rocky hill, and at the top I see him—he's digging a grave. I stop at a distance. He doesn't notice me or he doesn't care.

He's silhouetted against the television-gray sky. The ground is black, the hill of earth is black, he's dressed in black, a dark figure clear against the ceiling of clouds. An uneven lump wrapped in a gray sheet lies at his feet, waiting at the edge of the hole.

As if in a dream of my own, I drift toward him. I stand at the head of the grave, the dark man stands at the foot. I could be a ghost. He doesn't see me.

He stops, surveys the hole. It's deep enough. It's finished. This isn't the first grave he's dug. Just another in a long list of too many. This is his calling, his purpose, his name. Get close to him and die.

Ignoring me, he rolls the body into the hole. It thumps into the soft earth. He pauses a moment, considering, then begins covering the body, filling the grave.

I stand opposite, waiting. Perhaps I am a shy young man, an admirer, a fan, one of those enamored with anyone who still has power in this world.

At last, he stops, wipes his forehead, looks across at me, his expression somewhere between dispassionate and annoyed. "What?" he asks.

His body is wide, his shoulders are wide, his face is wide, his eyes are hard and black and penetrating. His nose is flat and wide, his lips are likewise flat and wide. An unusual face, compelling. He looks as if he has been pressed in a book. "What?" he repeats.

I shake my head. He is not interested in me as a boy. My hands in the pockets, I pull just enough and let my dark coat fall open, revealing my darker dress beneath, smooth, shiny. Adolescent curves. I shake my head again, this time to let my hair flow loose.

"I want to go with you."

"No." He glances at the grave. "It's too soon." The dark man turns and walks away, shovel still in his hand. I follow him anyway, keeping a careful distance. He knows I'm behind him, he ignores me, but neither does he tell me to stop following.

Down the hill, a long slope, and I have to wonder why he chose the crest of it for the grave. He had to carry the body all the way. And the shovel. I wouldn't have. But then, I'm not stocky, not strong like him. The attraction pulls me after.

A long row of broken buildings on one side of the road, emptiness on the other. At the end a dark brick tower, the only one with life. An ancient residence hotel, abandoned by all but the ancient residents.

I follow him up the stairs. Three flights. He says nothing, resigned to my companionship.

A narrow hall, the gloom presses in around unshaded orange lights. The walls are wrinkled, dark and burnished, from having been painted over too many times, the doors as well.

His last chance to shut me out. Instead, without expression, he holds the door open for me. Locks it behind us. The room is old and dirty, shadowed in red and indigo. Darkness crowds against the dirty glass of the window. A single bulb reveals a sagging chair, a rumpled bed, a stained carpet. Not his. He's just passing through. This is just a place to wait until the dark leaves and the gray returns.

I drop my coat to the floor, it collapses in folds around my ankles, and I turn to face him. Does he like what he sees? I wear the blush of femininity as an invitation.

He is dispassionate, unblinking—he never takes his eyes off me, a lidless reptilian gaze. Curious and detached at the same time. He watches with unreadable dark eyes. As uninterested as he was when I was a boy, he is equally uninterested in me as a girl.

I step forward and unbutton his black shirt, unbuckle his metal belt, unbutton his pants and drop them to the floor. I move to push his shirt down off his shoulders but he pushes me away. He steps out of his clothes like abandoning a shell. And still, he never takes his eyes off me. I am the proverbial bird caught in the study of the snake.

Stepping out of my shoes, I lead him to the bed. Wordless, he allows me to push him down onto the rumpled sheets. My dress flows like oil. I climb on top of him and stare down into his deep black eyes.

His body is cold and glistening, hard and wide and strangely flat. His skin has a pale glow. I study his chest, the lines and curves, tracing them with my fingertips. Down the slope of his belly to the first dark curls below his navel. His eyes unblinking, he watches my face. He remains unaroused, impassive.

And back up, my fingers glide. And touch and trace—and finally, it's time, a sharp red fingernail cuts sideways across his chest, leaving a redder slice. Tiny drops of blood appear—he grabs my wrist. "Don't do that."

"I thought you liked it."

"I don't."

I lean back, trying to withdraw. He doesn't let go of my wrist. I sense a new arousal in him, a different one. His expression tightens. "Enough—"

—and finally, I am in danger. It's written across his face. I slap him—hard!—to distract him, roll sideways off the bed—

He grabs at my dress, yanks me back, we both slip and tumble. I pummel at his face with my fists—he has me on the floor, punching at my head—his excitement rises, a ferocious grin lighting him up, his wide smile revealing sharpened teeth—

Not enough yet—I scramble backward, reaching—my hand wraps around a shoe, his—grab and swing, it comes around and thwacks hard against his temple, bits of black earth spattering off—

He looks shocked, he didn't expect that. Blinks. Finally!

—and renews his attack—both of us scrabbling around on the floor for traction, I scratch his cheek with sharpened nails—kick with one foot, then the other, again—he reels back, klunks his head against the bedframe, momentarily stunned, reaches behind himself, checking for blood—yes!

David Gerrold

I'm on my hands and knees, the rug sliding under me, somehow I'm up and fumbling at the door, screaming now—shrieking for help!

The dark man is behind me, he loves it, he feeds on terror—I kick back wildly, hitting him in the solar plexus, he doubles over—I work frantically at the lock, somehow, I get the door open—and run screaming down the hall, my dress is ripped, I'm holding it up to cover my breasts—

"Help me! Someone help me! Please! Call the police! He's in room six! Help me! Help! Someone!"

The hall is silent, as still as the inside of the grave. I stumble toward the end, toward the stairs—look back and he's there, still clutching his belly, but staggering after me—

Behind him, at the blunt end of the hall, finally a door opens. A man, half-naked in dirty T-shirt, torn and bloody, leans halfway out. He looks like a butcher, annoyed at the interruption. "What's going on out here?!"

The dark man turns and looks at him, bent into a feral posture.

The butcher hesitates. "Sorry. Never mind." He fades back inside, closes his door quickly.

A fleeting thought. Who hides behind these doors? What other horrors hide in this building?

The dark man swings around to face me again. He grunts and staggers forward, still gasping for breath—I really hurt him, but he has inhuman powers of recovery. He screams and leaps—I duck and roll, but he grabs me anyway. A sideways kick, I sweep his legs out from under him and we're both on the floor again.

Rolling together like lovers—and now he's on top of me, heavy and grinding, his knee pushing at me, parting my legs, his breath hot and foul. His huge hands find my throat, his face is red, his blood is raging, burning. Almost there—

Writhing beneath him, I arch my back, gasping, moaning, pushing him upward. He responds with a guttural cry. And finally, he's ready—

—and I explode, unfold, and rise to fill the hall, all eight limbs unfolding, darker than he will ever be—I rise, throwing him off of me. I come down on top of him, an avalanche of black, seizing, biting, stinging. My stinger curls around and under and up again, up through his ass, his intestines, his lungs, and finally to his heart—the venom paralyzes instantly, freezing the wide-eyed look of disbelief on his face—

Delicious.

Suck the fire out of him like spice.

Just the way I like it.

Eventually strength returns. I reassemble and reform. Renewed. Straightening, I rise. Drift through halls and out. Away and gone, wrapping darkness around me like a cloak.

Time to retire now, time to rest. Time to sink back beneath the ground. Return to the cycle of gray and night.

Wait and watch. Till hunger returns.

Dearly Beloved

by Bruce McAllister

I don't blame them. My parents, I mean. I don't view them as responsible for what happened, or for my new collection—which I'd actually started just before that summer. Maybe they should have looked into the camp a little bit more, asked around, but I wouldn't have if I'd been them. Why would anyone think an innocuous summer day-camp—one with basic crafts and activities and housed at an old school near the bay—might be the wrong place to send your kid. They were being good parents. They wanted to get their son out of the house, away from his snakes and lizards and books, meet people, play with other kids. Be sociable so that he wouldn't be teased so much for his red hair and mannerisms, his stamp and insect and match-book collections and, as one teacher put it, "his sometimes-embarrassing love of animals."

My mother, a teacher—and a very conscientious person—wanted me to grow up normal. My father, an engineer who worked for the city, was simply happy that she liked his summer camp idea. They drove me to the camp that first day and the next six, and picked me up too. I never told them what happened those first days. The big event—what happened the last day—they got to see themselves with all the other parents who picked up their kids. Camp ended that day. Death has a tendency to do that. The other things they didn't need to know about, I told myself. Some things you just don't tell your parents. I knew it by *feeling* if nothing else even at nine: *You just don't tell your parents everything... especially if you were there and didn't stop it...especially if you don't want them to take away what matters most to you....*

—

The school grounds were bright in the peninsula sun, nothing dark and moody about them. Hair didn't stand up on the back of our necks. Apparitions didn't float between the trees. There were no clanking chains or faint, feral howls in the distance. There was a main house—a big Victorian or Craftsman (what nine-year-old knows about such things?—it was a big, three-story wooden house, that was all)—and an endless, buckling asphalt parking lot that was returning to nature. By that I mean crooked grass was growing up in the cracks that covered it; there were only a couple of cars ever parked there; and you weren't really sure where the parking lot ended and the dead lawns of the actual school grounds began.

A long way from the big house and its shuttered windows were the classrooms, which looked more like abandoned laboratories, five of them in a row. Big, fixed tables in the middle of each white room. A Bunsen burner here and there. Lockers like the kind you see in school hallways attached to one wall. Lots of

Bruce McAllister

terrariums with reptiles and rodents—mainly white rats—which someone had to maintain, though we never saw who it was and were never asked to feed them or clean the cages. I wanted to stay with all of the animals—help with them—but I couldn't. We'd park our lunch bags and other belongings in the lockers and, our teachers calling to us, leave the classrooms immediately—to play outside. We could go back in to get our things, but we couldn't stay, and we had to eat lunch outside. It was summer. It was a summer camp. We were supposed to be outside playing.

Outside was a rusty jungle gym, but everyone ignored it. What grabbed everyone's attention—even though we hadn't played in a sandbox since we were little—was the amazing sandboxes the place had.

That doesn't capture it. *Sandboxes.* You get a picture, I'm sure, of a kid's sandbox. Small, 8X8 at the biggest. These were huge. They were endless worlds of sand. Someone had dug deep holes with a bulldozer, then brought the sand in with huge trucks, and they wouldn't need to come back until next year. The sand was at least two feet deep. You could dig forever and never hit earth. Each sandbox—and there were three of them—must have been thirty or forty feet square. They weren't for little kids. They were for building empires. We used short shovels—the school had them—to dig in the sand the way you would at the beach if you were making great forts and castles, and you could bring hoses into them to make watery worlds. The hoses were the longest I'd ever seen, stretching from faucets on the sides of the classroom buildings. You'd turn the water on, look to see if one of the teachers—mostly women, but a couple of men—was rushing toward you to stop you, but no one ever did. You got to do whatever you wanted at this camp—as long as it was outside.

Some kids built sand castles, some forts, some great road systems for the toy cars and trucks and tractors that were piled in a big wooden box by one of the classrooms at the start of each day. But the kids I found myself playing with were the tunnel kids. Kevin was our leader. He was ten and tall, with a moon face, eyes set far apart, and a scar on his chin. He took his clothes off twice the first day—something you didn't see many ten-year-olds do—and ran naked from the classrooms to the big house and back until the teachers caught him and made him put his clothes back on. He would do it again—no warning, just a sudden crazy laugh from him and his clothes would be gone and he'd be running—before those six days were over. But mainly he made tunnels in the sand, and those of us who liked tunnels, too, joined him in one of the sandboxes. The Tunnel Sandbox. The Tunnel Kids, we called ourselves. If you didn't want to make tunnels, you couldn't play in it. You had to use one of the other boxes.

There was a girl named Dot in our box. She'd make tunnels with me, and I thought nothing of it. When you're nine and the kind of kid I was, you don't think in terms of A Girl Really Liking You. You simply grow aware that someone who happens to be a girl is digging in the sand beside you, looking at you now and then, there every day, and it feels good, and you keep building tunnels together. If we looked at each other, we both smiled, and she seemed happy, but it never occurred to me that her happiness might be because I was there making tunnels with her. I was happy she was there, sure, but that was another matter—one I didn't think about either.

Because the sand was so deep, you could make your tunnels deep and wide, but you needed water to make the sand wet so it would stay together. If you made the tunnel big enough, you could run water through it and watch it come out the other side—which might be a long ways away if you made the hole with a broom handle. Your arm wasn't long enough. Dot would sit, her dress as sandy as her knees, at the other end of the long tunnel we'd made together and laugh when the water finally came rushing out. It was magic. What other sandbox in the world had tunnels you could send rivers of water through?

Sometimes, of course, the tunnels collapsed. The water collapsed them, or some idiot—one of the Tunnel Kids or some interloper from one of the other boxes—would step on a section and down the tunnel would go, water pooling in the hole.

Kevin would scream at the interloper or the Tunnel-Kids idiot who'd done it and then go back to his own tunnel making, which he never wanted help with. They were *his* tunnels. He would get tiny cars and trucks from the big box and push them through with a stick or broom handle, and you could tell this frustrated the hell out of him. He wanted the little vehicles to be able to move on their own.

One day he stood up and shouted, "They can run!" We thought he was going to take his clothes off again, but instead he ran toward one of the classrooms. We went back to our tunnel building.

When he reappeared, he had one of the white rats from the terrariums in his hand. It was struggling, though not in pain.

No teacher had seen him, but even if someone had, I don't think it would have mattered. A boy had one of the rats. He was going to play with it in the sand box. Playing was the point of the camp. What was wrong with a boy playing with a clean white rat in a sand box? No one really cared what we did. I understand that now. It was a money thing.

When we discovered what he wanted to do with the rat, we all got excited.

He made the rat run through one of his own tunnels first. When its white head and pink nose appeared suddenly at the other end of the tunnel, we cheered. Dot laughed and could barely contain herself. She jumped up and did the kind of dance that 5-year-olds do when they have a cookie in one hand and just can't stand it.

Then he put the rat through one of our tunnels—Dot's and mine—our biggest, longest one. When the rat appeared at the other end, we cheered again. Dot did another dance.

Kevin went back to the classroom, got two more white rats and was barely able to hold onto them as he returned to the sandbox.

Rats were running all over the place, but couldn't get over the high sidings. We'd grab them and put them in a tunnel and they'd reappear, trying to escape. We'd catch them and perform the tunnel magic again and again until it was time for our parents to pick us up in the parking lot.

—

This went on for days. White rats running everywhere, Dot laughing, Kevin shouting, the other Tunnel Kids looking on in wonder, impressed by Kevin's ingenuity and of course wanting the rats to go through their tunnels, too. Which Kevin allowed— as long as he got to run the rats.

At the end of each day, Kevin would be the one to return the rats—which now numbered probably a dozen—to their cages in the classrooms. This seemed to be enough for the teachers, who just wanted the rats back, alive even if sandy. The next morning the rats were as good as new—someone had cleaned them—which made me happy. I didn't want them hurt. No one did.

One day, Kevin started jumping and down in the sand screaming, angry, and we didn't know why.

"Did the teachers tell him *no?*" I asked Dot.

She knew what I meant. "I don't know."

"Do you see any rats?"

"No."

"Maybe they said he couldn't play with the rats anymore."

"Maybe." Dot went back to her tunnel building—which made her happy with or without rats.

Two days later I was digging with my hands in the sand and I felt something I'd never felt before. You never felt anything in the sandbox except metal or plastic or wood—a toy or piece of wood some kid had brought in. This was soft and wet.

I pulled it out and Dot screamed. It was one of the white rats. I held it by its tail. Wet and dead, it looked half the size it had looked when alive, but it was the eyes, which were closed, and the mouth, which was open, and the strange little feet with their bony bones that made me stare. I'd never really looked at those feet before. You couldn't when they were moving. They were made of countless tiny bones all connected together without much skin—pink skin. You had to have feet like that to escape through attics or trees or burrows from the animals that wanted to eat you, and you still had them if you lived in a cage. You were a rat, after all, and those feet couldn't save you from what someone might do to you in a sandbox with a hose.

I couldn't swallow. This wasn't supposed to happen. You weren't supposed to kill something by playing with it. Dot was feeling the same thing. I could see it in her face. She wasn't shrieking now. She was thinking: *Its eyes are closed and will never open again.*

I looked over at Kevin. He stared back, sullen, just as angry.

"It wouldn't come out," he said. "Three of them wouldn't come out. They wouldn't finish…"

I waited. I didn't know what to say.

"They had to be punished," he added.

I remembered how he'd jumped up and down in the sand, screaming, two days before, and I knew what he'd been doing. If you didn't do what Kevin wanted, you had to be punished.

I looked away quickly. Dot and the other girl hadn't heard what he'd said. They were still staring at the rat in my hand.

I got up, still holding it by its tail, and started walking. I grabbed a short shovel from the five that were tipped against the big mulberry tree by the sandbox, and in a moment heard Dot behind me, saying, "What are you going to do?"

"I'm going to bury it."

I wasn't mad at her, but I was mad at someone.

"Can I come with you?"

"Sure." I answered. It felt good to have her come.

—

Behind the first classroom was a dead lawn, bare earth here and there, leaves everywhere. The supervisors weren't gardeners. The ground in the Bay Area was soft, so I dug a hole and put the body in it.

We stood looking down. I thought Dot would say something—I wanted her to—but she didn't.

Finally, I started reciting *The Lord's Prayer.*

"Our Father, who art in Heaven..."

It was the only thing I knew, and I'd used it with dead animals before. A sparrow, a turtle. A month ago, our cat. Those times I'd cried. This time I wouldn't, but it still needed to be done, I thought—the burying and the prayer.

Dot tried to say it with me but didn't know it well. That didn't matter.

I kept thinking of the tiny feet—all bone and barely any skin—and how I'd dug up our cat a few months after I'd buried it to see what it looked like, amazed that there was just furry skin and bones left. I couldn't stop staring at those bones.

Later that day, I saw Dot talking to one of the teachers. The teacher kept looking over at me, then at Kevin, then at Kevin even more.

Kevin was watching them, too, the same sullen look on his face. When he glanced at me, the look got even harder, as if what was happening was my fault.

"You're the one that killed it," I wanted to say to him, but I didn't. I was thinking how he'd said *them*—how there must be other bodies in the sandbox. We just hadn't discovered them yet.

The next day we did. Two more wet white bodies. Dot didn't want to dig in the sand, so she sat on the siding and watched me do it. I wasn't digging to make a castle or tunnels. We both knew it. I was digging for the bodies, and I found them and buried them, Dot beside me, in the same place, using the same prayer because I didn't know any other.

—

Two days later, Dot's parents came to pick her up and couldn't find her. I'd seen her earlier in the day, in the Tunnel Kids sandbox, but not after lunch—which we ate at picnic tables at the other end of the grounds. She'd stayed in the sandbox after we'd left—that I remembered—but I couldn't remember seeing her at lunch.

Before my parents arrived to pick me up, the police came. Dot's parents were worried. I was worried, but I didn't know what about exactly. Dot was gone. Had she run away? Was she hiding? Was she afraid to go home because her family scared her but we didn't know it? I didn't know. I didn't know that when you're a parent you worry about terrible things, things kids can't even imagine.

I didn't know what to do, so I kept playing in our sandbox. I had this energy suddenly—which made me nervous—I didn't know what to do with it—so I started digging with the shovel I'd been using that day. I dug where I usually dug, but I also dug in the space I'd always thought of as Dot's and my place.

When the sand turned red at the tip of my shovel, I stopped. Another rat?

But a rat doesn't have so much blood, does it? I got down on my knees, picked up what lay at the shovel's tip—something it had cut off—and stopped breathing. It was a finger. Half of a finger.

I started pawing the sand. I didn't want to cut off anything else. I pawed and pawed and a dress, buried in the sand, brushed

Bruce McAllister

my fingers. I pawed frantically and found an arm, then more dress. I didn't want to find a face. I moved down, to a leg, to the shoes.

I stood up and started shouting, and there behind me was Kevin, with a shovel. He was swinging it.

As I turned to run, my foot fell into a tunnel, my body dropped down, and his shovel sailed over my head. I was holding myself up with my own shovel, and when I stood up, I swung it at him, connecting, blood everywhere.

Kids in the sandbox were screaming. Teachers were screaming. The police were running toward us. I swung again. He fell and dropped his shovel. I wanted to kill him, and I nearly did; but as I went for his hand with my shovel, jabbing and jabbing at it even though it was empty, the police grabbed the shovel from me and left me alone on the sand, crying, until my own parents arrived.

The camp was closed down, of course, and I had to talk to police at our house for a whole week. My parents kept apologizing for putting me there, at that "terrible place," and I finally had to get mad at them. "It's not *your* fault! It's *his* parents' fault! He shouldn't have been there!" I didn't know how to say what I was really feeling.

Police and volunteers looked for it. They asked me just once about it, and that was that. They knew I'd cut it off accidentally with the shovel—which meant that they just needed to look harder for it in the sand.

I buried it in our back yard two weeks later, saying *The Lord's Prayer*, and dug it up a few weeks after that. I boiled it clean when my parents were at work, and put the two bones in bleach for a day. They were beautiful, truly beautiful. Whiter than the classrooms at the camp. White as Dot's skin, when it wasn't covered with sand. White as her pretty face.

I went ahead and put them with the cat's bones—which weren't as pretty—in the blue enamel box I'd gotten from the attic, the one I have to this very day. I kept Kevin's for a while, but it felt wrong. I didn't want to see the whiteness of the bones. I didn't want to see beauty in them. Finally, I burnt it in our fireplace—in the hottest flame I could make—and put the ashes in an old pill bottle, so that I would still have it but not need to feel love.

The others I've collected since that day—from hands just like hers—are beautiful, too, but not as beautiful as hers.

Ms. Wysle and the Licorice Man

by Shane Nelson

"All right boys and girls, get out your pencil crayons," Ms. Wysle told her grade two students. "It's time for art."

An excited murmur passed through the students as they put their books away. A few smiled and laughed as books were closed and shoved into desks.

"Quietly! You know the rules."

While Ms. Wysle wrote on the board, her students gathered their pencil crayons. Ms. Wysle had just finished writing the words *My Favorite Holiday* on the board when she heard laughter and a scuffled thump. She turned and pierced two boys with her gaze. One boy held another's pencil crayons overhead.

"Mason! Thomas! What's going on?"

The boy straining for his pencil crayons flushed red. "Thomas took my crayons, Ms. Wysle."

"Thomas," Ms. Wysle said, "give those to Mason at once."

Thomas handed over the pencil crayons. Mason hurried to his seat, head down. He slumped forward, eyes darting to his teacher. She ignored him in favor of Thomas.

"You've only been in our class for two weeks," Ms. Wysle said. "But that's no excuse for not following the rules. Can someone tell me what Thomas did that we do *not* do in grade two?"

Hands shot up.

Ms. Wysle pointed at a blonde girl. The girl said, "We get our things quietly."

"Correct," Ms. Wysle said. "In here we are quiet and respectful. We do *not* touch things that do not belong to us." She glared at Thomas. His lower lip trembled and his eyes dampened.

"Thomas, you may stay in at recess," Ms. Wysle said. "Now take your seat."

Thomas *hated* Ms. Wysle. She'd had it in for him since his first day. She was always glaring at him from behind her glasses. She rarely smiled.

"Grade two," Ms. Wysle said, "Let's read what I've written here on the board."

Together, the class recited, "My Favorite Holiday."

"Very good," Ms. Wysle said. "I want you to draw a picture of your favorite holiday. Use your imagination and be creative." She picked up a pile of white paper and distributed sheets to the class.

Once every student had a sheet of paper, Ms. Wysle returned to the front of the room. She was aware of her students' expectant gazes and the way in which they sat, stiff-backed, waiting. They knew better than to misbehave, even when excited.

"You may choose any holiday you like, but it *must* be a holiday. We've discussed holidays. A birthday is *not* a holiday." She looked at Lacey Chambers, whose birthday was just days away. "*And...* everyone must explain their drawing and tell a story about it. So be sure this is something that is very important to you."

Ms. Wysle and the Licorice Man
Shane Nelson

Papers rustled and pencil crayons rattled as the students went to work.

—

When the lunch bell rang, Ms. Wysle's students put their things away. Their eyes watched the clock, eager to rush to the lunchroom. When the second hand completed a full revolution, Ms. Wysle said, "Leave your drawings on your desks. You may go for lunch."

Once the last of her children were gone, Ms. Wysle patrolled the empty classroom. A red pen crayon lay on the floor. She picked it up, identified its owner from the initials written on the side, and set it on that student's desk. She would be sure to speak to that student about being more careful.

The other teachers of W. J. Manfred School thought that Ms. Wysle was vindictive, as if she had to make up for years without a husband or children of her own. But they were wrong. Teachers today coddled children. They didn't set out rules and they didn't prepare the kids for life. Discipline was the key to teaching a child.

Ms. Wysle locked her classroom and walked to the staff lounge. It was half-filled, teachers milling about, preparing lunches. Ms. Wysle retrieved her lunch from the fridge, glancing out the windows at the brightly colored fall foliage. She could hardly believe that it was already October 30th.

The staff, like the students, had its unspoken cliques. Ms. Wysle distanced herself from most everyone and sat alone. Eventually other teachers, those close to her age or older, joined her.

Ms. Wysle ate her sandwich, listening to other conversations.

Some were discussing report cards while others talked about the mild fall weather. When some of the younger teachers got onto the topic of Halloween, her teeth came together with a jarring *clack*.

"Are you showing any movies in your class?" Paula Issacs asked.

"That depends," said Justin Ableman, the grade six teacher. "What's school policy on movies, Nicole?"

The principal was warming up her soup in the microwave. "Keep it school and age appropriate. I trust your judgment."

Ms. Wysle gave a disgusted snort that drew the attention of everyone at the table.

"Something wrong, Helen?" Justin asked.

Helen. Ms. Wysle *hated* that he had the gall to use her Christian name. She preferred that students and colleagues address her as Ms. Wysle. Still, sometimes one had to swallow a bitter pill.

"Yes, Mr. Ableman, something *is* wrong." Ms. Wysle said. "I have no idea why you encourage children to celebrate Halloween. Not only does it distract from proper lessons and good behavior, it's morally wrong."

"Maybe you think—"

"Yes, I *do* think, Mr. Ableman, and perhaps once you've gained some experience, you'll think as well. Halloween is the glorification of evil."

"They use their imaginations and have fun," Justin said. "What's wrong with that?"

"A lot," Ms. Wysle said, glowing with righteous anger. "You may think it's all right for children to believe in ghosts and monsters. *I don't.* I also don't think we need to turn our children into street beggars once a year, knocking on doors demanding candy."

"Don't you think that's a bit much?" Paula asked.

Ms. Wysle and the Licorice Man
Shane Nelson

"Not at all, *Ms.* Issacs. Children learn morality and behavior at an early age. Things are as they are because of a lack of good parenting and proper discipline. When I was a child, I understood respect and moral behavior."

"Oh, come on, Helen," Justin said. "You think Halloween is an evil day that makes children misbehave?"

"Yes," Ms. Wysle said. "It has no place in school. It isn't educational and it goes against good Christian morals. I think that the administration should be more professional and make sure—"

Nicole held up a hand. "It's the position of this division that Halloween *is* acceptable in the classroom as long as it is school appropriate. That means costumes and decorations and movies." Seeing Ms. Wysle open her mouth, Nicole went on. "However, it is up to the discretion of each teacher as to what goes on in his or her classroom."

"I think it's wrong," Ms. Wysle said.

Nicole took a seat. "That's your prerogative."

Fuming, Ms. Wysle finished her lunch in determined silence. She was certain that she would be the highlight of conversation once she had gone, but she didn't care. Let them gossip—that's what unintelligent people did.

Returning to her classroom, she marched to the desk upon which she'd placed the red pencil crayon. She picked it up and tucked it behind her ear. She would have a chat with this particular student about the importance of following the rules.

"All right," Ms. Wysle said, "we'll start with Robert's row. Come up, Robert, and show us your picture."

Robert's picture showed a family gathered around a green Christmas tree. The tree was decorated with blobs of various colors. As he talked about Christmas, Ms. Wysle sat at her desk. Other teachers had to patrol their class constantly. Not Ms. Wysle. She wrote marks in her daybook as the children droned on.

After years of teaching, Ms. Wysle knew the ins and outs of children. This art exercise would result in the same revelations—kids loved Christmas, some liked Easter. Some might choose Thanksgiving because it gave them a chance to draw a turkey. Ms. Wysle could half-listen and hear enough. She knew what each child was capable of and they would be marked accordingly. *It wasn't like she pre-judged the kids but sometimes a teacher just* knew *how a child would do...*

Ms. Wysle's pen scratched as the children presented drawings and told stories. It was only when Thomas Carpenter was half-way through his presentation—talking about someone called the Licorice Man—that she raised her head.

"But the Licorice Man isn't *really* made of licorice," Thomas said. "People think he is because he's all black and oily and has a funny smell."

Ms. Wysle walked to the front of her desk, where she had a better view of Thomas's picture. It seemed to show a giant spider hanging from the ceiling.

"The Licorice Man is all black, even his eyes. And he has long fingers and claws."

Ms. Wysle stiffened.

"He's so black and inky that he can hide in the shadows and in the dark. He can sneak under doors and through keyholes, though he doesn't like to 'cause it hurts."

Ms. Wysle and the Licorice Man

Shane Nelson

It was not a spider but a misshapen man hanging from the ceiling. He had long, gangly arms and legs, with hooked fingers and sharp claws. His head was elongated and his eyes shone. The man's mouth gaped open, showing off razor sharp teeth.

"He catches bad boys and girls—and mean grown-ups, too—and eats them. He eats everything," Thomas continued, oblivious to the looks of fear on his classmates' faces. "Skin and hair and bones. But he can only come out on one night the whole year, and that's Halloween. Halloween is my favorite holiday, and it's my mom's favorite too because she says—"

"Enough!" Ms. Wysle shrieked. "Thomas Carpenter, that's enough of your rubbish!" She marched to the front of the room, towering over Thomas. "Halloween is NOT a holiday!" she said, snatching the drawing from his hands. "It's an evil, immoral day. It's no surprise that a disrespectful boy such as yourself would like it."

"But I thought—"

"No, you *didn't* think," Ms. Wysle said. "We do *not* celebrate Halloween in this room. That is another rule, is it not grade two?"

A few heads bobbed, though most of the children were looking at their hands.

"You have *repeatedly* broken the rules in my classroom," Ms. Wysle said. "And because of that, you will spend the rest of the day in time-out."

Time-out was served in the cloakroom at the back of the classroom. Ordinarily it wasn't bad; it was clean and quiet. But during Thomas's previous time-out Ms. Wysle had turned out the lights and left him in the dark. It had been frightening.

She pulled him toward the cloakroom. "I'll be calling your mother. It's time she and I had a talk."

Thomas gave his fellow classmates a desperate look. His drawing rustled in Ms. Wysle's hand. He glanced at it, noticing how the rustling motion made his drawing of the Licorice Man appear to move.

What if he's in the cloakroom? Thomas thought. He countered that by telling himself it was impossible—the Licorice Man only came out on Halloween.

Ms. Wysle pushed him into the room and waved his drawing at him. "This is garbage, Mr. Carpenter, and that's where it belongs." She crumpled the paper and threw it into the trashcan. A moment later the cloakroom door closed. Thomas waited for the lights to go out.

They did.

Ms. Wysle heard the staccato tap of heels in the hallway and straightened her shoulders. The final bell of the day had rung thirty minutes earlier. Following the bell, she had telephoned Thomas's mother and demanded a meeting. Over the phone the woman had sounded quietly self-assured. Now Ms. Wysle would meet her face-to-face.

The *tap-tap* of heels paused and a moment later a tall woman appeared in the doorway. She wore knee-high leather boots under a paisley skirt. A peasant blouse accentuated her figure.

"Ms. Wysle?"

Ms. Wysle waved a hand at the chair she'd placed nearby. "Sit down, Mrs. Carpenter."

"It's Miss Forbes, actually, but you can call me Elana," Thomas's mother said. She crossed the room, her strides long and

Shane Nelson

graceful, and paused next to the chair. "I should have corrected you on the phone, but I was concerned about Tom." She looked around. "Where is he, by the way?"

"In the time-out room," Ms. Wysle said, gesturing to the cloakroom.

Elana moved toward the door and Ms. Wysle darted to her feet, intercepting her. "He's fine."

"I'd like to see him," Elana said, holding her smile.

"We have things to discuss."

Elana put a hand on Ms. Wysle's arm and eased her aside. Furious, Ms. Wysle watched as Thomas's mother opened the cloakroom door.

"Miss Forbes, I'd rather you—"

Elana dropped to a knee to hug her son. For a few moments mother and son had a whispery exchange. She brushed back his hair and wiped at his tears.

Ms. Wysle sniffed. "Miss Forbes, I must talk to you."

"Of course." As Elana moved to lead her son out of the cloakroom, Ms. Wysle shook her head.

"Grown-ups only."

"My son is the one in trouble, Ms. Wysle. He deserves to know why."

"I don't agree," Ms. Wysle said. "He has homework to complete and he can do it in the time-out room." She crossed her arms over her chest and cocked a hip.

"All right. Tom, finish your work. Mom and Ms. Wysle need to talk."

Thomas trudged back into the time-out room. Ms. Wysle closed the door, perhaps a bit too forcefully. The smile on Elana's face wavered.

"Take a seat," Ms. Wysle said.

Elana sat, crossing her legs and placing her hands in her lap. Ms. Wysle stared, giving the woman time to grow uneasy. But Elana seemed anything but uneasy. She smiled, tapping one foot.

"What did my son do?"

"I asked the children to draw a picture of their favorite holiday. Your son drew a Halloween picture and told the class a frightening story." Ms. Wysle tapped Thomas's drawing, which she had removed from the trash and now lay on the desk before her.

"I can tell him not to frighten his classmates, but I don't see—"

"This isn't about his classmates but about what is acceptable in this classroom. His drawing and story were *not* acceptable."

The smile slid from Elana's face. "Why is that?"

"We discussed holidays in class. Halloween is *not* a holiday. As well, Halloween is morally repugnant. Thomas flouted the rules and was disrespectful. The fact that irresponsible parents condone participation in Halloween is, sadly, out of my hands. But what goes on in this classroom is up to me."

There, Ms. Wysle thought savagely. *Take that.*

Elana sat silently, lips pursed. Ms. Wysle took the woman's silence for shame. Instead, Elana bared her teeth and said, "If you choose not to celebrate Halloween in your classroom, I'll respect that. But you will *not* judge my son or myself. And you *will* respect my son's feelings."

"He broke the rules."

"I don't care about that right now," Elana said. "I care that you've belittled my son. There's nothing wrong with a child drawing a picture for Halloween. Tom is a highly imaginative boy and I encourage imagination. Without it, what fun is childhood?"

Shane Nelson

"Not everything is about fun, Miss Forbes. You might do well to learn that yourself."

Miss Forbes raised her eyebrows. "Pardon?"

"Fun is what gets people into trouble," Ms. Wysle said. "Children. Young women, perhaps. Fun is a privilege. Your son needs to learn responsibility. It seems he isn't disciplined firmly."

"How I discipline my son is none of your concern."

"Where is Thomas's father?"

"I don't see how that matters."

"*That's* why Thomas is in trouble," Ms. Wysle said. "Because he needs a firmer hand. Perhaps he's never known his father, but regardless, his behavior—"

Elana got to her feet. The older woman's smug smile evaporated.

"I won't have you bad-mouthing me," Elana said. "You're a teacher, Ms. Wysle, not a parent. You can enforce your rules, but you will *not* make my son feel badly about himself. He drew a picture—that's all!"

"That most certainly is *not* all. I will not—"

Elana brushed past Ms. Wysle and opened the cloakroom door. Thomas, sitting at the table, his books stacked neatly in front of him, gazed at his mother in surprise.

"We're going now, Tom."

Tom gathered his things, stuffing them into his backpack. Ms. Wysle got to her feet and stood behind Elana, arms crossed. She had never been spoken to in such a rude manner, and if this young woman thought she could come traipsing into this classroom and treat people this way, she had another thing coming.

"Miss Forbes, we haven't settled this matter."

Elana took her son's hand. "There's nothing more to discuss."

Ms. Wysle said nothing as Elana led her son from the classroom. In the doorway Thomas threw one quick glance over his shoulder. Then he was gone.

———

Halloween.

Ms. Wysle came to school early, scowling at the decorations in the hallway. Soon the kids would arrive decked out in costumes—even some of the teachers would join in. Ms. Wysle was thankful that by tomorrow Halloween would be behind them.

Thomas's drawing was on her desk. She had forgotten to dispose of it after the confrontation with Miss Forbes. With savage glee, she crumpled the picture and threw it into the trash.

Young Thomas Carpenter is in for a surprise if he thinks he or his mother can behave like that in my classroom, she thought.

———

For a moment, Ms. Wysle thought Thomas wasn't coming to school. Had his mother decided to pull him out in a show of defiance? Then the second bell rang—the tardy bell—and Thomas came inside, backpack slung over his shoulder. His classmates were already at their desks, awaiting morning announcements.

"You're late, Mr. Carpenter," Ms. Wysle said.

Thomas hung up his backpack and jacket. "Sorry, Ms. Wysle."

"Sorry isn't good enough," Ms. Wysle said. "I'll see you at recess."

Thomas took his seat just as the morning announcements began. At her desk, Ms. Wysle smiled under her hand. Ordinarily,

Shane Nelson

she *hated* Halloween. Despised it. But perhaps today wouldn't be so bad after all.

By midday, Ms. Wysle had spoken to Thomas three times. When the bell rang to start the afternoon, she escorted him into the hallway.

"I won't tolerate any more nonsense, young man," she said. "You may think you have a license to misbehave because your mother has a smart mouth, but you do *not*. Am I making myself clear?"

"Yes, Ms. Wysle."

"If I have to talk to you one more time, you'll have afternoon detention."

"But Luke Jarvis is having a Halloween party and I—"

Ms. Wysle squeezed his arm. "I don't care about your Halloween party." Her eyes went wide, the tendons on her neck standing out. "Now get to your desk."

The children grew more excited as the afternoon passed. By three p.m., with the afternoon bell only ten minutes off, furtive whispers moved through the classroom. Ms. Wysle sat at her desk, hands folded in front of her, watching. She had the gaze of a bird of prey, just waiting for that one moment when she could swoop down and—

"Thomas!"

Thomas spun around in his desk, giving a startled cry when he saw Ms. Wysle marching toward him.

"I will not have you talking when you should be working!"

"But... I wasn't..."

Ms. Wysle loomed over him. "You weren't what? Were you talking?"

Thomas *had* been talking, but so had the rest of his class. The whispering had been going on for minutes and Ms. Wysle hadn't said anything. But now...

"Thomas?"

"I'm sorry, Ms. Wysle."

Ms. Wysle clapped her hands together. "Grade two, you may get ready for dismissal. Be sure you have your homework and that your desks are clean." As the students began to move, Ms. Wysle caught Thomas's eye. "You can stay in your desk. I'll talk to you after the bell."

—

"**You're a** stubborn boy and you need to learn how to behave."

Thomas remained in his desk, watching as Ms. Wysle erased the blackboard and tidied up. When she turned her back, his eyes jumped to the clock. It was twenty past three. Luke's party started at four.

"That's your mother's fault," Ms. Wysle said, setting the chalkboard brushes down and dusting her hands together. "She isn't a good woman, Thomas."

Thomas bit his lip.

"I can't allow you to act up in my classroom. You have to learn the rules if you are going to do well. You *do* want to do well, don't you?"

Thomas said nothing.

"Thomas?"

"Yes, Ms. Wysle."

Shane Nelson

"Good. You can start by getting your math book and coming with me."

Thomas grabbed his books from his desk. "I have to go, Ms. Wysle. I told my mother I would go straight to Luke's party—"

"I'm afraid you'll be missing Luke's party," Ms. Wysle said. "You'll be here with me, in detention."

Thomas stopped. "For how long?"

Ms. Wysle put a hand on his back, ushering him toward the cloakroom. "You'll stay until I dismiss you."

"My mother said—"

"What your mother said does *not* matter!" Ms. Wysle snapped. "You will listen to *me* and I'm telling you that you have detention."

Thomas jerked away from her. "You can't make me stay!"

Ms. Wysle recoiled as if slapped. She'd never had a child defy her so openly. She grabbed Thomas by the wrist. He dropped his books. As she dragged him to the cloakroom, she said, "How dare you talk back to me!"

Thomas squirmed but Ms. Wysle was too strong. Before he knew it she had shoved him into the cloakroom.

"You'll stay in here until I say otherwise."

Tears coursed down Thomas's face. His hands knotted into fists. "I hate you," he said.

Ms. Wysle closed the door.

—

Thomas had been silent for fifteen minutes. Ms. Wysle was surprised. She'd turned off the lights and sat at her desk, waiting. She knew that Thomas would either break down and cry or he would bang on the door and shout. She waited.

Nothing.

She went to the door. She could hear a faint whispery sound. Scratching. She pressed her ear to the door.

Scritch-scritch-scratch.

"Thomas?"

The sound stopped.

"What are you doing in there?"

Ms. Wysle thought that Thomas was ignoring her, but then the scratching sound resumed and he said, "Drawing." He sounded calm, as if he were sitting at home in his living room. "You really should let me out now, Ms. Wysle," he said. "You're going to get in trouble."

A chill ran up Ms. Wysle's arms. She hugged herself and let her anger push the trickle of fear aside.

"You have to learn how to behave, Thomas."

Scritch-scratch.

"So do you," Thomas said.

—

Ms. Wysle closed her daybook. The clock read four-thirty. Thomas had been in the cloakroom for an hour. Perhaps now he would be ready to apologize.

She got to her feet. That momentary bit of fear she'd felt earlier was gone. She was grinning, now, quite pleased with herself. She approached the door, reaching for the handle.

On the other side of the door, she could hear the faint sound of singing.

"Tonight is the night that dead leaves fly, chasing witches across the sky."

Shane Nelson

Ms. Wysle's brow came together in a tight V.

"Tonight is the night we see goblins and ghosts, demons and devils and all of their hosts."

The chill came back, raising gooseflesh on Ms. Wysle's arms.

"Good girls and boys do what they can, the rest is afeared of the Licorice Man."

"Thomas?"

The faint *scritch-scratch* stopped, as did the singing. She heard the shuffle of footsteps. Then, without warning, something struck the opposite side of the door with a heavy *thud*. Ms. Wysle jumped.

Thomas laughed. "Trick or treat!"

Ms. Wysle's face turned a deep red. With one hand pressed to her chest, she said, "That's it!"

She pulled open the door. The darkness waiting on the other side was thick and inky, almost alive. Ms. Wysle found the light switch and flipped it. The lights came on and she saw Thomas standing nearby, his back against the wall.

"All right, young man," Ms. Wysle said. "I've had it up to here with…"

The words trailed out of her mouth as her gaze fell on the wall behind Thomas.

While she had been outside, Thomas had been here in the darkness, drawing. He'd sketched an elongated stick figure on the wall, almost five feet tall. At first glance it appeared to be a misshapen thing, but as Ms. Wysle took a step closer she saw that it had shape and form. It had spider-like legs and long, tapering arms that ended in hooked claws. Its head was oval shaped and its eyes…

Eyes?

Yes, it had eyes. Though… how did Thomas manage to draw something like this in the dark? The image looked lifelike, stooped, shoulders hunched. It seemed almost three-dimensional on the wall.

Thomas was smiling, the stub of a pencil clutched in his hand. "I told you that you were going to be in trouble."

There was a slow, thick tearing sound, like something frozen being peeled off the ground. Ms. Wysle watched the drawing unfold itself from upon the wall. First one leg, then the other. Feet, long and three-toed, scraped the floor. There was another rending sound and one of the thing's arms reached out, trailing black, inky dust.

"Oh my God," Ms. Wysle whispered. "Thomas, what have you done? What is this?"

Thomas continued to smile as his creation pulled itself from the wall. It shrugged its shoulders and let loose a throaty growl. Muscles rippled as the pencil-sketch took on shape and substance. Its glassy black eyes, like polished onyx, blinked.

"This is the Licorice Man," Thomas said.

Ms. Wysle felt a scream rising in her chest as the black, misshapen thing turned toward her. A pair of elongated holes in its face flared. *It's smelling me*, she thought.

Thomas continued to smile. "You've been bad."

Ms. Wysle half-turned, uncertain where to go. Before she could move, Thomas darted past her. He slipped through the doorway and spun around, putting both hands against the door.

"Happy Halloween, Ms. Wysle," Thomas said.

He turned off the light and slammed the door.

—

Behind the cloakroom door, Ms. Wysle's gasps turned to whimpers. Then she fell silent and the only thing that Thomas heard

Shane Nelson

were wet tearing sounds. Something splashed against the door. Thomas sat in Ms. Wysle's chair and hummed under his breath.

"*Tonight is the night that dead leaves fly, chasing witches across the sky. Tonight is the night we see goblins and ghosts, demons and devils and all of their hosts. Good girls and boys do what they can, the rest is afeared of the Licorice Man.*"

Behind the door, the crunching sounds began.

"He eats everything, Ms. Wysle," Thomas said. "Hair, skin, teeth, even bones. He won't leave *anything* behind."

Finally there was nothing but silence in the cloakroom. Thomas opened the door and turned on the light. The room was undisturbed. The Licorice Man had eaten everything, from Ms. Wysle's hair to her shoes. There were only two things left in the room.

The stub of Thomas's pencil and a single sheet of paper. Thomas picked up the paper and looked at it.

It showed a dark, slouching figure standing inside a small room, grinning. Blood ran between its long, needle-like teeth. It held a jack-o'-lantern in one hand.

Thomas turned off the light and closed the door. In the top drawer on Ms. Wysle's desk he found two thumbtacks. Holding them in one hand, he grabbed his backpack and stepped out into the hallway.

He set his backpack down and stood in front of the bulletin board. It was decorated with the drawings they had done the day before. Bright, happy images of Christmas. Colorful pictures of Easter eggs. A Thanksgiving turkey.

Thomas found a blank spot and tacked the picture of the Licorice Man into place.

"There," he said. "Done."

Then he picked up his backpack and hurried down the hall.

THE HOUR IN BETWEEN

by Adam-Troy Castro

Oscar crept up on his sleeping wife and shattered her skull with five blows from a claw hammer.

The years might have robbed much of the strength from his legs and obliged him to do most of his walking these days with a cane, but his right arm was still almost as powerful as it had ever been. The first thundering impact struck Deanna with a crunch he could feel at the base of his spine.

There was still value in being sure, and so he raised the hammer again and brought it down a second time, burying much of its head in everything she had been: the toddler who had chased butterflies, the bride who had beamed in her wedding photos, the teacher who had taught English Comp for twenty years, the mother of one failed daughter and one merely defeated son, and finally the old woman who in her last years had precious little to say to her husband beyond businesslike reminders of whatever needed to be done around the house. He did not want her to linger, so he struck her the third, fourth, and fifth times, none of these three blows as accurate or as effective as the first two, but devastating enough between them to put out Deanna's right eye, and flatten her nose, and turn the crater he had made into a larger and wetter obscenity.

This, he understood once the deed was done, was the moment that would forever come to define him. Very soon, he would only be the man who, at the end, bludgeoned his sleeping wife before then joining her in death. It was only Deanna who'd be remembered in her fullness, Deanna whose passage through her last seconds would not become the image that defined her forever, but would instead be the sad footnote to a life well-lived.

As he'd always expected, nausea struck.

The room had been dim enough to protect Oscar from seeing everything his hammer did, and was now light enough to ensure a quick retreat to the master bath. Oscar hurried around the queen-sized bed, past the bookcase and bureau, and into the room he thought he needed.

For a second or two he thought he would not make it, but by the time he was ready to kneel by the toilet, the spasm had faded. The water in the bowl could remain unsullied.

He stopped at the sink to scrub his bloody hands and he almost got sick again when he flipped on the light. The face in the mirror was covered with a fine spray of red freckles, larger wet spots that looked like open wounds, and, sticking to the side of his face like postage, one shard of something that could only be chipped bone.

Washing his face was pointless. It would only get bloody again later, when he shot himself. But there were too many things still left to do, and the thought of continuing to do them while pieces of Deanna dried on his skin seemed beyond obscene. So, he turned on the water and grabbed the hand soap, working up a powerful pink lather in water just hot enough to burn. Afterward he used one of the hand-towels to clean the bloody hand print at the light switch, and another to clean the floor and counter of any blood that had dripped off him in the length of time it had taken him to surrender to this last, pointless vanity. His pajama top, drenched with Deanna's blood, went in the basket. So did the soap, though he'd washed it clean too. This was pure consideration for his son, Richard. He didn't know what happened to basic toiletries when a house had to be cleaned up after a murder-suicide, but the thought of Richard, or some other member of his family, innocently washing up with the same bar that had soaked up Deanna's blood, struck Oscar as almost as loathsome as the killing itself. So, he spared everybody that, at least.

A light moan escaped him when he turned on the bedroom lights and faced the aftermath of his crime. He'd already prepared himself to find Deanna's head reduced to an imploded bowl, and yes, that was pretty much as awful as expected. But he hadn't figured on all the blood he'd flung against the walls and ceiling with every upswing. The carved headboard was a spotty, dripping abstract. Her bedside lamp dripped pieces of her. The ceiling was a constellation of random red stars. The room where Oscar and his wife had slept for the last eight years, since the rising cost of retirement living had forced the two of them to sell the house he had never stopped considering their real home, had been marked in places he had never thought the murder could reach. There was even some marking the spines of the complete Dickens arrayed side by side on a shelf so far away from the bed that he could only marvel at how far blood could fly.

He hadn't expected the rising stench. Over and above the copper tang of blood were the more acrid smells of urine and feces, the last salvo of the final argument Deanna would ever have with him.

Oscar couldn't sit on her side of the bed. He did rest for a moment on his. If he had not had a few things still left to do he might have gotten the revolver and shot himself right then. But the moment seemed to require more in the way of last words, perhaps an apology or epitaph. He could not come up with one. What rushed to fill that empty space, in the absence of any legitimate eloquence, was a pair of before and after snapshots, one from the beginning of their marriage, and one of its last night: in the first snapshot, a soft-focus close-up of the early post-honeymoon days when he and Deanna had made sweet love more often than not; the second snapshot the final exchange of every evening for more nights than he wanted to name, including this night's, Deanna waiting until he was safely under the covers to ask him whether he'd made sure the front door was locked, and not feeling fully safe until he got up to double-check.

That had become every night's last conversation, in this house. It had been their final conversation, period. *Did you lock the front door?* Yes. *Can you check?* Okay. There had never been any point in saying that he had already made sure before coming to bed. It was not real for her, not safe, until he got back up and trudged to the front door and rattled the knob. Yes, he would say, coming back, I checked. Unspoken in the exchange was con-firmation that all dangers were now left outside; a sick joke, he thought now, given that she eventually lost her life to a husband who had always shared the fortress with her. Nor was that the only thing left unspoken. *Did you lock the front door?* Yes. *Can you check?* Yes. *Do you love me?* Unmentioned, for so long that he could not remember the last time either one of them had uttered the words. Now she was gone and here he sat trying to come up with something else he could say, something that could possibly make a difference to a cooling sack of flesh that could neither accept, nor reject, his excuses.

No, there was no point in saying anything, now. There would be epitaphs later, from people who had the right to say something. Any words from him would be an abomination.

He returned to the bathroom, moistened a washcloth, and returned to her side just long enough to retrieve the favorite photograph which sat framed on her nightstand. Deanna had been the one who insisted on keeping this photograph, one of the only ones they still had of all four family members together. He had caught her sitting at the edge of the bed holding it from time to time, and had known it was not the younger version of herself she was looking at, not the younger version of her husband or the younger, happier version of Richard. She was lost in the image of Erin, captured in an instant long passed that Oscar had always known said nothing at all relevant about his only daughter.

The frame he didn't even bother to try cleaning. It was an overwrought silver thing, sculpted with ivy and French curves and so ornate in its determination to honor whatever image it surrounded that some of the blood that had descended into its fissures would be next to impossible to remove from there. But for Deanna, and for Richard, who might be taking this photo home afterward, Oscar could spare the few seconds it would take to wipe the glass. He used the washcloth to scrub at the blood spots, first thinning them and then clearing them away, until a day thirty years past was once again clear.

The photo captured four people standing in sunlight, against the blurred, but colorful outlines of an amusement park merry-go-round. The parents stood in back: Oscar, wearing black glasses and slight moustache of a type that the verdict of time had decided ugly. Deanna stood next to him, tilting her head, her slight overbite adorable in the way it had always been, back then. Their grins were forced, as both had been fighting killer tension headaches. Richard and Erin stood before them, smaller versions of their parents. Fourteen-year-old Richard's smile guarded in the way that it would somehow always turn out to be guarded, well into his years as a man who could never free himself from the awareness that life could plunge him down a trap door at any moment. And Erin? Erin. Captured in a rare moment between screeching tantrums, between refusals to eat, between cutting herself and shoplifting and arrests for prostitution, before an adulthood that manifested as disappearing without word for years at a time, Erin here appeared as the platonic version of herself, her eyes bright, her smile uncomplicated, her warmth for the complete stranger the family had drafted as photographer so undiluted by her well of rage that it was possible, just from the image, to fall in love with her. Oscar would have liked to know that girl. He would have given an arm for a way to show her to the Erin he'd been obliged to raise, the Erin who might not still be alive for all he knew, and say, this, honey, this girl, this one here, that's who you were meant to be, and who you *should* have been.

The photo was one of those random moments of stopped time that tell the wrong story, that lie in the way that the wrong kind of grin can sometimes make the most exceptional paragon of humanity look, in that instant, like a creature depraved and evil. The actual day had been a nightmare. Nothing had made

Erin happy. The rides were stupid. The food was disgusting. Her parents were awful. Her brother was gross. She didn't want to be there. For half an hour, no more, the sun had seemed to come out and she'd seemed willing to forget the bottomless loathing she had for them, for her brother, for herself, and for life, really. She had said she'd try to have a good time, and held on to that promise long enough for the photo to be taken. But only half an hour later she'd be a storm of resentment again.

There were precious few other photographs of Erin. She'd destroyed many of them in her early teens, retaliating against her parents for one punishment or another; and had after fifteen become such an impossible terror, a nightmare of uncontrollable anger and sudden violence that the impulse to commemorate the moment had somehow never come up. A lone fleeting photo of Erin at sixteen, sticking her tongue out at the camera, trying to evade the lens and thus reducing herself to a blur, was the most recent image Oscar and Jeanne had; there were none of her as an adult, as she would never allow any to be taken during any of her rare subsequent appearances. Oscar had stored away as many of the remaining pictures as he could. He didn't destroy them and had no problem with them continuing to lie stacked in boxes he never opened or in albums he never cracked, but for the most part didn't want them hanging in plain sight, ambushing him at odd moments like evidence brandished by some angry prosecutor.

Deanna had insisted only on continuing to treasure this one. He had no idea why. But looking at the picture, really looking at it, Oscar was struck only by two things: one, that despite everything, Erin had been a very pretty girl, and two, that if she was in fact alive, it might be a very long time before word ever got to her about what had become of her parents. She might never find out. Or she might find out right away and storm into the funeral, to make it the same screeching atrocity she had made of everything else.

Either way, it was outside his power, and none of his business. That was the thing about death. It drew a curtain, made everything outside your own years a sequel that you would never be permitted to attend.

He stored the cleaned photograph in a drawer, protecting it from the spatter yet to come.

Tracking blood through the house but forcing himself to the knowledge that it really didn't matter much at this point, he went to the kitchen and poured himself a tall glass of ice water, from the dispenser on the refrigerator door. He drank that in a gulp and filled a second glass, to be nursed while he parked himself at the breakfast nook and peered out a window that, at this time of night, facing the woods the way it did, shielded from starlight the way it was, might as well have been painted black. It was a view he knew well, because he'd slept only fitfully in his old age and had made many post-midnight trips to this table and that view, finding in its very impenetrability an eloquence that spoke to him in ways that a more conventional landscape never could. Tonight, the view seemed even more illustrative. Nothingness. It was cleansed of everything that he would no longer see again: the glitter of sunlight on rippled water, birds cocking their heads at nearby sounds, leaves animated by errant breezes, clouds that looked like dogs, rainfall making ripples in tiny puddles, motionless frogs deciding for reasons of their own that it was time to head somewhere else.

Hell, forget the things he would never see again. The list of things he'd now done for the last time was even longer, and more primal. He'd never take another shower. He'd never read another book. He'd never issue another apology. He'd never eat another apple, never smell another flower. He'd never see another running child, never receive another kiss on the cheek, never squint at a bright light reflecting off another mirrored surface. He'd never encounter another appalling headline and would certainly never hear the words deficit, bipartisanship, gerrymandering, socialist, reactionary or global warming ever again.

The total number of steps he still had left to walk, once he rose from this table, were certainly less than one hundred and likely less than fifty.

Now, that was an interesting statistic. He felt some minor curiosity over the exact figure. He could count those final steps, if it mattered, crawl into bed for the last time aware at the end that his last mile had consisted of precisely thirty-two paces, or something like that. But no; such idle interests would serve him not at all, and were also therefore best forgotten.

His son, though.

His son remained.

Oscar returned to the refrigerator, filled his glass, and once again sat down at the breakfast nook, which was now forever just a nook because he'd eaten his last breakfast.

He had spent a lot of time, over the last few months of increasing resolve, debating just what kind of message he should leave for Richard. He had thought about writing a note, thinking about how a few words would never be enough and how pages on end would be far too much. He had put aside the idea of an apology and given up on ever providing a list specifying all the things that his final brutal act was not. *No, neither one of us was sick. No, I was not depressed. No, I did not act in anger. No, I did not hate her. No, life had not become too hard. No, I did not crave death; I just looked at the time that remained and saw that we were old and knew that every day still remaining to us it would less and less resemble anything worth living.*

Had Oscar been inclined to explain himself, he would have written something he'd learned early on: that life is a series of thefts, some small, some large, some gifts yanked away in moments of horrible trauma but most ferreted away in secret while you aren't paying attention. He would have written: our childhood sense of play goes away. The sense that everything's going to be all right goes away. The warm glow of youth goes away. Freedom from responsibility goes away, passion goes away, illusions go away, health goes away, potency goes away, the sense that life can still surprise you goes away, and so on, until you finally reach the point where you're left with nothing to do and four walls you know by heart.

He knew he didn't need to write this down because Richard already knew it. For as far back as Oscar could remember, Richard had faced life with a kind of resigned dread that stayed with him even as he did all the expected things, married and fathered children and been what other people would call a success, without ever shaking the melancholy that clung to him wherever he went. His joys had always been fleeting, his smiles those of a man shaking off an open wound. Oscar had never found his son really celebrating anything, not his graduations from high school and college, not his marriage to Delia, not his success in small business, and not even the coming of his own two children, without keeping some stored sadness in reserve. He was the one you spotted at family gatherings, in moments when he happened to be away from others, dropping his false face and revealing the trapped gaze of a trained animal, performing the expected tricks of adulthood without ever taking any special satisfaction in them.

Adam-Troy Castro

He was the one, sipping beer on the patio while he and his father watched the grandchildren bounce a ridiculous inflatable ball around, who had suddenly said, "They don't have a clue, do they? They too still think it's going to be fun."

Oscar had said, "You don't know. It might be."

Richard had shaken his head. "I don't remember the last time I had fun. I don't even remember the last time I wanted to have fun. I'm just acting out of habit. And part of me can't wait for it to be over."

Oscar remembered what it had been like being the father who wished he had known some wise and knowing thing to say to that. He hadn't any. He'd wound up commiserating. In not so many words, but in laments that had lasted much of the afternoon: *I agree, son. I wish it was over, too.* The two had wound up sitting in silence warmed not at all by the nearby laughter of children, knowing each other better than they had ever wanted to, the chief connection between them that of men who had forgotten what their lives had ever been for. Richard didn't need a note. Richard would be living through enough of a nightmare over the next few days, and beyond, but he didn't need a note. He wouldn't take what his father had done as an enigma. He'd see it as grim confirmation: just more of life's true shape, revealing itself as its false fronts failed.

Richard only needed to be alerted so he could do what he'd always done, and just get on with it.

The breakfast nook possessed the family's last corded phone, an antique now, not quite ancient enough to be rotary but certainly a relic of the days when push-button was still a new thing. A laminated list of frequently-dialed numbers sat upright on a wire stand that had once been used to display the table number at a relative's wedding. Oscar looked under the line for RICHARD (HOME) and the line for RICHARD (CELL) for the only line he could use tonight, RICHARD (WORK).

He was prepared to hang up in a hurry in the highly unlikely event that a human being was in the office to answer the call at this time of night, but after four rings Richard's recorded message replied, identifying the firm and inviting Oscar to leave a message.

Despite all of his inner rehearsal, Oscar found himself wholly unprepared to speak. "Um."

This was awful, communicating a hesitancy he didn't feel.

"Richard, this is me. Dad. I'm, um, calling a little bit after One AM. I…"

This really was terrible. He hadn't demanded eloquence from himself, but he had promised to deliver a sharp blow, instead of a parade of false taps.

"I'm sorry to leave this message on your office phone, but I didn't want to wake you with it. I'd rather you just get it when you make it into the office, in the morning."

He swallowed.

"I always felt terrible that I wasn't a better father to you and your sister. I did my best. I know it wasn't enough. You're better at it than I was. But I tried. I love you. I…"

Now his voice had almost broken, the image of Deanna's ruined face was rising in him like a cancer, and he found himself in serious danger of bequeathing his only son a message that spent too much time filling him with useless dread.

"I just killed your mother."

There. The rest would be easier, now.

"She didn't suffer. It was very quick. I made sure of that. I did it with love, whatever that means. I did it because I didn't think there was anything left for us. In a few minutes I'm going to join her. It's for the best." He almost hung up.

"I know you're going to be very angry with me but I want you to do what I say this one last time. You need to call the police and meet them at the house, but please, whatever you do, don't go inside yourself, not until we've been taken away. Your mother or I would never want you to see us like this. Please follow my wishes on that."

A last thought occurred to him. "If you see your sister again, don't let her think it was her fault. This has nothing to do with her. I'm serious. It has nothing to do with her, or with you. It was just that…the time had come. That's all."

He hesitated one last time, putting off the inevitable, aware that the two words to follow would be the last two words there would ever be.

Then he said, "Goodbye, son."

He hung up the phone, surprised that his overwhelming emotion now was not sadness, but relief. The most difficult part was done, with perhaps a few too many missteps and false starts, but with a level of rational calm that would help Richard hold on to his own in the difficult hours ahead.

The parade of lasts continued. That had been his last phone call and his last message to his son. There were any number of other last things he could do now, like perhaps straighten up a bit before pulling the trigger on himself, but for all he knew his son's office had night-time cleaning staff, not some recent immigrant legal or otherwise who couldn't understand enough English to comprehend the meaning of the alien words coming from the speaker, but someone with a command of the language who could take immediate steps to make sure the police got involved now and not hours from now. He had a deadline now. He needed to do whatever else needed to be done quickly.

He brought his glass to the sink (his last time doing that), and left the kitchen (his last time doing that), stopping at the thermostat to do the police a favor by turning the air conditioning up as high as it could possibly go (his last time, ever, fiddling with that little dial).

Returning to the bedroom, he walked right past the terrible carnage on the bed and into the master bathroom, where for the very last time in his life he stopped to pee, sparing his imminent corpse the least of its upcoming releases.

He flushed, put the seat down, and lowered the cover on top of it, aware that this was the last time he would perform any of these simple acts.

Out of custom, he washed his hands again, and forever.

He turned off the bathroom lights and got into bed beside his wife, discovering as he did that he had counted his remaining steps after all. Thirty-seven. That might not have been enough to get out to the mailbox and back. But he had taken the last of those while alive, and now he pulled the blanket up over himself for the last time.

He opened his bedside drawer and removed his revolver.

It was all too easy to keep fueling his obsession over the paucity of time he had left. What was it now? Certainly less time than it would take to listen to even the longest favorite song, possibly less time than it took to sit through the average commercial on television. How many breaths still remained? Ten? Five?

He could lose himself in counting, slicing the time in smaller and smaller increments until even the seconds had no more meaning than the last few years.

Adam-Troy Castro

The only remaining decision for Oscar, as he clamped his teeth around the barrel, was whether to fire at the roof of his mouth or at the back of his throat. He had read arguments in favor of both methods, differing on which one was less likely to leave him a hopeless vegetable or, worse, an intact mind trapped by misadventure in a body that couldn't see or hear or move. The consensus, he'd found, was that neither method offered absolute certainty of success. Freak trajectories happen. Sometimes people survived as warm meat, befouling their sheets years after a just God would have had them achieve ambient room temperature. From what Oscar understood, a controlled trajectory toward the back of the mouth offered the closest possible thing to a guarantee, though if he beat the odds and became something that had to be wired up to machines, he sure had no idea who he could see to invoke that guarantee for refund.

Doing the job while lying down made the shot he wanted more difficult than he'd expected, so he pulled himself up and scooted up against the headboard, using it as backrest.

The barrel was colder in his mouth than he'd imagined.

How much time left now? Twenty seconds? Ten?

He considered delaying long enough to say something pithy to Deanna, something that would communicate to the air if not to her spirit that he'd done what he'd done in full memory of how much he'd once loved her.

No.

His only remaining question was whether he would hear the shot.

As it happened, he did not.

He had the fleeting sensation of noise and light, but not enough time for his brain to analyze it and identify the only thing it could signify.

He was not aware of his bowels letting go, his heart stopping, the arm that held the revolver falling to one side and landing beside him, as if what he held was not a weapon but a novel that had put him to sleep. Guilt, memory, wonder, thought, sensation, and morality all became parts of his past. Right or wrong, it was over.

The haze swirled. All was darkness.

Then Deanna's corpse, speaking in a voice wet and polluted by fragments of itself, asked him, "Did you lock the front door?"

Oscar's corpse pursed its lips, bloodying them further, answering with the aggrieved reluctance of a thing that would rather remain asleep. "Yes."

"Can you check?"

His corpse sighed. "Yes."

It lifted a flap of blanket and trudged from the room, leaving shiny pieces of itself behind. It was not capable of emotion or conscious thought, and indulged in none on the way, but any witness observing its demeanor as it made its way to the front of the house and tested the knob would have found the implied attitude easy to read: a sense of the formalities being observed, and of the rituals being respected.

The errand took less than a minute.

Then what was left of the man followed its greasy trail back to bed, pulled the covers up over itself, and moved no more.

Always and Forever

by Greg Kishbaugh

*C*aleb's Journal. September

    Amy is hungry. So terribly, terribly hungry.

    I try to console her but she lashes out at me.

Naked teeth and blind aggression.

    I have not been outside the house for days, too dangerous. But I cannot wait much longer. She has never gone this long without being fed.

    I don't know what will happen to her.

    I just know that I cannot lose her again.

—

Caleb parts the curtains with his fingers, ever so slightly, *not too much*, and peers out into the midnight darkness.

    The streets are quiet. Yet he can *feel* them out in the gentle cushion of the night. Waiting for him.

    But he cannot hide behind these dim walls forever.

Amy needs fresh blood. Fresh meat.

And the only way she is going to get it is if Caleb journeys out into that lonely stretch of midnight and gets it for her himself.

Caleb turns the doorknob—slowly, *quietly*—and steps outside.

Caleb's Journal. September

It's not so much the way she gnashes her teeth. Or the black spittle foaming from her mouth. That's not why I want her to eat so badly.

It's that I miss her so terribly. I miss her touch.

And the only way we can be together again is if she has a full stomach.

That's the only way to calm the fury raging inside her.

That's the key to our happiness.

Every window in every home is a black soulless eye, staring back at Caleb, reminding him, whispering in silver tones, *you are alone.*

He can hear the graveyard muttering of Scabbers in the distance. Moaning. Searching for food.

Shuffling from abandoned house to abandoned house.

He moves deliberately, every step a conscious effort. He darts from tree to tree. A creature of the night every bit as much as the Scabbers.

A wind rises up, icy and unforgiving. It rattles the tops of the trees, sets them swaying, reminding Caleb of long-ago days, playing on these very same streets, many years before every one he had ever loved was dead.

Or worse.

The green suburban lushness falls away behind Caleb as he turns toward Main Street. It was once home to the bright lights of the Fountain Shop and the Glass Onion restaurant. Families gathered here, under the warmth of the summer moon, eating, laughing, children running wild into the soft night.

Now it is silent. Dark. A relic from a different age.

At the end of Main Street, he can hear the gentle hum of voices—human voices—coming from the general store. The store's shelves have been picked clean for months now, every single edible item long since carried away by scavengers and raiders, but the destitute and hungry still show up here, night after night, in the hopes that some crumb or morsel has been left behind, unseen, just waiting to be discovered.

Caleb approaches quietly, hugging the shadows of the storefronts along the way, pausing behind one of the Gothic arches at the entrance of the small post office to listen. He needs to know how many he is about to face. Anything more than three and he will be on his way. Just too much risk.

Caleb's heart trips in his chest, hammers arrhythmically. He knows the dangers of surprising survivors while they are foraging. If they mistakenly took him for a Scabber, they would most certainly shoot first and ask questions later.

Caleb is surprised when, moments later, a lone figure exits the store. Just another empty shell of a man left cratered by the world he knew falling down around his ears. Nothing left to do but mutter to himself.

"Gets more frustrating every day," Caleb says.

The man recoils, almost comically, backpedaling so quickly he nearly falls onto his tailbone. "What the hell…? I've got nothing… nothing you need or want…"

Caleb raises his hands over his head, a clear and incontrovertible sign of submission, and steps from behind the stone column. "Don't worry, friend. Just a forager like you. Didn't mean to startle you."

Caleb can now see the deadly wink of metal from the old single shot revolver the man has pulled from his coat. The man's hands are shaking; Caleb can hear the revolver's cylinder rattling against the barrel, tick, tick, tick, like fingernails tapping on a midnight-darkened window.

"You mind putting that thing away, friend. I'm unarmed."

"How do I know? Maybe it's hidden in your waistband. Or behind your back."

With one hand, Caleb lifts the tail of his shirt. "Nothing tucked away. Now, please. I'd hate to get a belly full of lead over a misunderstanding."

The man's eyes are rimmed red, a manic intensity that Caleb has seen many times before. Lack of food, lack of sleep, bone-breaking solitude. Sometimes it's too much for a man's mind to take.

"Please," Caleb urges.

The man lowers the gun, but keeps it firmly in his grip. A safety blanket he'd most likely clung to since his friends and family members began turning. Now, with no one left, he was left to wander the night, muttering to himself, hoping the waking nightmare he had found himself in would someday end.

"I've got food," Caleb says.

The man tilts his head, a dog that's heard a faraway whistle. "What did you say?"

"It's true. Back at my place. It's not much but you're welcome to get a little into your stomach. At least it'll get you through another day."

The man smiles, a wicked mad-dog grin. "And you're just gonna let me have some, huh?'

"Like I said, it's not much."

"If you have food, why you out here in the dead of night?"

"Batteries mostly. Generator died a while back but I've got some flashlights and a stack of books to get through. The thing about the end of the world is it lets you get caught up on your reading."

The man does not move. His face is frozen in a rictus of disbelief.

"I understand if you don't trust me. No offense taken, friend. I'll just be on my way. Take our separate paths and I'll wish you all the best on your hunt."

Caleb lowers his hands and steps back, once, twice. And then walks out into the midnight street.

He is several paces away, fading into the darkness when he hears a weak voice behind him, trembling with fear and hunger.

"Wait."

The Sterno crackles beneath the plate of beans, the quiet flame flickering white and blue.

The man—Caleb still does not know his name; it isn't important—has fallen into a waking slumber, slouched onto the kitchen chair, the flame lulling him into a sense of unexpected tranquility.

"Jesus," the man says. "That smell. It's the most glorious thing…"

"Nothing like a home-cooked meal. Just give me one more second."

Caleb spoons the beans onto a plate with a tarnished fork and sets them down before the starving man. Strands of spittle, foamy white, form in the corner of the man's mouth. Caleb still holds the fork in his hand.

The man bends toward the plate, ready to consume the meal in quick, slurping bites. Caleb knows he must act quickly.

He can't let a perfectly good plate of beans go to waste on this man.

He brings the fork down in a swift, powerful arc. It slices through the man's hand, the tendons crunching under the weight, before lodging into the wooden table, anchoring him.

The man screams, his voice unraveling.

"What are you…why…why…"

Caleb reaches for the shovel he keeps in the corner of the kitchen, a weapon he's been forced to use a number of times against stumbling, lurching Scabbers. He raises the shovel over his head. He has to show restraint; he knows that. Amy likes her meals to still be alive.

The shovel glances off the side of the man's head, a meaty thud, the sound of a slab of steak slapped to the griddle.

The man's screaming stops instantly. He slides from the chair and collapses to the floor. Caleb checks his pulse.

Weak. But still present.

Good, he thinks, he still has a little time. After all, he wants to eat the beans while they are still hot.

—

Amy can smell the food.

The door to her room shakes as she throws herself against it from the other side. Over and over.

Greg Kishbaugh

"Amy, I'm coming my love. But you need to be quiet."

Caleb has dragged the man from the kitchen, down the long hallway, his back burning, arms growing weary.

Outside, he sees shuffling figures, as ephemeral as shadows, moving through the neighborhood. The white eye of the moon peers through an embankment of clouds and in its silver light Caleb can see the Scabbers, hordes of them, a black mass, moving along outside his window.

The man's screams must have brought them. And now Amy throwing herself against the door isn't doing him any favors, either.

He has to move quickly.

Besides, Amy's meal is starting to wake up.

—

The man grumbles, huffs, rubs his head.

Caleb thinks of clubbing him again but he wants to be certain that Amy has a fresh meal. Something warm that will stick to her ribs.

Caleb knows that once he opens this door, he has very little time to act. Amy will be waiting, hunger clawing at her like a sickness. And she'll tear to shreds anything close to her.

"What...are...what..." the man speaks around a mouthful of marbles. His pupils are dilated, black as dinner plates. He struggles to move, to pull away from Caleb's grip but his muscles remain flaccid and inattentive.

Caleb throws open the door.

Amy lunges, a wild dog released from its leash. She bares her teeth. Stringy, blood-infused spittle runs down her chin. She reaches out with skeletal hands, fingernails black and shattered.

Caleb grabs the man's arm and positions it between himself and Amy. She has no choice. Even if her feeble, disease-addled mind could still contemplate what it is to make a choice.

She grabs the man's arm and sinks her teeth into the thin highway of tendons on his wrist. She rips the meat away ravenously, blood coursing from the fresh wound in tiny rhythmic spurts.

The man wants to scream; Caleb can clearly see that. The man's mouth is moving, an anguished circle, open, closed, but he emits no sound. Shock. Caleb has seen it too often.

When a Scabber begins to rip away someone's flesh, that first bite just shuts them down. Their minds simply go dark.

"Sorry, friend," Caleb says as he rolls, shoves, pushes, kicks the man into the room with Amy. For a moment the man's right leg becomes entangled on the door jamb and Caleb's blood spikes with fear. The door has been open for too long as it is. He cannot risk Amy slipping out.

He picks up the shovel.

"I was hoping I wouldn't have to use this."

Caleb raises the shovel high overhead, arms outstretched. He is going to need a lot of power to slice through the tibia. That will be the toughest part. It might even take more than one swing. After all, once he's worked his way through the tibia there is still the fibula and calf muscle to contend with.

Caleb brings the shovel down. Hard.

The man, once again, finds his voice.

—

Caleb's Journal. September

The man does not scream for long. Amy, surely, has ripped out his throat. That's always where she begins when I bring her a treat.

Then she works her way to the arms and legs, stripping them bare.

It's been nearly an hour. The disquieting sounds of chewing from behind the door as Amy slurps down her meal have grown silent.

That means she is full. Sated.

I slowly open the door. Push it inward.

The man, what remains of him, is heaped in the corner. He has been picked clean, bones bare. A pink strand of his intestines is unspooled across the floor, glistening.

Amy is huddled beneath the boarded-up window, knees to chest, a fine sheen of blood and gore coating the front of the nightgown she's worn since the night she passed.

"Hi, baby," I say. "Feel better?"

I cross the room and kneel before her. Her eyes have retained their faraway pallor, as if she is staring at a pinpoint of light a million miles from home.

This is when she is at her best. Just after she's eaten. She's as pliable as a baby, belly full and content.

I gently brush the stringy curtain of hair from her face. She is degrading at such an alarming rate. Her skin is not only covered in the wet scabs associated with this terrible plague, but her skin has now begun to fall away in thin sheets like wallpaper in an abandoned house.

The flesh on her fingers is gone. Whether it has sloughed off or, in a fit of hunger, she chewed it away, I do not know.

Blood has pooled in the corner of her eyes, and I can see several of her teeth, brown and cracked, have come dislodged from tonight's meal.

"Shhh…" I comfort her. "They will find a cure. We have to

believe. Have faith. The dawn is coming, sweet girl. I promise. We just have to remember that, despite everything, we still have each other. Always and forever. No disease can take that away. I still have as much love for you in my heart as the day we were married."

Amy grunts, coughs, and a small chunk of meat tumbles from her mouth. I brush it from her nightgown.

"Silly girl. Making a mess."

Everything I tell her is true. We just have to wait this out. Stay away from the other Scabbers that prowl through the night streets. As long as we have each other.

And now that Amy has eaten...

I unbutton the top button of the nightgown. Then the next.

"Love you always, Amy. Love you always."

I whisper this into her ear and I know she can hear me. I know she can understand.

I kiss her cheek, just above a line of scabs that throb with infection.

It's important that I show her how much I care. That, no matter what, we remain husband and wife.

Her nightgown is now open and I am ready for her.

And she, my beautiful wife, is ready for me.

Autophagy

by Ray Garton

Strange things have been coming out of my body lately.

I've been under a lot of stress, and that might have something to do with it. But who *hasn't* been under a lot of stress? In *this* economy? In *this* political climate? *Everybody's* stressed. Everything is falling apart and nobody knows how to deal with it. I haven't heard anyone else talking about strange things coming out of their bodies. But then, I haven't talked about it with anyone because it's...well, it's just so creepy. I'd like to tell someone, but it's so weird that I'm afraid I'll sound crazy. And that's what scares me the most—the possibility that I might be crazy.

Maybe I *am* crazy. I've spent a lot of time considering that lately. They say you're not crazy if you *think* you might be crazy. But a lot of the things They say are wrong.

I've been losing weight, too, and I haven't been trying. That's unusual for me. I gain it easily, lose it slowly and I've had a sedentary desk job for ten years. I don't have that job anymore, of course, but do I take advantage of my new free time to exercise? Of course not.

I can't help wondering if it has something to do with the things that have been coming out of me. It's almost as if they're pieces of me. But how can that be when they immediately *run away*? I try hard not to think too much about that...about those things I've seen and heard.

I've come close to telling Carly about it a few times, but these days, it's hard to talk to her about anything, let alone something that bizarre and unbelievable. She's made comments about the noises in the walls, though, so I know I'm not the only one hearing them. She thinks they're mice.

I don't know what they are, but I know they're not mice.

Things have been uncomfortable between us for a while. Nothing's been the same since we found out that I couldn't get her pregnant. We'd tried for a few years before we found out it was me. Then she started getting chilly. I suggested we adopt, but she wasn't interested. She wanted to have a child of her own. I looked into in vitro fertilization and found that it was *way* out of our financial realm. That's illegal now, anyway, so it wouldn't be an option even if we *could* afford it. Carly and I drifted from the subject and never returned to it. And then we drifted from each other.

It hurt, but it didn't come as a great surprise because I always thought it was too good to be true. She's so beautiful and sociable and funny, so sexy and alive. I'm a geek, a computer nerd, a shy, withdrawn guy who was never sure what she saw in me. She brought me out of all that and changed me. In the years after we met, I lost most of my shyness and became a lot more outgoing. Until we found out why she wasn't getting pregnant and things changed. I've been sinking back into my old self since then.

We had no real interest in getting married. We didn't feel we needed a license to validate our relationship. But we wanted to have a baby, and that was right after having children out of wed-lock became illegal. We're still together because it's a *lot* harder and more expensive to get a divorce now than it used to be. But we're more like roommates than a married couple. And if I don't find a new job soon, things are going to get a lot more uncomfortable.

With premarital sex against the law and abortion a capital offense now, people are getting married all over the place. If I were smart, I'd quit trying to get another job in the IT field and learn how to be a wedding planner. That's where the *real* money is these days. Well, that and government jobs. But to get a government job, you virtually have to sell your soul, and I'm not that desperate yet.

Before I met Carly, I spent a lot of time feeling lonely. Lately, I've been feeling that way again. That's why I started seeing Amber.

———

After Carly caught a bus to work, I put on my helmet and rode my bike into the city to meet Amber in the park for lunch. Riding a bike through the city isn't very safe anymore and I don't do it as often as I used to, but gas is far too expensive to drive a car unless absolutely necessary.

I met Amber at my former job at Sterling Systems. She'd survived the first big wave of lay-offs, and she'd managed to survive the second, although she had to take a sharp cut in hours and pay. She was a geek, like me, but one of those devastatingly attractive and sexy geeks who has no awareness at all of that fact. Petite, almost pixie-ish, with red hair and big green eyes that squinted behind her glasses when she was thinking. Not a conventional beauty, but *so* striking. I think I had a crush the first time I laid eyes on her. And back then, things were good between Carly and me. One of the worst parts of losing my job was the possibility of losing touch with Amber.

We stayed connected online, but only as friends, I thought. It never occurred to me that she could feel anything more for me. But when I began to tell her that things had gone bad with Carly, she opened up about how she felt. It was a big surprise to me. But a pleasant one.

It was the first week of March, but it felt like the worst part of August. The day was hot and muggy and the sun burned relentlessly through a thin layer of clouds.

Soldiers and military vehicles have become more common on the streets since the threat of terrorism—we've been told—has increased. It's hard to tell the difference between the military and the police these days because they look a lot alike and are equally armed to the teeth. A couple of weeks ago, a bomb went off in a car parked in a subterranean garage beneath a shopping center and six people were killed, several more injured. A few weeks before that, an IED went off in an outdoor café and killed three, injured a dozen.

But the presence of all those uniforms and all that firepower wasn't very reassuring. On my way to the park, I saw two soldiers beating a man on the sidewalk. That usually happened to homeless people who've wandered beyond the boundaries of the tent cities. This man didn't look like a homeless person, but so many homeless people were decently dressed lately that it was hard to tell who was and who wasn't. We'd been told that the homeless are likely terrorists because they're desperate and will do anything for a little money, which made them vulnerable to the offers of Muslim terrorist agents living secretly among us. But the only people the homeless were likely to hurt were themselves. It had been reported that suicides had skyrocketed in the tent cities around the country.

I passed a lot of empty buildings with FOR LEASE signs in the windows and even more with signs advertising going-out-of-business sales, so there would be more empty buildings soon. There seemed to be more of them every time I left the house. The streets weren't as busy as they used to be with gas prices so high, and the thin traffic gave the city a strange atmosphere. Sometimes it looked like it was in the process of being evacuated, or as if everyone were fleeing of their own free will. The only signs of growth were in the tent cities.

It seemed like this had happened suddenly, but it hadn't. I remembered when we elected our first black president. It seemed like such a hopeful sign, as if we had finally progressed to a point only dreamed of not so long ago. People *wept* the day of his inauguration because it seemed we had reached some long fought for goal. So many thought it would heal some of the damage done by the previous administration, which had been so unpopular. But we all know how that worked out. The damage was only accelerated. Then we elected our first woman president, another apparent milestone, seemingly a sign of progress, growth and maturity. Many thought it would usher in a wave of positive changes for our ailing country. Oh, there were changes, all right. Big ones. But they only made things worse.

For decades, there had been growing evidence that no one in Washington, D.C., was working for the citizenry. But we were too busy with our video games and all the fun new gadgets on the market, too busy keeping up with the latest talent competition on TV or the latest scandalized politician or celebrity, or surfing porn, or whatever it is we do instead of paying attention to the world around us. And those who *were* paying attention were too busy fighting over whose political party had the biggest penis to see that *both* parties were taking us in the same direction. The two-party system proved to be an effective distraction. It became more and more obvious that not only were We the People not a high priority, we weren't even on the *list*. But it took us far too long to see that, and when we did, it was too late to do anything about it.

Those parties never stopped saying the same things they'd always said, but it became pretty obvious it was all scripted—like the phony "reality TV" shows we knew so much more about than the workings of our own government—and nobody really knew *who* was in charge. We just knew it wasn't us. And it hadn't been for a long time.

Everything was upside down, inside out. We seemed to be in the middle of some major construction—the country was being rebuilt, but into what, and by whom?

It was like watching a foreign-language film without subtitles and trying to keep up with events that didn't make any sense. Just thinking about it all made my head hurt, made my stomach sick. But it kept my mind off of those things that were coming out of my body. As horrible as the country's situation was, it was much easier to think about than those things that dropped out of me and plopped into the toilet, then scurried out of the bowl and into the walls before I could get a good look at them.

To my right, I heard a woman screaming and I slowed down because the sound was rapidly getting louder. She ran into the road with a police officer close behind. He grabbed her long hair and jerked her to a stop, then raised his baton and hit the backs of her knees with it. She started to go down, but he broke her fall by dragging her out of the road by her hair and back to the sidewalk. She screamed in pain as I rode on.

The only difference between the police officers and the soldiers was the uniform. I didn't know whose side they're on, only that it wasn't ours.

Amber was waiting for me in our usual spot—the bench under the huge old oak tree by the duck pond—with our lunch in a brown paper bag. Behind the bench, I leaned my bike against the tree, wiped sweat from my brow with the back of my hand, then walked around to join her. She was crying.

"What's wrong?" I said as I sat down beside her.

She quickly tried to compose herself, but couldn't stop the tears or the small hitching sobs.

"My brother's been arrested," she said. Her younger brother Rob was gay. "He's being sent to one of the therapy centers."

Therapy centers were places that "cured" homosexuality using reparative therapy, once denounced by every professional medical, psychiatric and scientific organization in the country but now fully recognized and endorsed—even *mandated*—by the United States government as an effective treatment for homosexuality. The centers were set up in abandoned military bases and state hospitals that had been closed down. There was little information to be found about them and they weren't covered by the media. Rumor had it that not everyone who went into the therapy centers came out. Those who did weren't the same.

I got a queasy feeling in my stomach, as if I were in an elevator that had suddenly and unexpectedly dropped. I knew how close Amber was to her brother.

"I've been looking forward to this lunch with you," she said, "but now...this. I feel like...like I'm coming apart. Like

I'm just breaking up into little pieces. And it's not even the worst thing."

"What else?"

She shook her head hard, sucking her lips between her teeth. "It's too...I can't...it sounds so crazy. You'll think I'm...I don't know...*sick*, or something."

I put my arm around her. Touching her made me queasy, too, but in a good way. We'd done nothing together yet, although we wanted to. Desperately. It just wasn't safe.

I said, "I won't, I promise. How crazy can it sound? I mean, look *around* you. *Everything's* crazy now. The standard for crazy has changed. I've got some crazy stuff going on in my life, too. Stuff I, you know...keep to myself. Because it sounds so...weird. I know what you mean. Please tell me."

She turned to me and moved so close, I could feel her breath on my face. "I just want to be with you right now. Naked, in a bed, where we can hold each other. My plan was to take you back to my apartment so we could be together and just *fuck* the consequences. You know? But...I don't know if *I* can go back to my apartment because...because of what's there."

"What's there, Amber?"

"If I tell you, you'll think I'm—"

"No, I *won't*." I felt a sense of urgency suddenly, as well as dread. I turned toward her, clutched her upper arms and shook her gently as I whispered, "You have to tell me. Now."

She struggled to get the words out. "Well, things...really strange things...have been...coming out of my body lately."

I was not alone after all. Everything Amber told me was a summary of what had been happening to me.

It had started a few weeks ago with a slightly painful bowel movement, immediately followed by flopping, splashing sounds in the toilet. When I stood, there was another splash, then the sound of something wet scurrying over the tile floor and out the bathroom door, which was cracked open a few inches. It didn't happen with every bowel movement and followed no pattern. I was awakened in the middle of the night a few times by the sensation of something moving inside my throat and mouth, just in time to feel it scurry over the covers, then hear it whispering over the carpet as it rushed out of the bedroom.

All of the same things had happened to Amber with one difference. She told me—averting her eyes with embarrassment—that while masturbating on her couch one night, her orgasm was accompanied by the sensation of something exiting her vagina, followed by the sound of soft, wet pattering over the hardwood floor of her small apartment.

"Now I hear them in the walls," she whispered, leaning close to me. "It's like they're...gathering. Waiting for something."

"For what?"

"I...I don't know. Something."

"You think they're going to *do* something?"

"Not yet."

"When?"

She shrugged. "Maybe when there's enough of them."

That was a chilling thought.

"I took the rest of the day off work. Come home with me. I don't want to go there alone, and I just want to be with you, that's all I want right now."

We put my bike in the back seat of her car and drove to her apartment. It was old, small, and cluttered but clean. She stopped in the living room, just inside the door, turned to me and whispered, "Listen."

We remained still for about ten seconds, listening to the silence, until—

Something rustled in the wall to my right.

Amber's large eyes looked all around the apartment before she whispered, "I hear them every now and then. Moving around in the walls."

"Me, too. Carly thinks we have mice. I was just relieved that *she* heard them, too. I thought I was...I don't know..."

"Losing your mind?"

I nodded.

"Yeah. I was afraid of that, too. Kiss me. Please."

I kissed her. It wasn't the first time we'd kissed, but it was the first time in privacy, without the need to be careful or rush. She pulled away suddenly and said, "Wait." We went to the tiny kitchen and she put the bag and her purse on the counter, removed her cell phone and took the batteries out. Then she went to the living room and unplugged the television and satellite box.

"Call me paranoid, I don't care," she said. "If the place is bugged and they catch us, we'll both go to prison. And it'll be worse for you because you're married."

I did the same with my cell phone and put it on an end table. Everyone took it for granted now that the government was listening, watching and tracking everyone, everywhere. She grabbed my hand and led me to the bedroom, then turned and kissed me as she began frantically unbuttoning my shirt.

"Wait, wait," I said. "I'm really sweaty from riding my bike in the heat. I'd feel a lot better if I could take a shower."

"Oh, sure, sure," she said, catching her breath. "Right through that door."

I smiled. "Would you like to join me?"

"That shower's too tiny for two people. You go ahead. I'm gonna clean up in here. Towels and wash cloths are on the shelves above the toilet."

It *was* an awfully tiny shower, claustrophobically small. The pipes rattled and groaned and it took a long time for the water to stop being brown, and then to warm up. I found a bottle of body wash, lathered up, then rinsed off.

Amber's towels were thick, heavy and luxurious. I suspected she'd had them for a long time; they would cost a fortune now. I scrubbed dry, then wondered if I should put my clothes back on or just enter the bedroom naked. It's the kind of thing that always tripped me up in relationships. Having had so little experience with them, I was always afraid I was committing some kind of breach of etiquette. I compromised by putting on my boxers and my shirt, which I left unbuttoned.

When I entered the bedroom, I heard a strange sound. It was soft. Wet. Amber was lying on the bed. At first glance, I thought she was covered by a thick, rumpled blanket under which she was moving slightly, rhythmically. With the quiet wet sound accompanying that movement, I thought for a brief, titillating moment that she had started without me. But none of that was true.

I stood there for what seemed a long time, blinking a lot, I think, my jaw slack. Only seconds passed, but it felt like it took a long stretch of minutes to make sense of what I was seeing.

There was no blanket. Amber's body was covered with small, grey, starfish-like creatures, each about the size of a toddler's hand. They glistened as they made little humping motions on their body, and each creature made a faint, whispery sucking sound. There were so many of them, though, that the sound was loud enough for me to hear as soon as I entered the room. Beneath the layer of small, moist creatures, Amber's body lay perfectly still.

They shifted and moved over her, changing places as they sucked, never still, never staying in one place for long. Their movements increased as I watched, as if they were searching for something. When I got a glimpse of two of Amber's exposed ribs, streaked with blood, I understood that they were consuming her so rapidly that they were moving around to look for more flesh to devour.

Had she screamed? Had she called for help? Shouted my name? I couldn't imagine her *not* crying out when the creatures came out of the walls to attack her. But above the rattle of the pipes and the constant hiss of the shower, I'd heard nothing.

My stomach seemed to push itself up my esophagus and into my throat as I watched the creatures slowly, one by one, remove themselves from Amber. The sucking sound gradually diminished as they moved to the bed and surrounded her in a pool of wet, glimmering grey. They left behind something that used to be Amber, blood-smeared bones that had been cleaned of every last bit of tissue. Some of them remained inside, in the abdominal cavity and under the ribcage, still sucking and humping, still feeding. But it wasn't long before they, too, began to leave the skeleton and join the others on the bed.

I felt a rush of panic as I realized I was standing there, mostly naked, exposed to those creatures. But the fear that they would attack me next passed quickly. They weren't interested in me. They were done. I somehow understood that their hunger had been for Amber alone. This feeding was what they had been waiting for in the walls...waiting for that moment when—

...*there's enough of them*, Amber had said.

There was no time to feel anything. I had to get out of there and take with me any sign that I had been there.

—

Outside in the heat, I immediately began to feel the itchy sting of perspiration forming on my neck and back. I got my bike from her car and began riding. I took side streets and alleys, avoiding main thoroughfares. As I rode, I had to keep wiping away the tears.

They had come out of Amber's body, just as they had mine, and secreted themselves in the walls, waiting until there was enough of them to accomplish their goal. And mine—whatever they were—waited for the same thing. We couldn't be the only ones, Amber and myself. There had to be others. Were the walls at home also hiding things that had come out of Carly's body? Things she hadn't told me about, just as I hadn't told her? Things that were waiting to do to her what had been done to Amber... and what would be done to me?

Maybe everyone had them. Maybe they were everywhere, hiding, waiting. And we had been so frightened by their arrival that we blocked them out, occupied ourselves with other things, because we just didn't want to face up to the truth that something that horrible was really going on.

I rode my bike aimlessly through the city for a while, but then decided to go home. There was no point in putting it off any longer.

SEXUAL EXPLORATION IS A CRIME

by Alan Peter Ryan

t was Jerry Crenshaw's first time in Brazil. It was his first time anywhere, really. He was thirty-four, had done well in college, and now made good money successfully running his own business, but he was not a well-travelled man, had never visited the great capitals of Europe, never bought a vacation package on a Caribbean island, never taken a skiing trip, never eaten a taco in a Mexican border town. Until that first trip to Brazil, he had never been out of the United States and that trip had come about purely by chance and with no great planning on Jerry's part.

When Jerry was twenty-three and just two years out of college, a drunk driver had killed his parents as they were coming home from his cousin's wedding on a Saturday evening. Jerry, following in his own car, had seen the accident. He was an only child and so, at a young age, he suddenly found himself in sole possession of a large house, a flourishing business, a good inheritance, and quite a lot of insurance money. His father had been as hard-working, as thrifty, and as methodical as he was unimaginative. He had started out in life working at a plant nursery, saved his money and later borrowed more and then opened a flower and plant shop. He built that up steadily and then opened a plant nursery like the one where he had worked. He developed that successfully and soon expanded it into a landscaping business. He knew little of the world, but he knew flowers and grasses and bushes and trees and planting and blooming seasons and the cycles of weather in the Midwest. For eight months of the year he worked long hours at the nursery and with landscaping clients and only grew a little restless in the winter months when business was slow. He had never taken a vacation and the most adventurous thing he had ever done was to name his business Beautiful Midwest.

Jerry was just like him. He worked hard and lived a quiet life. He had no passionate interests. He was not a reader. He liked pop music and some rock, but not hip hop or reggae, and he had only been to a concert once when he was in college. He had seen John Denver and really enjoyed the show and thought he might go to other concerts but never did. He liked movies but usually preferred to wait and watch them on DVD or television. He rarely went to a mall or multiplex. Action and suspense films were his favorites. He could never quite follow what was going on in ordinary dramas and romantic comedies. He preferred honest American foods. Occasionally, when he got together with a few college friends, someone would suggest foreign food—Chinese or Mexican or Italian—and Jerry would go along to be agreeable, but he would never think of eating such exotic food or going to such restaurants on his own. His gastronomic interests did not extend much beyond the menu at Denny's.

"Jerry," a date had said to him once, gently and affectionately but firmly, "you're dull." Jerry thought about that for a long time

Alan Peter Ryan

and he had to admit that she was right. He did not at all feel that his life was dull—after all, he was busy all the time, wasn't he?—but he could see that his tranquil and uneventful life was not interesting to other people.

And it was especially not interesting to young women. Jerry understood and accepted this but did not see what he could do about it. His life was his life. He also understood that he did not feel any urgent need to do something about it. By the time he reached his thirties, all his old school friends were either married or living with somebody or at least had girlfriends. Jerry would have liked to have a girlfriend too, but it was more a desire for company and companionship than a burning need for sex. He was not a virgin and he supposed—his experience was limited—that he enjoyed sex as much as any other guy. He just didn't have the constant, urgent awareness of sex that some of his friends seemed to have. The times he'd had sex—he could remember each of them—it had come about at least as much because of the girl's urging as his own. More, probably, it seemed, if he really thought about it.

But a frequent female companion and occasional sex just did not seem to be in the cards. From time to time he met someone he found attractive but dating was always a little awkward for him. The only subject he could really talk about for more than a minute or so was his business, but young women, whom he had always understood to be interested in flowers, seemed only minimally interested in the actual growing of them and even less in the nurture of grasses and decorative borders. He could see their eyes grow dark, their smiles grow stiff, and their attention wander. Yes, that one date had said it all when she told him he was dull.

But then one day, Jerry suddenly saw a glimmer of distant possibilities.

One day in early October, at the end of his busy season, he stopped by the house of a client. One of his landscaping crews had just finished a job there and Jerry wanted to be certain that the large garden and extensive lawns were all taken care of properly to survive the winter. Mrs. Douglas was at home and she introduced Jerry to her son Phil. While his mother answered a phone call, Phil walked around the garden with Jerry. It was a chilly day and Phil offered Jerry a cup of coffee. They were about the same age but Phil, Jerry saw at once, seemed very wise in the ways of the world, very knowledgeable, and very self-confident. It was obvious in the way he talked and moved. He had stopped by his parents' home because it was on the way to the airport. Phil had a large suitcase with him and he was flying to Brazil that evening. Jerry didn't know a great deal about Brazil, but he marveled at Phil's imminent adventure. He asked if Phil spoke Spanish and Phil smiled and said they spoke Portuguese in Brazil. Jerry was a little embarrassed. He supposed Phil was going there on business.

"Oh, no," said Phil. He was going to Brazil for the girls. "You're up to your balls in girls there," he said. "Up to your eyeballs, in fact," he added and laughed at what seemed to be a joke. "You never saw so many beautiful girls in all your life. They specialize in brunettes. They call them *morenas*, brown hair, brown eyes, coffee-colored skin. But they've got everything. Black or white and every color in between, all of them beautiful with incredible bodies. And they love to show them off. I go to Copacabana in Rio. You should see the beach. Unbelievable girls. And talented too, if you know what I mean," Phil said. "Easy to meet. *Really* easy to meet. And they love Americans.

An American guy there with a couple of dollars in his pocket can take his pick."

Jerry was fascinated. How many times have you been there? he asked Phil.

"I've been going for ten years," Phil told him, "usually twice a year. I go for three or four weeks each time."

"Do you have a girlfriend there?" Jerry asked.

"I always have a girlfriend there," Phil said. "Sometimes I call one from before or I just go to a bar or a club and look around. I always meet somebody the first night. Never fails."

Before Jerry could formulate another question, Phil started laughing. He was pouring more coffee for both of them.

"They have these signs at bars and luncheonettes," he said, "all the places where tourists hang out. I guess the city puts them up. They're in English and they say, 'Sexual Exploration Is a Crime.'" He laughed again.

"I don't get it," Jerry said. "What's sexual exploration?"

Phil explained. "Portuguese, of which I have picked up a little, doesn't have as many words as English, so one word often has several meanings. There's only one word in Portuguese for 'explore' and 'exploit,' so Brazilians can't tell the difference. When they put up the signs in English, what they meant is 'Sexual Exploitation,' but what the signs say is 'Sexual Exploration.' It's a big laugh among the guys who go there."

Phil took a little of his coffee and shook his head. "It's a wacky country," he said. "Those signs are a joke. You can't even tell down there who's exploiting who. See, they have these girls called *garotas de programa*. Program girls, but that doesn't mean anything in English. They just have boyfriends, you know, one after another, tourists, I mean. You meet one, she stays with you if you want, as long as you're there. Does everything you want, has dinner with you, goes to the movies, goes to the beach, whatever. You want to go away for a week, travel somewhere in Brazil, maybe in the mountains or to Club Med near Rio, she goes with you, if you want. She's your girlfriend. You want to buy souvenirs or clothes, she'll help you, whatever. Of course, it costs you some money. You have to feed her and maybe buy her some jewelry and clothes and help her out with some cash, you know—everybody's pretty poor down there—but basically, she's yours. And she won't go fooling with anybody else while you're there, either. She's your girlfriend."

Jerry's mind was busy. "Do they speak English?" he asked.

"Enough," Phil said with a grin. "Enough to tell you she needs a new dress or shoes or a pair of jeans or a new bikini and she wants you to help her pick it out. Or to tell you she needs a little money to help her sick mother buy food or pay the doctor. All the girls I know speak a little English, enough to get by, anyway. But you can do most of the talking. They're not like American girls. They're really good at listening. Believe me, you talk about anything you want and your girlfriend will be fascinated. Just feed her and buy her a few things and she'll treat you like a king. And when you head for the airport to come home, she'll cry a little and tell you to come back soon because she'll miss you. And she'll mean it." Phil shook his head again. "Those Brazilian girls," he said. "They just never quit."

After that day, Jerry continued as before with his uneventful life but he could not get that conversation about Rio de Janeiro and Copacabana and the Brazilian girls out of his head.

So, you had to spend money on a girlfriend. Well, you always had to spend money with women, right? It cost money just to go out and eat and do things. He had money and he was willing to spend it but American girls never found him interesting. Maybe Brazilian girls really were different. He could not get over the way Phil had talked. Those Brazilian girls, he had said. They just never quit.

Before the end of the following week, Jerry went to see a travel agent.

He had taken a look online, but he wasn't very skilled at the internet except for ordering plants and landscaping supplies. It was better to talk to somebody in person who could help him with the bewildering array of choices. The travel agent he visited was very helpful. When it turned out that Jerry didn't have a passport, the agent gave him the forms, helped him fill them out, and went ahead and booked a trip to Rio for him, three weeks in November which, he said, was glorious summer in Rio de Janeiro, far away from the ice and snow of the Midwest.

So, only a matter of weeks later, Jerry Crenshaw found himself putting his shorts and T-shirts in drawers in his very pleasant room at the Savoy Othon Hotel in Copacabana, Rio de Janeiro, just one block away from the famous beach. He went out for a walk. He was astonished at the beach and the ocean—it was, in fact, the first time he had even seen an ocean—and the three-mile curve of white sand and breaking waves was magnificent with the big sheer rock of Sugarloaf rising up at the end of it. And the girls on the beach! Never in his life had he seen such good-looking girls or so much female skin exposed without embarrassment. On his way back to the hotel, he stopped at an open-air luncheonette and successfully ordered a hamburger and a glass of orange juice. He had changed some dollars at the airport and he paid his bill correctly with Brazilian currency. He felt he was turning into quite the world traveler, discovering new and unknown resources within himself. Back at the hotel, he asked the English-speaking desk clerk where there was a good bar or disco. The clerk told him there was a good place, very big, just two blocks away, facing the beach. "All the Americans go there," he said. "It's best after eleven o'clock."

Jerry went up to his room. He lay down on the bed to rest up a little for the evening ahead and to think with pleasure about the new self-confidence he was feeling. The problem of finding a place to eat dinner hardly daunted him at all now. If he could get a hamburger at a luncheonette, he could get dinner at a restaurant. And after dinner he would head off to the disco.

He smiled. Somewhere out there, he felt sure, there was a girlfriend just waiting to meet him. He wondered what she would look like.

—

She was gorgeous. She had long thick dark brown hair, brushed to a smooth and lustrous shine. Her eyes were a warm, welcoming, wonderful brown too, very slightly almond-shaped. Her eyebrows were perfectly lined, her skin smooth and glowing and the color of lightly toasted bread. Her lips were full, her teeth as white as pearls, and her smile as big as all outdoors. She was a living cliché of standardized popular modern beauty. Her figure took Jerry's breath away. Her short skirt revealed long slender legs. While her push-up bra pushed up, her top plunged downward, revealing a dizzyingly deep crevice. Her fingernails and toenails were perfectly manicured and painted. But, to Jerry Crenshaw's way of thinking, the single most beautiful thing about her was the fact that she spoke to him first.

Alan Peter Ryan

It was not easy to hold a conversation inside the disco with the thundering music and the flashing strobes, but it was made easier for Jerry because the girl did most of the talking. Her name was Renata and she spoke enough English to communicate basic ideas. Jerry was relieved. It was a new experience for him to talk with a girl who took the initiative like this. Mostly she asked questions and they were questions Jerry could answer. How long had he been in Rio, had he been here before, did he have any friends here, how long was he staying? His answers seemed somehow to please her and she looked delighted when he said he was staying for three weeks. They walked over to the bar and got a beer for him and something called *guaraná* for her that looked a lot like ginger ale. Jerry was having a good time. Renata really seemed to like him.

Jerry hardly knew how it happened, with the deafening music and his total lack of Portuguese, but soon they had agreed to go outside to the street where it would be easier to talk. As they passed through the entrance, Jerry noticed on the wall a sign that said, "Sexual Exploration Is a Crime." He smiled and hurried after Renata to take hold of the hand she stretched out to him. Phil had certainly steered him straight. Everything in Brazil certainly seemed to be exactly as he had said.

Standing outside on the broad black-and-white mosaic sidewalk of Avenida Atlântica with palm trees rustling lightly overhead, Jerry had a chance to take a really good look at Renata. She was very pretty and her teeth were really amazingly white. She was wearing high heels. Large silver hoops hung from her ears and rhinestone studs decorated the waist and seams of her skirt. Jerry's mother would certainly have said that she looked "tarty," and Jerry supposed she did, a little, but she was also a knockout. He had little experience or skill in describing women to other guys or even in his own mind, but Renata was definitely great-looking.

Her English was quite good, Jerry thought gratefully. She asked where he was from. She didn't seem to recognize Minnesota, although she looked quite curious about it, but when he said Minneapolis she looked delighted. Her heart's desire might have been to meet a nice young man from Minneapolis. "We have cities in Brazil with names like this," she told him brightly, "Teresopolis, Petropolis, very near here, very nice, very pretty, you could like to see them maybe one day, in the mountains, very beautiful mountains." Jerry said maybe he would. He said he'd like to see Rio and the beach but, sure, he liked mountains well enough, he guessed. Maybe they could go to the beach tomorrow, Renata said. That would be great, Jerry said.

He had never known a girl like Renata. She was friendly and vivacious. She stood very close to him and looked up straight into his eyes and kept one hand resting lightly on his arm. Once or twice her breast brushed lightly against his arm. She asked him questions and he answered them. He asked her a few questions. She lived in the Zona Norte—Zona Norchee, she pronounced it—with her mother. It was two hours away and the bus and the train were expensive for her, but a girl had to have some fun and go to a disco sometimes, didn't she, even if she had very little money because she had just lost her job in a dress shop. But she would love to come back tomorrow to go to the beach with him, if he would like that.

Within little more than an hour after leaving the club, they were in Jerry's room at the hotel. The night was a revelation to him. Although he had often wished to have a girlfriend, he had always been a little vague about the details of such a relationship, especially the sexual details. Renata opened his eyes. She was gentle and passionate at the same time. She was happy to lead or to follow, and Jerry was happy to let her lead. She knew how to do things that it had never even occurred to Jerry to do at all. It had been a very long day for him and the most fascinating of his life and it wasn't long before he slept, but when he closed his eyes he was a happy man.

—

Renata moved into the hotel with him. She was his girlfriend. They were a couple, and Jerry didn't mind paying the additional charge when, a few days later, the desk clerk asked politely if he would like to pay now for the extra guest in the room. Renata went home briefly and came back with a small bag containing clothing and shoes and cosmetics. The casual presence of all these feminine things in his room gave Jerry a warm glow. He loved to watch Renata brush her hair. He was proud to go to the beach with such a beautiful girl and to walk with her in the street. They ate in buffet restaurants and Renata helped him choose the simple foods he liked best. By the third day she would fill a plate for him herself with all the things he preferred. She would have fed it to him right there in the restaurant if he had allowed her. It was obvious that she loved being with him.

One afternoon as they were coming back from the beach, Renata said sadly that she didn't know what she was going to wear that evening. She was running out of clothes. Jerry jumped at the opportunity. He would take her shopping and she could get some new things. Would she let him help her choose? Of course she would! She was delighted! They changed quickly at the hotel and went out immediately to some small shops she knew in Copacabana. She showed him jeans and stretch tops and dresses and they bought a good selection. She took him to a shoe store and she got three pairs of shoes. "What about a new bikini?" Jerry asked, and Renata clapped her hands like a child. He was astonished at the prices of bikinis but they bought three of them, all chosen with Jerry's hearty approval. It was amazing. Every day he spent with Renata was better than the day before.

She made certain Jerry saw the sights too. They took the cute little train to the top of Corcovado and the Christ statue and rode the cable car to the top of Sugarloaf. There really weren't any other famous sights but Renata said with a knowing smile that maybe, because Jerry worked with plants, he would like to see the Botanical Gardens and the collection of tropical plants from all over the world. Jerry actually exclaimed over the exotic flowers and trees, the gigantic stands of bamboo, and the towering Imperial palms. Renata smiled happily at his pleasure. She really was a wonderful companion and the very best sort of girlfriend.

It really was too bad that her poor mother was so sick, a thought that darkened her beautiful eyes from time to time. Her mother could not afford health insurance and had to wait for hours and hours at a clinic to see a doctor. And all the medicines she had to take were so expensive. Jerry wondered how much the medicines cost. Renata named a figure in the hundreds of *reais* per month, but when Jerry translated it approximately into dollars, it didn't seem quite so high. The next time he changed money, he pressed some *reais* on Renata and, though her eyes were glistening with tears of gratitude, he would hardly let her say a word of thanks.

SEXUAL EXPLORATION IS A CRIME
Alan Peter Ryan

After living his life in Minneapolis, Jerry was not accustomed to going to the beach every day and, in fact, since he was such a hard worker, he was used to a much more active life. He asked if there were any other sights near Rio that they could go to see. Renata said there weren't, really, but there was a Club Med. Jerry would have happily gone there if Renata wanted to, although Club Med would only mean more time at the beach. But then, seeing his hesitation, Renata had another idea, a much better idea, she said. There was another place in Brazil that a lot of Americans liked to see.

She called it the *Caminho de Ouro*, although Jerry couldn't quite make out what she was saying. The Road of Gold, she told him in English. It was in another state, but not very far away. Many years ago, she wasn't really sure how many but it was in historical times, really long ago, gold was found there and all the great wealth of Brazil came from the gold mines. There were six colonial cities there and they had famous churches and inside the churches everything was covered with gold and there were lots of little shops in those cities that sold things made of gold and one city, Belo Horizonte, another name Jerry couldn't make out, was famous for its cheap clothing. The trip would take about a week and they would have to rent a car. Jerry thought it was a great idea. In fact, he had been a little worried that Renata would get tired of going to the beach every day, just as he was getting a little tired of it himself. And if she got tired of the beach, maybe she would get tired of him and of Copacabana. But if they went away for a week, then she would stay with him that long and they would have all sorts of interesting things to do.

They packed up—Jerry bought Renata a new suitcase for the trip—and they set off the next day. He was astonished at the way Brazilians drove—like a bunch of drunken teenagers—and he couldn't make heads or tails of the roads and signs. He had no idea where he was going but Renata knew the way—a cousin of hers, she told him, had once lived near the Road of Gold—and she was an excellent navigator. Once they got out of the city, the roads were fast and narrow and twisting. They were soon in the mountains and Jerry noticed that in many places there were no guard rails or that old ones had been torn up by accidents and never replaced. Twice in the mountains part of the road had collapsed down the hillside. They passed through some very poor-looking towns where big-eyed children watched the car go by. On smaller roads there were sometimes farm machinery and horse-drawn wagons. On still smaller roads, there was no pavement. And everyone drove so fast! But Jerry was having a good time. The weather was beautiful, he had a great car, his girlfriend was with him, he was exploring a foreign country, and he was having the adventure of his life. They had been on the road about nine hours and they were nearing a small city that Renata called Black Gold in English. She said she had been there once before, long, long ago, and she remembered a very nice *pousada*, a little hotel, where they could stay.

They found the hotel and there was a room available. The hotel had a dining room and they ate dinner there. Renata ordered for him and he couldn't get over how good the beef was in Brazil. He didn't know what it was called but it was the best he'd ever had. After the long and tiring drive, he slept well.

Breakfast was included in the room rate and they lingered over it in the morning, comfortable with each other's company. Jerry thought he was actually getting to like papaya and mango. When they finished, they went to the car and started off on what they both agreed would be an easy day of sightseeing in Black Gold.

SEXUAL EXPLORATION IS A CRIME

Alan Peter Ryan

They weren't ten minutes from the hotel when the accident happened.

—

Later, when Jerry became aware of his surroundings and his vision had focus again, he could not comprehend the situation or its details. He was surrounded by movement and faces and voices that made no sense to him. At the scene and for quite some while after the world began to calm down a little, he did not know quite what had happened. The only things he understood for certain were that there had been an accident, that he was alive and unhurt, and that Renata was dead.

The day passed in a swirl of incomprehensible images. People talked to him and asked him questions in Portuguese. He could not understand a word. People lifted him, carried him, supported him by holding his arms. At one point he knew he was sitting on a low stone wall, but he did not know why. He thought of Renata. She could help him understand all this confusion, she could figure out what was going on, but she was nowhere around. Later he became aware that the big bulky men in gray and black with cold eyes and gruff voices were policemen. He noticed that some of them were carrying machine guns and directing traffic around some obstacle in the road—he had seen them do that in Rio—but his mind seemed not to be working very well. He put his head down and closed his eyes.

It was nine or ten hours later before he completely understood everything clearly

A young woman named Cristina who taught English at a nearby high school was called in to translate. She stayed with him all day, translating for him and for the police. She explained it all to him.

Jerry had been driving toward the main square of the town. A side street entered the street he was in from the right, at an angle. A flatbed truck carrying a load of reddish-brown clay building blocks had come speeding from the side road. The view of the main road was limited, the truck had not slowed down, and it hit the right side of the car with tremendous force. The car was pushed all the way across the road and onto the sidewalk. Quite a number of people had witnessed the accident, including eight officers of the *Polícia Militar*, the state police. The battered car had ended up right in front of their barracks. They had been lounging outside, preparing to go on duty, and had to scamper out of the way when the car and truck came at them.

It was a good thing, Cristina told Jerry, that the accident had taken place where it did and that it had been witnessed by eight *policiais*. That way there could be no mistake about who was responsible. Besides, said Cristina, the driver of the truck, a man who was barely literate, had admitted at the scene that he had been drinking *cachaça* half the night and had hardly slept. He was bleeding from the head and barely understood what he had done. What concerned him most was that he would lose his job. He was under arrest. The police had not handled him gently. Cristina said she did not think his future was very bright.

The truck had crushed the right side of the car. Jerry's passenger, the young woman, had been killed instantly. That was a mercy, Cristina said, because she had been cut up very badly and crushed and one of her legs had been completely severed by the impact. Cristina recounted all of this to Jerry in a very matter-of-fact manner. She had already determined that the young woman was not his wife or sister or any other relative, that she appeared to be Brazilian, and that she was apparently no more than a casual friend. Cristina knew about young American men who came to Rio and what they liked to do when they were there. And she knew about young Brazilian women like Renata too, if that was her name. Jerry listened, took in as best he could what Cristina was saying, and tried to make it all seem real. Even so, he kept wishing Renata was there to help. She would know what to do.

Did Jerry know Renata's real name? Cristina asked. Jerry looked puzzled. This was late in the afternoon and his head was a little clearer. Wasn't her name Renata? Cristina said the police had been through her bag and had also gone through and taken away with them all her things from the hotel room. She had no identification at all, no CPF card, no *Cartão de Identidade*, no driver's license, nothing that showed a name or address or date or place of birth. Had Jerry known her long? No. Cristina was very kind and understanding but the police wanted to know all of this. She said she was not just an English teacher. She was also a certified translator which meant that anything she translated from English, any document or transcript, once impressed with her official seal and signature, became an official and authentic legal document. She kept careful notes on everything Jerry told her. Jerry's head was swimming. It was hard to keep up with all of this. She asked him more questions about Renata that he did not know how to answer. Then he heard a term he thought he recognized. *Garota de programa.* Hadn't Phil used that term? Jerry raised his head. Program girl, Cristina said in English. "Yes," said Jerry. "Yes, I guess so."

Cristina was really very kind in an efficient sort of way, very different from that of Renata. She was doing a job for the police, of course, but she saw how bewildered Jerry was and she was genuinely trying to help. She said that, if he would pay for the meal, she would have dinner with him and she could advise him better then. Jerry understood that she meant no more than exactly what she said. The police would not reimburse her for a meal. "If I ever get paid at all," she added. When Jerry looked puzzled, she shrugged and said, "that's the way things are in Brazil. You can never be sure of anything. We live with disorder and confusion here," she said. "I know you're not accustomed to this, it's different in America, but that's the way it is here. Everything here is a big confusion."

They had dinner in the hotel, in the same dining room where Jerry had eaten with Renata only the night before. The thought of that upset Jerry but Cristina said gently that he had to eat and he did manage a little and, to his surprise, felt better for it. "What would happen with Renata now?" He asked. Cristina shrugged again. "The police will take care of everything," she said. "What about identifying her?" Jerry asked. He was thinking more clearly now. "Can they use fingerprints?" he asked, "or do it some other way? How would they notify her mother in Rio?" Cristina looked down at the table. She told him that nobody would even try to trace Renata. There was no way. "This is Brazil," she said. "And a girl like that, a program girl, almost certainly had no mother or family in Rio de Janeiro. She was probably from the northeast of the country, probably from the state of Ceará. It was common for poor girls to come to Rio and become, well, program girls to make a living." Jerry listened in silence. It was all very sad.

Cristina said he should spend another day or two in the hotel to get over the shock. She did not think the police would need to talk to him again, once she filed her translation of his statements. She would call the car rental company in the morning and deal with them. When he felt better, she said, he could rent another car and drive back to Rio. But when she saw his face, she realized that Jerry could do none of those things alone. She promised to come by the hotel the next morning, between her classes, to see how he was doing. Then the following morning, she would take him to the *rodoviária*, the bus terminal, and put him on a bus to Rio.

Somehow Jerry got through the next two days. He managed to eat meals in the hotel, he went out and took short walks, he turned on the television in his room and felt better when he stumbled on CNN. He was not interested in the news of the world but at least it was in English. He was learning a great deal about his own feelings. He could not stop thinking about Renata, or whatever her real name was, but he was getting a better perspective now on his relationship with her. He had never been in love with her. Such a thought had never entered his mind. Certainly, he liked her and was grateful to her for her good company, and he did not at all resent the money he had spent and all the things he had bought for her. After all, it cost money to go out with any girl and it cost more money still to have a girlfriend. And that was all that Renata had been, a girlfriend, a temporary girlfriend, and, as delighted as he had been to have her with him, she had never been more than that. But oh, he really did like her and she was such good company and she had helped him so much. And the sex. He would probably never have sex like that again in all his life. He would never forget Renata. Despite the sadness he felt at her death, the memory of her and the good time he'd had with her brought a little smile to his lips.

The next evening, Cristina came to look in on him at the hotel and to arrange to take him to the bus terminal in the morning. He took her to dinner and, as he always did with any woman, he let her do most of the talking. She had already dealt with the car rental company about the accident and filed the police report with them. He should have no trouble about that, she told him. She was very nice. She said she would pick him up at ten in the morning and reminded him to eat a good breakfast.

By nine o'clock that evening, Jerry was back in his room. He packed up his clothes and toiletries in preparation for leaving in the morning. He was always very methodical about this sort of thing. He turned on the television and found CNN. He wished Renata was there with him. He was going to miss her for a long time to come.

There was a knock at the door. He couldn't imagine who it might be. He knew no one in the city except Cristina and she had already helped him settle his bill at the front desk and then gone home. He opened the door.

His room faced the hotel's small pool and there were paper lanterns in the trees around it. The colored lights shone strangely on the two *policiais* who stood in front of him. One of them was holding a black bag which he extended toward Jerry. The policeman said something but Jerry had no idea what it meant. Clearly, however, they had come to give him the bag. Unable to say anything in Portuguese, Jerry nodded and thanked them and took the bag. He thought it must contain Renata's clothes and belongings which they were now returning. The poor girl must be buried by now and the case closed and they no longer had any use for her things.

The bag was oddly heavy as he carried it into the room and set it on the bed. He listened for a minute as he heard the police officers having a little difficulty getting their car started. Then he heard them drive off. He sat on the side of the bed and pulled the bag closer. He supposed he should look inside it but he was reluctant to handle the clothes. He sat there for a while and then, with a sad sigh, pulled back the long zipper on the bag. He certainly didn't recognize the bag. It looked old and rather battered and dusty, as if it had been crushed into a closet, maybe at the police station, for a long time. It was all very odd. He looked inside and saw a shiny black plastic garbage bag. This was very strange. He could not imagine what was in it. He pulled out the plastic bag. It was heavy. He felt for the opening, pulled again, and put his hand inside. He felt toes. He felt a foot.

His heart pounding, he reached into the outer bag and lifted out the inner bag and set it on the bed beside him. He could not believe what he saw. He reminded himself to breathe. He could not see all of what was in the plastic bag but he knew it was Renata's severed leg. When the police sent Renata's unidentified body off for burial, they must have forgotten it. Disorder and confusion were routine here, Phil had told him and Cristina had repeated. Or maybe the morgue or the mortuary had neglected to bury it and had simply sent it back to the police and the police, having no desire for it, had sent it on to him. Jerry reminded himself again to breathe. He stole another look. Yes, it was her left leg. No. He looked again at the foot. Her right leg and, judging from the shape in the plastic bag, it went to just above the knee. And it was definitely Renata's leg, no question about it. Jerry recognized the design on her toenails, red and white divided diagonally and with little stars of the opposite color on each half. Jerry just stared, far more surprised than he was horrified. He could hardly move.

What was he going to do with Renata's leg? If he brought it over to the manager of the hotel, the poor woman would be shocked. He could never find the number of the police and, even if he managed to make the call, he could not talk to them in Portuguese. If he waited until morning to do something, Cristina would be horrified and he might miss his bus besides. And he would have to spend the night with the leg in his room.

The questions tumbled through his mind. But the need to deal with practical matters and the continuing murmur of English from the television calmed him considerably. He stopped to think. He took another look at that right foot and its decorated toenails. He remembered something very unusual and very pleasant that Renata had done with that very foot, with those very toes. He smiled.

He pushed the plastic bag farther up the leg, past the ankle, and then past the shin, almost as far as the knee. Renata had very nice legs. Hesitantly, gingerly, Jerry touched it. The flesh yielded a little beneath the tip of his index finger. It felt neutral, neither warm nor cold. It was quite light in color with a golden tinge just as Renata was, had been, all over. Slowly he ran two fingertips a couple of inches along the leg. He felt the solid bone within. The skin itself was as smooth as silk, just as it had been in life.

He withdrew his hand and turned his head toward the television screen. If you had told me I would be in this situation or doing something like this, he thought, I would have said you were crazy. He sat for a while, staring at the television and letting the strange mix of thoughts, both happy and sad, drift slowly back and forth in his mind.

He felt an odd sensation on his thigh. A touch. A gentle pressure. A slow stroke. He looked at Renata's leg and the right foot with its bright nails. It had somehow slid a little farther from the plastic bag and moved closer to him. Those brightly painted nails were now touching his thigh. As he watched, fascinated, the foot arched itself slowly, relaxed, then flexed again, coming closer. The toes wiggled a little, and again, and then they began slowly to stroke his leg.

Much to his own surprise, Jerry burst out laughing. He remembered the signs that Phil had told him about and that he had seen for himself: "Sexual Exploration Is a Crime." Apparently, as he had been told, anything at all could happen in Brazil. Once again, he was reminded that Phil had really steered him straight in more ways than one. Jerry shook his head. These Brazilian girls, he thought. They just never quit.

LUCIEN'S TALE

by David Niall Wilson

From the text of The Chronicles of Lucien Vanderslice Volume the First "The Rat"—San Valencez, California—1978:

"Sometimes lessons come from disparate sources. Book binders use PVA as their adhesive of choice. It's a wonderful synthetic blend with good strength and quick adhesion. It is not, however, the best. Society often obscures quality through an inability to deal with certain truths. It is warm, living bodies that bind reality into a solid fabric—warm flesh, flashing synapses, and bone.

From a cabinet maker's notes:

"This is almost the oldest glue known to man. It's made, as the name suggests, from bits and bobs of animals boiled down to a dark brown sticky substance, and sticky it is. For this is an extremely strong glue and in the right situation I would trust its strength in preference to PVA, or Cascamite. It is gap filling, which is useful—not that we ever have any gaps as long as it's applied properly—is very resistant to all the changes of humidity and temperature that a piece of furniture might experience. It is, however, not especially resistant to damp or moisture or alcohol. Put your piece of high-glued furniture in a damp wet barn for a few months and you might find joints being affected, but for general use it is a very nice glue to use. It has an awful lot of properties that make it attractive."

Building a book is not unlike building furniture. You get what you pay for. The materials can be plain, exotic, functional or bizarre. The only measure of what is possible is in the talent behind the craftsmanship—and the vision behind the concept. Once the fundamentals are mastered, the real work begins. Only in truly understanding each detail can a work be fully brought to its highest form.

My first project was *The Rat*. It isn't a rat, of course, in the literal sense. It is *all* rats. It contains their essence. I began it as a science fair project, but when the time came to display it, it wasn't complete, and by the time it *was* complete, my days of science fairs were far behind me, and I was working on new things. Bigger things. Art is a constantly evolving state of mind and being. If it grows stagnant, there is nothing left. The world spins—you continue to waste oxygen—but all useful progress is at an end. I am a work in progress, and I began with *The Rat*."

David Niall Wilson

I

Lucien stood in the shadows behind the rusted water heater in the basement. His eyes had begun to accustom themselves to the darkness, and shapes melted slowly from the shadows. The only illumination shone in through a crack in a dusty window above his head. The window was the old crank style with a handle you wound in a circular motion to tip the panes at an angle. Its mechanism had long since rusted shut and was caked with dirt. The glass was dark with soot, dust and filth, but the thin crack let in a sliver of light.

The basement was musty and smelled of cardboard left too long covering puddles of mud, animal excrement, and rot. Lucien's grandfather was too old to manage the steps, so the basement had become Lucien's private place. It had been a long time since any thought had been given to cleanliness. Lucien had other concerns.

In one corner an old refrigerator hummed and wheezed. Behind it, clambering over a small pile of wooden crates and forgotten tools, a small, dark form poked its nose into view. Lucien stood patiently, and watched.

The rat was cautious. It was a big one, crafty and sly, and it had survived the baited traps, the neighborhood cats, and other predators long enough to grow strong. For Lucien's purpose, it was perfect. In the center of the floor, as though dropped by accident, lay a small chunk of buttered bread. It could have fallen from a carelessly chewed sandwich, or dropped from a bag of garbage. The rat stared at it, nose twitching. The creature must have sensed that something was wrong. Unfortunately for the rat, such sensory perception could not rule its hunger for long.

One cautious step after another, it crawled from the shadows. Lucien stood still as stone. He was fascinated by the odd curvature of the rat's spine, the constant motion of its nose and whiskers, and the way its eyes managed to capture and reflect light, even when there was so little available. He took mental notes, willing his breathing to slow and his heart to beat as silently as possible.

Another foot, two, and the rat reached the bread. It snatched the morsel greedily from the muck, held it between incredibly dexterous forepaws, and ate quickly. Lucien stepped from the shadows. For just an instant, the rat froze. The remnant of the bread fell away, and it turned. The poison worked quickly. The small creature toppled to one side, hit the floor with a wet thump and scrabbled weakly with all four legs. Its body no longer functioned, but as Lucien leaned in close, he saw that the eyes were alive and alight with terror.

He reached out and stroked the dark fur behind its ears carefully. He had no intention of being bitten, but he wanted to share the moment life departed. He wanted to sense the cooling touch of death licking the rat's face with its icy tongue. More than anything, he wanted to be certain to see death glaze its eyes.

The reality was a momentary disappointment. The rat's breathing grew shallow and rapid, and its spine arched so far it appeared it might snap. Its mouth opened and Lucien saw first its sharp, pointed teeth, and then its squirming tongue. A tiny rattle of breath—almost imperceptible—ushered it off to oblivion. Lucien stood still a moment longer, then scooped up the still warm body and carried it to the workbench at the far end of the basement.

David Niall Wilson

In contrast to the dank, abandoned aspect of the area near the old refrigerator and the stairs, the small section of basement surrounding the workbench was pristine. The floor had been swept, mopped, and then carefully scrubbed. The surface of the bench glistened. There was a battered fluorescent lamp he'd found in a thrift store clamped to the corner—the type with the round magnifying lens and the circular bulb. It hovered like a hinged metal insect.

The horizontal surface was covered in clear plastic. It was carefully taped down over the edges so that no part remained bare. Lucien laid his burden carefully on the slick plastic and reached down to a shelf beneath the bench. He brought out a slab of wood that had been sanded smooth. He laid it in the center of the bench and swung the light around so the board was illuminated brightly.

He lay the rat's corpse belly down on the board and spread it out, so that its extremities nearly touched the edges of the wood. From a small bowl on a shelf to his right, he pulled out several long finishing nails. The hammer hung on a hook beneath the shelf. He examined one of the nails under the light. It was bright stainless steel and needle sharp, the kind of fastener used to hold paneling to a wall with a counter-sunk head. He'd wanted to use pins, but none that he'd found were large enough for the job.

He placed the head of the first nail dead center on one paw, drew the hammer back carefully, and swung, driving the glittering metal through dead flesh and into the wood beyond. He repeated this on each of the remaining paws, pulling the rat's body taut until the nails held it firmly in place. He drove two more of the nails through the sides of the rat's neck to immobilize the head, and did the same on the sides of the tail. He didn't want to take any chances it would move once he'd started. There was only a small window available before rigor set in, and he knew that after that the job would be much more difficult.

Lucien had done his homework; he knew what needed to be done. From another shelf he pulled down a folded piece of silk. He unfolded it and pulled out his grandfather's straight razor. The old man hadn't shaved in over a year and would never miss it. Lucien had cleaned, oiled and polished it. He flicked the razor open, pressed the blade deftly between the rat's shoulder blades, and sliced it open to the tail. Then, very slowly, he peeled the skin back from the center. He used a vertical slice in the skin to channel the blood onto the plastic and away from the wood.

Despite his caution, the rat's ruined flesh was slick with blood. He reached out and stroked it gently. That first caress sent a shiver through him that stood the hairs on his arms, his back, and his neck on end. He closed his eyes—just for a second. Then, with careful precision, he began his life's work.

From the text of The Chronicles of Lucien Vanderslice Volume the First "The Rat"—San Valencez, California—1978

"The simple fact is, though they call the spine of a book a spine, it's something of a misnomer. The science fair came and went without my project, and the reason was a very simple one. I disassembled the skin and bones of a dozen rats. Some were larger, some smaller, and from each I extracted, along with everything else, the spine. I tried innumerable times to glue the bones in place and stretch the hide, but each time something went wrong. Bones are brittle, and they break easily. Rat bones are small and delicate. The hide of a rat can be tanned and stretched, but the smaller bones of the spine are sharp. If you pull the hide over them too tightly they cut through the leather; if you manage not to cut the leather, the pressure of unfolding the book case—the assembled boards and spine—snaps the bones.

It took me a long time to realize what it was that I'd missed. A rat is a rat, and a book is a book. I thought that if the book was to represent the rat, it would have to become a rat. What I missed was the other half. The rat must also become the book, and the act of creation brings a third, separate entity to life. When the image of what needed to be done crystallized—that was the moment I truly began to create."

—

The basement had changed since that first day. The old refrigerator still hummed with life, but the floor had been finished with wood planking and then covered in long, rolled sheets of vinyl. The walls had been dry walled and painted. A two-foot strip of the same vinyl that covered the floor ran down the walls. The seam where this met the flooring was carefully caulked and sealed, then covered by trim. The beams of the ceiling were covered as well, the drywall painted an antiseptic white and long, brilliant fluorescent lights hung down the center.

Lucien had framed a wall separating his workbench from the rest of the space and replaced the old, broken porcelain sink with a stainless steel deep sink. He worked two jobs, both of which served him well. He delivered newspapers to the paperboys so early that you could count the people you passed on the street on one hand. He liked the crisp newsprint and the scent of fresh ink, and he liked the solitude. After school, he clerked at the public library, a huge old stone edifice left to the city by an eccentric millionaire back in the 1920s. The stacks, where Lucien spent his hours cataloging and sorting, were deep and shadowed. Many of the books were old and rare, fragile or in need of repair. The city maintained the library, but lacked the funding to fully staff it, and entropy threatened to destroy the words of several centuries.

The head librarian was a crook-backed old man named Mortimer. Mortimer had worked the stacks when their mahogany gleamed and the leather, gold-leafed spines of the books glistened under crystal chandelier lighting. Mortimer and the library aged together, neither of them quite as straight or attractive as they'd begun, but the years did nothing to quench the man's enthusiasm for books.

Mortimer found a student and kindred spirit in Lucien. When he pulled one of the particularly valuable old books from the shelves for repair, he kept the boy close at his side. Lucien gravitated naturally to maintaining the stacks as his co-workers, craving less strenuous activity and interaction with others, worked the front desk. Eventually, Mortimer came to trust Lucien implicitly, and in that trust, Lucien gained the two things he cherished—knowledge, and solitude.

He learned to disassemble a leather-bound book and carefully recreate it, reinforcing the inner hinges, replacing the boards and the spine. At first he did only simple repairs, but with each project he learned more, until one night, when everyone had left and only he and Mortimer were left in the stacks, he took the bits and pieces of a dozen old books and—from those tattered remnants—he created something entirely new—a book that had never existed. He used a story from a collection published in the early 1800s, an article from a text on physics from the turn of the century. The only criteria were that the pages were the same size, and that the books they'd come from were beyond repair. He had bins of such material, destined to be discarded or destroyed.

Mortimer watched him as he worked, and when it was done—when the signatures had been sewn, the case manufactured and attached to the spine—the endpapers meticulously glued and creased—the old man inspected it carefully. He ran his fingers over the leather—flipped through the pages—held it to the light and checked to be certain edges were square and pages straight. He looked for ripples in the glued endpapers and then—finally—he set the book on its spine and let it fall open to test durability. It was very nearly perfect—a thing of beauty. Mortimer handed it back to Lucien with a smile.

"Never forget," the old man said. "Your work—it's like a part of you. It defines you. That book will be a thing of beauty when you are no more than a whisper of dust in the wind. Most of the words inside were written long before I was born. It's not as important what you are working on as it is how you go about that work. Never halfway. Never without thought and planning. Never without a vision in your mind of what it should be in the end."

When Lucien created his first masterwork, he carefully inscribed those words, just as he remembered them, onto the acknowledgment page. He took his time on each letter, copying the print from the pages of a nineteenth century book on calligraphy. He wrote the words three times before he was satisfied, carefully destroying each page that didn't meet his standard.

On the title page, the book read—simply—"The Rat."

The casing gave him the most trouble. Tanning the hides proved simple enough, but stretching and sewing them into a single sheet of leather large enough to cover the boards took time. It was the tanning and preparing of the leather that drove him to install the deep sink. He also added carefully filtered ventilation.

For the spine of the book, in the end, he took a thin strip of pliant book board and laid it out on his bench. He sorted through the bones he'd gathered, separating out the ribs. From the three hundred plus rib bones he'd collected, he chose eighteen that were so close to being identical it was impossible to tell them apart, even with his magnifying light.

He lined them up on the strip of book board and glued each in place, clipping off any excess beyond the edge of the board. On a book at the library, he'd have covered this with buckram, or leather. This spine he covered with the cured and tanned rat skin, leaving flaps on either side to bind it to the book's boards. He worked the hide around each of the ribs so they formed a raised, rippled effect. It was not unlike the protruding vertebrae of a spine.

As he stroked the final bit of leather down around the last of the tiny bones, he heard a loud thump from overhead. He laid the finished work on his bench to dry and flicked off the magnifying light. He stripped the latex gloves off carefully and dropped them into a stainless-steel bin in the corner, letting the lid close tightly.

The sounds from above grew frantic. Lucien frowned. He turned a last time and studied his work in progress. On the pegboard above his workbench, the preserved hides of several rats dangled from clips. Canisters and boxes of bones covered the bench in well-organized lines. A reference book lay open and braced by a paperweight in one corner. He felt the sense of something important coming together—the sense of accomplishment on the verge of completion.

He turned off the overhead light, then closed and locked the outer door of his workroom. The main basement room, sterile and cleansed, smelled slightly of disinfectant and bleach. Its floor and walls glittered under the overhead fluorescents. He crossed the room, flipped off the remaining lights, and ascended to another world.

Things had changed since his graduation from high school. His grandfather, once a necessary evil, had become something of a liability. The old man had lost most of his mobility, and along with that a great deal of his mental acuity. He spoke often, loudly, and seldom made sense. He required a number of medications that had to be administered on a strict schedule. He had to be assisted to relieve himself, feed himself, and return to his bed at night.

Lucien remembered another man. He remembered the man who'd first shown him the magic of books. He remembered coming to this place, his parents dead and no one else willing to be troubled with a lone, abandoned child, no matter what promise he showed. His grandfather had taken him in. Unfortunately, that man had left the building three doctor's visits back to be replaced by a recalcitrant, gray-haired child.

At the top of the stairs, Lucien carefully locked the door, then used a thick brass key to lock the deadbolt. He pocketed the key and turned down the hall to his grandfather's room. He couldn't get the image of the book's spine out of his mind. He felt the soft hide under his fingers and the ripple where it crossed each tiny bone.

He opened the door and the thing in the wheelchair spun to face him. Its eyes were wide, its hair disheveled. Nothing that resembled his grandfather remained. Lucien closed his eyes. He began to imagine a book—a tribute to things lost. He imagined bones and leather, hair and organs. He opened his eyes. The thing met his gaze.

Lucien crossed the room, grabbed the handles of the wheelchair, and rolled the old man into the hall. He wheeled the chair past the bathroom and stopped at the head of the basement stairs. He fished the keys from his pocket and opened the deadlock. When the second lock clicked open, the thing in the chair cursed.

"Who the hell are you?" it screeched.

Lucien remained silent. He opened the door and spun the chair so it faced the stairs.

"What are you doing? I need my vitamins. Do you hear me? I need my vitamins. The doctor says I can't be well—can't have my beer—unless I have my vitamins. Who the hell *are* you?"

Lucien gave the chair a push.

The old man screeched. There was a horrible clatter and crash as the wheeled contraption caromed off the stairs, tumbled forward, and plummeted into the darkness. Lucien stood very still. A loud, wet thud cut off the screams. All sound ceased.

Lucien closed and locked the door. He snapped the deadbolt in place. He turned away, concentrating on the work to come. The rat would be delayed, but only long enough to save the materials for his next creation. It took time to tan leather, and he would need to replenish the chemicals in the vat where he cleaned the bones.

Silence settled around him like a warm, comfortable blanket.

The Carbon Dreamer

by Jack Dann

I.

I t had been snowing for the past four hours. The water was unusually quiet, at least it seemed so to Fleitman, who was standing in the sand behind the breaker rocks. The foam splashed over the rocks and drooled into puddles in the brown slush. The water blended into the sky, a white canvas turned grey with dust. The snow enveloped Fleitman as he watched the ocean.

The girl nearby continued to scream. A thread of blood tinted the eddies swirling around her trapped ankle. Her knit coat was pulled behind her shoulders, hiding her ribboned ponytails. Her crinoline dress was torn and folded back, revealing a tent of skin, goose-bumped and grey. A man, his overcoat open, crawled over her, muffled her mouth with his palm while neatly spreading his coat over the rocks. Only two faces now, expressions much the same, turning and stabbing at each other. The little girl fainted and the man continued, spasmodically bringing himself to completion. He remained on top of her, stretching his coat over the rocks.

It had stopped snowing. The man stood up, wrapped his coat around himself, and slipping on the ice-covered rocks, reached the sand.

Fleitman was hidden by the rocks. He watched the man leave and waited for the tide to come in. It would soon be suppertime. The wind was stabbing at his face, catching the wrinkles and blowing through the microscopic crags and mountains of his skin.

The man turned around and stared at Fleitman. Fleitman noticed that the rocks no longer gave him cover; the man had walked a diagonal. And then he disappeared.

She was still screaming. But she had fainted, Fleitman thought.

Fleitman had left out the middle. He had pieced together the beginning and the end. She had not stopped screaming. Her tiny voice cut into the chill air; she was still scratching at her attacker. Fleitman knew that she was twelve, but he did not dwell on it: the tide would be in soon.

Patiently, feeling like a patriarch, a wizened father, Fleitman waited for the tide. It was past suppertime. The shore lost an inch. That was enough, leave, she'll freeze, but you can't remember; you've got to give a piano lesson. Was the man still looking? The piano was couched in the corner of the room, under an old oil painting. It was warm in here; the wind could slice through the building, but not through this room.

The ocean, rocks, sky merged into walls and over-used carpet. He fell asleep in the cold, dreaming of warmth, as the sand disappeared. He awakened a second later, waved his hands in the air, and began home.

He had forgotten something very important.

2.

He sat on the piano stool, his back against the piano. It was dusk and the breakers pounding on the beach seemed to grow louder. She should be here...*now*, he thought as he watched the door, waiting for the glass knob to move. Now, the door is open. Come in. A draft from the window tickled his shoulder. He gazed out the window. The sea mist—a monochrome of grey streaked with an occasional daub of white—shrouded the reconverted summer house, pressed against the uncaulked timbers, chilled the unheated rooms.

It began to snow again, slowly at first, and then in great sticky drops. The grey snowflakes silently crashed against the windows and then settled on the sill: a grey melting latticework. The constant rumble of waves falling on the rocks became a distant hum, overshadowed by the wind wheezing past the house.

Fleitman stared into the mist, unfocused his eyes, permitted the motes and particles outside to grow into giant balloons glowing with color. He still had his coat on. He buried his face in the collar. The chill consoled him. As he fell asleep, the gray dissolved into azure and appeared again as cylinders of vermillion stacked side by side. Numbness tickled his fingers, pushed through his arms, and languished before passing into the thickness of his body. Rotted, rotted old man. Sleep. Wagon wheels driving tracks into the snow, into the grey sand.

He yawned and the night seemed to merge with his dream of the beach, the same dream he had every night. It would only take a few seconds.

It is evening. Fleitman stands in the sand beside an abandoned beach house. The house smells the same: rotted wood, smell of chicken somewhere. The basement windows are covered with sand. The stars are pressed judiciously against the sky, and the calm water reflects the icy pinpoints. The water splashes against the wharf before him. Out of the corner of his eye he sees an old woman standing in the shadow of the house. She holds an orange shawl against her face to conceal blue climbing veins. She stares at him as they walk toward the wharf...

"Hello Fleitman." A large hand clasped his wooden shoulder. "Didn't mean to just walk in. Come on. Shit, it's only Paddy... Beer?" he asked as he sat down on the bed. "Goddamn building's without heat again. Sandy's in bed with the youngest just to keep warm. Here, take a beer." He took a can from his six-pack and handed it to Fleitman. "Come on, take it. I just came to see if little Suzy was up here to play your piano. She has one of your lessons today, doesn't she?"

Fleitman took a sip of beer. She had never missed a lesson before. "Your wife is alright, isn't she? Suzy should be here. She's never missed a lesson. You get your check today?"

"No. Look, if Suzy comes up or you see her, let me know. I'll be in the rec room. Sandy's really worried. Enjoy your beer."

Fleitman turned to the window as the door clicked shut. Paddy was neat, even in his filth, he thought. His stains were somehow purposeful—an emblem of his manhood. Fleitman would have wanted him in his youth. He had that swollen appearance that Fleitman used to seek, a decadent beauty that grew in revulsion. Dream Fleitman. Right yourself. It's over. He let the dream resume.

The wharf is silhouetted against the black water. The old lady walks faster. She runs along the rotted, wooden planks. Fleitman crawls along the sand. She is now at the end of the wharf, the black water and sky merging behind her. Her long white hair clings to her shoulders. She is smiling. Bending over, she clutches her ankles and pulls herself inside out. Her reversible skin is a map of crawling blue veins and arteries. But Fleitman must get to the water. He waits for her to move. She will stop him.

"Paddy was looking for you. You see him?" asked Eva Pedon, a dark Puerto Rican woman who lived across the hall from Fleitman.

Fleitman was now hunched over a table in the rec room. His coat was unbuttoned. His head was lolling over his right shoulder. He was sweating.

He often walked in his dreams; he merged them with reality. "Come on, old man. Wake up."

It was warm in the rec room. Fleitman enjoyed a few more seconds of the dream. The old lady was speaking to him: *I love you for yourself, bravo.* Frank, a tall lanky man playing the pinball machine, shouted at Paddy who had just walked in. Paddy was slapping at the snow on his coat. His wife walked in behind him.

"I don't know where the hell she could be," Paddy said as he sat down beside Fleitman. "Still sleeping, hey?" he asked Fleitman. "We've been looking everywhere. Any heat in the rooms yet?"

"No," Eva replied. "And stop staring at me," she whispered to Paddy. "When is George going to fix the boiler?"

"He's not," Frank said, leaving the pinball machine and sitting down at the table. "Right, George?" he shouted.

The manager appeared behind the food counter. "The thing's cracked too bad for me to fix. The soonest I can get someone over to fix it is tomorrow. So, we'll just have to suffer."

"Sonovabitch," Paddy said.

Walking past the wharf, the damp sand sticking to his legs, he can hear the wheezing of the squall rippling the water. He walks along the pier, his head down, watching the sand bunched up in the cracks of the wharf. A little further, the elevation increases; he can

see the rills of sand through the wooden slats, and then the cold dead
water below him. The old lady is at the end of the pier. She sidesteps
to meet him. She fences him off before he can reach the end...

Fleitman rippled the pages of the old Schuam book. He did
not know why he had taken it. He thought about taking a walk.
It was cold, he told himself. But he took a walk every evening.

3.

He opened the rusted latch and let the door fly open, relishing
the onrush of cold wind against his face. He heard Paddy screaming, "Shut the goddamn door," but the sharp wind melted his
words into the wheezing of the trees. She had missed her piano
lesson. That was the first time. He watched the ground as he
walked. He carried the Schuam book, full of happy memories
interlocked with the simple chords and arpeggios, under his arm.
Somehow, he felt that it was protecting him.

The beach was different at night. At night the shadows became
lords of their objects. The cold white sand and snow would darken
and merge with the sky, leaving only the luminescent seawater to
crash on the rocks. But tonight, the snow was a neon roadmap of
light and shadow—a bright heap of sand here, a well of shadow
there. Magnifying itself through the clouds, the full moon illuminated the crashing foam and silver rocks. Fleitman felt a chill
as he passed through the open gate. He lost sight of the painted
backdrop of houses and streets as he walked toward the shore.

He overlays his dream on the hard surface of his surroundings.
He hears the screams of the old woman, but he pushes them back into
his sleep. He remains awake, following an unconscious impulse to see
the rocks before he returns home to his bed.

Jack Dann

The rocks stood out pale white against the background of black churning water. A glistening layer of freezing rain had smoothed out their harsh angular contours. The rain acted as a fixative for the snow. It had stopped raining in time for Fleitman's walk. Soon it would start snowing again, Fleitman thought. It would probably snow all night. He shivered and continued his evening walk: it pushed his dreams a little further away.

He watched the waves splashing between the rocks. He stepped carefully over a small ridge. The little body was nestled between the rocks before him, submerged under a thin layer of ice and snow. Fleitman did not want to look. Her stiff coat, pulled behind her shoulders, disappeared into the sand. Her face was white; the snow did not blanket the dainty features etched into the mask of ice. And she screamed. Fleitman saw the tiny bubbles at the corners of her mouth. He waited for the scream to pass through the ice.

The ice cracked and the screams, trapped for hours under the ice, escaped with one concentrated shriek. Fleitman held his hands to his ears, but the sound was already in his head. He joined it with a scream of his own and pushed himself into the rocks. The hard edges and shards of rock broke the skin, pulling warmth deep inside him to the surface. As he closed his eyes, he retained the retinal image of blood streaming from her trapped foot. That too was suspended under the ice, he thought. He dreamed of joining it, but the old dream of the quay returns.

The old woman has beaten him again. He turns away as she tears off protruding organs and throws them at him. He cannot reach the sea. She will grow new parts to throw. A glistening white fin cuts through the water behind her.

In his dream Fleitman is only an observer. He could not completely forget the rocks and the rain. If he did he would freeze to death—no one would find him for days. The dream receded and Fleitman stiffened with cold. He did not move and the numbness returned with the dream, but the dream was a blur and Fleitman was too far above to make out the tiny details. It began to snow again.

Standing up, he felt the shock of cold, recognized the numbness radiating from his hands and feet. A flap of coagulated blood hung from his cheek. He did not touch it. His trousers were torn and stained. His awareness brought more pain. Stumbling over the rocks, he reached the sand. Its softness brought on a sympathetic wave of nausea. She shouldn't have gone outside, he told himself. She should have stayed inside until her piano lesson was over. He felt for his Schuam book, but he had left it on the rocks. Hurrying past the gate, he walked on the grass beside the sidewalk to avoid slipping. The snow swirled around him, pressing him to dream, drawing off his consciousness.

As Fleitman approached the apartment house, the images of his dream covered everything with a warm glow. As he opened the front door, everything began to blur. There was no one in the office. Blowing streamers of icy smoke through his nose, he edged along the wall to the rec room. The hall was strewn with newspapers. Fleitman felt a tightness in his stomach and watched amazed as he vomited against the rec room door.

He screamed as he fell to his knees, pushing the door open. "She's in the ice, in the rocks. I left my book there." As he listened to himself he felt embarrassed. The cold floor felt good in contrast to the overheated room. No suspicion, he thought as he heaved again. She's already frozen. I couldn't do it. I gave her piano lessons. They know.

Jack Dann

Paddy had his palm behind Fleitman's neck. Fleitman chuckled as his perception suddenly cleared, but he gagged before he could verbalize it.

"Fleitman, where is she? Where on the rocks, you crazy sonovabitch?"

Fleitman waited, enjoying Paddy's warm breath on his face. It smelled pleasantly of beer and brought back memories of laughter and young girls. He contemplated feigning unconsciousness for a few more minutes. The dreams returned, stronger than before.

It is very warm. In the nineties. Fleitman has all the windows open, but the air is stagnant—there is not the slightest breeze. Fleitman leans out the window. He can smell chicken frying upstairs. Or is it chicken soup? But it is so hot. The fire escape is cool to the touch...

"On the rocks, Paddy. Near the wire fence. Near the old World War Two cement bunker. The one that the Eaton kid fell off of last summer."

"You sonovabitch."

"I feel sick."

"What were you doing out there, you goddamn old pervert?"

"On the rocks. I always take a walk." He knows that, Fleitman thought. He knows, but he's upset. She missed her piano lesson. And the Schuam book.

"Come on, Paddy," Sandy said. "I want my baby."

Eva Pedon pushed a damp cloth against Fleitman's face. Fleitman could smell his vomit. He opened his eyes and shut them. Eva was pretty, but her features were too coarse, too leathery. She would have been good—at one time. Fleitman mused over the prospect of making love, but his dreams contained more reality.

"Get a doctor," Eva said. "He's an old man. Christ, he's probably already got pneumonia."

Paddy ran out of the room, followed by everyone except Eva and a woman behind the counter. Eva left the cloth on his face and called for a doctor.

She returned, rested her hand on his forehead, and talked to him. But he could not understand Spanish. He tried to remember how he had felt when his body was hard enough to be touched. He could remember only by trick of reason, by sterile imagination. His past had been excreted with the growing of new skin, withered grey skin, dropped in folds under dim eyes that barely perceived the brown girl sitting beside him, pitying him.

He sank back into his dreams, and the little girl wiping his forehead shrank into a little brown cockroach pedaling across the floor.

Up the fire escape. It is the apartment above him. Fleitman loves the old lady cooking the chicken, although he has never seen her. It is chicken soup, Fleitman is sure. He pulls himself out the window and begins to climb. He is very hungry, He is in love…

4.

Fleitman did not pay any attention to the doctor prodding his chest with a stethoscope. The sheets of his bed were cold, reminding him of pieces of ice that would melt in his hand. He savored the cold trickle of sweat that ran off his palm. He did not move his fingers. He could hear the rattle of the electric heater that Eva had brought in, and he could smell gas. The oven was turned on to heat the room.

"No, he's awake, aren't you Mr. Fleitman? Those cuts and bruises look worse than they are. The main thing is to keep warm. Have him take these pills. I've given him a sedative. I'll look in on him tomorrow. He should be all right; he seems to be in good health. Don't get out of bed, Mr. Fleitman. And take these pills. And keep warm."

The doctor left. Fleitman was hungry. He waited for the soup. Doctor said you're healthy, Fleitman thought. You take walks, every day. Yes, she missed her piano lesson.

Sometimes, in his dreams, Fleitman can smell colors.

As he climbs he smells yellow. It is always the same color. He remembers as he dreams. The steps are smooth from wear, the ground is magnified below him. Fleitman closes one eye and looks between the slats. He is not very high. But he has been climbing for hours. He can see yellow clouds wafting out of her window...

It was chicken soup. Fleitman finished it, placed it on the floor next to his bed, and pulled the covers over his head. It grew warm as he inhaled his own breath. He shivered. The fire escape was cold.

5.

Someone was trying to open the door. It rattled. Fleitman looked out the window, hoping for light. It would be morning soon. He was perspiring; the oven was still on and the electric heater was coughing. The knob did not turn. Not so soon, Fleitman thought. He would not be here so soon. They would get him. Fleitman could not remember his face, but he remembered that he was a neat man: he had left the little girl in order under the ice.

Fleitman counted for the morning. The sound of the water and the predawn grey made him shiver. He was coughing, spitting gobs of phlegm into tissues. Throwing the tissues at the garbage can and missing. Fleitman covered his chest with his arms; he stopped shaking. He took another pill. The alarm wasn't set; he would sleep.

He tried to resume the dream. He could feel the warmth of a summer day, the coolness of the fire escape. But the yellow smell of chicken revolted him. He thought about fat boys and shuddered. He spat into the tissue. The dream would have to end, but he could not do it now. The man kept pushing at the door, but Fleitman wasn't worried: it was too early.

⬤

Fleitman did not remember the next day. He took his pills and the doctor saw him again. But Fleitman had stopped dreaming: there was nothing to hold onto. He did not change his pajamas. It was still grey outside and the streets had turned into brown slush.

But you remember him. No I don't, Fleitman said to himself. He sat up in the bed, his skin shiny from accumulated oil. The man was about thirty. No he wasn't. Remember Fleitman? He was older.

Fleitman looked out the window. His eyes were wet; everything blurred. He squinted. It was sunny. Fleitman pretended it was summer. The oven was still on, although the heat was now working. Fleitman refused to shut it off. He would not blink his eyes. They began to sting, and Fleitman could almost see the rainbow-hued gas puddles shining in the gutter and the plastic umbrellas held aloft as protection from the rain-heavy leaves that shook and turned in the fitful breeze. And he could see the young girls pacing to the beach gate, carrying boomboxes and dark stained army blankets, waiting for the sun to seep through the clouds and turn them into nut brown Cinderellas. The young

Jack Dann

boys followed, cigarette packs tucked and rolled in the short sleeves of their snow-white T-shirts.

Fleitman shivered. But the cold was leaving his body.

In the distance the water, dotted by ships defining make-believe horizons, merged into the grey sky. The foam breakers wafted soap bubbles and tar smears onto the matted beach. A blanket was already pinioned in the sand; books, shoes, purse, and a bottle of suntan lotion held the corners in place. A young girl tiptoed into the water, unnoticed by the crowd that would soon form.

Fleitman, you're dreaming.

He leaned against the headboard, head propped up on pillows, covers drawn over his chest. Fleitman whispered to himself: do it right. Dream it. Dream it first.

You can do it later.

Fleitman walks along the beach. The hot white sand doesn't burn the soles of his feet—they are calloused. Past the swimmers, past the sitters and the show-offs, Fleitman walks toward the rocks. The water is green; it could easily have been blue. Fleitman skirts the rocks and notices a Schuam book, suntan lotion, and a paperback novel lying in the wet sand.

The girl nearby continues to scream. A thread of blood tints the eddies swirling around her trapped ankle. Her knit coat is pulled behind her shoulders, hiding her ribboned ponytails. Her crinoline dress is torn and folded back, revealing a tent of skin, goose-bumped and grey. A man, his overcoat open, crawls over her, muffles her mouth with his palm, while neatly spreading his coat over the rocks.

Fleitman steps over a puddle of water and sits down in the wet sand. He remembers that the man is neat. Fleitman will have to wait. He thinks about the fire escape and the old lady, but there is no time for that now. Fleitman picks up the paperback and studies its red and green cover. He remembers reading it. He turns the pages. Not much time. You should be done. Hurry. Fleitman is beginning to wake up.

The man leaves. He turns around and stares at Fleitman. Fleitman is still thumbing through the book. He looks up in time to catch a glimpse of the man before he turns around and runs.

He has grey hair, bleaching to white, like you, Fleitman. He is fifty-five or sixty, Fleitman thinks. His eyes are deep set like mine and he is frightened. But why a little girl? Fleitman was bending the paperback. As he begins to understand, the book crumbles, the beach turns grey with snow, and Fleitman has no chance to walk home before he awakens.

—

Fleitman was hungry. Eva should have brought him something by now. It was almost one o'clock. Exactly right. A knock at the door.

"Come in," Fleitman said. "The door is not locked."

Of course it's not locked.

How did the man comb his hair? Fleitman wondered. Was it parted down the middle like mine, or did he part it on the side to cover a bald spot? You should have run after him. You haven't touched the piano. Fleitman reached for his pills on the night table—the bottle was almost empty. But you saw him twice.

Fleitman giggled at the detective pulling a chair next to his bed. Eva was there—he could smell food. "These men have to see you about little Suzy," Eva said as she laid a tray of soup and cold fish on the night table. Too fat, Fleitman thought as he watched the detective sitting beside him. And he had a tic in his eye, a tiny insect crawling under his skin.

Jack Dann

"You take a walk every day, don't you, Mr. Fleitman?"

A uniformed policeman stood in front of the bed. He was much younger than the detective. He loosened his tie and took off his hat, revealing short cropped hair. Fleitman once had a brush cut. He remembered how it used to scratch his palm when he combed it. You're old, Fleitman told himself. That's a good enough reason. He's sure to come for me, he thought. Tell them. He's sixty or so. I'll be seventy-five.

"Did you see anyone else on the beach?"

She had probably been dead for hours, Fleitman thought.

He answered the questions as he dreamed. He curled inside himself. He didn't listen to his answers.

He pauses for breath. How many steps has he climbed? Everything has turned to specks below him. He looks out at the ocean. He can see the curve of the horizon. It is tinted slightly yellow. Watch the water, Fleitman. It will still change its shape, flow and ebb. Only a little more fluid than the metal handrail you're leaning on, already dead, slowly decaying into something else, to ferment and build new fermenting shapes. All shape, Fleitman. All illusion. There, it moves again. Subtly changing into air, adding an atom to the jellyfish glistening on the hot sand. Keep your eyes on the slippery foam; it's a thousand-fold reflection of your insides— it's dying and rebuilding and separating and decaying. And so are you—but you have the illusion of consciousness. Fleitman looks up and the steps shiver under him. He remembers something important and forgets it again...

Fleitman wanted to tell them something. He was in danger. But from what?

The detective had finished asking questions. Fleitman wondered if he had answered them correctly. Had he forgotten anything? He ate his soup and tried to remember. He tried to remember the scratching at the door, but he was too tired. He thought about the man's age. Say sixty. I'll be seventy-five, he thought. And he's sure to come for me. He looked right at me. Fleitman was still a bit chilled. He would remember what he wanted to tell the detective tomorrow.

6.

A blink, the shudder of an eyelid, an ill-timed glance at a coat billowing in the wind, and the world might end and instantaneously build itself again upon the excretion of the old. Fleitman had missed many endings. As he stood before his window facing the storm-fed sea, he counted the possibilities. Each death and rebirth changed his world subtly, pushed him back a moment in time, changed the curve of his path slightly. Dimmed his vision softly. But he was too young to be senile. He was here at the window, basking in the winter sun, soon to bury itself in the waves of the horizon.

How old are you really, Fleitman? Fleitman felt a subtle change as the world built itself again on the sand-corpse of the last, a little dimmer, a little more complicated.

Eva told him all she knew about the incident. Fleitman compared her gossip with what he saw and his dreams. He felt better, relieved. He could not tell the police anything. He could not tell them now that he had seen it all. Could he tell them he had forgotten? That he was dreaming at the time? Things had become clearer lately. And that shouldn't be, Fleitman thought. Yet, everything had also become more complicated.

He would not reveal his secret, even though he was in danger.

"Paddy's been drunk since it happened," Eva said. "Sonovabitch made another pass at me this morning. Sandy just cries. Poor baby. But there's nothing to do for her."

Fleitman gurgled for effect. Her blouse was always half unbuttoned, he thought. It felt good to watch her.

"You heard what the doctor said. You can start getting around now. No more food—and you owe me some money. Your check came in today." She opened another button. Fleitman turned to the wall.

"Well, the rest of the meals you get yourself. And here's your goddamn check."

—

After she left, Fleitman made himself some tea and turned on the radio. The music was loud and didn't make much sense to him. That's why he did it, Fleitman thought. *Because* he was old. Overcompensation. Then why don't you take Eva? Because you're afraid you couldn't do it. That would be worse than knowing. But a little girl.... Even if you couldn't make it, it would be an act of love. Fleitman felt a slight sympathy for the man. But how could he continue when she screamed? And he left her, a crumpled rag doll.

But you left her, too, he told himself. But I was dreaming. That doesn't count. And Fleitman dreams.

Imagine the wharf, the old worm-ridden wharf extending into the puddle sea. Imagine the quiet evening and the house in the sand. The same wood, the same hour labors under the weight of the little woman on the quay. She steps aside. Fleitman can walk to the water now, but he doesn't move. This dream is over. He should not have returned again.

"Hello, Mr. Fleitman. Can I come in?"

Lenny Thompson stood in the doorway with a sheaf of music under his arm. "I'm supposed to have a lesson. It's Friday. You want to change it? Ma wasn't sure if I should come. You know, with all that stuff that happened."

Fleitman put his teacup in the saucer, spilling tea on his trousers. It was sticky and Fleitman was immediately uncomfortable. He would try not to move his leg. The wet spot was suctioned against his skin. "Yes, come in, Lenny. We'll have a lesson."

The spot turns cool, then cold. It is a shiny icicle impaled in his leg. Fleitman dreams of ice, large shimmering cubes heaped on the floor. Budding stalagmites press against the blocks. They will soon support the ceiling, growing heavy with sister stalactites. Fleitman touches the large blocks, careful not to break the pointed buds beside them. He finds room to sleep...

"They had a fight about you."

"Who did?" Fleitman asked.

"Mom and Dad. You know, because..."

"Well, let's forget about that for now. What exercises did you prepare?"

"Which book?"

"The Hanon." Fleitman took a notebook from the top of the piano. "Sit down, Lenny." He pushed back the fallboard. The keys were badly yellowed. One day, he thought, he would have it tuned. "E" and "A" were flat, and High "C" responded very slowly. "You were supposed to prepare Exercise Number Twenty-three. Did you do that one?"

"I don't know that one very well. I haven't had much time to practice. There's been too much noise."

"Well, begin."

He sucks in his cheek and begins. When he stumbles, he goes back to the beginning and plays the piece over again. Fleitman doesn't stop him. Fleitman understands that he must finish the piece perfectly. Once the boy made a mistake, there was no sense in going on.

"You're not using the right fingering," Fleitman said. "It's five-four-three-four-five in the left hand. You're starting with your fourth finger."

Fleitman listened as the boy ground his fingers into the keys, pushing and stabbing at the music like a baker kneading bread. Children are so small, Fleitman thought. He felt the man on the rocks crying. But once she started screaming, it was too late. That ruined it, broke the container. Fleitman watched the man cry, the tears trapped in the hollows of his eyes. He should not have tried to scrub himself with the child.

Lenny played the exercise over and over again. And then he played the next one, stumbling and beginning again. Fleitman waited until the required time had passed and then stopped him. "That's not bad, Lenny—for not practicing very much." He leafed through the pages of Lenny's books quickly—he felt another dream forming. He fought it.

"Move over, I'll play this for you. This is your next assignment. It's difficult."

Fleitman had always liked Schubert. And "The Erl-King" had been one of his favorite pieces when he was a child.

"See, it's *presto agitato*, that's very fast." He began playing. He did not need the music. "Can you hear the horse's hoofs pouncing? And now very soft, and loud for the Father's Theme. He is riding home with his sick child. He is racing with death. And now the Erl-King's theme, at first very soft. And louder, then the child. Notice the pedaling. The key changes. It is faster, death is gaining. And *lento* and the last chords were *forte*. Did you watch the pedaling?"

Lenny nodded his head.

"Well, it's marked. Be very careful with the pedaling. Did your mother give you any money?"

"No, I'll bring it the next time."

As Fleitman watches Lenny leave, he discovers a small piece of ice in his palm. Bands of ice are wrapped around his legs: he is frozen to the chair. The little piece of ice in his hand traps his fingers. He leans his head against the wall—it freezes in a comfortable position. As Fleitman falls asleep, he remembers that it is Friday. He always has dinner with his nephew on Fridays...

7.

He will probably do it again, Fleitman thought. He already has little Suzy's mouth. That one screams louder than most. Maybe the next time will be better for him. He will certainly try again. And if the next one goes bad, he will have another mouth to yell and scream inside his head. Surely, it could not be much louder than Suzy's. He probably collects them: each little girl leaves him a little charm.

Fleitman could hear Suzy's screams, but he had become used to them. He had collected a mouth himself. Probably by mere proximity, he thought. He could examine her little white teeth. They were slightly uneven. She was so small. How many other tiny malformations and potential diseases did her body contain? How long would she have fermented before they matured? Fleitman listened to her teeth chatter while he thought about her.

The man would eventually fill his head with those little mouths and become deaf. They would scream until his eyes watered. But there was nobility in those gross movements. Maybe the rocks lent charm to the man from Brooklyn. The man's image became clearer after Fleitman had given him a residence.

And he probably was from Brooklyn, anyway.

—

Fleitman dressed and took a subway to Manhattan. His nephew lived in the West Village, on McDougal Street. He had moved in after Fleitman's brother had died. Like father like son, Fleitman thought. The streets were crowded. Fleitman pushed his way through tourists wearing heavy fur coats, week-end hippies in Friday night outfits, businessmen who had lingered for a drink after work, office workers browsing, children playing in the crowd, chased by their mothers. The old locals were here somewhere, Fleitman thought, but he could not see any.

A group of boys pushed past him. They all wore jeans and carried guitars. Fleitman smiled: one of the boys wore his beard Van Dyke fashion. As a youth, Fleitman had sported a beard. He remembered combing and trimming it, contrasting beard and sideburns, skin and hair. Then short hair. Brush cuts became stylish. The man on the rocks wore a brush cut, Fleitman thought. He kept it a little longer than Fleitman thought proper, but then Fleitman had let his hair grow out once too.

There were twelve- and thirteen-year-olds all over the streets. They were purposely scruffy. A few of them smiled as they passed Fleitman. He paid no attention to them. He concentrated on watching the clothes waving past him. Coats thrown open to reveal orange shirts, blue waistbands tied around leather jackets. An azure T-shirt contrasted with grey skin.

Fleitman pretended that colored sailboats were racing past him. He did not look down at legs; that would break the illusion. The coats and open jackets glided along the cement. Children were the hardest to control: they were too little. Every time Fleitman looked down at them, the tangle of legs surrounded him.

All these children, Fleitman thought. All running around, bumping into each other, getting lost, stoned, laid. They were all anonymous. They were all little mouths surrounded by flesh. All screaming and laughing, tasting and mashing. They were so unlike little Suzy. He could still hear Suzy yelping, her little mouth popping in and out. This is where the man should be. Suzy could certainly scream louder than these ragamuffins.

Fleitman looked for his nephew. He usually waited in front of his building. Fleitman walked the five flights slowly. A young girl standing in the hall mumbled something to herself. Fleitman stepped over a plastic garbage bag. The super would find it. He kicked it down the stairs.

Before Fleitman could knock, Stuart, his nephew, opened the door. "Hello, Uncle Jake. Cold as hell outside, isn't it?" It was a very small apartment. Fleitman gave Stuart's children a kiss and five dollars each and then sat down in his favorite easy chair in the living room. Stuart's wife Fran waved hello from the hallway as she called the children into the kitchen.

Jack Dann

That's better, Fleitman thought. He could sense the fire escape, almost see a wavering image. He talked with his nephew until Stuart's wife called them to dinner. He listened to mother and daughter talking, preparing for grace. The little girl acted very grown up—she copied her mother. "One more year," Aileen said, "'and I'll be in the same school as Stephen." Her brother didn't seem to notice. He just stared at his plate.

Aileen was Suzy's age. Fleitman looked away from her mouth, which was constantly moving. He watched his hands as he ate, watched his fingers curling to hold his fork, arching to push his knife, pinching together around a falling napkin. As he concentrated on style of movement, on tilting his wrist at the proper angle, his movements became jerky. He cut himself.

Stuart and Fran fluttered around him; the children continued eating, looking up once in a while. As Stuart wrapped a bandage around Fleitman's finger, Fleitman noticed that his nephew's eyes just seemed to stare in whatever direction he turned his head. They had no life of their own.

"There," Stuart said. "It could have been a lot worse. You have to be careful. Let's have a smoke."

They sat down in the living room while Fran and the children picked up the dishes. Fleitman didn't usually smoke, but he took a cigarette. He didn't want to disappoint his nephew. Stuart lit Fleitman's cigarette. Fleitman waited for his eyes to blink.

"What's the matter, Uncle Jake? Honey, bring the dessert in here. And send the kids in, too."

Stuart was like the children outside. He was anonymous. The glazed eyes and bent nose were for effect. Like the man on the rocks used nobility to good effect. His eyes still did not blink. It could just as well have been Stuart on top of Suzy. But Stuart had no reason, Fleitman. He is young.

Stephen came into the living room holding a metal tray. "Strawberry shortcake," he said. "Ma says you can put the whipped cream on yourself." Fleitman noticed that one of Stephen's eyes was glazed.

"I have to take him to the doctor. He's having trouble with that left eye again. The drops helped some, but then the same thing happened again."

Fleitman nodded. "Yes, you'd better take him back."

When Fleitman finished his dessert, Aileen sat down on his lap. "Is your finger alright now?" she asked.

"Just like new," Fleitman said, bouncing her up and down. She was not at all like Suzy. She would not have screamed. She would just whimper and die. Fleitman felt sorry for her; she was like her father. She would have no reason to kick and scream; she would have no identity to hang on to. Fleitman bounced her a few more times. She was too soft; she had no bones. This could not provide love. This would be no challenge. And Suzy was lost. How could anyone find chastity in this? She was no more chaste than a piece of chewing gum. Fleitman thought he understood something, but he quickly forgot. He wanted to leave: there was no reason to stay any longer.

"The steak was very good," he shouted to Fran. Aileen was holding on to his belt. Fleitman lifted her from his lap, swung her around, and sat her down on the couch. She was laughing and gurgling. Her little body seemed to bulge around his hands—he quickly let go.

Fleitman promised to come again next Friday. He waved good-by to Aileen; Stephen had disappeared. Fleitman hurried to his subway station. The streets were too crowded. All those faces painted and accentuated for effect. All the same person. The tiny distinctions were affectations. But there were real people scattered about. They would never smile or nod to Fleitman as they passed. But Fleitman could tell they were real. He tipped his hat to an old lady walking a Pekingese. She was real. She quickly picked up her dog and cradled it in her arms. He also found a real beggar and gave him a quarter.

It was quiet in the subway station. A train had just pulled in. Fleitman walked down the platform until he found an empty car. He sat down next to a window and watched his reflection in the glass.

The steak has bloated his stomach and he rests, dreaming about the ice pillars growing in his room. They are growing over him, fusing into a lattice of prisms. Crystalline trees hang upside down from the ceiling, breaking the sun into rainbows. The room is petrified. Fleitman watches the crystal splinters grow along a crack in the far wall, vitrifying into a gilt design. The furniture is covered with a glacé sheath. Fleitman is chilled. The food in his stomach is freezing. His organs grow transparent. Fleitman slowly turns to glass. He dreams about Suzy. She is warm. She contains everything he has lost. But she is lost, too, Fleitman.

The conductor woke him up. It was the last stop. Fleitman took a bus from the station. He would take a walk on the beach before going home. It took him a few minutes to get used to the darkness. Trees blotted out the lights. He could hear the waves splashing on the rocks and the scrunching of his new patent leather shoes in the sand. He would have to clean his shoes when he got home—they would be covered with tar slick.

Fleitman could make out the outlines of the beach. In the distance the rocks were grey, intermittently covered with black water. Fleitman could hear voices, then discern faces. They all looked unfamiliar.

"I don't know exactly where it happened," said a girl wearing jeans and a navy pea-coat. "Maybe where that ledge is." She passed her cigarette to a tall boy standing beside her. He inhaled loudly.

"Hey man," he said, "you know where that little kid got molested?"

Fleitman quickly walked past them. They were all laughing. Another boy tried to say something, but he could not stop giggling.

"Hey, fucking child molester," said the girl. "Come back and show us where you did it."

Fleitman walked along the water. There was another exit further along the beach. They were still yelling and laughing, but Fleitman couldn't hear them. He could only hear Suzy screaming. It grew louder. She was biting her tongue inside his head. As he passed the rocks, the voice became a whisper and then died. Fleitman's hands were cold.

The tall boy could have done it, Fleitman told himself as he walked toward the gate. Or even the other one. They were real. But you saw who did it, Fleitman. He was an old man. But why couldn't he be young, Fleitman? Because I saw him. But he could have been anybody. It could even be Stuart, and he isn't even real. Fleitman could have seen anybody. He stopped at the gate: it was locked. He thought he saw somebody. He would let it be one of the kids for a while. They were available, at least.

Fleitman skirted the fence. If he could find a tear in the wire mesh, he could reach the avenue through someone's back yard. He didn't want to walk back to the other gate—the kids might still be on the beach. Fleitman found a spot where the fence was loose. He lifted the wire as best he could and crawled under. He hurried across the yard.

Two drunks were arguing under a street lamp. Fleitman would have to wait until they left, before he could step into the street. He crouched behind the bushes that fronted the yard and listened.

It could have been one of them, Fleitman thought. That's no stretch of the imagination. Fleitman could feel the presence of the man that did it. He could smell the strong, musty odor of the man. But it was the screaming that convinced Fleitman. He could hear all those little mouths screaming and wheezing. So, the man did have a collection of them. But you could be wrong, Fleitman. Suzy's screams were loud enough to make up for five or six little girls. Fleitman was sure of it: only Suzy was screaming. Her little mouth was an orchestra.

Fleitman was breathing heavily. He held his mouth. The man must not find him. He controlled his breathing. He was shivering with cold. His legs ached from crouching. He kept his eyes closed until the drunks left the vicinity of the streetlight. He knew what the man looked like: he had seen him on the rocks. Fleitman didn't want to look at him again; his nearness had been too overpowering.

—

Fleitman did not relax until he reached his apartment. He bolted the chain lock and wedged a chair against the door. He was not sure if the chair was positioned correctly; he had only seen it done in the movies. The presence of the piano made him feel better. He left the lights on and lay down on the bed. Suzy was screaming very softly.

Fleitman heard footsteps in the hall. He didn't move. They stopped in front of his door. It could have been Eva or even Paddy, he told himself. The door creaked. Someone was pushing against it. Then Fleitman listened to footsteps hurrying away.

He turned toward the wall for security. The man would be back, Fleitman thought. He would wait for the right time. But Fleitman understood. He tried not to fall asleep: he would wait.

The sun has disappeared behind a puff of cloud. It is suddenly cooler. Fleitman is climbing, two steps at a time. But the steps are creaking. The fire escape is shaking. A shard of metal hits Fleitman on the shoulder. He hangs onto the handrail for support. He can see the ground undulating below him. He will hold on and wait...

8.

Fleitman had changed his habits. He would stay awake all night and sleep in the day. Fleitman had learned to enjoy sleeping in the day. He could watch the clouds scudding past his window as they changed into familiar shapes. Sometimes, as he watched the dust drifting in a band of sunlight, he felt as if he were swimming underwater without a mask.

At night Fleitman waited for the man. But lately he had begun to doubt the man's existence. But he must exist, Fleitman. Someone had to do it. But Fleitman didn't care. He was no longer afraid to stay up at night. The shadows, the noises, the groaning of settling wood were comforting. It was a private show, and

Fleitman was the only one awake to enjoy it. He could watch the world build itself and then scratch and crumble into something different. Everything changed many times at night, even Fleitman. Sometimes Fleitman was aware of the changes and he would count them. But Fleitman did not know that every time *he* changed, he had to start again.

And Suzy was his orchestra. He had been correct: she could easily scream loud enough to make up for five or six little girls. He had become used to the screams; he learned to filter them when he played his radio. Fleitman found that his tastes in music were changing: Suzy preferred Cage to Haydn, Joe Cocker to Gianni Poggi. He could feel her little mouth pucker up, move into a more comfortable space in his head. She would snarl quietly as he listened to his radio.

When Fleitman tired of the radio, he would try to make words out of Suzy's screams. Sometimes, he thought he could hear *no*. Lately she scolded him. She often grumbled. Fleitman isolated *choose*; he could hear it over and over again. But usually it was a voice and nothing more, sound without sense.

Fleitman could not understand why the man did not come. Because I chose not to believe he would. Fleitman felt at ease. He chose to keep Suzy for himself. You've stolen everything, Fleitman; her mouth hangs only in your head. He studied the crack in the door-stile and waited for an answer.

None came.

Well, I'll stop thinking about him now, Fleitman told himself. Why? He killed little Suzy. But you don't care, Fleitman. You've stopped feeling sorry for him. Why? Because you've stolen his girl?

Fleitman left his apartment and went for a walk. It was late. Everything seemed muted: the crashing of the waves was dulled, the splashing water seemed to drift in the air, removed from Fleitman's arbitrary time sense. Only you can hear her screams, he thought. They were too concentrated to be spread between two people.

Fleitman walked slowly, letting his heels drop into the sand. The snow glistened on his boots. The screaming had stopped. Why didn't he notice before? Fleitman tried to bring the screams back.

He hurried home. He was afraid again. He did not want to think about her; her little mouth was a grotesquerie. He knocked on Eva Pedon's door. There was no answer. Could she be with a man? Fleitman asked himself. He knocked again, harder. He heard a groan.

"Who Is it? Paddy, if that's you, get the hell out of here."

"No. It's only Fleitman."

She opened the door slightly. "It's four o'clock in the morning. What do you want?" She rubbed her eyes. The hollows under them were grey. Fleitman looked at the floor. He could leave now, bolt and run. But she was already laughing, her beautiful olive pit face was cracking. "Well since it's you, Fleitman. Come on. But I only do it because you're old. As a favor. For very little."

Fleitman sat down in a chair and watched her take off her nightgown. She was slightly flabby; her hips were too fleshy. It's no good, Fleitman thought. She's like me.

"Remember, Fleitman. You don't tell anybody."

She's ugly, Fleitman. He tried to wrap himself up in a dream, but he had stopped dreaming. Why hadn't he remembered? He could not let her touch him; he would have to pull away.

She curled up on the bed. "Come on. Let's do it."

Fleitman could taste saliva, then vomit. She's so ugly, he thought. She's turning grey. Her skin is sliding off the bed.

He vomited and bolted for the door. He had trouble opening it. She had used the chain lock. He turned the key and the chain dropped free.

"Why you sonovabitch." She jumped out of bed and slipped on the vomit. She kicked at him, but he was already in the hall "You faggot sonovabitch." Tears slid over her cheeks, each taking a different path. Her face was too smooth and coated with oil. She was almost a little girl, Fleitman thought as he fumbled for his key. As she cried, he could hear a whispering inside his head. But her skin is falling off. She is flaccid like you. She grows jowls. Her hair is white. "You sonovabitch."

Fleitman closed his door. The whisper grew louder, turned to table talk, then a scream. The little mouth inside him opened up, curled its lips over uneven teeth, and screamed. Fleitman leaned against the wall, allowed the screams to pass through him. He thought he could hear Eva, but Suzy would not permit that.

It was getting light. It would be a dull dawn, he thought. The cold grey water would splash against the rocks and coagulate into ice in secret hollows. There were too many changes that night, but it was not quite day—there was still time. It was still damp. The hoarfrost on the window sparkled.

It would be a very cold day.

Fleitman was very tired, but he could not sleep. At first the screaming demanded all his attention; then, as he became used to it again, it calmed. It left him time to think. He didn't want that. He played with the radio, turning the selector knob. Country Joe and the Fish. The screaming became louder. He changed channels. Prokofiev's *Cinderella*. He could picture the dancers quarreling over the shawl they were embroidering. The two sisters, Khudyshka and Kubyshka, depart, leaving Cinderella alone on the stage. The screaming grows louder. Fleitman does not have to think. He listens. The screams become a roar. A shout interrupts the Portrait Scene. Fleitman can also hear a news program crackling in the background.

And then the screams stop. Fleitman is alone. You could not have done it, he told himself. You picked the little girl, like the man did. No, Fleitman thought. The man will come. Even your nephew could have done it—and he had that dead eye. Remember the bushes, Fleitman? Of course, one of those men did it. Because you were listening. It follows you, Fleitman.

Of course it followed, Fleitman thought. He turned the radio off—the screams returned. Fleitman could feel the little mouth wedged inside his head. It goes wherever I go. And he remembers. He sinks into his chair and dreams. It is very bright outside; the light permeates his closed eyelids and provides a damask background.

The girl screams. A thread of blood tints the eddies swirling around her trapped ankle. Fleitman tries to pull off her coat, but she fights him. He pulls it behind her shoulders. He gropes for her dress; it tears and he folds it back, revealing a tent of skin, goose-bumped and gray. Fleitman opens up his overcoat and crawls over her. He muffles her mouth with his palm.

Make it up, Fleitman. Fill in the spaces. He cannot remember. But that was the best part, Fleitman. You scared her. You took away her littleness. Now she's bones, a receptacle for insects. Like you, Fleitman. Except you're aware of your decomposition.

Someone slapped his door. "You sonovabitch. I hope you drop dead," It was Eva Pedon's voice. He listened to her footsteps click down the hall. He could feel Suzy's mouth moving inside his head. He felt a sharp pain.

THE CARBON DREAMER

Jack Dann

She was chewing on him, biting him with her uneven teeth. Don't worry, Fleitman. It won't be long. Her teeth will crumble.

It had been snowing for the past four hours. The water was unusually quiet, at least it seemed so to Fleitman, who was standing in the sand behind the breaker rocks. The foam splashed over the rocks and drooled into puddles in the brown slush. The water blended into the sky, a white canvas turned grey with dust. The snow enveloped Fleitman as he watched the ocean.

Fleitman felt faint. he tried to sleep, but Suzy began to cry. And then she screamed; long needles of pain gently passed through his skull. Whimpering, she clicked her teeth together and tore his flesh. She chewed it carefully. Took another bite.

Then continued to scream.

Red Earth

by Blu Gilliand

When I was six, I nearly died in a mud puddle.

To understand how such a thing could happen, or almost happen, you have to understand how different things were back then. 1950s rural Alabama might as well be in a different universe than the world we live in now—especially when it comes to the raising of children.

As I recall, we'd just finished Sunday lunch. We were visiting my Aunt June and Uncle Darby, this being my Ma's sister and brother-in-law. They lived in a little town called Eustace, right up in the northern corner of King County, Alabama. They were Southern Baptists, like we were—I have since lapsed a bit—which meant we'd spent most of that morning listening to a preacher go on about the eternal struggle of sin and the hot coals of Hell and whatnot. I remember wondering if Hell could possibly be hotter than Aunt June and Uncle Darby's little church, which had yet to discover the salvation of indoor air conditioning and instead relied on open doors and the flapping of church bulletins to combat the August heat. Thought about asking my Ma that, but every once in a while common sense would intervene on my behalf, and that was one of those times.

Sunday lunch had been a big one, as we were company and thus had the full spread laid out before us. Judging by Uncle Darby's generous belly, which protruded over and above his beltline in defiance of the rules of gravity and the physics of corduroy, I reckoned they ate like they had company every night. After we'd had our fill we retired to the big front porch for "visitin'." "Visitin'" mostly consisted of my Ma and Aunt June catching up on family gossip, while my Pa and Uncle Darby talked about how good the fishing had been and how good they hoped deer season was gonna be. As a budding out-doorsman myself I listened greedily to their conversation, but soon enough they wandered into the high weeds of politics and I lost interest.

Aunt June and Uncle Darby were childless, so there were no cousins for me to run around in the yard with. Darby was a kind and perceptive man, something I didn't appreciate until much later in life, and that day he noticed that I'd drifted away to the porch steps, sitting all folded up the way only the very young can manage, with my chin resting on my knees, just staring off into the distance. It was Uncle Darby made the suggestion that nearly got me killed.

"There's a nice creek runs through there," he said, pointing a crooked and calloused finger at the woods creeping up on the right side of the house. "'Bout a mile down that path. Might be fun to ramble down to it. What do you think, Paul?"

Pa was puffing on his pipe, trying to get a bowlful of cherry-wood tobacco to fire up. He spoke out of the side of his mouth and kept puffing at the same time. "Alright by me," he said. "Ask your Ma."

I swiveled around and looked at Ma. She already had that face on; you know the one. The one that said, "Men are good for nothin' but foolishness, and for passing that foolishness down to their sons and nephews." I knew her well enough to know that face was also as good as a "Yes," so I was halfway down the stairs by the time she nodded in the affirmative.

I made it around the corner and nearly to the woods before Uncle Darby whoaed me up. I'd took off so fast I didn't even notice him getting up to follow me. I will admit my heart sank a little at the sight of him lumbering after me. He never could stand completely straight long as I knew him. He had a bad hip, too—a frequent conversation piece between he and my Pa—so walking was a painful endeavor for him to undertake, and for others to watch.

I was afraid, I'm ashamed to say, that he wanted to go with me. I had a lot of energy pent up on account of sitting in church all morning, then sitting at the lunch table waiting on the grown-ups to finish eating, not to mention the hour-long car ride it took to get to Eustace. I was about to bust, and if I was going to have to slow-walk that trail down to the creek, waiting while Uncle Darby picked his way over rocks and around tree roots…well, hell, I might as well go back and sit on the porch.

"Just hold on a second," Uncle Darby said. "Got somethin' for you."

He fumbled around in his pockets, an act accompanied by all sorts of jingling and jangling. Men of all ages are prone to fill their pockets with prodigious amounts of shiny metal doo-dads, something me and Pa and Uncle Darby held in common.

"Here we go," he said, and he brought out a pocket knife. It was the folding kind, and as soon as I saw that silver blade tucked into that wooden handle, I was head over heels in love.

I held out my hand, too surprised to say anything. He laid it across my palm, and what I remember most is the <u>weight</u> of it. It had a heft to it that no toy could replicate. It was my first glimpse at a future in which I would stop being a boy and become a man; someone who would be trusted with weighty things.

"That's yours," Uncle Darby said. "Not on loan. To keep. Done talked to your Pa about it, and he to your Ma. They's alright with it, but you gotta use it proper. Don't go carvin' your initials in the kitchen table or some such foolishness. And for God's sake, try not to cut yourself. I gave it to you, but your Ma and Pa are well within their rights to take it away if they see fit. Okay?"

I nodded. He showed me how to open it, how to fold the blade all the way back until it locked in place, and how to close it. When he was done I hugged him tight. I looked up and noticed his eyes had gone a bit shiny, and I felt bad for hoping he wasn't trying to go to the creek with me. He'd given me the knife because he loved me, but also because he'd never have a son of his own to give it to, and that made me sad.

I asked him if he wanted to come to the creek with me, but he said no, he was gonna play cards with my Pa and Ma and Aunt June. He told me again to be careful, and walked in his painfully peculiar stride back toward the house.

I slipped the knife into my pocket, marveling again at the pure solidity of it, and turned and ducked into the woods.

I believe I mentioned before that it was hot that day, but once I got under the leafy green canopy of the woods, it cooled off some.

The trail was covered in a soft carpet of pine needles, and I longed to kick off my shoes—constrictive, claustrophobic things—but I knew I'd have to put them back on before I went back to Uncle Darby and Aunt June's house, and I knew I'd probably forget to do it. Or, worse, I'd leave them by some tree in the woods, never to be seen again, and that was a whipping-worthy offense. So I kept them on and did my best not to scuff them against the rocks and roots that occasionally poked through the pine needles.

Sweat sprung on my brow as I skipped and darted down the twisting, sloping path. I passed an oak with a knot on its trunk as big as my head, and I stopped for a minute and ran my hand over its gnarled surface. There was something mossy in the grooves of the knot, and I got out my new knife and scraped some out and sniffed it. It smelled both fresh and decayed somehow; bitter and sweet all swirled together. I wiped the blade on my pants leg, clicked the knife closed and dropped it in my pocket, and continued on my way.

I know a lot of times when people tell stories about finding weird things in the woods—and just about everybody in King County has a story about finding something weird in the woods, I have come to find out—they talk about how quiet it went, like all the birds and critters had taken the day off or something. It wasn't like that for me.

I hit a stretch of the trail where the branches overhead were bunched so tight it looked like dusk, and I swear the temperature dropped ten degrees. Up in those branches were birds, hundreds of them by the sound of it, and they were raising cain. I never heard such a thing before. I had my neck craned back, trying to see if a snaked had crawled into a bird's nest or something, and that's how I missed the mud puddle.

It was as wide as the path and way too big for me to step over even if I had been looking where I was going. I wasn't looking, though, and next thing I knew I was in mud up to my ankles.

I felt that cold mud close around my feet and immediately went to calculating how much trouble I was going to be in. I reckoned it to be a considerable amount. For one thing, this wasn't a little dirty water—this was a stew of rain and red clay. Clay like that gets on your hands, they're stained for at least two or three lye soap scrubbings. For another, there was a good chance my shoes weren't coming out of that mud. It had a good hold on them, I could tell. As I shifted, I could feel my feet wanting to slip out of them. If I did get them out, I didn't know how they'd ever get clean. You think red clay mud is bad on your skin? It ain't no good for your clothes, either.

I wiggled my feet side-to-side, trying to loosen the mud's grip a bit. The puddle was big, but I figured I could step backwards if I could just get a foot free. I went to lift my right foot out but felt it coming loose from my shoe.

Nope. Them shoes were done for.

I thought about how Ma usually let Pa handle the whipping portion of my discipline program. I figured she might be inclined to try her hand at it once she realized I'd lost my shoes.

I stood there for a moment, feeling a bit sorry for myself. That wasn't doing me any good, though, so I finally took a breath and pulled my right foot free. Feeling my foot slide out of that shoe, knowing that was the end of that shoe and, maybe, probably, the end of me, was not a good time. I stepped back, expecting to feel the solid trail behind me, only to have my foot sink back into mud.

I looked back over my shoulder and saw that the puddle had spread out behind me. I'd only taken one step in, but now I was in the middle of a puddle that went all the way back to the bend in the trail—back to where I'd first noticed how frantic the birds were acting up in the trees.

I was trying to figure out how that could be when I felt something cold and wet spiral up over my pants and around my leg. Felt like a snake at first, and I hollered and reached down and started swatting at my legs, and that's when I saw the tendrils of mud that had curled around the outside of my pants. While I watched, they kept moving, wrapping around me like vines, growing thicker and climbing higher.

I brushed at them and smeared them, but the mud kept flowing, filling in the spots I knocked away. Mud wound around me in little cables, up to my stomach, sliding up my chest and over my shoulders. Cold, grainy streams of the stuff began to ease down my back. My arms were circled with bands of mud, and they kept winding around 'til mud covered my hand like a glove.

Panic was setting in fast. The tendrils were more like roots now; big, twisty, knotty lumps that wrapped me almost completely from the neck down. They weren't tightening up on me —I could still breathe fine, and I could still move my arms, but the mud down below held my feet firm, so I could do little more than swing my arms and rock back and forth.

At a point I quit worrying about my shoes and my clothes and started wondering if I was gonna die. My breath sped up and my heart went to galloping in my chest, and the cold fingers of mud traced their way up my neck and began exploring my face. Mud plugged my ears and matted my hair and slid across my lips. I tasted grit and earth, and a little cold water trickled into my mouth, and when I opened my mouth to spit it out, the mud darted in.

It hadn't covered my eyes, not yet, so I was able to see the mound of mud that rose up in front of me, swirling around and around like clay on a potter's wheel. It started out round, like the columns on a plantation home, but began to change as it reached the same height as me. Little pieces of it fell away in some places while lines appeared in others. It started to take shape, the way a piece of wood that fell under my granddaddy's knife would take shape. Unseen hands were whittling away at that column of mud, and soon I realized what the whittler was making.

That column of mud now looked more like a person. A six-year-old boy, to be exact. As those gritty lines continued to crawl over my face, I saw my own features begin to appear on the blank canvas of the mud boy. A stub of a nose, even as my own was coated and sealed with cold, gooey grit. Big barn door ears. Mud flowed over my left eye, and I saw an identical eye open in the mud boy's face, little muddy eyeball swirling madly while the unseen sculptor tried to lock it down, make it look right.

I don't know why it took so long, and I don't know why it happened at that moment, but that's when I thought about the knife in my pocket. I could still move my arms, so I slipped my hand into my pocket and felt for the knife. I pulled it out slow, not wanting to drop it, not wanting the mud boy to spy it with his little eye. I didn't know if it could actually see or not, but that eye had stopped spinning around and was locked on me, and it sure felt like it was looking at me. So I pulled that knife out slow and thumbed the blade open, which was hard because the knife was new and still a little stiff. I got it open and slid my hand up slowly and, with the mud just about to seal me off for good, I plunged that knife into the mud boy's eye.

It rared its head back and its new mouth opened as if in a scream, but nothing came out, which was good; I think I might've lost my last shred of calm if it had made a sound. When it jerked back the knife slid out of the eye, and for a second a long rope of mud hung, suspended between blade and boy.

Then the mud boy came undone. It was like somebody taking a hairdryer to an ice cream cone. All the fine details it had been filling in slid away. In seconds it went from a pretty good likeness of me to a featureless pile of goop. I stood there, gawking, knife clenched in my hand, and watched it all spill down into the puddle. Then thee puddle itself began to recede, like something underneath the earth was sucking it down with a straw.

Before I had time to cry out, it was gone. The mud that had come up over my ankles had drained into the ground, quicker than you can sneeze. When I replay it in my mind, it's like that old effect they used to do in movies, running the film in reverse and at a high rate of speed. It was almost comical, the way that stuff run away from me and my little ol' knife.

It left me alive. It also left some of itself behind; not on the ground, but on me. I was iced head-to-toe in red Alabama clay. It tried to look like me, and, foiled, left me looking like it: a column of mud.

So, I had maybe, probably, just cheated death. Now I had to go and face my mother.

I trudged home, and let me tell you, I wasn't in no hurry. Yes, I wanted to get the hell away from them woods, and whatever had come up out of the ground to take me, but I wanted no part of having my parents see me this way. But, it was either that or live the rest of my life in them woods, and that wasn't going to happen.

So, I walked back up the trail, and very soon I was back in Aunt June and Uncle Darby's yard, and then I was rounding that corner and there they all were on the porch. Someone had drug a little folding table out there and they sat around it, playing cards. Uncle Darby spotted me first and his eyes got real big and I think I saw the corner of his mouth turn up, but just a little, because then my Pa followed his look and saw me, and his mouth flew open and his pipe fell out, spilling tobacco all down his shirt, which caused Aunt June to look up and scowl, of which I took only a second's notice because then my Ma spotted me and let loose with a holler that silenced the birds in the trees and froze my poor young heart.

A House for the Wee Ones

by Michael M. Hughes

"Isn't it pretty?" Leila asked.

"Amazing," I said.

Cheryl got down on one knee in the dewy grass and held Morgan so he could see it, too. "That's really lovely, Leila," she said. "What do you think Morgan?"

The baby stared blankly, oblivious. Leila, who had just turned six, had become fixated on building fairy houses the summer before when we were vacationing in Maine and found a picture book—*Houses for the Wee Ones*—in a used bookstore. Her current construction looked more like a lean-to made of bark, sticks, and leaves than the artsy houses pictured in the book. But it had a rough, childish charm.

—

"It has a moss bed," Leila said, sticking her finger into the structure. "And an acorn sink so they can wash their faces."

"They're going to be some very happy fairies," Cheryl said. "When are they moving in?"

Leila smiled. "Tonight. After I do my welcome dance for them they're having a party."

Morgan blew a spit bubble and pointed at the house with his tiny finger. "It looks like Morgan wants to move in, too," Cheryl said.

Leila glared. "No. This is for *my* fairies. He'll break it. He breaks everything of mine." She stuck her tongue out at her baby brother.

Morgan squawked and started crying, and Cheryl hefted him into her arms. "Now be nice, Leila. Your brother loves you."

Leila glared, then turned back to the house, whispering to herself.

—

"Mitch, are you okay?"

Cheryl was staring at me. She brushed her hair out of her eyes and squeezed my arm. "What are you yelling at?"

I was standing at the bedroom window, facing the darkness outside. The curtains lifted and waved in the breeze. "I told the neighbors to shut off the music and go to bed. They're going to wake up Morgan." I was feeling a little woozy and still half-asleep. The noise and the lights had been unbearable, but now I heard only the sound of the crickets and insects.

Cheryl blinked. "What party? I didn't hear anything."

Leila walked in the room. "Daddy, why are you yelling?"

"Are you sick?" Cheryl asked. She held the back of her hand against my forehead.

Michael M. Hughes

"No." I pushed her hand away and rubbed temples. "Just go to bed. Everybody go to bed."

Morgan started wailing from his bedroom. "Shit," Cheryl muttered and left to get him. Leila stepped next to me at the window. "They're done now, daddy," she said.

—

When I woke up the next morning my head ached. I heard Leila playing outside. She was dancing around the fairy house, skipping and swinging her arms and singing. When I stepped into the kitchen Cheryl was sitting by the window, watching Leila and nursing Morgan. "Coffee's made, but it's cold. You'll have to nuke a cup."

"I'm sorry about last night," I said. "All the racket was driving me crazy."

Morgan detached from Cheryl's breast and gurgled, then went back to the nipple. "You were dreaming," Cheryl said. "There wasn't any party."

I poured coffee into my WORLD'S GREATEST DAD mug and stuck it in the microwave. "The hell there wasn't. That new couple down the road must have had some friends over."

"No. They didn't. They're not even there this week—they're in Florida. Remember?"

"Well, maybe their kids had a party."

"They don't have kids, Mitch."

The microwave beeped. "I know what I heard. It woke me up. I wasn't dreaming."

Cheryl sighed and rolled her eyes, then turned back to the window. "I wish Leila had some friends around here."

"She's fine," I said. "She'll make friends when school starts." Cheryl was always worrying about something. "She likes being alone. Look at her."

Leila had stopped dancing and was sitting in front of the fairy house, talking to her invisible friends. She held up something that looked like a stone, then placed it in the shadowy interior.

"I worry about her," Cheryl said. "Being by herself so much. It's not healthy for a kid her age."

I laughed, and immediately felt bad for doing it. "Come on. She's smart and imaginative." I sipped my coffee and scalded my tongue. "Maybe she'll grow up to be a writer like her mother." Cheryl had taken the summer off to work on the third book in her *Parenting Without Tears* series.

"God, don't wish that on her," she said. "Can you go grab her and bring her in for some breakfast?"

Leila didn't hear me as I approached. She startled when I touched her shoulder. "Daddy," she said. "You scared me."

I rubbed the top of her head as an apology. "What's new with the house?" I asked, squatting next to her. My knees cracked.

"Look," she said. "I put the *durgin* over top the door."

"What's a *durgin*?" I asked.

She stared at me as if I were stupid. "Daddy. Every fairy house has to have a *durgin*." She pointed. "Right here."

A bird skull sat above the oval doorway, its eye sockets dark black holes, the beak jutting. "Hmm," I said. "Isn't that a little gross?"

Leila rolled her eyes. "You don't know anything, do you?"

A House for the Wee Ones

Michael M. Hughes

That night I woke up at 3:33 a.m. The damn music was playing again, glasses were clinking, and the neighbors were laughing and chattering, though I couldn't make out what they were saying. I threw off the sheet and saw lights flicking outside the window. Cheryl was snoring. I thought about waking her up so she could see I wasn't making it up this time. But as soon as my feet hit the floor the music stopped. A woman's laughter faded, and then the chorus of night insects and peepers swelled until that was almost deafening. I stepped to the window. Fireflies blinked low against the ground, but the neighbor's house was lit by only the small porch light they always left on.

I had a sudden urge to check on the kids. Leila was asleep, thumb tucked in her mouth. Morgan was standing in his crib, staring out the window as the curtains lifted and fell. He was smiling. "Ja ja," he said, pointing his tiny finger. "Ja ja."

I was making spaghetti while Morgan slept in his bouncy seat on the kitchen table. Cheryl sat on the porch staring at her MacBook's screen, drinking an iced tea. I hadn't seen her type anything or heard the rattle of the keys, but I'd long ago learned that her process of writing sometimes meant staring into the air for hours on end.

The screen door banged. Morgan flinched and his eyes fluttered. Leila ran into the kitchen.

"Shhh," I said, pointing to her brother, who squirmed in his seat, eyes closed but perilously close to waking.

Her eyes were wide. "Daddy, look what Nysha left for me." She held out her hands.

I forced myself to smile. "Well, isn't that...neat."

It was another skull, this one larger—a chipmunk, maybe, or a small squirrel. Tiny, bright blue pebbles had been stuck inside the dirty eye sockets, and the bone was daubed with a pattern of dots of what looked like red mud. "Isn't it pretty? It's a *pyshatz*."

"Go show Mommy," I said.

She ran into the porch. "Put that outside. And go wash your hands," Cheryl said.

"But Mommy, it's a present," Leila whined. She stomped through the kitchen and into her bedroom. Her door slammed.

Cheryl turned to me, her brow twisted in worry. "Do you think she can get impetigo from that?"

I laughed. "You tell me. You're writing the book."

She closed the laptop and stuck her middle finger in the air.

Morgan started crying.

———

"Honey, Daddy's going to need to take that down," Cheryl said. Her face was scrunched in disgust. Morgan was bundled across her chest, his features shadowed by a yellow sunflower hat.

"No," Leila cried. "You can't take their house down. They won't have any place to live."

I put my hand on her shoulder. "Leila, sweetie, I think some kind of animal has been living in there." I waved a fly away from my face. "It keeps bringing dead things inside. I know you like to leave food for the fairies, but food attracts bugs and animals, too."

"You can get sick," Cheryl said. "And then Mommy and Daddy and your baby brother can get sick, too."

Michael M. Hughes

"You can't take it down, they'll get mad at you," Leila shouted. She was crying now, her face livid.

I poked a stick into the house. A blur of flies emerged. When I removed the stick, there was a little bundle of twigs and dried grass hanging on the end. It had been twisted into what looked like a little human puppet. Flies crawled over the tiny figure, and between the brown sheaves of grass I could see white worms writhing.

"Daddy's going to get the hose," Cheryl said, backing away and waving below her nose. She instinctively covered Morgan's face.

"No!" Leila screamed. "You'll ruin everything. They *like* it like that."

"Leila, baby doll—"

"Don't call me that!" She stomped her feet. "They're my *friends. My* friends. My *only* friends. And you're going to take away their house and they're going to get mad and go *away.*" She glared, hot tears running down her cheeks. A fly landed near her eye but she didn't flinch.

"Go inside," Cheryl said. "Now."

"I hate you," Leila said. "I hate you and Daddy and my stupid baby brother. I don't want to have a family anymore." She started screaming and ran to the house.

Cheryl bounced Morgan on her hip. "We need to talk tonight."

I caught the smell of rot and dropped the stick. "Yeah," I said. "Yeah, we do."

<hr />

That night we drank two bottles of wine and decided to make an appointment with a child psychiatrist Cheryl knew in Monroeville. I waited until Leila was asleep and dragged the garden hose out to the fairy house. The assemblage seemed to have hardened, and it took repeated blasts of water from the hose to break it apart and make sure anything dead and rotten had been washed out and into a nearby thicket. Then I grabbed a bottle of bleach from beneath the kitchen sink and sloshed it into the lump that had been the home for Leila's friends. It was now a pile of sticks and rocks, but at least it wasn't going to make anyone sick.

—

I had terrible dreams that night. The neighbors were at it again, yammering and laughing and playing stupid, repetitive music. A bunch of their kids swarmed our yard, and when I looked out the window they all stopped playing and turned to face me. Stone still. They were all thin and tiny, their skin gray and mottled, bony bird faces with shiny pebble eyes.

—

The next morning Leila refused to come out of her room for breakfast. Morgan was cranky and kept throwing up his milk, and no amount of holding and rocking him would get him to stop his incessant, low-grade whining. Neither Cheryl or I broached the subject of the night's destruction. I knew she felt as terrible about it as I did.

"I think I might take Leila to visit my mom's," Cheryl said. "Just me and her. For the night."

I nodded.

"I pumped enough for Morgan. Do you mind? I think she really needs it. We can watch movies and paint our toenails."

Michael M. Hughes

"You don't think Morgan's sick?" I asked.

"He's fine. No temperature." She waited. It was clear there was only one answer. I hefted Morgan and kissed him. He wiped his snotty nose against my shirt. "Looks like it's you and me tonight, little man."

———

I had two old fashioneds and listened to the baseball game on the radio while Morgan sat in front of the TV watching Curious George with the sound down. I heated a bottle of milk and fed him as the deep orange, early-evening sun knifed through the trees. With Leila gone I realized how demanding and dominant she was, and how much I had been missing time alone with the boy, who tonight was full of giggles and nonstop blabbing. He was asleep as soon as I placed him in his crib.

I figured I'd find something to read, but when I got to the bookshelf I saw the *Houses for the Wee Ones* cover facing me. Cheryl must have removed it from Leila's room. I picked it up and glanced at the author photo on the back. A pretty, sharp-faced young woman with dark hair. Leila had wanted to know about her, so Cheryl had googled her and found out she had disappeared while hiking shortly after the book was published in the 80s. We didn't tell that to Leila. I flipped through the pages and stopped at a black-and-white illustration of a bird skull. It had feathers arrayed around it like a headdress.

I put the book down. Maybe I'd watch TV instead.

———

I woke up to the sound of glass breaking. Not a loud crash, but a sharp crack and then the tinkle of falling pieces. I walked into the kitchen. Moonlight from the window pooled in a rectangle on the floor. When I stepped toward the window I noticed a hole in the center pane, about the size of a golf ball. Below it, on the sink, sharp bits of glass twinkled.

I reached into the nearby drawer and pulled out one of our heavy, expensive knives. When I flipped on the exterior light the yard was empty. I stood quietly and listened, scanning the tree line. Nothing but the peepers and hum of the crickets. Beyond the light the woods were a deep, featureless black void. I locked all the doors and windows, turned off the TV, made myself a nightcap, and went to bed with the knife on the bedside table.

—

The next morning, I woke up with an unexpected hangover. I ate breakfast and watched a documentary about the Black Plague on the History Channel while Morgan slept on my chest. When he took a nap after his bottle I went outside and found a rock below the broken window. It was white, quartz-like and oval with a black spot in its center. It looked like an eyeball. I wondered if one of the kids from the neighbors' party had thrown it at the window, then realized those kids had been part of a dream. I had never seen a kid within miles. Maybe a drink would make me feel better.

The remains of the fairy house had been whitened by the bleach and the sun. The sticks looked like piles of broken grey bones, the rocks tiny skulls. I picked up a nearby stick and poked at the refuse. Leila was going to be pissed. I wondered if Cheryl would write about this epic parenting failure in one of her books.

A House for the Wee Ones

Michael M. Hughes

Something moved in a small hole in the dirt. Brown, like a beetle. I pushed the stick into the hole. Maybe I would need some more bleach to kill whatever was left. I pushed the stick in deeper.

Bugs started crawling out. Then alighting and buzzing.

I dropped the stick and stepped backward. "Fuck," I hissed.

Wasps.

—

Cheryl walked in the door and her jaw dropped. "Jesus, Mitch."

"I'm okay," I said. "Got stung by some wasps."

"Your eye! The whole side of your face."

I covered the swelling with the icepack. "I'm fine. I took a couple Benadryl."

"Where were you? Did you walk into a nest or something?"

Leila walked in, dragging her fairy backpack. She dropped the bag and looked up at me. "I told you," she said. "I told you they would be mad."

—

Cheryl woke me that night. She wrapped her arms around me from behind. Her breath was sour and hot against my neck. "I had a nightmare," she said.

"Sorry," I whispered.

"There were a bunch of kids outside. Playing with Leila. I was afraid she would leave with them and never come back."

"Just a dream," I said. I had taken a Percocet for the pain of the stings and was having difficulty talking.

We both jumped. We heard it at the same time—a whistle. Like a flute.

I got out of bed.

Cheryl's eyes were wide. "What was that?"

We heard it again. Three soft, high pitched notes, from down the hall. I wrapped my robe around me and stumbled to Leila's room. Leila blinked when her light turned on and covered her face with her sleeve.

"Did you make that noise?" Cheryl asked.

Leila didn't answer.

"What's in your hands?" I asked.

Leila held something to her lips. Blew two high, shrill notes. She held out her hand. I took the object. It was feather-light, a thin, off-white tube. I turned to Cheryl. "A whistle." I turned it over in my hands. "Looks like it's made of bone."

Cheryl took the whistle from me. "Leila, go wash your face. And brush your teeth."

Leila grimaced and stuck out her hands. "Give it back," she shrieked.

———

Leila wouldn't talk to the psychiatrist. On the way home she told us she wanted to run away and we were no longer her family. We took her to get ice cream anyway, then after we finally got her to bed Cheryl sat on the porch smoking cigarettes. I poured myself a vodka and tonic and half-watched a show about Peruvian mummies. I knew that night that our family had broken. Maybe even irreparably.

A House for the Wee Ones
Michael M. Hughes

——

A few months later I had to file the restraining order. My lawyer said it was my only option.

From that terrible July morning—the morning we found Morgan sucking on a bird skull in his crib—Cheryl believed our baby boy was stolen and replaced by someone else. That she knew this child was not the baby who grew in her womb. I would watch her holding him but unable to look at him, nursing him and crying quietly while he stared at her, his cheeks moving in and out. Then her milk dried up. Or so she said.

Her mother's testimony helped me get full custody, and Cheryl's breakdown in the courtroom most likely sealed the deal. Leila lived with Grandma for a few weeks while I tried to get Cheryl some help, but I failed.

I never talked about that morning with anyone, not even my lawyer or my therapist. I was as out of my mind as Cheryl when we found him. Anyone would have gone off the deep end, seeing what we saw, and I knew it was best to just pretend it never happened.

Leila was in Morgan's room, blowing her bird-bone whistle, when the first dim purple sunlight rimmed the windows. When we looked in his crib, in the shadows, we didn't understand what we were seeing. I thought he had pulled off his diaper again and had what we called a *shitcident*. But it wasn't his feces smeared around him, but dirt. Black soil, writhing with earthworms. He was holding something in his mouth, sucking on it and smiling at us, his eyes wide with mirth. And tied around his head, in a braid of thin, green grass, was a crown of purple flowers and moss.

"They took him," Leila said, smiling triumphantly. "Now he's a prince."

———

Leila and I haven't talked much since she graduated from art school a month after her mother died. That was almost a decade ago.

The Atlantic interviewed her about her book last month. I have the article on my fridge, with two quotes highlighted in bright yellow:

I have always been a shaman, even as a little girl. There were these people, these beings, who lived in the woods, and they wanted to come and play with me. How could I have said no?

And below it, towards the end:

An artist is a conduit that bridges the worlds. I connect children with the very real beings who live alongside us. We are creating homes for things that live in our imagination and bringing them into our realm. Parents think it's just pretend, but we—the children and I—we know better.

Morgan lives with her now, and he doesn't speak to me, either. He dropped out after his first year of college and now he plays guitar in a doom rock band. I follow the band on Facebook, but I can't listen to the music. It makes me physically ill, all that heavy bass and feedback, but the fans say it carries them to other places. I'm sure it does.

The last time I saw them both was at an opening at a gallery in Syracuse. I watched through the window as Leila showed the slides of her fairy houses, then as she helped dozens of children build their own to take home. She invites parents to bring

Michael M. Hughes

their kids to all her events and provides plastic tubs full of sticks, leaves, and moss, and containers of crystals and smooth, colorful river rocks. Sometimes she'll even bring a box of tiny, thin bones, which she assures the parents are well-bleached and sanitary.

I watched the children through the glass, entranced, as their parents mingled and drank wine. With the kids occupied, the parents seemed to have forgotten they even existed.

Morgan sat in the back of the room in the shadows, alone, with a black notebook in his lap. Although his eyes were hidden by his long, bleached-white hair, I knew he was watching the children, too. And taking notes.

THE GORGON

By Lisa Morton

Stheno can't hold in a harsh laugh when Perseus slays Medusa.

She doesn't care if any of the other customers are irritated; these days most of them are too busy looking at their phones anyway.

The movie was bad before this, but the ridiculous computer-generated monstrosity being decapitated by a pretty man-child in plastic armor is too much for her. Her sister was both more terrifying and more beautiful; the real Perseus was also a lovelier creature than his current cinematic counterpart.

After all, his father was the king of the gods.

Stheno is nearly overcome by a sudden wash of sadness as she thinks of Zeus, and of her own parents, Ceto and Phorcys; of her other sisters and brothers; of the accursed Athena, who had assisted Perseus; and the rest of the gods and heroes she once moved among, all gone now, dead or faded or hidden away. She thought, a few years ago, that she'd glimpsed the Maenads, playing loud music in a video with more views than it deserved, but otherwise she might be the last of the divine Greeks.

Well, and maybe Perseus.

Stheno studies the figure now strutting across the screen, holding a bulging cloth sack that contains Medusa's head, and a sword still dripping blood. The thought of Perseus causes her blood to boil and her head-snakes to writhe and hiss beneath the scarf she wears. Perseus, the murderer who she and Euryale chased three thousand years ago; Perseus, the deceiver who escaped them with a helm of darkness given to him by Hades. Soon after, Euryale gave up the search for Perseus, but Stheno didn't. Mythology never recorded the time she caught up to him, years later, but nearly found her *own* head severed by his adamantine sword. She set aside her plans for vengeance after that, although the burning of it never left her. When she finally heard of the death of Perseus, she rejoiced.

But Perseus—the first great Mycenaean hero—hadn't given up so easily. A hundred years after his death, Stheno had seen him from afar, leading a great army, young again, his name new…but with her same eyes that could turn men to stone she'd recognized him in an instant. When he'd died in battle before she could reach him, she'd once again cursed her failure.

But he'd shown up again, in another century. And again. And again. Always the hero, always in a different form, with a different name, but still him. Sometimes he died before she could reach him; other times she lost his trail. Once he'd injured her badly with the aid of the last centaur, and she'd been forced to flee; she might be immortal, but she felt pain. Stheno continued in her own body while Perseus was reborn generation after generation, always taunting her with the promise of retribution she never achieved.

And so she'd pursued him over the millennia. She learned to walk among humans, to hide her head beneath scarves and hats, her eyes behind glasses or simply kept lowered. Upon occasion, if she needed to appease her anger or her material needs, she removed her glasses and locked gazes with a victim, enjoying the power that filled her as she silenced a screaming man forever, watching his skin turn to white marble or gray granite. Stheno had learned to be cautious with this particular pleasure, however; it wouldn't do to leave a trail of uncannily-realistic statues leading straight to her.

Stheno watches the ridiculous film to the end. As she exits the theater into the wet Seattle night, doing her best to stay away from other patrons, she feels quite certain the actor playing Perseus *is* Perseus. She's seen his soul change slightly over the long years, whittled away with each passing reincarnation, lessened as each fresh era displayed less use for heroes, until he'd dwindled down to the vain, useless fop she'd just seen on screen.

Still, she's never found him this easily before. Despite his stature in the movie business, she knows she could get to him. He doesn't know what or who he really is, so he'd be easy to kill.

This time, at last, she might find her revenge.

—

Daniel is especially tired tonight. He worked at the restaurant until 7 p.m., clearing tables and hustling dishes; then he rode his bike home as fast as he could since his mama wouldn't be home from her job until after 9 p.m., and his Tia Lupe would be bored watching his six-year-old sister Alicia. He'll send Tia home, then do his homework while he gets Alicia fed and into bed. Normally he can get a few hours to himself, from ten until midnight, when he drifts off to sleep, but he's exhausted after what happened at school today.

He stood up to the bullies threatening his friend Ken.

Ken is small, not good with confrontation, an easy target for the class bullies. Daniel has always stood up for him, but today there were three. One—Raul—is big, broad-shouldered, without an ounce of compassion or regard for another human being. Daniel ducked his first punch, but took a blow to the shoulder before his charge caught Raul and his two minions off-guard. Raul went down hard, got back up swearing vengeance, but Daniel was more worried about Ken.

Ken was okay. And no teachers saw the fight, so Daniel needn't fear disciplinary action.

Ken called him a hero today. It wasn't the first time Daniel had heard that. He's never really thought of himself in that way.

After Alicia is in bed and Mama is home, Daniel looks at his shoulder in the bathroom mirror—it's purple, the discoloration inches wide.

His phone bings just then; a text has come in. It's Ken, checking on him. He snaps a quick picture of his shoulder and sends it back to his friend. "Dude that is LOCO," Ken types back, and Daniel isn't sure if that's a compliment or Ken is just grossed out.

The rest of Ken's text is better: his Uncle Lee says he can get them work as movie extras tomorrow night. It's an action movie starring Justin Day. They have to be at a rock quarry in the Valley at 6 p.m. for an all-night shoot. It pays $150.

Daniel's never made that much money in a single day. Even though he's tired, he stays up to text the restaurant and Tia Lupe.

His aunt is excited to hear he'll be in a movie with Justin Day, star of *Sword of the Gods*.

Daniel, though, is happy that he'll be able to add a three-digit check to his college fund.

—

Stheno swims south from Seattle, gliding through the Pacific faster than anything else in the water. Her parents, after all, were sea monsters.

She enjoys her time in the ocean, but it also saddens her (as so much else does these days). She can remember when the world was still new, the water so clear you could see for miles. In those days it was inhabited by nereids and gods, by great Poseidon with his trident that was longer than the first ships. It was an enchanted place. Now the depths are murky, full of humankind's ugly offerings, inhabited by nothing more magical than dying starfish.

She reaches the shore of Malibu before dawn. Crawling up out of the surf like some evolving primordial organism, she finds a wealthy house before her.

Too easy.

Thirty minutes later, she's leaving the house, dressed in designer clothing and driving an expensive car. She laughs as she imagines the owner's friends coming to see her and exclaiming over the incredible likeness of the marble statue they'll find in the bedroom even as they wonder where she's gone.

Stheno's been to Los Angeles before, but it's been years and it—like everything else—has changed. It's slower, dirtier, more crowded. Still she can sense her prey ahead of her. His aura surrounds him like a pheromone net, and Stheno's snake-hair hisses in excitement. They can already taste the life as it passes out of him, replaced by the stone of Stheno's hard heart.

This promises to be an excellent visit.

—

Daniel and Ken arrive at the location at 5 p.m. The guard at the front gate of the quarry frowns—"You guys are early"—but waves them in.

They reach the heart of the rock quarry to find that the central pit has been transformed into a rave, with tiers of dancers and lights lining the sides of the quarry. Daniel's not much of a movie fan (who has time for movies?), but he's impressed by the way the quarry has been remade.

"Extra work's easy," Uncle Lee told them. "You just do what they tell you, and you get a free meal and a little money. What's not to love?"

He did warn them about the waiting around—apparently there was a lot of boring down time between takes—but Daniel doesn't mind because he's got books loaded onto his phone and he can study then.

They check in with an assistant director, who briefly explains the scene (they'll be positioned near the top of the quarry, swaying to music when the hero, played by Justin Day, comes in looking for the bad guy). He tells them they don't have to speak, just look like they're enjoying a rave. Daniel says he can do that.

At 6:30 p.m., Justin Day arrives. Daniel's mildly surprised—he's not as big as he looks onscreen, and he seems kind of tired ("Hungover more like," Ken notes with a smirk).

They've been told not to approach Mr. Day. That's fine with Daniel; he's not interested anyway, although he may have to make up a story for Tia Lupe. He notes only that the star goes to his own trailer at the top of the quarry, and then Daniel returns to his biology textbook.

Uncle Lee was right—making movies *is* boring.

—

It's night before Stheno finds the location. She leaves the car on a side street nearby, adjusts her scarf and glasses, and walks along the fenced perimeter of the quarry until she comes to a place where the lighting is dim and the traffic non-existent. It's an easy matter for her to scale the chain-link and barbed wire, and then she drops down on the other side.

The quarry is big and dark, but it's not hard to follow the lights and sound to where the filming is happening. Stheno has to admit the redressed quarry is spectacular, with a hundred young extras gyrating along its walls. She glances at a row of trailers parked nearby, and feels her blood heat up when she sees a name plate on one:

JUSTIN DAY

An amplified voice booms out. "Cut!"

The music stops playing. The dancers quit. A knot of voices is raised in argument. As Stheno steps back into shadows, a man walks up out of the quarry, moving with rapid rage. He goes into the trailer designated for Justin Day and slams the door behind him.

Stheno stands back, watching, as other men pour out of the quarry. One of them pounds on the door of the trailer. "Justin, you can't do this. We've got to get this scene in the can *tonight*. We're burning money that's not in the budget!"

From within the trailer, Justin shouts, "Fuck your budget! I'm not shooting this shit until those lines are changed!"

The man gives up; turning away from the trailer, he converses quickly with the other men. One of them throws a script to the ground and strides off furiously. The other two go after him.

She hears more voices coming from within the pit, but no one else comes up.

It's time for her to meet Justin Day.

"**Wow, dude,** Justin Day is a fucking *jerk*."

That's Ken, pulling Daniel away from learning about mito-chondria. "Huh?"

"Didn't you see that little shitstorm he just threw?"

Daniel didn't pay much attention. "Oh. Yeah."

Ken glances in the direction of the trailers. "What a *pussy*." Laughing, Ken gives Daniel a playful shove. "You could *so* take him."

Daniel smiles, but he's already turned away. He's more interested in cell structure than in Justin Day.

Stheno doesn't really breathe, so there's no need for her to take a deep breath before entering the trailer. But she nevertheless hesitates, more to relish this moment than compose herself.

The long hunt ends tonight.

She opens the door and steps up into the trailer.

Justin Day is sprawled on a bunk inside, playing a mindless game on his phone. He doesn't look up as she enters. "Are those lines changed yet? I hope so because otherwise you can just turn your ass around and walk right back out."

When there's no response, he looks up. "Who the fuck are you?"

"My name is Stheno."

"Ohhhhkaaay." He utters an exaggerated sigh and sets the phone aside. "And whose agent are you?"

"I am no one's agent except perhaps…death's."

He gapes for a few seconds before picking up the phone again. "Uh-huh. Guess it's time to call security—"

In an instant, Stheno has his phone in her hand. She flings it into a corner of the trailer. With satisfaction, she sees the first flicker of fear cross Perseus/Justin's handsome features. Then his arrogance and petulance return, and he rises from the bunk, trying to make himself big like any less-sophisticated predator. "Oh, you wanna play rough?" He reaches out a hand for her.

In that instant she tears the scarf from her head. Dozens of snakes lunge at him, hissing, their hinged jaws open wide, drops of venom spraying from extended fangs. He gasps and staggers back, colliding with a table, stumbling, barely catching himself. "How…how are you…"

His lips curl up in a smile as he draws himself up. "Oh, I get it: a *Sword of the Gods* fan, right? Hey, I gotta give ya credit— those snakes are good. *Really* good."

"Shut up, Perseus," Stheno says. She hisses like one of her snakes.

"I'm not Perseus, you crazy bitch."

She laughs before saying, "You don't even know, you fool. You *are* Perseus, or at least what's left of him. Granted, your soul has withered over the centuries, but you're still the slayer of my sister. I've chased you, through all your different forms, but you always eluded me...until tonight."

She's pleased to see real fear in him now. Some part of him hears and knows that she's telling the truth.

As she lowers her glasses, he screams.

—

Ken is occupying his time hitting on a lovely young woman who is telling him that she's only doing extra work until she can get speaking roles. Daniel hasn't eaten since morning, and he figures Ken would like a little space, so he excuses himself to go in search of the craft service table he's heard about.

He finds it located near the trailers: two long tables full of vegetables, candy, and chips. He's just reaching for a protein bar when a scream from nearby stops him.

Daniel's first thought is that it's his friend, but he doesn't slow down even when he realizes it's not. He forgets the free food to race to the source.

The scream is coming from inside Justin Day's trailer.

No one else is coming.

Daniel runs forward, flings the door open, steps in—and stops at what he sees.

—

Now.

Stheno removes the glasses and looks into Justin Day's/Perseus's eyes.

392

Their gazes meet.

Lock.

Justin begins to harden.

Mad joy threatens to overwhelm Stheno, but she can't risk turning away for even a second. She trembles with released fury as Justin stops screaming, stops moving, his skin altering, turning gray, his arms held out before him, arms now made from unyielding stone.

It's done.

Stheno wants to howl, dance, ride the night winds as a mad shrieking thing, join the Maenads in their demented revels—but she hears something behind her, a small human sound.

She turns, and there's a young man there, halfway in the door, staring in panting disbelief at the granite figure that was once the mighty Perseus. The boy starts to look up at her. She doesn't know who he is, but her bloodlust has been unleashed and she prepares to bind this one's soul to eternal stone next.

Something tells Daniel to look away. Whether it's because of that scene in *Sword of the Gods* or some far older instinct, he doesn't know, but he drops his gaze, even though he wants to look up (did he see real *snakes* on her head?). He wishes he had a weapon, something to defend himself with. He should turn and run, let the crew's security handle this, but running's just never been his style.

The boy looks away.

Stheno utters a small cry of disappointment and steps forward, ready to *force* him to look. It would be easy; she's done it so many times before.

But something stops her.

She looks at the young man, who now stands resolutely in the doorway, blocking her exit. His head is lowered, his chest is heaving, but he's silent, strong. Strong in a way that she hasn't seen a long time. Strong in the way that Perseus once was, before most of him was hacked away by progress.

The boy is a hero.

Stheno finds herself looking down the long future to come, when there will be no more purpose, no Perseus to keep her in the forward slipstream of time. She thinks of her sister, Euryale, also immortal (as Medusa wasn't); she remembers how Euryale gave up, traveled down to the bottom of the deepest crack in the oceans and stayed there, abandoning the world. How long will it be now before she joins her sister, seeking that release, that oblivion?

Unless...

There is a new hero to pursue.

—

"**What's your** name?"

Daniel has no reason to answer the monster, but his tongue betrays him. "Daniel Ortiz."

"Well, Daniel Ortiz..." Out of his peripheral vision, he sees her moving toward him. He tenses as she reaches out, but her hand is moving to her own face. "I've put my glasses back on. You can look up."

He shouldn't, but he does.

She's smiling as she ties the scarf back around her head, quieting and hiding the writhing serpents. "Daniel Ortiz, I'm sparing you this time but we will meet again. Study your mythology and remember my name: Stheno. Next time, you'll need to be prepared because I won't be so generous again. Especially not if *you* come after *me*."

She pushes him aside so she can leave, and he lets her. As she's stepping from the trailer, she pauses to speak softly into his ear, causing him to shiver. "Look at Perseus over there, remember his fate and remember my name: *Stheno*."

She's gone then.

Moving on legs of ice water, Daniel staggers from the trailer, his mind struggling to parse what has just happened. He tries to grab hold of the sense that he's stepped into some age-old cosmic drama, that he has a part to play—an *important* part, a part that Justin Day wasn't up to.

His life has just been unveiled. He's been told what to do, and he'll do it.

"And *you* should remember *my* name," he mutters, "Daniel Ortiz."

He'll be ready.

(With thanks to Dan'l Danehy-Oakes for the suggestion that started this)

THE DUNGEON OF COUNT VERLOCK

by Norman Prentiss

[Note: This anonymous "novelization" of a long-lost movie written and directed by Bud "Budget" Preston, was scheduled to appear in issue 101 of Monster Project *magazine. The story was uncovered by Norman Prentiss during research for a book,* Life in a Haunted House, *which fictionalizes elements of Preston's life and filmography.]*

"Come back to the couch." Reece patted the cushion beside him. "Sit with me."

"Maybe later." Julia Dougherty stood at the windows, her fingers absently touching the tassel that held back one of the green curtains on one side.

"I bet you like what you see." The two adjoining windows overlooked the back yard, but in nighttime darkness the glass became more of a mirror. Reece winked at her. "I sure do."

"Stop." She half-smiled, but managed to resist his predictable charm. Would she even be here if she didn't feel like she needed him?

Her reflected stare provided no answer, her skin translucent in the sheen of glass...her eyes bright and blank...hair wisping like a torchfire atop her head. She wore a dark blue shirt that absorbed the interior room's light, making her neck appear severed at the collar. Her head floated in the dark of Reece Farraday's back yard.

"I think about that line of trees at the edge of your property," she said. "Those woods...You never know what's behind them."

"More trees."

"Yes, of course. And the path to the abandoned house further back...the mansion you told me about. We *know* what's supposed to be there. But when we can't actually see it..."

"I guess the dark is always kind of scary." Reece stood and moved beside her. In the reflection, his arm disappeared behind her missing torso...he hugged empty air beneath a severed head.

"I'm not just talking about the dark," Julia said. "During the day, too...that line of trunks...limbs and leaves intertwining. It's like a wall. The world behind that wall could change, and we'd never know."

"What you don't know, won't hurt you."

Julia shrugged away from him. "How could you say that? Especially now..."

"I'm sorry." His arm was no longer around her waist, and it was as if he didn't know what to do with it. Reece started to reach out to her...embarrassed, he changed his mind and lifted his hand to run fingers through his slicked-back hair. "I'm sorry."

"Tell me why I'm safer here," Julia said.

He summoned up easy, rehearsed arguments. She'd heard them before, but he guessed it would comfort her to hear them repeated. "I've got solid locks on the front and back doors. I'll keep you in eyeshot or earshot at all times...while you're sleeping,

I'll be right down the hall. Just shout and I'll come running." Then the clincher: "They were alone. The girls who disappeared were all alone when they were taken."

"God, yes, I'll set it to music for you." She slipped into a mocking sing-song voice, a quick twirling dance move as accompaniment. " 'A Woman Alone at Night Was Abducted.' " Julia lowered her arms from the ballerina pose. "That'd be a great tune for the radio, wouldn't it? They'd play it every hour."

"It's a warning. They're just repeating the truth."

"And repeating, and repeating, and repeating, and repeating. Oh, I'm not mad at you. But sometimes we girls *want* to be alone…or at least, when we're with a guy we want it to be our *choice*. Not because we're scared."

"Oh, I get it," he pouted. "You'd rather not be here with me."

"That's *not* what I said." Julia crossed back to the windows, closer to him. She might have guessed he was playing at being wounded…but she could play along. "It's a kind gesture. And I took you up on it, so I must be okay with it on some level."

"On *some* level."

"I'm just being honest. Look, Reece…We haven't been dating that long. Certainly not long enough for me to be spending the night at your place. Maybe we'd get there eventually…I don't know. But this…this awful *situation* in our town…it's kind of moved things too fast between us." She took his hands between hers: a gesture of friendship or gratitude, rather than a lover's clasp. "Some maniac kidnaps women, and hey, *I'm* a woman, so suddenly I'm not safe in my own home anymore. I've gotta be locked up with you."

He broke away from her platonic gesture. "You make it sound like a prison."

"Maybe it is."

"Some prison's aren't so bad. Think of those 'country club' prisons, where they send crooked politicians or corrupt business-men. You get fine meals, a soft bed, all the comforts of home." He tried another wink, the mock lechery actually working on her a bit this time. "And you've got an 'in' with the warden. Special privileges, you know."

"Yeah, that prison talk doesn't quite get me in the mood." But she smiled. In the window her flame-top head floated closer. His arm again disappeared behind her dark-clothed torso.

Their faces pressed closer. He tilted his neck in position to kiss her...

But she turned away... Again, staring out the window, squint-ing at darkness and her own reflection.

"What? You can't see anything." Reece reached for the closest tassel and unhooked it, letting the curtain drop into place on this side. He went to the adjoining window and repeated the process. "There. Now you won't be tempted."

"I wasn't," she said dryly.

"Very funny." They were joking at the moment, like they were on the same wavelength. Maybe she would let him kiss her now. In her words: let it be her *choice,* rather than because she was scared.

He tried again, an arm around her waist, a tilt of his neck, closing his eyes...

She didn't struggle out of his grasp. They kissed.

He felt her lips slide away from his...closed tight...turning toward the curtained windows.

Reece opened his eyes. She slipped away from him.

He'd never seen anyone who was hypnotized, but that's how Julia looked to him now. Her expression was glazed over, facial muscles loose as if she was asleep…but her eyes stayed wide open, drawn to the obscured windows.

Never wake a sleepwalker…But she wasn't asleep, not really. He considered grabbing her as she walked past. Shaking her.

Instead he said her name, the gentle way you'd rouse someone in the morning: *Your alarm has gone off. You'll be late for work.*

She continued to the window, reaching for the closed curtain.

"Julia? There's nothing to see out there."

She pulled the dark green fabric aside…slowly…slowly.

The black back yard appeared, and the reflected room superimposed.

Julia moved closer to the glass…close enough to fog the image.

"It's your face," he told her. "Your pretty face."

She ignored him, staring into her own eyes.

Then a slam like a gunshot, a sudden shake of the glass that distorted her face with the warp of a funhouse mirror. Her own frightened reaction intensified the effect, and she jumped back, almost knocking into Reece.

"I got you," he said.

He steadied her, and she let him. She touched her face, as if to ensure her features hadn't been rearranged. "What happened?"

"You were in a kind of daze," he said.

"No, the window. Something hit the window from outside."

"Stay here. I'll check."

"I'm not supposed to be alone," she reminded him with a hint of sarcasm.

So the two of them went outside.

Neither of them carried a flashlight, but they could see well enough in the glow from the house. They looked inside now…a framed view of the room, and where they'd just been standing.

"Whoever was out here," Julia said. "This is how easily they could watch us."

"Now, don't jump to conclusions." Reece looked at the window and shivered...from the chill night air, or not wanting to admit the possible truth of Julia's statement. "It was probably a bird. They're stupid about glass. They see the light, and think they can fly right into the house, then, *bang!*" He shifted his angle to get a slant view of the window, and a smear of blood seemed to appear at the level of Julia's face...right where her face had been, that is, when she peered out into the yard. "It's your fault for opening the curtain again."

"Where is it, then?" Julia waved her arm at the tufts of grass around their feet, at the shrub bushes that pressed against the side of the house. "Where is this bird I supposedly lured to its death?"

Reece pointed at the blood on the window, then drew a line with his finger to the bush beneath. A glisten of red painted a section of leafage. He moved a branch, peering down.

Julia stood next to him, following his gaze. A round gray-white shape appeared deep in the clutter of branches and leaves.

"Feathers," she said, confirming his guess about a bird. A dead bird, curled up like a ball.

Reece pulled the branch wider, and something like a banded tail appeared behind the curled shape. "Or fur," she said, because she realized her eyes might have played tricks on her, with wet, matted fur simulating the grain of feathers.

Some awful rodent. But that didn't make sense. Without wings, how could the creature have flown at the window?

Reece pulled again at branches from both sides, spreading them wider. More of the shape revealed itself. The tail was larger than she realized, with a calico pattern rather than the stiff banded coils she'd attribute to a rodent.

A kitten or a small cat. A child's missing pet, no doubt, white with gray stripes, and a red collar about its neck. It had hit the window with such terrible force. Someone must have thrown it at the house...

Reece opened the gap even wider, revealing more to the shape than she expected. The calico tail had been some trick of the dim light, shadows cast by the branches and leaves...not a tail at all, but a small pale leg overcast with bands of shadow.

No fur, no feathers.

Skin.

"C'mere, little guy," Reece said, reaching in with both hands to lift the fallen infant.

Careful to avoid scratching the skin with the branches...careful also not to snag the cloth diaper (the original rounded shape she'd seen).

Reece held the infant. He *cradled* it in one arm, a cupped hand beneath the neck to support its head. The idea crossed her mind, then, that he might make a good father, if they ever reached that point.

But why did he cradle the head so gently? It was clear the infant's neck was broken. Its head was smashed in on one side, the tender still-forming skull flattened and the brain bashed beneath.

And there was the strange red collar circling the infant's neck. A line of varying thickness...a sticky, liquid ribbon.

Two violent circles at the widest point in the ribbon. Bite marks...Punctures.

"C'mon now. You're okay." Reece shifted his grip on the infant, his fingers working the arms from beneath, a puppet master bringing life. The arms flapped like wings.

He was moving the arms. The baby couldn't possibly still be alive...with that much blood loss, with that much damage to its head.

She remembered the awful, echoing thump as the baby was thrown against the window glass.

Suddenly, a screech in the night, from the forest behind her, from the strange abomination cradled in Reece's arms. The child's mouth opened, but the mouth looked like a ridged beak, then it opened wider to reveal the tiny animal teeth of a rat...a kitten...a bat.

Another shriek, a human infant in pain, starving to death. Tiny arms continued to flap...with the leathern flutter of bat wings.

"Go on," Reece said. "Go on." He bounced the cradled shape up and down, offering it to the night sky.

He tossed the child into the air.

It flew away.

Julia screamed.

———

"Drink this." Reece handed her a mug. "It'll make you feel better."

"I'm afraid it will keep me up. I already know I'll have trouble sleeping." Julia accepted the mug with both hands and brought it slowly to her lips. "Too hot." She set the mug on the end table, and adjusted a blanket over her legs. She hadn't bothered to change into the pajamas she'd brought in a small overnight bag, but had simply loosened the collar of her canary-yellow blouse to make the day's outfit easier to sleep in.

"My bed would be more comfortable," he said. "I don't mind the couch."

"I'll be fine here. Warm blankets. Lots of pillows. Did you save some for yourself?"

"I'm good." His expression showed such concern for her. A side of Reece she hadn't really seen before…a genuine tenderness, without that ulterior motive guys usually followed… "You gave me quite a scare out there," he said.

"Oh, *you* got the scare."

"Well, I was scared *for* you, okay?"

"Was it…" she said. "Was it really a bird, the whole time?"

He nodded. "A dirty white pigeon. A divebomber, I guess. Musta had a pretty hard noggin, since it was able to fly away."

She tried again with the too-hot coffee, taking a small sip. Reece had made it strong…probably hoping to clear her head. "I saw more than that. I could have sworn."

"Well, it was dark." Reece sat next to her on the couch…at a respectful, rather than amorous distance. Too far away to try that old chestnut, where he'd fake a broad yawn and then "accidently" put his arm around his date's shoulders. "I think I'm starting to understand what you were saying earlier," he said. "You know, how the radio and TV get you gals so excited about danger."

"Us *gals?*"

"It's like a hypnotic suggestion or something. Preconditioning. No wonder you expect to see something awful in the dark. They're making you jump at every sound and shadow, you know?"

"But you're immune."

He shrugged. "It explains what I saw: just a dirty ol' divebombing pigeon. Which one of us do you think is right?"

Julia took another sobering sip of coffee. Inside a bright house, wrapped in a blanket, surrounded by pillows, it was easy to dismiss what she'd seen...*thought* she'd seen. "You're right," she said. "I know you're right." She passed him the mug. "That's enough for now. This *gal* needs to get some rest."

Reece smiled as he stood from the couch. "I can take a hint. If you need anything, call me. I'll come running."

"Thank you," she said, and meant it. "Thank you for being a gentleman...for taking care of me...for not saying you think I'm crazy."

"Leave the light on," Julia said as he paused near the wall switch. She hated to feel so vulnerable around him.

Reece's next remarks seemed to sense her insecurity...covering it for her: "It's an unfamiliar room. You don't want to stumble around if you get up in the middle of the night."

"Exactly," she said.

And he left her alone.

A phrase she'd earlier set to music began to run through her head: "A Woman Alone at Night Was Abducted."

—

Julia tried to sleep. She tossed and turned, punching pillows and rearranging blankets. She undid another button on her blouse to loosen its fit. Her rump sank into a gap between sofa cushions, and she switched to lying on her side...then her hips fell even farther into the gap.

The overhead light was too bright.

Why not turn it off? No need to act like an immature child. She was inside, locked up tight. The things that frightened her might as well be miles away...years away...it all seemed so long ago, like a dream.

Nothing really happened, anyway. There wasn't any screeching, bloody baby with leather wings.

The curtains remained closed over the windows beside the sofa. Maybe she could look into the back yard one last time, to reassure herself.

If she turned off the light, she could see outside better.

And nobody else would be able to see in.

Julia pushed the blankets below her waist then kicked them to the end of the couch. She swung her legs around and sat up.

She walked to the light switch at the other side of the room… clicked it off.

She stood, waiting for her eyes to adjust to the darkness.

She crossed to the adjoining windows. A small line formed where the curtains didn't quite overlap.

The curtains were thick fabric…she remembered how heavy they felt in her hand. Even so, the panel on the right fluttered slightly, as if stirred by a faint breeze.

She reached for the dark gap between curtain panels. Another phantom gust of wind anticipated her fingers, and the gap widened…then closed.

It moved like the gills on a gasping fish.

The fabric rustled. The cloth curtain was a stiff polyester, with a rough burlap backing to help block the light.

Why, then, did it rustle like leather wings?

Julia drew back her hand. A faint squeak sounded from outside…the mewl of a kitten or screech of a bat…a sweaty fingertip rubbing against glass.

At a strange height, a bulge began to form beneath the closed curtain. Julia watched it from where she stood, the same distance she'd stand when inspecting herself in a full length mirror.

She put a hand over her belly.

At the corresponding height, a pregnant bulge swelled beneath the curtain, nearly the size of a basketball.

Julia reached beneath the bottom of her loosened blouse. Her fingers tensed, gathering the flesh of her stomach. She squeezed.

The swelling in the curtain flattened on one side...air deflated from the basketball.

She heard the cry again...too much like the wail of an infant, now. Julia squeezed tighter at her stomach, felt an awful crackle inside, heard the snap of tiny bones.

The curtain fell flat.

Julia released the gathered flesh of her belly. The snap of tiny bones continued to echo in the dark room.

Not bones.

Tapping. Tapping on the other side of the window.

A bird's beak against glass...rodent teeth...feline claws...the tiny fingernails of a human infant.

Leather wings flapping in a steady, wounded beat.

A summons of some kind.

Which animal was it? She pulled back the curtain...peered into the dark of the back yard.

Julia saw nothing. She leaned closer to the glass, and her own eyes stared back. Her eyes were bloodshot from the evening's earlier fright...from lack of sleep.

She blinked, and the bloodshot eyes in the window blinked, too, in exact time.

Maybe a split-second behind.

Julia saw nothing, but the tap and rustle and crack of bones continued. She put her palm flat against the window, and felt rhythmic vibrations through the glass.

Norman Prentiss

She followed the sound outside.

——

"**Did you** call me?"

Reece knew she hadn't called, but he still thought he should check on her periodically during the night. He bumped against a chair as he walked into his living room. "Hey, I thought we decided to keep a light on."

The sight of blankets gathered at the end of an empty couch gave him immediate cause for concern.

The open curtain worried him even more. He ran across the room, cupped his hand on either side of his face and pressed against the window.

He stared into the yard, squinting for the line of trees behind his house.

In the distance, he just managed to spot a flash of yellow...a clothed figure as it disappeared into the trees.

It had to be Julia.

——

She found herself in the middle of the dark woods that stretched behind Reece's home.

Julia was staying with him, so she wouldn't be alone. Reece was protecting her, and she resented that protection, a little...she was strong enough to take care of herself...and then she'd had some kind of scare. A loud noise, an investigation, then a strange animal that changed its horrible, wounded shape as she watched.

No...that had been a trick of the dark...a distortion brought on by fright.

She'd pulled herself together...back to reality. Safe, indoors, sleeping on Reece's couch so he'd be close if she needed him.

So why was she here, now, alone in the woods?

Alone.

She wore her same clothes from earlier today...yellow blouse and tan slacks...but she didn't have shoes. Her stocking feet felt damp against cold, packed earth.

Had she been sleepwalking?

There were no clear signposts. Darkness frustrated her ability to read her surroundings...walls of trees pressed close, confining her to a thin path worn in the dirt. The path curved ahead and behind, making it impossible for her to get her bearings.

One or the other direction might lead her back to Reece's house...but which one?

Julia glanced up at the sky, hoping for a hint...some constellation shaped like an arrow, pointing toward safety. There were no obvious patterns in the dim stars...not that she could read them, anyway. She wasn't a sailor or astronomer.

A scythe moon offered minimal light. A cloud partially covered the crescent shape.

The cloud moved in midnight wind. It seemed heavy... sharper than expected.

It *flapped*.

The shadowy cloud broke away from the moon with a leathern rustle. The sky rippled like a black tarp snapped in the gusts of an approaching storm.

There was a shape in the sky after all...not a constellation, but a hovering breathing thing that passed over stars, winking them out as it moved closer.

Wind through trees, the violent rustle of air, the rhythmic flap of wings bearing closer.

She heard the shriek of an animal, then a thud on the ground…so near that she could feel the earth shake beneath her stocking feet.

Julia tried to pinpoint the location of the sound…on the path, slightly past a curve that disappeared into the trees. Before, she hadn't known which direction she should face to return to Reece's home…now, that goal no longer mattered…

That sound needed to stay behind her. She needed to run the other way.

Because there were footsteps echoing beyond that curve in the path. They sounded a steady scuff of leather-soled shoes in the dirt…but she could hear a muffled brush as well, like the rough pads of an animal's feet…and a staccato click, the curl of claws flexing with each step.

Julia ran, almost blind, following the path that led away from the pursuing threat. Her shoeless feet hit the ground hard, sharp rock edges occasionally scraping her arch or heel, but she ran…all the time fearing she'd run into a dead end.

The footsteps grew closer. Julia reached a straight stretch of the path, followed it long enough to know, if she turned her head, she'd see what kind of menace drew closer…closer.

She was too afraid to look. But she imagined it…a creature with muscled legs and arms, its leonine body covered with dark fur…a wide span of wings stretching behind, their tips clipping against tree limbs on either side of the path…animal eyes that shone with a bright red fire…a cold, black snout…a long jaw, open wide with a drool of anticipation, sharp teeth glinting in the dark…

Sometimes, they say, a monster you imagine is much worse than one you can actually see.

A gust of warm wind shook the surrounding trees. It misted the back of her neck, like the hot breath of her hungry pursuer.

She was still too afraid to turn her head…but she felt it… felt a dark shape growing closer…heard the rapid click and fleshy pad of animal feet…felt another hot, wet gust against the back of her neck.

She ran…

Until something caught her.

—

Reece probably lost some time retrieving a flashlight from the back of a kitchen drawer, but he'd need it to search for Julia. He'd hurry, before she had a chance to get too far…the light would help him discover clues along the trail.

And he could signal with it, too. He'd wave the light, and she'd be drawn to him.

He entered the woods at the location where he thought he'd last seen her. The trees were like anonymous faces in a crowd, impossible to distinguish from each other…but he hoped some tracking instinct would kick in to guide him.

There were paths once you got deeper. He remembered them from when he owned a dog, and used to take short walks…

He also remembered how easy it was to get turned around unawares…how easy it was to get lost.

One path, which he'd told Julia about, led to a large abandoned mansion. He'd asked around town, but could never find out how long ago it had been occupied…or who might have lived there.

For some reason, Boxer had never wanted to follow that path.

The Dungeon of Count Verlock

Norman Prentiss

Reece moved his flashlight across the ground in front, hoping to locate fresh disturbances in the earth. Failing that, he searched for odd rocks or overgrowth or shapes in tree trunks, hoping to trigger some half-buried sense of direction.

Because he felt certain Julia would be headed toward that abandoned house. She'd made that strange comment about the woods, earlier...some weird fascination...

A shriek echoed in the night air. Julia, he thought, but sounding so scared that her voice lost some of its human quality...

The direction of the echo was hard to locate, but he felt like he'd stumbled into the mansion path. Something about the way it curved behind a gathering of leaning trees...clicking an uneasy memory into place.

He ran toward the sound...

And tripped. He hit the ground with a heavy thud that knocked the wind out of him. His flashlight tumbled ahead of him, its back compartment snapping off and the batteries rolling away... Reece stood, quickly dusted himself off, then rushed forward...leaving the useless flashlight behind.

A clue, perhaps, if people later tried to locate him...

He hurried, as fast as he could safely travel in dark and unfamiliar territory, hoping he was on the right path.

Reece grew more optimistic as he distinguished footsteps in the hidden distance ahead.

Still winded from the fall, he pushed himself forward. He panted from exertion as his footsteps scuffed along the winding dirt path. He opened his mouth to call out to Julia, to beg her to slow down, but he couldn't quite catch his breath.

A few times, he saw the subtle glow of a yellow shirt, glimpsed at a gap between trees, or at some tantalizing bend in the path.

Once, a large shadowy shape passed over the shirt, then retreated.

He reached a long straight stretch in the path, and he could see Julia at the far end of it. The yellow shirt, moving with a trance-like sway.

As Reece hurried closer, he expected her figure to get larger... Instead, the closer he got, the smaller she seemed.

An optical illusion...a trick of perspective. She seemed farther away, because he'd judged the shirt would be the size of her full torso. Instead, the patch of yellow was a smaller piece of cloth... part of a sleeve that had torn off, tangled in the fingered overhanging branch of a nearby tree.

Reece stopped, breathing heavy. He picked up the yellow patch of cloth, tilted it in the faint moonlight.

Were those drops of blood on the fabric?

—

Julia broke through a clearing at the edge of the woods.

She hadn't doubled back to Reece's house. Instead, she faced the ominous front of a large mansion.

An *abandoned* mansion, Reece had told her. But this one looked lived in.

Her feet were damp and sore and scraped from the unforgiving ground. Her arm hurt, too...four parallel scratches along her forearm. She'd gotten tangled in a tree limb, back when she thought some creature had chased her. The branch had seemed to grab at her...hold her back...and she'd fought it, pulling away, her shirt sleeve ripping as she escaped and continued to run.

Run from *what?* Nothing followed her...and she realized she'd been having another fright-induced hallucination...there was no real danger in these woods.

All the same, she had wanted out. She wanted to escape from the maze of forest paths...the smothering mass of tall trees all around, closing in, blocking the night sky. She wanted a cool grass lawn under her feet, or the predictable smooth surface of a sidewalk or asphalt road. She wanted the comfort of a suburban neighborhood filled with familiar, interchangeable houses.

Instead, she got a strange mansion. It might provide some shelter, though...if she could manage to get inside.

The large structure sat at the edge of the clearing, another bank of trees stretching behind it. She crossed an unkempt yard, dry grass cracking against her sore feet as she headed toward the mansion's ornamented entryway. The structure was three stories high, with several sets of tall windows on either side of a columned porch. A bas-relief frieze spanned atop massive double doors, a brass lion's-head knocker at the center of each.

She climbed the stairs onto the porch. She reached toward the ring beneath one of the lion heads, then thought better of it.

"Is anyone here?" she whispered...then paused as if she'd spoken loud enough to prompt an answer.

Why was she certain the mansion was inhabited? The house was quiet...shades closed...lights out.

"I feel like someone's been watching me," she said. A whisper, again...a dare. "Show yourself."

She reached again for the door knocker. "It's the middle of the night. If there *are* people here, they should be asleep."

Julia grasped the ring, tapped it gently. She stepped back and waited.

Louder now, explaining her situation to a paneled slab of wood. "I'm sorry to bother you. I got lost in the woods. My feet and arm are injured. May I use your phone? May I stay here and wait for help?"

No answer.

Julia recalled her musings from earlier in the evening, about the mysteries beyond the woods' edge. You can't see past the line of trees. Even if you know what paths stretch behind them, you can't be certain.

Doors are the same way. You knock on them, expecting someone to answer. It's often a familiar home, and your parent or best friend would answer and invite you inside. But a stranger could always open the door. Disturbing variations passed through her mind:

- A beautiful young woman bars the entrance, saying... "Your boyfriend doesn't want to see you anymore. He's with me, now."

- A doctor... "Your mother's inside, but too sick to have visitors. She's dying."

- A police officer..."Miss, can you tell us why you're here? What is your relationship to the victim?"

Julia shook her head, concentrating again on the door in front of her...stubbornly opaque...unmoving.

She again reached for the brass ring. Lifted it, then let it drop.

A sudden chill came over her. She hugged her arms close to her chest. She stamped her feet, which had begun to feel numb.

"Please answer." She barely spoke aloud. She was too strong to ask for help, so instead she asked: "What do you want? I'll do—"

A loud snap, like the breaking of a bone. The slide of a latch... the door creaking inward.

Candlelight flickered from a three-pronged candelabra. The man who held it looked like he was dressed for a formal dinner...a black tuxedo with a frilled white shirt at the open collar. A red broach hung about his neck...a cluster of jewels like small berries, full of juice.

"Ah, come in," he said. "I am Count Verlock." As the man smiled his greeting, his teeth shone bright and large. He was about the same age as Reece, but with a maturity her boyfriend lacked. Perhaps it was an illusion brought forth by the formal clothing, making him seem part of a long gone, more serious era.

"A count...?" Julia felt self-conscious now, in casual dress, hair disheveled from sleep, shoeless, a sleeve torn from her blouse and the arm bleeding. She wondered if there was some etiquette she should follow...eyes lowered, bowing before majesty...or if she should stand straight, a soldier at attention, awaiting some command.

"Come in," he told her, stepping back and waving an arm toward the interior of his home.

She stepped forward cautiously, but paused at the line of the doorway.

Wasn't there something about counts and invitations, about crossing thresholds? A vague memory about books or movies struggled to the surface...a supernatural threat, requesting entrance...the victim foolishly unlocking the door...a gracious hostess to her own doom.

Yes, that's right. She'd gotten it backwards. The danger was inviting a monster into your *own* home. This situation was perfectly safe.

She lifted her gaze...stared directly into Count Verlock's eyes. His expression was so welcoming. She didn't want to offend him.

Julia stepped into the antechamber. The marble floor was cold against her wounded feet. She glanced down...saw a smear of blood she'd dragged across the elegant tile. "Oh, I'm so sorry. I've ruined..."

"You're hurt." Count Verlock waved the candelabra closer to inspect her. She felt the heat of flickering candles as it passed over her face, over her chest, along the scratched, exposed arm.

And a heat of shame, too. "I don't quite remember how I got here," she said. "I should be better dressed."

The candles were almost close enough to singe the fine soft hairs of her forearm. With his free hand, the Count touched her elbow. He positioned his fingertips at the top of the four long scratches...then he traced the length of the bloody grooves all the way to the underside of her wrist.

"I'll need to clean this...and bandage it." As he removed his hand, the pads of his fingertips wore small circles of Julia's blood.

"Your feet," he said. The Count dropped to his knees setting the candelabra on the ground next to him. His position reminded her of a man proposing marriage...coupled with his elegant clothing, perhaps he was more like the fairy-tale prince, ready to test the fit of Cinderella's glass slippers.

At the same time, he reminded her of an awful predator lying in wait...a crouching animal, ready to pounce.

He supported her calf as he lifted one foot for inspection, then the other. His fingertips prodded gently at the soles of her feet, and the sensation was at once pleasant and worrisome.

Julia's stockings had been torn as she raced over the rough forest path. The Count's probing fingers moved bits of torn cloth aside...and she wondered if some of those shreds were actually strips of torn flesh.

She tried not to think about it…turned her head away, as she often might during a doctor's examination.

"Clean and bandage," he said. The candle flames flickered, and shadows danced across his face, distorting his handsome features. She looked down, and the Count's fingertips were no longer bloody. Instead, they seemed…wet.

Still kneeling at her feet, he smiled up at her. If he intended the gesture to be comforting, he failed miserably. Flickering shadows cast an illusion of gristle over his wide mouth of white teeth… flames illuminated the brooch of ruby jewels about his neck, aiming a reflection of bright red flecks onto his moistened lips.

"I will take care of you." He stood, then passed behind her to close the latch on the front door. It snapped into place with an echoing clang. "You will be safe here."

The Count stood next to her, pointing the candelabra forward to direct her into the next room. He touched her elbow, lightly prodding her forward.

Julia threw one last glance behind, at the solid oak door she'd previously stood on the other side of. As before, she couldn't see through it. The outside world might have disappeared, for all she could tell.

Or, Reece might be coming to find her. She imagined him running to the door, banging on it, slamming down the ring of each brass knocker, calling out her name, crying *Let me in, I want to help you*…and getting no answer.

She had made her choice, she realized. Her choice.

Julia allowed Count Verlock to lead her deeper into his mansion.

Reece stumbled out of the woods and raced across the dry lawn.

He recalled visiting this place a few years earlier, his dog struggling on its leash, alternating between angry barks and fearful whimpering.

"Calm down, boy," he'd said, placing a firm hand on Boxer's collar to hold him in place. "Nobody's home. Nothing here to worry about."

And the dog barked and whimpered at an abandoned house.

Now, Reece bounded up the steps to the front porch. One of the boards creaked beneath him, and his foot fell part-way through the rotted wood.

"Careful," he told himself. He tested the firmness of each new step as he crossed to the double doors.

One of the age- and weather-worn doors listed crooked in its frame. A rusted brass knocker hung in the center of the other.

He rattled the knob of each door...pushed his shoulder against them in turn, throwing his weight into it. When they didn't budge, Reece put his fingers in the gap caused by the ill-fitting door, trying to separate them further.

No success. He searched the junk and debris that had gathered on the porch over the years, and found a tree limb. He fit one end between the doors, and pushed and pulled.

The doors wouldn't budge. The limb snapped when he renewed his attempts.

Enraged, he banged at one of the doors.

He wasn't sure why he felt so desperate. If he couldn't get inside, then Julia wouldn't have been able to, either.

Why was he so certain she'd come here?

He reached in his back pocket and removed the scrap of clothing he'd found in the woods.

Norman Prentiss

The blood-stained scrap of clothing.

And then one of the doors creaked open.

—

Count Verlock had been gone a long time.

He had been leading Julia down a long staircase...so deep that she couldn't see the bottom from her current position. The Count had used his candelabra to light wall torches along the way, but the ones beneath remained dark.

A sound had caught the Count's attention, and he'd cautioned her to remain still. "Don't attempt to go forward on your own. There's no railing."

How long did he expect her to wait?

Julia moved next to the wall, taking comfort from the heat and light offered by the nearest torch.

She wondered again why he was taking her towards a basement. The house was three stories tall...surely there were more comfortable rooms above. And in her condition, with injured feet, these hard stone stairs seemed to make matters worse.

But she'd trusted him. The Count's deep voice had soothed her..."Clean, then bandage. A few more steps." He was a gentleman, and she felt safe with him. The idea that he might be connected with the town's recent disappearances had never crossed her mind.

Had it?

Now, Julia ran her hand along the wall. The stone felt cold, even the area around the torch. She lifted her hand and held it near the flame.

On the wall, the shadow of her hand repeated her movements. She flexed her fingers, curled and uncurled.

She brought her hand closer to the flame, and the shadow on the wall grew larger. Julia wriggled the digits again, then counted them.

"Too many," she said, then dropped her arm.

The shadow remained on the stone. Its eight digits wriggled.

A large spider scurried down the wall.

Julia jumped back. She stumbled, accidently kicking a rock over the edge of the railless staircase.

After a brief pause, she heard the rock hit bottom.

Where was the spider? She shivered at the thought of stepping on its plump, bristled body...its venomed mandibles clicking at her bare feet, drooling thick poison into open wounds.

Julia wondered what sound the spider's legs would make against hard stone...the fingers of a silk glove sweeping crumbs off a marble tabletop.

She moved back toward the torch again, grabbed it...rocked it back and forth...snapped it from its place in the wall.

As she waved the torch, all the shadows seemed to move like silken fingers...the plump legs of spiders.

Julia spun in a circle with the flaming weapon. She lowered it to the ground to warn away any venomous threat.

"I can't stay here," she said, giving voice to her anxiety. The way back...the way the Count had headed when he abandoned her...was already lit by other torches. But now that she held her own torch, Julia was free to illuminate her descent. "Which way?"

She listened, hoping to hear whatever had drawn the Count's attention. Far above her, she thought she could distinguish two male voices, arguing. One of them was Count Verlock. The other one sounded like Reece.

Then a woman's voice. "Verlock." A weakened voice…a whisper that seemed to echo all around. "You animal."

From nowhere…from everywhere: the sounds of a struggle… an angry splintering of wood…a frustrated clatter of metal.

"Release me." The same voice…so weak, like a hundred-year-old woman on her deathbed.

All around her, the woman's whisper…the quarreling men… the rattle of chains.

Julia hesitated. She thought of the women in her town who had disappeared. She considered her own plight, the weakness in her scratched arm, her tattered feet. A rush of empathy for the faint, whispering woman flooded over her. That could be her *own* voice, crying out for help.

Despite the confusion of echoes, Julia knew the whisper had to be coming from the bottom of the stairs.

———

An old man stood on the other side of the door.

Reece immediately assumed the man was a vagrant. A decrepit bum squatting on the abandoned property. He was dressed in an ill-fitting tuxedo that looked like it had been fished out of a dumpster.

A white shirt beneath had faded to filthy tatters, and a dark gravy or ketchup stain marred the patch above his chest. An awful smell rose up from the man, and Reece had to wave his hand in front of his face.

"Step aside, Pops," Reece said, attempting to muscle his way in.

The vagrant didn't budge. "I am Count Verlock," he said. "You are trespassing."

"Listen, Bub, nobody's owned this place for a hundred years." Reece pulled a strip of yellow cloth from his pocket...waved it like a flag. "My girlfriend ran this way."

A haughty expression crossed the vagrant's face. He reminded Reece of an ignorant low-life who tried to adopt the snooty posture and voice of an aristocrat. "Your girlfriend is not here." The man dismissed the torn cloth with a wave of his hand...a spoiled patriarch sending an ill-cooked meal back to the kitchen. "Perhaps she was running away from you. You seem rude." The self-appointed "Count" looked him up and down. "Unimpressive."

If Reece had time for games, he might have slapped the old man's face and challenged him to a duel. Instead, he decided to return to his original plan...pushing the man aside and searching the dilapidated building.

Reece looked at the frail man, judging how hard to shove him. He'd easily fold at a punch to the stomach. Or he could kick his legs, knock his feet out from beneath him.

His feet...

Discarded dress shoes, rescued from a dumpster. Laceless... the sole flapping on one...on the other, a large toe with a filthy unclipped nail, protruding from the tip.

But around these feet...

Rotting wood on the floor, and glistening streaks of red.

Fresh blood.

—

Julia stepped onto the landing at the bottom of the stone staircase. A wooden door reinforced with metal bars waited at the end of a short hallway. A small slot was carved into the door at eye level…and an inset door at the bottom, similar to ones she'd seen in houses that allowed separate exit or entry for small pets.

The woman on the other side whispered again…a harsh sound that emerged through the door slot and echoed through the steep chamber. "You abomination. Release me."

Julia raised her torch to the eye-level slot, but the interior of the room was too dark. She cleared her throat, as preparation to offering soothing words to the prisoner. Before she could speak, the other woman began to panic. The rattling of shackles…a sickly thump of flesh against unyielding stone.

"Verlock," the prisoner shrieked. "You're killing me!"

More rattling…the woman on the other side apparently thrashing about like a beached fish.

"Verlock…I know you're there!"

Julia looked over her shoulder.

She thinks I'm someone else, Julia thought. It was an awful feeling she never thought she'd experience. *The woman's terrified. She's terrified of* me.

And the prisoner shrieked now…a song of pained, incoherent syllables.

Again Julia attempted soothing words…a scratch still in her throat caused by her own discomfort throughout this night of horrors. She planned to say, "I'm here to help."

Instead, the words tumbled together in a gurgling hiss.

Behind the door, a horrible gasp…a frightened silence…a pleading moment of calm. "Oh god, not the *beast,*" she whimpered. "Anything but that…I beg you…"

Julia finally gained control of her voice. "No. You don't understand—"

Suddenly...the inset door flipped open...a skeletal hand reached through...it grabbed Julia by the ankle.

"Let go," Julia shouted and, nearly dropping the torch, she kicked with her other foot...knowing it was wrong...that she'd bring the tortured prisoner more pain...this woman's brittle fingers scraped and streaked with blood, a dark bruise encircling her wrist...and Julia's foot coming down, a horrible snap as she pulled her ankle free from the surprisingly resilient grip.

Julia tried reason again. "I want to..."

"I know what you want," the prisoner whispered. Instead of drawing back her arm, the woman slowly began to rotate it... palm upward...the underside of the wrist exposed.

Seeing the dark bruise around the woman's wrist, Julia had earlier attributed the injury to metal handcuffs or shackles...they cut off her circulation, and she'd fought against them, breaking free to reach under the door to her prison cell.

She held the torch closer. The underside of the woman's wrist was different. The skin here was cleaner than the surrounding area...white and pale.

Except for two crusted scabs at the center. Their raised shape, like the domes of two identical moles...the way they were positioned...

They looked like bite marks.

"Go ahead, Verlock." A hopeless resignation was evident in the woman's weak voice. "Feed."

—

She badly wanted to rescue this unfortunate woman.

At the same time, she wanted to be elsewhere.

The Dungeon of Count Verlock

Norman Prentiss

In her mind's eye, she ran away.

She imagined escaping the dungeon of Count Verlock. She ran up the long staircase, the steps seeming to stretch endlessly above her.

Finally she reached the main floor of the building. She remembered a high-ceilinged dining room, the walls decorated with elegant tapestries.

She imagined herself reaching the front of the house…pausing outside the vestibule, looking in…

She saw:

—

Reece stands there, holding Count Verlock by the collar…that beautiful frill shirt bunched in Reece's angry fists. "What have you done to her?" Reece yells. "You better start talking."

Julia is so proud of him, the way he's come to her rescue…so rough and strong…

"I mean it." Reece shakes the Count again…almost seems ready to throw him against the wall. "Where is she?"

The Count is undeniably handsome, but how could she ever have been fooled by this well-dressed weakling? He's a milquetoast… especially in comparison to Reece. "I'm right here," Julia tells him.

And Reece is a statue frozen in place…the Count on tiptoes, nearly lifted off the ground from Reece's rough treatment.

Julia blinks her eyes.

The room…looks different.

The elegant chandelier so glamorous overhead…now many of its crystal hangings missing, cobwebs stretching from one broken candle to the next.

The gold trimmed tapestry on the wall...gone now, and the wall beneath chipped, stained, water-damaged.

The beautiful hand-woven carpet...rolled away years ago, to reveal a rotted, wooden floor.

"Reece," she says. "I'm right here."

Finally the statue moves. He turns his head.

His head lolls. His eyes are empty.

A large gash appears in Reece's neck...a chunk of flesh ripped out...bitten out.

The two men have changed position. Reece is the one nearly held in the air...

The Count's arm lifts...Reece's body rises.

Count Verlock holds Reece over his head with both hands. The fiend closes one hand about her boyfriend's throat...tightens his fist as if squeezing the last drops of water out of a sponge.

Verlock's vile fanged mouth catches these drops.

He tosses her boyfriend's emptied body aside.

Before her eyes, Count Verlock's elegant clothing begins to shred into wrinkled rags. His skin wrinkles, too, as if he's suddenly aged into the oldest person she had ever seen.

"Let's tend to your wounds," Verlock says.

———

Julia felt gentle pressure along the scratches in her arm. Later, an antiseptic ointment washed over the abrasions in the soles of her feet.

She'd been sleeping. She kept her eyes closed.

"Let's tend to your wounds," someone said. She heard the clatter of sterile instruments on a metal tray.

Norman Prentiss

Next, she felt bandages rolled and tightened over her cleansed wounds.

The bandages clicked into place...over her wrists, over her ankles.

She opened her eyes to find herself in a dungeon, shackled to the wall.

Count Verlock stood close, inspecting her. He wasn't the handsome gentleman who'd first greeted her. This was an old man...a hundred years old...hundreds or thousands.

The old man who killed Reece...who'd been kidnapping women in their neighborhood.

Julia looked to one side, and saw another woman shackled to the wall. Her face had grown worn and thin, her eyes sunken into shadow, but Julia recognized the woman from a missing-persons report on the news.

She turned her head in the other direction...saw another of the missing women, bound as Count Verlock's prisoner...

His food...

The Count scratched at Julia's arm, making the wounds bleed anew. He picked bits of flesh off the bottoms of her feet.

Daylight.

Two police officers paused at a forked path in the woods.

Outside a dog barked, straining at the end of its leash.

"Hey Sheriff, give him a chance to refresh the scent," said the younger officer...the one holding the leash.

The older man removed a yellow scrap from a sealed bag... held the cloth under the dog's nose. "Here you go, Boxer."

The dog barked again, more certain this time, leading the officers down the right-most path.

Eventually, they emerged into a clearing. The abandoned mansion awaited them.

"What's the matter, boy?" The junior officer kneeled next to the animal. It whimpered now, its back legs shaking. "You brought us here. Why so skittish now?"

"I'm checking the ruins," the sheriff said. "Bring Boxer along, will you Fremont?"

They crunched across dry grass to the front of the decayed house. Fremont practically had to drag the reluctant dog along with them.

When they reached the porch, the dog began barking again. The officers climbed up the unsteady wooden stairs, then paused at the landing.

A section of the porch in front of the double doors had collapsed.

"Hold back a second." The sheriff knew his own weight was risky enough...the splinters suggested that the porch boards had snapped recently.

He leaned over, carefully peering into the freshly made pit. "Poor guy." A short distance below, a crumpled body was impaled on gory bits of rotted wood. "It's the boyfriend."

The dog started barking uncontrollably, the smell of Reece's blood driving the animal towards frenzy.

"Not him," the sheriff said. "Found him. Now we need to focus on the girl." He pulled out the strip of cloth...rubbed it under the dog's nose.

Boxer strained at the leash again, as if ready to jump over the pit and attack the double doors.

The Sheriff reached across the gap and tested one of the doors. It opened easily. "Let's go, Fremont."

"Do you think we'll find her?"

"I don't know *what* we'll find." He turned on a flashlight, then stepped over the gap and inside the abandoned property.

—

Julia heard steps approaching.

"Verlock," she said, hating to hear the name aloud. Hating the weak rasp of her fearful voice. "You abomination." She shook at the manacles on her wrists…kicked her feet and the chains rattled.

The footsteps grew closer. "Release me," she hissed in a pained whisper. "You're killing me." The footsteps paused outside her dungeon, and she stared at the reinforced door. A shadow moved over the eye-level slot, and she thought she caught a gleam of white…a horrible fanged mouth, smiling in anticipation of the next meal.

Why was he taking so long to enter. Was this terrifying delay part of her torment? "I know you're there," she whispered.

Julia waited, her own teeth chattering from fear…from some unholy chill. She listened.

From the other side of the door, she heard…*panting.*

Then a weight fell against the door…the pad of an animal's feet…the frantic scratching of claws.

"Oh god," Julia screamed, finding her full voice. "Not the *beast!*"

She could never bear the Count's ghastly feedings. Each sucked drop of blood stole more than her life's energy…it stole her sense of self...her belief in humanity...in rightness. It buried any dim hope that she could ever escape.

And whenever he appeared to her in animal form, that experience was always the most horrible.

The door finally opened. Julia screamed as the beast came bounding into her cell.

A dog stopped short at the end of its leash. Two police officers entered.

The younger of them ran toward her...covered her with a blanket.

The shoulder belt of the police car pressed secure across her chest. Julia looked out the window as the scenery rushed by. The cemetery passed on the left, then a church.

A siren wailed...a strobe light flashed as the car raced forward.

"We'll get you to the hospital as quick as we can."

The driver was the older of the two men. She recognized him from newspaper photos as Sheriff Hazelbury.

Julia had a foggy memory of this man helping her...using some combination of pliers or bolt cutter or wire-picks to snap or unlock her shackles. And the younger man, so strong...carrying her up that long flight of steps and out of the mansion. Through the woods, past the back yard of Reece's house to a waiting squad car parked out front.

The world moved past her as she was carried...just as it moved past her now from the car. She'd worried that the officer would get tired from carrying her, but he never complained.

Maybe she wasn't that heavy of a burden. She'd lost so much blood, after all.

Julia looked toward the backseat of the car, but it was empty. "Where's your partner? Is he helping the others?"

The Sheriff half-turned to respond, keeping one eye on the road ahead. "Others?"

"Those other kidnapped women. In the dungeon with me."

He didn't respond. The scenery scrolled past…the cemetery on the left, then the church.

Julia almost wanted to unbuckle her seatbelt and jump from the moving car. "We have to go back for them," she said. "And Count Verlock. Did you find him? Did you arrest him? Kill him?"

"Calm down, now, miss." The sheriff…kept one eye on the road, but looked more worried.

Julia strained against her seatbelt and shoulder strap. They felt heavy, reminding her of the persistent weight of metal chains, the confining cuff of shackles over her wrists and ankles.

The cemetery passed on the left, then the church. She knew she'd seen them before. The scenery was looping past like images projected onto a screen.

The screen of memory.

Julia started to wail. She pulled at the latch of her seatbelt…grabbed at the handle of the passenger-side door. Neither would budge.

The sheriff pulled the car over, bringing it to a stop. Julia was shaking, thrashing in her seat like she was in the middle of an epileptic seizure. Sheriff Hazelbury put his arms on her to comfort her…to steady her…to keep her from hurting herself. He leaned his body over hers, to restrict her movements.

More weight. The Sheriff smothered her like the chains, like the shackles...like the press of Count Verlock's body looming over her, taking an unoffered gift of her life's blood.

"I'm still there!" Julia screamed. "The Dungeon of Count Verlock! Oh God, someone save me. I'm still trapped there!"

Mama's Sleeping

by Brian James Freeman

Someone had shoveled the crumbling sidewalk and Jacob *was* grateful for that small favor as he made his way toward the brick apartment building, but he was also fairly certain he should have called off sick like most of his coworkers apparently had. Temperatures in the teens, wind chill less than zero, and most of his stops so far had required him to trudge through two feet of snow from the previous week's storm.

He wondered again what he was doing with his life. This was no way to make a living. Not only was the pay significantly less than the vo-tech program had promised, but people genuinely seemed to hate him. Sometimes kids threw snowballs or chunks of ice at his distinctive red and white work van with the VeriNet logo on the side. Adults yelled things he couldn't hear over the drone of the engine, although he was surprisingly good at reading lips when it came to the nasty names he was called.

Jacob had spent time in the joint and he never would have guessed that "cable repair technician" might end up being the

435

most despised thing he could be known for. Some days he felt like public enemy number one, as if people thought he was personally responsible for the lies the flashy VeriNet advertisements used to get suckers locked in for two years of substandard service.

That said, he had a job to do—a job he *did* appreciate having, given his record—so here he was, making his way past the battered cars sleeping in the snow valleys their owners had excavated. There were also dozens of vehicles still cocooned in dirty mountains of ice, either because they were abandoned or because no one cared enough to liberate them. This had once been a nice part of town, maybe fifty years ago, but now you wouldn't want to be caught walking these streets after dark.

Jacob entered the lobby of the apartment building. Three of the overhead lights were busted and a fourth flickered as if taking a few last gasps of breath before dying. The green tile floor was wet with melted snow. A trashcan overflowed with junk mail. There was a dark puddle that Jacob slowly realized was blood no one had bothered to clean up.

"Jesus," he muttered. He checked the work order one more time—J Smith, Apartment 6B—and he groaned when he saw the date the troubleshooting call was logged. Four days ago. *Christ.* Folks were usually plenty pissed if one day had passed before someone arrived to fix their cable, let alone four.

He started up the stairs to the sixth floor, taking care not to slip and fall on the narrow steps. His health insurance plan was useless and he couldn't afford a trip to the emergency room. Hell, he wouldn't be able to pay his *regular* bills if he had to take time off to go to the hospital.

As he passed the door to the second floor, he heard Mexican rock music blaring. Thanks to his time in prison, he *habla un poco de Español,* just enough to get by, but not enough to follow anyone speaking too quickly or a singer screaming over heavy guitars and drums. The song was probably about chasing *señoritas* anyway; most of that music was in his experience. Nothing wrong with that. He loved the *señoritas* very much. Who didn't?

The door to the third floor did nothing to block the noise of kids running and shouting in the hallway in a mix of English and Spanish and Spanglish. There were wails and piercing shrieks, the likes of which only children could produce, sounds that might be blissful happiness or profound anger or both. Jacob shook his head, wondering how the neighbors tolerated the commotion.

By the time Jacob reached the sixth floor, he was sweating. He located apartment 6B, knocked on the door twice, and announced his presence and his company's name, as was standard operating procedure. Then he waited to discover how bad his day might get. Sometimes he was greeted with a stream of profanities about how late he was, how long the customer had been without service, and everything else that was apparently his responsibility and burden. That said, sometimes the customers were gracious and appreciative of his work. There was no way to guess which way the service call might go. Nice part of town, bad part of town, it didn't matter. You met angels and assholes in both places.

After a minute, Jacob knocked again. The scheduled appointment window was huge, 11 AM to 4 PM in this case, so it was possible the customer wasn't home, which would absolutely suck given the stairs. He would have to make his way back to his van, report to dispatch, and wait fifteen minutes before trying to contact the customer again. If there was still no answer at the door, he could log the appointment as a no-show and let this be someone else's problem on a different shift. Or perhaps he would be back tomorrow. You never knew how the cards of customer service might be dealt.

As Jacob prepared to knock for the third and final time, he heard the click of a deadbolt unlocking. The door opened a crack and a metal chain sagged in the opening. At first Jacob thought no one was there, but then he spotted the eye peering out at him, halfway down the door, nearly at his waist. The eye of a child.

"Hello, I'm Jacob from VeriNet." He tilted the ID badge pinned to his parka toward that watching eyeball. "I was sent to check on a problem with your cable."

The door opened further, enough so Jacob could determine he was speaking to a little girl. Her yellow dress was dirty and there was a smudge of peanut butter on her face. Her hair was in a ponytail, but it hadn't been washed in a while.

"Mama's sleeping," the little girl whispered, raising one finger to her lips.

This wasn't an entirely surprising statement, not on this side of the tracks where half the kids had no fathers—immaculate conception babies some people called them—and their moms lived on food stamps and state assistance. Sleeping in until noon was probably pretty common in this building, in fact. Yet Jacob was shocked by the size of the televisions he saw in some of the most dilapidated apartments in town. Between what those luxuries cost to purchase—or more likely rent—and the price of the services VeriNet sold these people, he wondered why they needed so much help from his taxes.

The little girl stared at Jacob and he began to feel uncomfortable, as if she had somehow heard what he was thinking. Those eyes were both beautiful and haunting, and they were not trusting.

Jacob forced the thought from his mind and returned to his standard script for these situations. "There's a service fee if VeriNet has to send someone else again for the same problem. When does your mother usually get out of bed?"

"I don't know." The little girl sniffled and Jacob realized her eyes were wet with tears. "She hasn't woken up in days."

Oh shit. Everything clicked. He had heard stories of technicians finding customers dead, sometimes in bed and sometimes on the toilet and sometimes in the garage with the car still running, but it hadn't happened to him. Not yet, at least. He took a deep breath.

"How many days?" he asked, keeping his voice calm and casual.

"Three. I think."

"It's okay," Jacob replied when he couldn't think of anything else to say. "Maybe she's just real tired, right?"

The little girl closed the door without another word. Jacob wasn't sure of his next move. He doubted anyone was home in the other apartments on this floor. They were too quiet compared to the rest of the building. His cell phone was locked in the glove compartment of his work truck, per company policy. And that little girl was in there, all alone, with her almost certainly dead mother.

Jacob was still debating what to do when the door swung open. He stepped inside and the little girl closed the door behind him. The living room was neatly decorated with shelves of books, several potted plants, two side tables with reading lamps, and a couch. There wasn't any clutter and the apartment smelled clean. The furniture wasn't fancy but it was well cared for. Maybe he had misjudged the people who lived here.

"Where's the television?" Jacob asked out of habit.

"Mama's room," the little girl whispered. "She has the television. I got the radio."

"Okay, just stay here. I'll check on her."

Jacob forced his best smile, set his workbag next to the couch, removed his heavy winter gloves, and entered the apartment's lone hallway. There were three doors. To the right was a bathroom and to the left was a bedroom where he could hear the local pop station counting down this week's hits. Straight ahead was the master bedroom.

Jacob's heart accelerated as he approached the bedroom door. He was almost certain of what he would find and he didn't know what he would do then. He certainly hadn't expected to be put in this situation when he left his apartment this morning.

Jacob knocked on the door. No answer. He struggled to remember the name of the customer on the work order, which he had left in his bag in the living room. A common name...

"Hello, Ms. Smith? This is Jacob from VeriNet. I'm here about the problem with your cable."

No answer. He knocked and spoke louder. Still, no answer.

Jacob turned the doorknob, stepped into the room. The curtains were drawn and he walked toward them, keeping his eye on the figure under the comforter on the bed. The sheets did not rise and fall. He didn't attempt to muffle the impact of his work boots, but the person in the bed did not react.

Jacob pulled the curtains open, allowing the blinding winter sun to flood the room, and as the light illuminated the bed, he was convinced the woman was dead. He didn't need to examine her any closer to be sure. Her skin looked like wax and she wasn't breathing.

Oh shit, Jacob thought, stepping out of the bedroom and closing the door. As he made his way down the hallway he did his best to keep his expression neutral, but he had no idea if he was successful. The little girl stood by the couch.

"What's your name?" he asked.

"Elizabeth. How's my mama?"

"You were right, your mother's sleeping." The words were a spur-of-the-moment decision. He saw a telephone in the kitchen. There hadn't been one in the master bedroom. He knew what he needed to do next. "Did I hear the radio in your room?"

"Mama says it's okay so long as I don't bother the neighbors."

"That's very smart of your mother. Can you show me your radio?"

"Okay, I guess."

Elizabeth opened the door on the left side of the hallway and Jacob followed her into the small pink and white bedroom. The radio perched on the petite dresser was a little bit louder now, but the music was still so soft the girl didn't have to worry about any neighbors complaining. Some teenage pop star Jacob couldn't name if his life depended on it was belting out a tune that sounded like every other song on the radio these days. Even the soft parts of the music were loud.

"Are you sure my mama's okay?" Elizabeth asked, her voice conveying suspicions that all was not well in her world.

Jacob knelt before her, wiping a tear from her cheek. He took her small hands into his much larger hands. He squeezed in what he hoped was an encouraging manner, and the sensation of her tender flesh touching his callused skin sent an electric jolt through his body. He released her hands and his face flushed.

"Everything will be okay if you're a *good girl* and don't make a fuss," Jacob said as he reached under her yellow dress.

Elizabeth's eyes grew wide in horror as Jacob's fingers looped into her cotton underwear and yanked them toward the floor. She squirmed backwards, but he grabbed onto her arm and squeezed hard. The struggle set his entire body on fire, sending more electric thunderbolts through every muscle. This was the burning hunger that had landed him in prison, keeping him away from temptation for several very long years — and yet his time in the concrete cellblock suddenly felt like it was so very long ago.

"Mama!" the little girl yelled. "Mama!"

Jacob slapped her across the face and shoved her hard to the floor. She landed with a grunt.

"I said to be *good*," he growled as he fell upon her. She gazed up at him in fear. Blood trickled from her nose.

The radio on the dresser beeped and a broadcaster interrupted the music for the first time Jacob could remember since 9/11. The voice on the radio was nearly frantic. Something major had happened, a catastrophe of some kind, but Jacob barely heard what the man was saying. He was too focused on seizing this opportunity.

"Be a *good* girl," he whispered, caressing the girl's face, smearing the blood across her cheek as she struggled.

Instead, she cried: "Mama!"

Jacob grinned. "Honey, your mama is *dead*. She's not coming to help you."

The radio broadcaster was speaking even more urgently, and this time some part of Jacob's brain heard the words, but he still didn't understand them. They made no sense.

Then a cold, dead hand gripped Jacob's shoulder and began to squeeze.